Ab

Siobhan Curham is ... born and brought up in North West London. She has since emigrated to South Staffordshire where she lives with her husband and son and an extensive range of Wolverhampton Wanderers' pants.

Siobhan Curham

Sweet FA

CORONET BOOKS
Hodder & Stoughton

copyright © 2002 by Siobhan Curham

First published in Great Britain in 2002 by Hodder and Stoughton
A division of Hodder Headline
A Coronet paperback

The right of Siobhan Curham to be identified as the Author
of the Work has been asserted by her in accordance with
the Copyright, Designs and Patents Act 1988.

2 4 6 8 10 9 7 5 3 1

A CIP catalogue record for this title
is available from the British Library

ISBN 0 340 82369 0

Typeset in Sabon by Hewer Text Ltd, Edinburgh
Printed and bound in Great Britain by
Mackays of Chatham plc, Chatham, Kent

Hodder and Stoughton
A division of Hodder Headline
338 Euston Road
London NW1 3BH

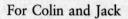

For Colin and Jack

Acknowledgements

Acknowledgements

I hold the following people solely responsible for this book making it into print (so if you don't like it blame them not me!)

Firstly, a huge thank you to my parents, Anne and Mikey, for sharing with me their passion for reading and writing and providing an endless source of encouragement and support. Thank you to the rest of my family: Bea and Chris for keeping Clintons in business, Luke – my fellow Rayners Lane nutter – for all the pep talks and Alice for the fabulous foot rubs (a packet of Chewits is winging its way!)

Thank you to Ginny for being the best friend a girl could wish for – 'These characters are fictitious and any resemblance to any persons living or dead is entirely coincidental', etc., etc.!

Thank you to Jeanette, my fellow 'widow' for all those nights down the pub plotting our revenge.

Thank you to my agent (!) Judy Chilcote for all of your help and support – I will be for ever grateful – and to my fantastic editor, Sara Hulse, and all at Hodder for their overwhelming warmth and enthusiasm.

Thank you to Steve Haslett at IMA for sharing

with me your extensive knowledge of Wigan slaughterhouses.

And a massive thank you to Colin, Jack and Harry-Billy for providing me with such an endless source of love and inspiration!

Prologue
Throw-in to Chelsea

'How about her?' Belle enquired, pointing to a woman loitering by the goalpost nearest the carpark.

Ginny and Maz watched through the windscreen in stunned silence as the woman lit a cigarette with one hand and discreetly fished her knickers from between her buttocks with the other.

'You are kidding?' Ginny snorted. 'Look at the state of her.'

At that moment a football came flying through the air, landing with a crunch on the gravel behind the car. Like undercover cops on a cheesy B-movie stake-out, Belle, Ginny and Maz slunk down into their seats as the focus of their attention began tottering her way towards them.

Her hair had been bleached to within an inch of its life, the roots appearing jet black in contrast and the ends frazzled from an outgrowing perm. Each of her earlobes was laden with large hoops, shrewdly purchased in the same cheap gold plate as the wide range of sovereign rings adorning her fingers. Inspired by Pepsi and Shirlie in her favourite Wham! video, she had tied a knot in the front of her figure-hugging Arsenal top to reveal a tantalising roll of deathly white midriff. Her legs (repeatedly nominated in magazine quizzes as the part of her body she would most like to change) were clad in woefully Lycra-free leggings, cut off just below the knee; cut off just above a pair of purple dappled calves, creating the rather unsavoury impression of two joints of corned beef, straining to control the seven-inch stiletto-heeled sandals beneath them. As she half sashayed, half stumbled her way past the car, Belle groaned in recognition.

'Oh no – it's Milwall!'

'Chelsea,' Maz corrected from her crouched position on the back seat. 'Oh, Mary mother of Jesus, she's only going to try and throw it back!'

By now most of the players had congregated by the goal and were waiting for their ball to be retrieved. Chelsea staggered a few steps forward and then, tattooed arms flailing wildly, flung the football high into the air. Unfortunately it plummeted straight back down, landing just a foot in front of her. Even more unfortunately, the strain of running on the gravel proved too much for her sandals to bear, causing one of the heels to snap off completely.

'Oh, bleedin' 'ell!' Chelsea muttered as she bent to retrieve the ball, revealing a provocative glimpse of greying gusset in the process. 'Oooh, sorry, lads,' she simpered, fag dangling from lip, and, picking up the ball with one hand and her heel with the other, she limped slowly back towards the pitch.

1

It was a sweltering August day, and as the summer simmered to a close a new football season was just beginning. But Belle hadn't brought Maz and Ginny to the ground of non-league Rayners Park to watch the match – far from it. No, they were on a mission, a 'recruitment drive', as Belle had optimistically described it, and so far it was not proving too successful.

'Oooh, sorry, lads!' Ginny mimicked, removing her Chloe sunglasses to give her face a quick spritz of Evian – at least, that's what it said on the label; the others weren't to know she had long since refilled it with tap water. 'Who the hell was that?'

'Chelsea – Chelsea Watson. Rayners Park's number-one fan and well-known local bike,' Maz replied bitterly, unwrapping a Mars bar and promptly showering herself in molten chocolate. 'Oh, Jesus mother of Joseph!'

'How could you even consider asking her?' Ginny turned to look at Belle accusingly. 'She's wearing a football top, for Christ's sake.'

Belle winced as she unpeeled her bare legs from Ginny's leather upholstery. She was seriously beginning to regret insisting upon a fourth member. The whole point of the exercise had been to escape from the damned game, and yet here she was wasting valuable sunbathing time holed up in a football club carpark. 'I didn't realise it was her,' she offered lamely. 'She's the last person I'd ask – she loves football.'

'More like she loves football *players*,' Maz muttered, trying in vain to remove the unsightly brown stain from her canary-yellow pedal-pushers.

'What do you mean?' Ginny asked warily.

'I mean, she pretends to be really into football, hanging around here week after week when all she's really after is a damned good rogering!'

Ginny cringed.

'Oh, come on, Ginny, you know the type,' Belle said, well aware that Ginny had probably never come into contact with a Chelsea Watson in her entire life. 'She thinks that shagging her local midfielder will make her Harrow's answer to Posh Spice.'

'That's so tacky.' Ginny shuddered. 'Why didn't you warn me that kind of thing went on here? When Mike asked me if he could play football this season I thought he'd be running around a field with a load of blokes called Dazza, Gazza and . . . and—'

'Bazza?' Belle offered helpfully.

'Precisely,' Ginny replied. 'I had no idea he'd be targeted by the local trollop!'

'Oh yeah, it happens all the time at non-league clubs,' Maz uttered solemnly while winking at Belle.

4

'The old slapper offered my Darren a blowjob twice last season.'

'Only twice? She offered Johnny one for every goal he scored,' Belle responded, staring out of the window and thinking of Princess Diana, Marilyn Monroe, Tiffany from *EastEnders* and the tragedy of untimely death – anything to stop herself from giggling.

'You're kidding?' Ginny whispered, visibly paling beneath her Estée Lauder tan.

'Shit, wasn't Johnny last season's leading goalscorer?' Maz asked, devouring the last of the chocolate from beneath her fingernails.

'Yeah, I think he finished on forty-three.'

'Forty-three?' Ginny stared at Belle, mortified. 'She offered to . . . forty-three times?'

Belle nodded.

'So what position does your Mike play in?' Maz enquired nonchalantly as she produced a packet of cigarettes from her handbag.

'Centre-forward, I think.'

'Oh dear!' Belle and Maz groaned in unison.

'I can assure you there's no way Mike would even contemplate letting someone like her near his . . . near him,' Ginny retorted. 'My husband has standards, you know. Look at the state of her, look at her hair. Good grief, has the girl never heard of reapplication?'

They all stared smugly at Chelsea's two-tone hair and then took a moment to consider their own comparatively stylish coiffures. Belle twirled one of her Titian curls around her finger, Maz ruffled her chunky crop, which this week was resplendent in blackberry blush, and Ginny cast an admiring glance at her pristine platinum bob in the rear-view mirror – thanking God she had kept her appointment with Toni and Guy that morning.

'So, do you think Johnny spotted you?' Maz enquired, removing a gold plastic pistol from her bag and proceeding to light her cigarette with it.

'I doubt it. I could run across the pitch naked and he probably wouldn't notice me,' Belle replied bitterly. Once, during a particularly dull *Match of the Day*, she had performed an impromptu striptease right next to the television. It had been for scientific rather than sensual purposes, and the results of her experiment had confirmed her worst fears. To her husband, football was indeed better than sex. Rather than hitting the stand-by button on the remote control and ravishing her on the sofa, Johnny had simply requested that she 'put them away, love, the Wolves game is coming up next'. Then, adding insult to injury, he had actually turned the volume up, conveniently drowning out the slamming doors and stomping feet of his frustrated wife storming upstairs.

Belle drummed her fingers on the dashboard and sighed loudly. 'Shall we make a move? I could murder a drink. Anyway, it's not as if we *have* to have another member, is it?'

'Hold on – how about her?' Ginny asked, pointing to a young woman pushing a buggy across the carpark.

'I don't know, she looks a bit miserable.'

'Exactly!' Ginny exclaimed. 'She's coming to a football match and she looks miserable – I'd say that makes her an ideal candidate. And at least she's got decent hair.'

Belle watched as the woman trudged towards the pitch. Her pale blonde hair was pulled back into a ponytail, but a few stray strands had worked their way free and plastered themselves to her flushed face. She looked tired and hot and as if Rayners Park football ground was the last place on earth she wanted to be.

'Well, she isn't wearing a football top – I suppose that's something,' Belle conceded.

'Let's just do it,' said Maz, heaving herself out of the back of the car, leaving a cloud of smoke in her wake.

Tutting loudly, Ginny turned to douse the back seat in Dior. 'It's going to smell like an ashtray in here for weeks now,' she hissed to Belle. 'You'd have thought she could have waited until she got out. Well, come on, then – don't forget the envelope.'

Belle sighed as she somewhat reluctantly retrieved an envelope from her bag. This was the first time she had approached a stranger about her idea. It was all right telling the others – she had known Ginny for years and Maz was game for anything – but who knew what this flustered woman would make of it all. She hardly looked like the game-for-a-laugh type.

2

As she traipsed across the carpark, Anna felt a surge of panic welling up inside of her. She was twenty minutes late – not the best start to the new season. Why did Grace have to do a crap just as they were about to leave the flat? As if that wasn't bad enough, after changing the nappy at breakneck speed she'd gone and got herself lost. They'd lived on the estate for two months now, but the football ground was in completely the opposite direction to the local parade of shops and the park. As soon as Anna entered the uncharted territory beyond the lock-up garages underneath the archways she'd panicked. Every road looked identical – a confusing rabbit-warren of tatty front gardens and boarded-up windows. When she had finally found the ground all hopes of slinking in unnoticed were soon dashed. Grace's buggy sounded more like a bulldozer crossing the carpark as it churned up the gravel in its wake. To cap it all, Grace had decided to herald their late arrival with a blood-curdling howl. There was no way Tom wouldn't have noticed.

As soon as Anna reached the grassy bank next to the pitch she stopped and crouched down beside the buggy. She could hear the players just a few yards away from her screaming, 'Man on! Man on!' but she couldn't bring herself to look up in case she caught Tom's eye. Grace's howls were becoming increasingly insistent, her chubby little cheeks glowing with rage as she pummelled the sides of the buggy with her fists. It was too hot for a toddler to be outside – it felt too hot for a twenty-four-year-old to be outside. Anna opened her battered canvas rucksack and her heart sank. In her rush to leave the flat she had completely forgotten the bottle of juice sitting ready and waiting on the kitchen counter. She rummaged about desperately in her bag. Why couldn't she be one of those mums who never left home without a portable branch of Mother-care swinging merrily from the pram handle? She sighed as she examined the mess inside. Several hundred used bus tickets, a crumpled scratch card, a packet of chewing gum and a badly misshapen disposable nappy. Just as Anna contemplated gumming Grace's howling mouth shut with a stick of Wrigleys she spotted a half-eaten lollipop sticking out from between the pages of a Jehovah's Witness pamphlet. Saying no to the clipboard-wielding, leaflet-thrusting army patrolling Harrow town centre every Saturday did not come easy to Anna, as the pile of unused mail-order catalogues currently barricading her hallway testified. Peeling as much paper as she could from the sticky glucose, Anna thrust the lollipop into Grace's mouth, instantly corking the deafening whine.

As Grace sucked eagerly on the lolly, Anna sank down on to the grass and sneaked a few furtive glances around the ground. It was certainly an improvement on the last one, with its tree-lined pitch and proper, purpose-built clubhouse. It even had floodlights. The supporters seemed pretty familiar, though. The two old men standing next to her looked exactly like Arthur and Ted from Uxbridge Town, the way they stood there shaking their heads and muttering 'load of bloody crap' over and over again, and yet they were bound to be at every match come rain or shine until the end of the season. Then there was the obligatory group of teenagers to Anna's left having animated conversations about drugs on their mobiles and making fun of the greasy-haired anorak hovering by the sideline. Uxbridge Town had a resident anorak too; a spotty forty-year-old called Davey who used to shout 'Wotcha' at anyone walking past – to the annoyance of many a poor linesman. Rayners Park's anorak seemed more interested in the tarty blonde by the goal, who appeared to have one leg several inches shorter than the other, than any action taking place on the pitch. Yes, it looked as if this new ground would be just like a home from home.

Just as Anna started to relax she spotted three women heading her way. Oh God, football wives. She began reading her Jehovah's Witness pamphlet intently and waited for them to pass. 'A New Millennium, A New Beginning', the leaflet promised over a rather naff meadow scene. A shadow fell ominously over the dancing children and frolicking lambs in the picture.

'Hi,' came a cut-glass voice from above. 'I'm Ginny.'

Anna stuffed the pamphlet back in her bag and looked up. The three women loomed over her, dark silhouettes against the brilliant sunshine. Anna panicked. What should she say? What should she do?

'Hi,' she managed to squeak, clambering awkwardly to her feet.

On cue Grace flung the lolly stick on to the grass and began to whimper.

'It's hot, innit,' said a plump woman with bright purple hair. 'I bet she wants a drink, doesn't she.'

'Yes. I, er, left her juice at home.' Great, Anna thought to herself. Don't even pretend to be a competent mother.

'Go and get her a lemonade, Ginny,' said Purple Hair, pointing to the clubhouse.

Ginny shook her head and frowned. 'I can't go in there,' she whispered, seemingly horrified at the mere suggestion. 'Will she drink Evian?' she asked Anna, fetching a bottle of water out of her brown leather bag.

Anna nodded and took the bottle gratefully. 'Thank you.' She hoped they didn't notice her fingers shaking slightly as she unscrewed the cap and held the bottle up to Grace's mouth.

'I'm Maz, by the way,' said Purple Hair. 'And this is Belle.' A third woman, with porcelain skin and a mass of copper curls, smiled at her weakly. She reminded Anna of those china dolls her mum liked to order from Sunday colour supplements.

'So how old's the nipper?' Maz asked.

Anna's mind went blank. How old was Grace? For a split second she didn't have a clue. Oh my God, she must look like the world's most useless mother. When was Grace born? May last year. So that would make her . . .? June, July, August. Anna's brain whirred into action. 'Fifteen months!' she exclaimed. 'She's fifteen months.'

Maz smiled and stroked Grace's cheek. 'So what's her name?'

'Grace,' Anna replied, thankfully recalling her daughter's name rather more quickly than her age. 'My name's Anna,' she added as an inspired afterthought.

'So, Anna,' said Belle, glancing surreptitiously at the pitch, 'does your partner play for Rayners Park?'

Anna nodded, then, realising she really ought to be a little more forthcoming, she said, 'Yes. Tom. Tom Grant. It's his first game for them.'

'Oh, really? It's my husband Mike's first game too!' exclaimed Ginny, as if it were the most amazing coincidence since Geri Halliwell declared her undying love for Chris Evans the week before her new single came out.

An awkward silence fell upon the group. Ginny coughed loudly and Maz nudged Belle. Belle coiled one of her curls around her finger as if she were playing with a telephone wire. 'So, do you like football, then?' she asked, rather more abruptly than she had intended.

Once again, Anna froze. She longed to be honest. She wished she had the guts to tell this walking, talking china doll exactly what she thought about football, but she'd made enough of a fool of herself already.

'Yes, I suppose so,' she replied flatly, her eyes fixed on the pitch to avoid Belle's scrutinising stare.

'Our old men all play for the Park too,' Maz said with a smile. 'That's why we're here.'

'But not to watch the football,' Belle interrupted.

'Oh.' Anna wasn't exactly surprised. Hot sunny days had always brought out a handful of wives and girlfriends at Uxbridge Town too. It was the ideal chance to top up their tans and catch up on gossip. They'd never bothered making conversation with her, though.

'We're here to recruit one more member for an organisation I've recently founded,' Belle continued.

'Oh.' Anna's heart sank. Was there no escape?

'It's called the Football Widows, and it's for women who are sick and tired of constantly coming second best to that pathetic game.' Belle nodded disdainfully towards the pitch. 'I don't know if it applies to you or not, but you'll find all the details on the leaflet inside.' She handed Anna an envelope. 'Whether you decide to join us or not, I'd appreciate it if you didn't show this to anyone else, especially your husband.'

'No, of course not. He's my boyfriend.'

'What?' Belle looked totally bewildered.

14

'Tom – he's my boyfriend, not my husband.'

'Oh. Right. Whatever. Well, have a read and if you like what you see come along next week.'

Anna nodded silently. Why the hell had she said that? What difference did it make to Belle whether Tom was her husband or not? Anyway, they might as well be married, they'd been together five years and had a child. And why oh why had she said she liked football? If only she'd told the truth. Anna stared at the ground disconsolately.

'Right, well, see you, then.' Belle turned and began walking briskly towards the carpark.

' 'Bye, Anna, 'bye, Grace.' Ginny bent down to air-kiss Grace before heading after Belle.

'You will try and come, won't you,' said Maz, giving Anna's arm a gentle squeeze. 'It should be a right laugh – it's about time us girls got our own back on those selfish gits.'

Anna nodded blankly. She couldn't believe she'd finally been given a leaflet she might actually be interested in, and what had she done? Instead of nodding enthusiastically and agreeing to everything they'd said, like the time she'd gone to Harrow for some sterilising solution and inadvertently ended up becoming a Betterware saleswoman, she'd mumbled and stuttered like a gormless idiot. She sank back down to the ground in despair. Checking to make sure the women were a safe distance away, she took the leaflet from its envelope and began to read.

THE FOOTBALL WIDOWS

Does your heart sink at the start of every football season? Do you feel like you constantly come second best to football? Are you sick of asking your partner to spend more time with you?

Do you feel as if your whole life revolves around football fixtures and is dependent upon football scores?

Do you find yourself repeating the following sentences over and over again, but to no avail?

'It's only a game!'
'What the hell is the offside trap anyway?'
'I don't care if they won ten–nil, where the hell have you been until three in the morning?'
'But EastEnders *is on the other side.'*
'No, we cannot remortgage the house so you can go to the World Cup/European Championship/ pre-season tour of Finland!'
'That top cost how much? But it's exactly the same as last season's.'
'If you only play football as a way of keeping fit why do you drink seventeen pints after each match?'
'But the Second World War finished sixty years ago.'
'No, we cannot go on holiday to Bayern Munich.'

IN SHORT – ARE YOU A FOOTBALL WIDOW?

If you have answered 'yes' to two or more of these questions then you most certainly are.

But do not despair, football widows, the time for grieving is officially over. It's time to come together and even the score.

For more details, join your fellow widows at our first meeting, 3 p.m. next Saturday at:

22 Emerald Avenue
Rayners Park
Harrow
HA2 7ZU

Back in the car Belle was in a vile mood. 'Well, that was a roaring success!'

'I thought she was sweet.'

'Maz, you just need to see a baby and you turn into a gooey mush. There's no way she's going to come. Did you see the way she was looking at me? She made me feel like I was a Jehovah's Witness or something!'

'She was a bit on the quiet side,' said Ginny, running a comb through her hair.

'I reckon she'll show up,' Maz stated confidently.

'No way.'

'I bet you a bottle of vodka she'll be there.'

'You're on. Speaking of which, let's get out of here.' Belle pictured an ice-cold vodka and tonic waiting for her at home, condensation frosting the glass and a slice of lemon bobbing on the surface. 'If we stay much longer I may well break out in some kind of hideous allergic reaction.'

3

'How much longer are you going to be?' Belle screamed at the bathroom door.

'Steady on, love, I haven't even got to the second division yet.'

It was Sunday morning and Johnny was conducting his usual post-match analysis, which involved studying the sports sections of at least four different newspapers in minute detail. Belle wouldn't have minded so much if this weekly ritual took place out of the way in the back garden or the garage, but for some reason tradition decreed that it had to take place on the toilet.

'Well, I'm coming in – I've got to go over to Ginny's and I need to bath Harry.' Belle took a deep breath and flung the door open. 'Jesus!'

Every available square inch of bathroom floor was completely covered in newspaper, with every single football table from the Premiership to the Unijet Sussex League on display. Hunched over them on the toilet, shorts around ankles, sat Johnny, a look of deep concentration upon his face. Seemingly oblivious to the gut-wrenching stench permeating the air, and without averting his gaze from the paper in front of him, he reached out for a can of Coke balancing on the edge of the sink. Belle stared at him for a second – with his tanned skin and muscular physique she knew she must once have found this man attractive; she just couldn't remember when.

'You are truly disgusting,' she finally uttered, flinging the window open and leaning out for a gulp of fresh air. 'How can you possibly turn crapping into a social event? You've even brought some refreshments in with you. Maybe you'd like me to fix you some breakfast? A croissant while you crap, perhaps?'

'Do you realise, if Wolves carry on at this rate we'll get promoted easily.' Johnny had learnt long ago to turn a deaf ear to Belle's rants. Besides, nothing could spoil the euphoria he was currently experiencing.

'You've only played one match, for Christ's sake.'

'Yeah, but we'd be top of Division One today if we didn't begin with W.'

'What the hell are you talking about?'

'Well, Portsmouth were the only other team to win three–nil, but they automatically go to the top because they begin with P and we begin with W.'

It was only the first Sunday of the football season and Belle was already getting that familiar sinking feeling, but this year was going to be different, of that she was certain.

'It's a pity they aren't called Aardvark United, then. You'd be guaranteed to come top.'

Johnny frowned at Belle. 'I suppose where your mother's from there actually is a team called Aardvark United. No, don't tell me, the Arkansas Aard-varks? Well, we take our football a little more seriously over here.' Johnny smiled smugly and returned his gaze to the paper on the floor.

'Wolves, aardvarks, what's the difference? They're both animals,' Belle pointed out as she began running a bath.

'You know full well that Wolves is short for Wolverhampton Wanderers. It's you Yanks who have to give all your football teams cute little animal names. Euurghh!' Johnny strained over a particularly arduous bowel movement before continuing his onslaught. 'Not only that, but your nancy-boy players have to wear shoulder pads and tights and your fans aren't happy unless there's a break every fifteen minutes and the score is at least thirty-five–twenty-seven. Christ!' Johnny wiped his brow with the back of his hand.

'Oh yes, there's nothing more thrilling than freezing your arse off for ninety minutes for a nil–nil draw,' Belle retorted.

'I'll have you know, last season's nil–nil draw at Grimsby was one of the tensest matches I've ever been to.'

'Oh, for God's sake.' Belle couldn't believe she'd been sucked into yet another pointless argument about football. 'Look, can you please take your riveting read elsewhere while I fumigate the bathroom and wash your son.'

'What's he done this time?' Johnny enquired as he

got to his feet and glanced casually into the toilet bowl. 'Bloody hell! Take a look at this, Belle – it's a monster!'

'Flush it away this instant,' Belle commanded, refusing to look anywhere near the toilet. 'Your son,' she continued, 'has decided to have ketchup on his Frosties and managed to get most of it in his hair.'

On cue their three-year-old son Harry appeared in the bathroom doorway. Tomato ketchup was trickling from his hair down on to his face, making him look like the victim of a particularly vicious bludgeoning.

'All right, son? Wolves won yesterday,' Johnny announced, directing one final admiring glance down the toilet before flushing the contents away.

'Wolves are dog's poo!' Harry declared, dripping ketchup all over the Doc Martens League, Division One.

Belle smiled – her intensive programme of anti-football brainwashing appeared to be paying off. In a huff, Johnny gathered up the piles of newspaper from the floor and retreated to the bedroom.

As Belle rinsed the ketchup from Harry's hair she wondered what on earth Ginny could want to see her for this early on a Sunday morning. It was unheard of for Ginny to show her face over the bedclothes until at least midday on a Sunday – one of the many luxuries her childless state allowed her.

Belle didn't ever regret having Harry, but there

were times she wished she hadn't fallen pregnant right in the middle of her twenties. Sometimes, as she wiped yet another grubby paw print from her increasingly battered Calvin Klein jeans, or scraped the melted chocolate buttons from the inside of her handbag, she felt a pang of envy for Ginny's high-flying, Gucci-accessorised lifestyle.

From the moment they met at university, Ginny had lived her life as if it were a demonstration for an organisational skills workshop. Advanced level. The only thing the two girls had in common was the location of their adjoining rooms in the halls of residence – B corridor in Rathbone block. Rathbone was the only hall to offer the luxury of one bathroom for every two students. When Belle had first walked into their bathroom she had wondered whether the university were following the example of hotels and providing complimentary toiletries, such was the professionalism with which Ginny had arranged her side of the shelves. Sets of lotions and potions for hair, face and body were lovingly displayed in neat, symmetrical clusters, and even though they were different brands, every single bottle and jar was blue. Even the toilet cleaner was in Ocean Spray. Belle had despaired; a room-mate who purchased toilet cleaner did not bode well for the late-night drinking and gossip sessions she had been anticipating. Suddenly the 'Virginia Gallagher' who sounded so glamorous and full of promise on the name card on her door conjured up images of hairnets and nylon housecoats. Belle was therefore pleasantly surprised when, some time later, a slim, sophisticated blonde arrived at her room, introducing herself as Ginny.

'I thought you might like one of these for your bedroom,' she had said, handing Belle a magic mushroom air freshener (in forget-me-not mist).

Belle and Ginny were like chalk and cheese in almost every way. Rather than relying on somebody else's photocopied notes, like Belle, who had charmed various young men into providing such a service, only to discover with horror upon revising that she couldn't translate a word of their illegible scrawl, Ginny attended every single lecture of her marketing degree in person. Each night she would file her notes methodically in colour-coordinated folders – red for market trends, blue for unique selling points, and so on. In the bustling kitchen at the end of their corridor, Ginny would whip up a well-balanced pasta dish in the time it took Belle to burn a round of toast. And, rather than lurching headlong from one disastrous affair to another, Belle style, Ginny remained ensconced with Toby from Saffron Walden until two months before her finals (her meticulously planned revision timetable unfortunately not accommodating affairs of the heart).

Despite their differences, the friendship that was initially born out of curiosity – *I've never met anyone quite so irresponsible*, thought Ginny; *I've never met anyone quite so anal*, thought Belle – soon became a strong bond in the highly charged atmosphere of university.

Their friendship continued past graduation – Ginny got first-class honours, Belle a third – surviving a year's separation when Belle travelled to the States to spend some time with her family, two manic years as flatmates upon Belle's return, the trauma of Belle's unplanned pregnancy, and even now, as Ginny clambered ever higher up the corporate ladder while Belle floundered in a world of nursery school outings and dinosaur-shaped chicken nuggets, the bond remained as strong as ever.

As Belle raced over to Ginny's her imagination went into overdrive. Most Sundays all she had to satisfy her insatiable appetite for drama and gossip was the front page of the *News of the World*, and that just hadn't been the same since Princess Diana died.

Reaching Ginny's house in record time, Belle swung her car into the drive and instantly realised something was very wrong indeed. A pair of Y-fronts hung from the branch of a weeping willow, flapping gently in the breeze like a flag to fashion faux pas. Ginny was far too neat to let a stray weed spoil her garden, let alone a pair of pants. As Belle turned off the engine she noticed various other articles of men's clothing strewn across the manicured lawn. A higgledy-piggledy mass of corduroy trousers, knitted sweaters and a particularly nasty Aran cardigan. A heap of socks littered the rockery and a pair of polka-dot pyjamas floated mournfully in the miniature pond. It was all terribly apocalyptic. Belle was thrilled.

Ginny had been very abrupt on the phone. 'You've got to get over here now,' she had whispered ominously, before hanging up. While Belle contemplated the possible cause of such carnage, Harry released himself from his supposedly secure child seat and began enjoying a fun game of dress-up on the lawn.

'Look, Mum!' he shouted as he ran about in a shirt, sleeves trailing along the ground behind him, and what looked suspiciously like a pair of Arsenal pants on his head. Arsenal pants? Belle pondered this latest development. Surely they couldn't be Mike's clothes?

4

Mike, or Captain Sensible as Johnny called him, was one of the nicest, most laid-back people Belle had ever met. In the five years he and Ginny had been together they had only had one serious argument. It had been over Ginny going out with friends. Mike, having read an essay by Germaine Greer on the importance of female camaraderie, had suggested that she socialise more with women. Ginny was outraged – how dare he imply that she had no mates? After all, plenty of women had only one friend – didn't they?

Ginny's relationship was another thing Belle envied. She and Mike had done everything by the book – going out for a year before moving in together, investing in a cashback, fixed-rate mortgage rather than squandering exorbitant amounts of money on rent, and delaying having children so they could spend quality time with each other. They were so organised they had probably cleared a window in June 2003 for the conception of their first-born. Ginny was probably already on the folic acid while Mike carefully monitored the potassium levels in his diet and ensured that he wore loose-fitting underwear. No – they couldn't possibly be Mike's Y-fronts on her son's head.

'Come on, Harry!' Belle shouted as she strode up the drive, practically drooling for further information. As she approached the front door she was startled to hear a low, strangulated moan emanating from a rhododendron bush to her left. Belle and Harry stopped in their tracks and peered into the branches.

'It must be a monster,' Harry announced, solemnly.

'Shh,' said Belle, trying to part the branches to get a better view. A pair of wild, staring eyes glinted back at her from deep within the bush. 'Run!' she screamed to Harry as she prepared to beat a hasty retreat to the car, but to her dismay Harry dived into the undergrowth.

'Get your hands off my child!' Belle shrieked as she launched herself after him.

'Look, Mum, it's Uncle Mike, he's playing hide-and-seek.'

Belle forced the leaves from her face to discover that the eyes did indeed belong to Mike, a very tired, bedraggled-looking Mike.

'What the hell?'

Mike's thick curly hair was strewn with leaves and bits of twig, his face was streaked with mud, and, although he was fully clothed, his whole hunched-up body was shaking quite violently.

'About bloody time too!' All three of them jumped

as Ginny flung open the front door and yelled down the garden. 'Belle, get out of that bush and come inside now!'

Belle had never heard her normally ice-cool friend sound quite so forceful and so very, very angry.

'Sorry, Mike, love to stay and, er, chat, but . . . Come on, Harry.'

'I want to play, I want to play,' Harry protested in vain as Belle dragged him up the gravel path towards the house. Once they had been bustled inside by Ginny, who promptly double-locked and bolted the front door behind them, Belle could barely contain her excitement.

'What the hell's going on?'

Ginny paced up and down the immaculately designed living room, sprinkling some kind of white crystal on to the floor. Belle nearly wet herself – this was well worth missing the *Hollyoaks* omnibus for!

'What is that stuff? Why are there pairs of pants all over your garden and what the hell is Mike doing hiding in a bush? If you've called me over here to take part in some kind of kinky sex game you childless couples play out here in suburbia, then I'm sorry but . . .'

'Mike has moved out.'

'What?'

'Or should I say, Mike has been thrown out.' Ginny flung the bag of white crystals down on to the black marble coffee table. 'It's rock salt – it absorbs negative energy, and God knows there's enough of that around here today!' She stormed over to one of the gleaming chrome shelf units flanking the enormous wide-screen television and grabbed a set of tiny silver bells which she proceeded to jangle aggressively. 'I wish I was single. I wish he would disappear. I wish football had never been invented.'

'What the hell are you doing?' Belle had gone from feeling deliriously excited to extremely concerned. Could Ginny be having some kind of breakdown?

'I'm reciting my wish list – having created a protective seal of rock salt against Mike's negative vibes. Would you like a drink?'

Belle nodded, speechless. She'd always assumed that they'd gone on that feng shui course for a laugh. Ginny marched over to the drinks cabinet and poured them both a stiff snowball. Belle stifled a smirk. That was the problem with a house not used to drink problems or relationship crises – you ended up drowning your sorrows in cooking sherry or the chosen drink of twelve-year-olds.

'I don't know what you're smiling for,' Ginny admonished. 'This is a very serious matter.'

'Oh, I don't doubt that for a second. I'm just finding it difficult to imagine what he could have done. Don't tell me – he's insisted you take a year off work to find yourself while he foots the bill.'

'I would really appreciate it if for once in your life you didn't take the piss out of what is an extremely serious situation.'

'No, of course, I'm sorry.'

Suddenly there was an almighty crash as Harry sent the bottle of advocaat toppling off the coffee table. Belle watched, horrified, as the thick yellow liquid seeped into the plush white carpet.

'Harry! Oh, Ginny, I'm so sorry, I should have kept an eye on him.' Belle fumbled around in her handbag, trying desperately to find a tissue of some description.

'Don't worry about it. Believe me, at this moment in time I am far more concerned with the state of my relationship than I am with the state of my carpet.'

Belle sat back in amazement – Ginny's arctic-white shagpile was her pride and joy.

'As you know, yesterday was the fifth anniversary of our taking out a joint mortgage and Mike had booked a table at that Ethiopian restaurant we go to in Islington.'

Belle nodded, by now well aware that this was not the time for any obvious wisecracks.

'Anyway,' Ginny continued, 'things got off to a pretty poor start when he turned up at the station late and drunk.'

'Mike turned up drunk?'

'Yes, absolutely roaring, but that's not the worst of it. All the way up to London he's singing football songs and' – Ginny lowered her voice to an appalled whisper – 'belching!'

Belle's heart sank – it was starting to sound like an average Saturday night to her. Ginny took a sip of her snowball and continued.

'By the time we got to Green Park I'm, like, dying of embarrassment and he's bellowing the most appalling song.'

'Which one?' Belle asked, as casually as she was able.

'Oh God, I don't know if I can bring myself . . . oh, all right, it was something like, "My old man said be a Tottenham fan, I said fuck off, bollocks, you're a . . .' Once again Ginny lowered her voice to a whisper. '*cunt*!'

'Fluck off, bollocks, you're a cunt!' Harry hollered, shattering the stunned silence.

'Oh my God, Harry, you mustn't say those words, they're naughty. I'm sorry, Belle, I'm just not thinking straight this morning.'

Belle nodded, completely speechless. The worst 'C' word she'd ever heard Mike utter was 'crumbs'. The first time Johnny met him he'd been mortified. 'What kind of a bloke says he needs to go for a wee-wee?' he had asked Belle when they got home from the pub, shaking his head in disgust. Since then, however, their shared love of football had led to them becoming quite good friends. Belle grew worried – what if Johnny's bad behaviour had started rubbing off on Mike?

'Anyway,' Ginny continued, 'suddenly this guy wearing a Spurs top appears out of nowhere and Mike staggers to his feet shouting, "Come on – if you think you're hard enough!" Oh, Belle, I could've died, everybody in the carriage was staring at us.'

'What happened? Did Mike get hurt?' Belle pictured a six-foot-tall skinhead pummelling Mike's head, sending his glasses flying and blood gushing all over his Marks and Spencer polo shirt.

'Did he get hurt? Oh God, Belle, that's the worst part – the guy was only about twelve and he was with his grandparents. It was so embarrassing. He could have been one of Mike's pupils. You should have seen the way they were looking at us – I felt like we were two of those awful guests on the Jerry Springer show!'

'So what happened next? Did you come back home?' Belle asked, praying that they hadn't.

'Oh, if only. Well, we got off at Covent Garden. As you can imagine I had completely gone off the idea of an Ethiopian, but I couldn't face getting another train back home while he was still in that condition, and I thought if he got some food inside him he might sober up a bit.'

'So where did you go?'

'Well, I thought if we went to TGI's it would be noisy enough to drown out any more football chants.'

'And was it?'

'Well, yes, it was, but that was irrelevant anyway, because by the time we got a table he'd gone really quiet.'

'Oh no. He didn't puke all over the waitress, did he?' Belle asked, recalling a particularly embarrassing Indian she'd had with Johnny the night Wolves lost to Crystal Palace in the play-offs.

'No, but I was really worried that he would, so I made him go to the toilet just in case. After he'd gone I sat back and downed nearly a quarter of my cocktail in one go. Just as I was starting to relax I realised that everyone seemed to be laughing at something behind me. So I turned round and . . . oh my God . . .' Ginny shuddered. 'Mike was standing there, in the middle of the restaurant, having a piss up against a rubber plant.'

Belle fought furiously for control of her facial muscles, knowing the slightest hint of a smile could bring about the end of her oldest friendship.

'Oh, Ginny,' was all she dared squeeze out.

'Oh, Belle.' Ginny suddenly looked dangerously close to tears. 'It's that bloody football team. It's making him act so . . . so working class, mixing with Neanderthals three times a week, he's beginning to sink to their level. No offence – you know I love Johnny – but I did not spend three years of my life at university and I did not attend all of those self-assertiveness workshops to end up some sort of . . .' Ginny was lost for words.

'Football widow?' Belle suggested helpfully.

'Yes, football widow. You know, when you first suggested this football widow thing I must admit I didn't take it all that seriously – I thought it was another one of your hare-brained schemes, you know, like the time you tried to organise that Students Against Oppression rally at university. But after what happened last night I want you to know that I am so behind you. I mean, why should we put up with this sort of bollocks?'

'Bollocks,' Harry echoed from the floor, where he sat making bright yellow advocaat swirls with his hand.

'That's exactly what I've been trying to say,' Belle cried, excited at finally having some genuine support for her idea. 'Believe me, Ginny, what happened last night is just the tip of the iceberg. God, Mike's only played there for a week and he's acting like that – Johnny's been there for three years now and I can tell you it doesn't get any better.'

'Oh, it will do – there's no way I'm going to put up with another nine months of that sort of behaviour.'

'Ginny, believe me – it won't work. I've tried everything in the book – sulking, shouting, screaming, threatening to move out, threatening to move my mother in. I've practically begged him to take up badminton or something else that we could play together, I've withdrawn conjugal rights and pretended I'm having an affair, but nothing ever works. I'm sorry, Ginny, but making Mike sleep in a bush and throwing his clothes all over the garden won't make a blind bit of difference. It just makes you more wound up.'

'So what the hell am I supposed to do, then? Just sit at home and play the little woman while he's pissing in rubber plants and terrorising twelve-year-olds?'

'No – that's the whole point I'm trying to make.

It's time we got even and gave them a taste of their own medicine.'

'How the hell are we going to do that without sulking or shouting?' Ginny asked, totally bewildered.

'Just wait and see,' said Belle as enigmatically as she could. 'Just wait and see.'

5

'You found him stark bollock naked? You're winding me up!' Maz threw back her head and let out one of her customary foghorn roars, causing a shopper in the frozen food section to drop their fish fingers in fright. 'So? Did you see his John Thomas?'

'Er, not exactly,' Belle replied, instantly regretting her slight embellishment of Sunday morning's events. 'Too much foliage. Anyway, you'll never guess what happened next . . .'

As they slowly ambled their way around the supermarket Belle regaled Maz with the juicy details, stopping by the tinned meats to re-enact Ginny's creation of a protective seal of rock salt.

'What the bleeding hell is feng shui anyway?' Maz asked. 'I heard some posh bird talking about it on the telly the other day and I thought she was ordering a Chinese takeaway.'

'It's an ancient art of furniture rearranging for people with more money than sense,' Belle explained. 'Basically you pay an "expert" a load of money to come into your house and tell you to face your sofa eastwards and keep your toilet lid closed.'

'But why?' Maz asked, accidentally placing a

packet of veggie-burgers in her trolley, such was her state of bewilderment. 'Bloody hell, better put these back – the boys'll go mental,' she said, hurriedly replacing Linda McCartney with a huge box of economy beefburgers.

'Well, it's supposed to create a greater sense of harmony and bring more prosperity into your life.' Belle couldn't decide which shaped chicken nuggets to go for this week. Tank engines were probably the best bet – Harry was heavily into Thomas at the moment.

'So what did the poor sod do to get the old chop-suey treatment? Ruffle her hair? Hide her knicker starch?' Maz snorted.

Piling her trolley high with tins of Postman Pat-shaped pasta, strings of cheese as chewy as rubber, and smiley faces allegedly made from the finest fluffy potato, Belle recounted the train journey to London, the drunken singing, the attempted child abuse, and last but not least . . .

'HE PISSED IN A RUBBER PLANT? MIKE? FUCK ME!' Maz shrieked at the top of her voice, almost dropping her twenty-four-pack of Coke in shock.

Belle winced. Maz wasn't the subtlest of people. Ginny would go mad if she knew half of Tesco's had now heard all about her husband's recent indiscretions. 'You must promise not to breathe a word of this to anyone,' she hissed as they reached the check-outs. 'Especially not Darren.'

Maz grinned and winked a heavily made-up eye at Belle.

'Don't worry, darling, mum's the word. Who'd have thought it, eh? And him a schoolteacher an' all.'

Belle watched Maz unloading her week's supply of junk food.

'Oh well, this'll keep 'em in zits for another week.' Maz sighed, heaving a sack of oven chips on to the conveyor belt. 'Pissing in a rubber plant, eh?' Her size-eighteen frame shook with laughter, causing the multicoloured bangles lining her arms to jangle wildly.

Everything about Maz was colourful, from her chameleonesque hair to her eccentric clothes – Vivienne Westwood and Dolly Parton were her two main influences. Belle had first met her at the Rayners Park Football Club Christmas party two years previously. Johnny had spent the entire night reliving old games with his team-mates, leaving Belle furiously sipping her vodka and tonic, wishing the ground would open up and swallow her whole. To avoid the dirty looks of the cliquey wives and girlfriends, she fixed her eyes firmly on the deserted dance-floor. The cardigan-clad DJ, 'Vince Dean – the Music Machine', seemed entirely unaffected by the lack of disco fever his endless Jive Bunny megamix had caused. Just as Belle thought she would scream if she heard 'Colonel Bogey' once more, she saw Maz.

'Come on, everybody, c-c-come on, everybody!' Jive Bunny yelled, and suddenly a woman with canary-yellow hair protruding from beneath a tinsel-strewn Stetson hurtled across the dance-floor. The fringe of tassels on her beige suede jacket and skirt quivered wildly as she shook her way through the Hippy Hippy Shake. The other women rolled their mascara-clogged eyes in disgust. 'Who the hell does she think she is?' they seethed over their martini and lemonades. 'Fat tart,' they hissed, clamping their stomach muscles rigid and gazing down at their spindly legs. Belle, however, smiled with relief, and as Jive Bunny launched into the twist for the sixth time that night, she made her way on to the dance-floor to join Maz.

They spent the entire night dancing and daring each other to request increasingly naffer tunes from Vince.

'This one's for the two lovely ladies down here at the front,' Vince murmured over the opening chords to such classics as 'Silver Lady' and 'Living Next Door To Alice'. When 'Sweet Caroline' came on, Belle nearly burst into tears. Neil Diamond was her childhood hero, but this was the first time she'd found a DJ willing to play him. Vince was delighted at such an enthusiastic response from two women under sixty. He'd always known if he waited long enough Neil Diamond would make a comeback with the youngsters – that techno garage rubbish was so overrated. By the end of the night – and after more than a few double vodkas – Belle and Maz were convinced that Vince Dean was a total legend. Their shared love of Vince and loathing of the other Rayners Park wives created an instant bond. Belle was overjoyed to have finally met somebody she liked at the football club. Maz was warm, funny and brilliant company, but she was also extremely loud.

What if she blabs to Darren and he tells the whole team? Belle thought, in her panic asking the confused checkout girl for five hundred pounds cashback.

'I won't say anything,' Maz reassured her once again as they loaded the shopping into their cars. 'Bloody hell, Ginny's hard enough work as it is, I'm not likely to do anything to make things worse, am I?' Maz clambered into her clapped-out Datsun and wound down the window until the 'Country and Western Lives' sticker disappeared from view. Leaning out, she bellowed, 'I still can't believe you've seen his knob! See you Saturday.'

And with that she zoomed off, leaving a fading blast of Kenny Rogers and a red-faced Belle in her wake.

Later that night, when Belle had finally got Harry into bed – it had taken her one hour, twenty minutes to get him to eat two tank-engine-shaped chicken nuggets – she returned to the living room to find Johnny deep in thought. For once the television was switched off and the remote control was not fixed to his hand. It was on the floor next to his feet. The terracotta-washed walls, combined with the last fading rays of sunlight, gave the room an almost magical glow. Johnny was dressed only in a pair of shorts, and his hair and skin seemed to shine gold against the cobalt blue of the sofa. As he absent-mindedly scratched his toned stomach, Belle experienced a stab of physical yearning so strong and unexpected it jolted her right back to the day they first met.

It had been a run-of-the-mill Monday morning sales meeting at Global Telecoms, and after the standard talk of 'running things up the flagpole and seeing if some fucker salutes it', Simon, the red-braced, Bugs Bunny-necktied sales manager, had asked them all to 'give it up' for Johnny Farraday, the newest member of the account management team. Belle had taken one look at Johnny with his closely cropped hair and mean-looking face and it had been the equivalent of downing four espressos laced with Pro Plus. Her customary post-weekend hangover vanished as every single nerve-ending in her body sprang back into life. Coughing just loudly enough to attract his attention, she then treated him to one of her finest smouldering gazes coupled with sultry leg-crossing manoeuvres, lifted staight from *Basic Instinct*. Sharon Stone had eaten her heart out, and Johnny's face had broken into such a devastatingly handsome grin that Belle had been instantly smitten. At last there was a man in the office who looked like a man rather than a well-scrubbed mummy's boy. She was mortified when he opened that perfect, mean-looking mouth and whined in a thick West Midlands accent, 'All roight, how's it gooing?' Belle couldn't believe that this bronzed Adonis could sound so much like Barry from *Auf Wiedersehen, Pet*. Undeterred, as soon as she got back to her desk she looked up elecution lessons on the Internet. At least an accent could be altered, she reasoned, whereas character flaws tended to be set in stone.

Johnny fascinated Belle. The first member of his working-class family to make it to university, he was the only man she knew who read the *Guardian* and called women 'birds'. Belle smiled as she remembered the hours they spent in the pub those first three months, ripping their arrogant work colleagues to shreds and putting the world to rights. Within days she was convinced that she'd met her soul mate, the one, her life's partner. A man who actually hated James Bond, a man who loved to read – even if it was mainly sports autobiographies. So where had it all gone wrong?

Belle looked at Johnny, his bright green eyes staring dreamily into the middle distance. He was thinking about her, she just knew it. Maybe it wasn't too late, perhaps she'd been overreacting with this football widows thing. Standing by the end of the sofa, ready to fall into his arms, Belle felt the time was right to make the peace.

'A penny for your thoughts,' she murmured softly.

Johnny jumped. 'Oh, I was thinking about Wolves. They're going to get promoted to the Premiership this season, I can just feel it,' and as Belle sank down on to the arm of the sofa in despair Johnny leapt to his feet punching the air and yelling at the top of his voice, 'COME ON, WANDERERS! COME ON, WANDERERS!'

6

With every faltering step she took down Emerald Avenue, Anna's heart beat a little faster. By the time she got to number sixteen she felt dangerously close to vomiting in one of their immaculately pruned rose bushes, she was so nervous. She was just four houses away from Belle's. Four houses away from the Football Widows meeting. Slackening her pace, she glanced furtively about her. Emerald Avenue. Never had a name seemed more apt as the warm rays of the late August sun shimmered on the leaves of the neatly clipped hedges and ranks of sycamore trees lining the pavement.

As Anna drew level with number twenty she stopped and pretended to look for something in Grace's bag. Playing for time, she rummaged through the assorted snacks, bottles of juice, nappies and wide selection of wipes – she was taking no chances this time. The bag had been packed by nine o'clock that morning and placed on top of the pile of mail-order catalogues beside the front door.

For the first time ever, Anna thought of her cluttered, shabby old flat with something close to affection. Why the hell wasn't she there now? Watching the *EastEnders* omnibus on UK Gold. The prospect of an afternoon with Pauline Fowler seemed far, far better than what awaited her at the end of the conifer hedge she was currently crawling past. Suddenly the women she had spent all week imagining as potential new friends seemed about as inviting as a firing squad. Once she got to the end of the hedge there would be no turning back – she would be in full view of Belle's house. Anna glanced down at her lilac sundress. Back in the gloomy recesses of the flat it had made her feel jaunty and summery, but under the glaring spotlight of the sun she felt naked and vulnerable and as pale as a ghost. Tom had been right – it was far too skimpy for her.

Just as she contemplated turning the buggy around and beating a hasty retreat, an unknown force seemed to propel her on to Belle's garden path. Unable to raise her gaze, Anna followed the trail of colour emanating from the flower-beds to the assorted terracotta pots standing guard by the porch.

Taking a deep breath, Anna pulled the porch door handle down. It didn't move. She pulled again, this time a little harder. It still didn't budge. Oh God, how embarrassing. What was she doing wrong? She studied the handle. It seemed pretty run-of-the-mill as door handles went. Perhaps it was one of those you had to lift up rather than down, she pondered, attempting to raise the handle, but it remained rigid. She peered into the porch for some kind of inspiration. In one corner a box overflowed with muddy trainers, a variety of flip-flops and a pair of children's Wellingtons. In the other corner a garden gnome dressed in a football kit was bending over to reveal a pair of pert china buttocks. On the wall directly above the gnome a brightly painted sign cheerfully proclaimed that she was at 22 Emerald Avenue, right next to a doorbell, hopelessly out of reach. Perhaps there had been an emergency and the meeting had been called off. Or maybe there never had been a meeting and she was the victim of an elaborate hoax. They were probably all hiding behind the curtains right now, clutching their sides and stifling their giggles as she tried in vain to open the locked porch door. Anna's face began to smart and she felt the onset of tears stinging the corners of her eyes. Just as she was about to turn and flee she heard a clattering from inside the house. Moments later the front door flew open and Belle burst into the porch.

'I'm sorry,' she mouthed through the glass, fumbling with a key in the lock before flinging the door open. 'I have to keep it locked to stop my son escaping. I'm so glad you could make it. Here, let me help you.' Belle took the buggy and led Anna into a large, airy hall. Framed prints of film stills lined the jade walls. Anna followed her past a pouting Scarlett O'Hara into the living room.

A deliciously cool breeze swept through the French windows, rustling the piles of paperwork stacked on the dining-room table and dancing its way through the silver wind chimes hanging from the archway into the living room.

Anna watched nervously as Grace toddled over to inspect the rubber plants clustered around the fireplace in multicoloured ceramic pots.

'All right?' said a voice to Anna's right. She looked down to see Maz beaming up at her, a vision in fuchsia sprawled on the outsized blue sofa.

'Hi,' she replied in a voice that was bearly distinguishable from a mouse's squeak. Sat at the far end of the sofa was Ginny, punching away on some kind of electronic organiser. She looked up briefly to smile at Anna before returning to her frantic keying.

'Can I get you a drink?' Belle asked politely.

'Oh, yes, just a juice, please,' Anna replied, eyeing the bottles of wine on the coffee table nervously.

'Are you sure?'

Anna nodded and perched warily on the edge of one of the enormous armchairs. Just then a little boy of about three came tearing into the room. When he saw Grace he stopped dead and his mouth fell open.

'A baby,' he whispered, awestruck. 'Mum, can I play with it?'

'Yes, Harry, you can play with her, as long as you're careful.' Anna watched nervously as Harry prodded Grace's stomach. To her surprise, Grace gurgled with delight.

Belle handed Anna a glass of orange juice. 'He's going through a bit of a baby obsession at the moment,' she explained. 'Much to Johnny's dismay.'

She turned to Ginny and Maz. 'He's finding it a bit hard to accept that a son of his could possibly prefer pushing a pram to kicking a football.'

Maz chuckled. 'Worried he might have produced a nancy boy, is he?'

Belle smiled and gave Grace and Harry a bowl of crisps each. Returning to her armchair, she cleared her throat. 'Well, thank you all for coming and a special welcome to Anna. I thought we could start the ball rolling, so to speak, by reminding ourselves exactly why we're here. So let's each take a turn to talk about the one thing that really pisses us off about football, or rather our sad, football-obsessed partners.'

Anna gulped nervously. She was going to have to talk to three complete strangers. Why hadn't she asked for a glass of wine?

'Okay, well, I'll start,' said Belle, gathering her mass of curls into a scrunchy. 'The thing that really, really bugs me about Johnny is when he watches a match on Ceefax.'

'How can you watch a match on Ceefax? Don't you mean when he checks the scores?' Ginny asked, as she put her Palm Pilot back into her bag.

'No, Ceefax do this thing called Live In-Vision,' Belle explained. 'One night when Wolves were playing, and for some reason the match wasn't being shown on one of our twenty-seven sports channels, Johnny announced that he'd have to watch it on Ceefax instead. I went mad – there was no way I was missing *EastEnders* to look at a page of Ceefax. It was the one when Saskia got clumped with the ashtray as well.'

Maz nodded sympathetically. 'Too bloody right.'

'But Johnny says, "Don't worry, love, I'll watch it on Live In-Vision." Then he starts fiddling around with the remote control and the next thing I know this little box appears at the bottom of the screen saying Wolves nil, Reading nil.'

'Oh my God!' Ginny exclaimed.

'But that's not the worst of it,' Belle continued, revelling in Ginny's horror. 'I'd just got used to having a football score at the bottom of the screen and Steve Owen's just about to brain her when Johnny suddenly leaps up screaming. I nearly had a heart attack. I'd never seen him get so excited over a soap.'

'It was a blinding episode, though,' Maz mused.

'Yes, but he wasn't screaming at *EastEnders* – he was screaming at the damned box at the bottom of the screen which now read Wolves one, Reading nil!'

'Oh my God, that is so sad,' said Ginny. 'He'd better not share the joys of this Live In-Vision thing with Mike – there's no way I'm having *Frasier* interrupted by a bloody football score.'

Belle nodded. 'The worst thing is, you get absolutely no warning when the score's going to change. One evening we were watching a documentary about Mother Teresa and they were showing footage of her hugging a leper or something when Johnny suddenly yells, "You fucking bastard!" at the top of his voice. I thought he'd gone mad – until I looked at the box at the bottom of the screen and saw that one of the Wolves players had scored an own goal.'

As Ginny and Maz shook their heads in disgust, Anna stared at the floor. The last time Tom discovered Arsenal had lost on Ceefax he had flung the remote control at the wall so hard that batteries and shards of plastic had showered the room.

'Okay,' said Ginny, taking a sip of her spritzer, 'I've got one. How about when you go away on holiday or even for a weekend break and you somehow always end up visiting the local football ground?' The living room resounded with groans of recognition. 'Now I wouldn't mind so much if it was some world-famous stadium, like New Trafford or something.'

'Old Trafford,' Belle corrected, instantly feeling ashamed.

'Yeah, whatever, but it's always some piddly insignificant ground in the middle of nowhere. For example' – Ginny paused to rearrange her perfectly bottle-tanned legs – 'last year Mike and I went on a get-away-from-it-all trip to the Scottish Highlands. You know the sort of thing,' she said, turning to Maz, 'log cabin, a spot of salmon fishing, glasses of Scotch in front of a roaring fire.'

Maz nodded and forced a smile. What the hell was wrong with fish and chips on Southend Pier? The stuck-up cow.

'But the whole trip was ruined by his sudden obsession with Scottish football grounds. On the way up we stopped at no fewer than five different grounds. I was, like, going out of my mind. It must have added at least another four hours on to the journey and the worst thing was when we got to each ground they'd all be totally deserted and he'd just stand there staring dreamily at the pitch as if he'd come on a pilgrimage to some kind of sacred shrine!' Ginny slumped back into the sofa, exasperated.

Anna busied herself rummaging around in Grace's bag for a bottle of juice, terrified Belle would pick her next.

'Okay – here's one for you,' said Maz, pausing to drain her glass of wine. 'How come wherever you happen to be on a Saturday night and whatever you happen to be doing they always manage to get home in time for *Match of the* bloody *Day?*'

'Yeah,' Belle agreed, sullenly.

'I mean, we can be out having a great time somewhere and suddenly Darren'll go, "That's it, we're off," and before I know it I'm being whisked out the bleeding door and we're back home just in time for the opening credits.'

'Don't you Videoplus it?' Ginny enquired, topping up her drink with some Perrier water.

'What?'

'Mike always Videopluses it. Mind you, I suppose it's easier to get home in time from the places you drink in than it is for us to get back from All Bar One or Brown's.'

Maz grabbed a bottle of wine from the coffee table and for a split second Anna thought she might be about to smash it over Ginny's head.

'Okay, so how about you, Anna,' Belle said swiftly. 'What drives you mad about . . . sorry, what's your partner's name again?'

'Tom,' Anna replied, shifting nervously in her chair. 'Well, I don't know where to begin, really.'

Maz laughed heartily. 'Tell me about it, darling. I could write a book about the things that piss me off about my Darren! I tell you what – let's all have a refill. Stick some music on, Belle, and then you can tell us what else you've got in store for us.' Maz took the bottle over to Anna and, ignoring her murmured protestations, filled her glass with wine.

'Right, you've asked for this,' Belle said, leaping to her feet and heading for the huge CD rack in the corner. Anna watched wistfully as she rooted through the CDs. How could Belle wear a slip dress so unselfconsciously? Although her skin was fair she didn't resemble a ghost suffering from a severe case of anaemia like Anna. She was so full of energy too, clapping and laughing as Neil Diamond's unmistakable drawl filled the room. Neil Diamond? Anna was momentarily stunned. She would have had Belle down as an All Saints or Madonna fan. Neil Diamond was one of her mother's favourites, along with Barry Manilow and Daniel bloody O'Donnell.

Shutting her eyes, Anna took a huge gulp of wine. She sighed as she felt the alcohol trace a warm path from her mouth right down into her empty stomach, slowly replacing the tension in her body with a gentle glow.

The shrieking voices of Belle and Maz singing along to 'Sweet Caroline' snapped Anna from her daze. 'Come on,' they were yelling, pulling her to her feet until they all formed a circle in the middle of the living room. Belle, Ginny, Maz, Harry, Grace and a somewhat embarrassed Anna, dancing round and round, faster and faster.

As Belle and Maz punched the air shrieking 'Da! Da! Da!' and Grace and Harry giggled uncontrollably, Anna found herself in the unlikely position of agreeing with Neil Diamond that good times never had felt so good.

7

Two 'Sweet Carolines' and one 'Cracklin' Rosie' later, Belle, Maz, Ginny and Anna collapsed back into their seats, exhausted. Belle watched Ginny and Maz comparing nail varnish on the sofa and smiled to herself.

'Fuchsia is just so you,' Ginny schmoozed, while Maz conceded that French manicures weren't so bad themselves.

Belle had known Neil Diamond would save the day – even Anna seemed more relaxed as she bounced a giggling Grace on her knee.

'Okay – let's get down to business,' Belle said, rifling through a file of papers on her lap. 'Take one and pass it on,' she instructed, handing the papers to Maz. One by one they began to read while Belle looked on anxiously. To her relief the room was soon filled with murmurs of agreement interspersed with the occasional giggle.

FOOTBALL WIDOWS – THE RULES

1. Never, ever learn the offside rule.
2. Never wear a football top of any description – not even to decorate in.

---

3. Never attend a football match in person or watch one on the television.
4. Never watch any programme featuring Gary Lineker.
5. Boycott Walker's crisps.
6. Never agree to wash the team strip.
7. Refuse point blank to quiz your partner on past FA Cup Final results or other football trivia – this is a pointless and immature exercise and only serves to feed his obsession.
8. Never again beg your partner to stop playing football – begging is for wimps.
9. Complete at least one 'Passion Pursuit' by the end of this football season.
10. Take part in one act of 'Widow's Revenge' each week.

'Could you define exactly what you mean by "act of Widow's Revenge"? I trust you're not going to be inciting us into acts of terrorism?' Ginny enquired, not quite managing to conceal the look of concern enveloping her face.

Belle laughed. 'No, not at all, but I think we'll all agree that there's nothing quite so sweet as revenge. I thought it would be fun if we took it in turns each week to come up with a way of getting our own back on football.'

'Such as?' Ginny asked.

'Okay, follow me,' said Belle, getting to her feet.

They all followed her out into the hall and upstairs to a large, sunlit bedroom. Belle marched over to a gigantic antique pine wardrobe and flung open the doors.

'Take a look at this,' she said, gesturing inside.

The others gathered around. The wardrobe was crammed full of men's clothes: trousers and suits hanging on one side and assorted shirts and tops on the other. Belle pointed to the tops. 'Do you notice anything?'

They all peered more closely into the wardrobe. At first glance the tops seemed pretty normal. Denim shirts, cotton shirts, sweatshirts and polo shirts – one by one Belle flung them on to the king-size bed for closer inspection. Suddenly it was obvious – each of the tops displayed exactly the same orange-and-black motif of a wolf's head above the inscription 'Wolverhampton Wanderers'. Ginny sniggered.

'And if you think that's bad,' said Belle, marching over to a chest of drawers by the window, 'take a look at this.'

The top drawer was crammed full of various football strips, all slightly different in colour and design but again carrying the same black wolf's-head motif. Belle slammed the drawer shut and opened the next one down. This contained a variety of orange-and-black pants, boxer shorts, briefs and even a thong in the shape of a wolf's head that Belle brandished in disgust before discarding on the bed. 'Absolutely pathetic, isn't it? Look at this.' She stomped over to a tie rack hanging on the back of the bedroom door, where once again there seemed to be an overwhelming predominance of orange and black. Belle held aloft a particularly hideous bright orange tie, the centre of which was emblazoned with a black wolf's head. 'Can you believe he actually wore this tie to a job interview?'

'No!' Ginny sank down on to the bed in shock.

'Did he get the job?' Maz asked, studying the wolf thong intently. She quite fancied seeing her Darren in one of these – if only it didn't have those naff whiskers.

'Of course not – he probably blinded the interviewer,' Belle replied, hanging the tie back on the rack. 'I honestly don't think I've ever seen Johnny not wearing at least one article of Wolves leisure wear – it drives me nuts. It wouldn't be quite so bad if it wasn't such a god-awful colour. He insists on calling it "old gold", but there's no denying the fact that it's orange and, let's face it, has orange *ever* been in fashion?'

'I've got some quite nice orange combats,' Maz offered.

'Hmm,' said Ginny. 'So what are you going to do, Belle – bomb the Wolves leisure-wear factory?'

'No, but I'm going to make a small stand,' Belle replied, producing a rather old-fashioned-looking football shirt from the back of the wardrobe. 'Now to you or me this may appear to be just another football top, but to Johnny this is in fact' – Belle adopted a high-pitched West Midlands accent – 'a vintage 1974 League Cup Final replica.'

'Is that supposed to mean something?' Ginny asked, neatly folding a Wolves shell suit.

'God, yeah – I think it's the last time Wolves

actually won anything. It's his pride and joy, his top for really special occasions, like Harry's christening.'

'What?' Maz dropped the thong and joined Ginny, Anna, Harry and Grace on the blanket of Wolves leisure wear now covering the bed.

'Don't ask. Anyway, it's about to get the wash of its life – follow me.'

Belle led the others back downstairs and into the kitchen. Slinging the vintage 1974 League Cup Final replica into the washing machine, she then ceremoniously poured two measures of bleach into the top drawer and turned the programme dial to setting C – 'Boil Wash'. Maz led the shrieks of excitement and high-fives as Belle hit the ON button.

Anna stood in the middle of the kitchen in a state of shock. 'What are you going to tell him when he sees it?' she asked incredulously.

'Oh, I'll just blame it on him – tell him he must have put it in with the tea towels by accident or something,' Belle replied breezily.

As the washing machine began whirring through its programme of destruction, they all filed back into the living room.

'Okay,' said Ginny, once they were all seated, 'I like the sound of number ten, but number eight's a bit unrealistic, isn't it? Why should we stop demanding they spend more time with us?'

'Yeah, what's the point of moaning about football if we aren't allowed to give them hell?' Maz agreed.

'But don't you see?' Belle cried as she got to her feet

to refill everyone's glasses with wine. 'What have we ever really achieved by moaning? Let's face it, we've all shouted and stropped about football, but if it had got us anywhere we wouldn't be sitting here today, would we?'

'No, we'd be out browsing around an art exhibition or shopping in Paul Smith like normal couples.' Ginny sighed wistfully.

Maz raised an eyebrow and helped herself to a large handful of peanuts from a dish on the coffee table. If Darren ever announced that he wanted to spend his time browsing around the Tate or some poncy boutique she'd probably frogmarch him to the first football pitch she could find.

Belle picked up the peanuts. 'So what I'm getting at is this. While they're busy enjoying themselves doing something they love, why the hell should we sit around sulking and miserable? Anyone want a nut?'

Anna leaned across and took the bowl from Belle – all of a sudden she had developed a ravenous appetite.

'So what are you saying we should do?' Ginny enquired. 'Just smile sweetly and take it?'

'No. I'm saying we should follow their example. Which is where rule number nine comes in.'

'What? Start playing football?' Ginny's jaw fell open in indignation.

'Don't be silly. No, I mean follow our own dreams, pursue our own passions. Look, every Saturday when they run around that pitch pretending to be

David Beckham we may think they're being pathetic, but the concept isn't – it's brilliant.' The room fell silent. 'Every one of you must have some kind of dream or ambition that you haven't fulfilled. Maybe you've been too scared or too busy, or perhaps you haven't had enough support.' Belle got to her feet. When she'd been rehearsing this part of her speech earlier she'd found that standing up gave her more of an air of authority. 'So,' she continued, walking authoritatively to the centre of the living room, 'I think we should each come up with an unfulfilled dream or ambition and share it with the rest of the group and in doing so . . .' Belle paused for full dramatic effect. '. . . we can help each other to realise our dreams and leave the men to their dreary, pathetic little game!'

Belle sat back down slightly deflated. In her rehearsal this was the point where the others burst into spontaneous, rapturous applause rather than sat in a state of silent confusion.

Finally Ginny spoke. 'I think I see what you're getting at,' she said, nodding thoughtfully. 'For some time now I've been thinking I ought to do more for charity. You know, put something back. Admittedly being an events manager for the Wembley National Stadium Group does allow me to bring a considerable amount of joy into a lot of people's lives, but sometimes I do stop and think to myself, surely there must be more to life than Boyzone playing five nights at Wembley Arena. Mustn't there?' Ginny looked at the three other women staring at her blankly. 'Anyway, maybe a bit of charity work would make me feel more complete as a person. I mean, it worked for Princess Diana, didn't it? Perhaps I could take some of last season's clothes to the Oxfam shop or something. Would you believe I still possess about three pairs of leggings?'

Belle felt her enthusiasm rapidly begin to ebb. 'Anyone else?' she asked feebly. 'Anna?'

Anna hurriedly swallowed her mouthful of peanuts. 'I suppose my main ambition is to be a good mother to Grace,' she mumbled as a surge of blood flooded her cheeks.

Belle felt like crying. 'Maz?'

'Oh, I'd really like to do more for world peace and all the little animals out there who are so neglected and mistreated,' Maz replied.

It took a second for Belle to realise that Maz was in fact joking, but when she did her heart leaped – perhaps all was not lost. 'Look, when I told you to think of an unfulfilled dream I meant something that was really personal to you, something that you really wanted to do for yourself. Not that there's anything wrong with charitable work.' Belle glanced at Ginny. 'Or being a good mum, for that matter.' And she smiled at Anna. 'But the whole point about the Football Widows is that we can help each other achieve something really dear to our hearts, something that we've never had the guts to do on our own. You don't need any moral support to walk into an

Oxfam shop, now, do you?' Belle thought of Ginny's chronic retail snobbery. 'Okay, maybe in some cases you do.'

'So what are you saying?' Ginny asked huffily.

'I'm saying what is it that you really want to do with your life? When you're old and decrepit, what would you really regret not having done? As a child, what did you want to be when you grew up? What type of life did you want to be leading? What type of person do you really want to be?'

Belle slumped back into her chair. She was starting to run a little short on inspirational zeal.

'I always wanted to be an artist.'

Everybody turned to face Anna, who sat wringing her hands in her lap.

'Really?' Belle asked, hoping she didn't sound too disbelieving. 'So what happened?'

Anna took a deep breath and raised her eyes just high enough to communicate with Belle's knees. 'Well, I got a place at St Martin's College in London doing art and design but things didn't really work out.'

'How long were you there for?' Belle asked. Talk about hidden depths.

'Just over two years.'

Ginny sighed. 'Oh, what a waste.'

'What made you pack it in?' Maz asked, slightly insecure at being surrounded by so many ex-university types.

'The other students, really.'

'What do you mean? Did they pick on you or something?' Ginny stared at Anna intently. She could just imagine the frail little thing being a frequent visitor to the Student Welfare Counsellor.

'Oh no, nothing like that.'

'What was it, then?' Belle enquired, her curiosity well and truly aroused.

Anna took a deep breath. 'I just had nothing in common with them really, and then I met Tom and I ended up spending more and more time with him and less and less time at college.'

Belle sighed. 'How romantic. Sacrificing your education for love. So what kind of art do you do? Do you still do any?'

Anna thought of the boxes in the hall housing her fading pictures and drying-out jars of paint. 'No. I haven't been near a sketchpad for ages – not since I was pregnant with Grace. I used to like doing cartoons and comic strips, that kind of thing.' Anna couldn't believe she had said so much and not embarrassed herself once. Taking a congratulatory swig of wine, she settled back in her seat.

'Right, so this could be the perfect opportunity for you to start drawing again,' Belle said, picking up a notebook from the arm of her chair and scribbling something down.

'Oh, I don't know, I don't really have the time, what with Grace and everything.' Anna hadn't allowed herself to think of drawing for so long she felt a little afraid of what she might have unleashed.

'Does Tom have the time to play football?'

'Ye-es.'

'And does he have the time to go training twice a week?'

'Yes.'

'And does he have the time to follow his favourite team?'

'Yes.'

'Well then, you can find the time to paint. I can always help with Grace, or at least Harry can.' They all turned to look at Harry, who had constructed a bed of cushions on the floor and was busy tucking Grace up in a blanket made out of a tea towel.

'Okay, good, so that's Anna. Now how about you, Maz? I take it you won't be opening up a rival to Battersea Dogs Home?' Belle looked at Maz and grinned.

'Mine's going to seem a bit crap and boring, I'm afraid,' said Maz, blushing slightly. 'As you can probably tell, I've never really been into books and studying and all that.'

Ginny nodded a little too enthusiastically.

'But the one thing I've always really wanted to do since I was a kid was design and make my own clothes.'

'You mean you don't already?' Ginny asked, eyeing Maz's bright fuchsia top and pedal-pushers suspiciously.

'No. I dyed these and I make alterations to things

all the time, but I've never actually made anything from scratch. That's what I'd love to do, design an outfit and have my own sewing machine to make it on. That would be wicked.'

'Excellent,' said Belle, scribbling on her pad.

'Okay, Ginny, how about you? Or is it still going to be making your first trip to an Oxfam shop?'

'Ha, ha, very funny,' Ginny replied, giving Belle an elegant one-fingered salute. 'Well, I suppose if I'm really honest it would have to be learning to become more relaxed and laid-back.'

'You're kidding?' said Maz in feigned surprise.

'No, honestly,' Ginny replied earnestly. 'I know I may seem a pretty cool person to all of you, but I am actually rather . . .'

'Uptight?' Maz offered.

'Highly strung,' Ginny corrected. 'I know I need to chill out a bit more, but I just don't know how to do it.'

'Right, so you want to learn how to relax and let go a bit?' Belle enquired, chewing thoughtfully on the end of her pen. Perhaps there was hope for Ginny yet.

'Yes, well, I don't really have any unfulfilled ambitions on the career or financial front,' Ginny replied, smiling smugly at Maz.

'Okay, that's fine,' said Belle, writing 'GINNY – CHILL OUT!!' on her notepad. 'Well, that just leaves me, then.'

'Yeah, enough of putting us on the spot. What great unfulfilled dream do you have, apart from shagging Neil Diamond, of course,' said Maz, letting rip with one of her bellowing laughs.

'Oh, gross.' Ginny shuddered.

'I,' Belle declared, 'am going to have a mad, passionate affair!'

8

Belle's mother, Rosalie, was ultimately to blame for her current predicament. Naming her only daughter Marybelle Scarlett Ashley Elizabeth certainly hadn't helped. Sounding like she'd sashayed straight off the pages of a bodice-ripping blockbuster made Belle's insatiable craving for romance almost inevitable.

Rosalie, an auburn-haired beauty from America's Deep South, was a true romantic of the highest order. At an extremely early age she realised that being raised on an Arkansas farm was not the best possible start to the life of romance and splendour she so coveted – so deserved. Not for her the endless quilt-making and cookie-baking that seemed to satisfy the other women of her small home-town. Besides, beauty such as hers would be wasted on a dungar-ee-clad, straw-chewing farmer named Chuck or Billy-Bob. So at the tender age of eighteen she travelled four thousand miles around the world to Swinging Sixties London under the cunning guise of visiting an elderly aunt, never to return home again.

A modelling contract with a Bond Street fashion house soon procured her a bed-sit off the King's Road, and within weeks her admittance to the London social set was virtually complete. One night she even attended a party hosted by Lionel Blair. All that remained was to ensnare a member of the English aristocracy – her own personal Heathcliff – and all her childhood dreams would be realised. Unfortunately Rosalie couldn't help feeling slightly let down by the members of the aristocracy she came into contact with. Quite frankly she found the pompous cads who hovered around her like well-heeled bees around a honeypot as tiresome as the boys back home. Which was why, when she ran into a small-time East End drug dealer named Jimmy 'the Biscuit' Price, the attraction was instant. Jimmy was rugged, he was manly, he spoke with a genuine cockney accent.

He was also a compulsive liar. Not only had he never met the Kray twins, he also had no intention of withdrawing before he came. 'Whoops!' he'd whispered almost apologetically, as he rolled off Rosalie and lit up a joint. Rosalie hadn't been unduly concerned when she got up to use the bathroom and felt the warm trickle down the inside of her thigh – she was far too stoned. It was only when, six weeks later, she unexpectedly threw up all over the front row at a fashion show that her world was turned upon its head.

Jimmy promptly disappeared back into the East End underworld, leaving Rosalie to face single parenthood in sixties Britain – neither a romantic nor a particularly splendid prospect. Rosalie, however, was made of stern stuff. Now that she had come so far, how could she possibly let the small matter of an unplanned pregnancy interfere with her destiny? By the time she was four months pregnant she had found her alternative hero in the form of Bill Tapworth. Not quite a member of the English aristocracy, but a manager of Woolworths, and one of their largest branches at that. Bill, a plain man who liked to iron his socks, couldn't believe his luck that someone as attractive and vivacious as Rosalie would agree to go on a day trip to Worthing with him, let alone be his wife. By the age of forty-five he'd resigned himself to living out his days a confirmed bachelor, doomed to meals for one on a tray in front of *Crossroads*. His sense of eternal gratitude to Rosalie for providing him with a ready-made family and filling his house with fragrance and frivolity made him more than willing to turn a blind eye to her frequent nocturnal indiscretions.

For years Belle thought her mother got all dressed up simply to put her to bed at night. 'Honey, y'all are just sooo precious to me,' she would drawl into Belle's hair, tucking the bedclothes around her snuggly. 'If anything ever happened to you I would just die!' And Belle would inhale deeply, almost tasting the sweet mixture of cocoa butter and Chanel No. 5 emanating from Rosalie's creamy skin. As her little hand clasped her mother's tightly in the dark, Belle felt as if it was the two of them against the world. Although she loved Bill dearly, she knew he wasn't

71

her dad. Rosalie had wasted no time in telling her all about her real father; the American soldier who had died so tragically and needlessly on a top-secret military exercise shortly after she was conceived.

It was unavoidable that Belle would become hooked on the sense of romance and drama that shrouded Rosalie like a cloak. While the other girls in her class became obsessed with Enid Blyton, Rosalie fed Belle a diet of Mills and Boon. When her class-mates daydreamed of tuck boxes, boarding schools and ponies, Belle's head was awash with tales of timid little creatures called Emily or Susan being relentlessly pursued by powerful and slightly danger-ous businessmen with glints in their eyes and names like Guy Manley.

Then, one fateful night, when Belle complained of not being able to sleep and a fully made-up Rosalie was eager to escape to the loving arms of her latest beau, a twenty-year-old Italian fashion student, she recommended her own alternative to counting sheep.

'Honey, if y'all can't sleep, why don't you play my favourite game?' And she whispered mysteriously, 'Romantic Liaisons.' Belle gazed up at her in awe. How did Rosalie manage to make everything sound so exciting? 'Okay, now all you have to do is think about the boy you love . . .'

'He's not a boy,' Belle interrupted. 'He's a man.'

Rosalie looked down at her ten-year-old daughter and sighed. Sometimes she could be so precocious. 'So who is this *man*?'

'Mr Butcher, my teacher,' Belle confessed, sinking beneath the covers to conceal her blushes.

'Excellent choice,' Rosalie murmured thoughtfully. Mr Butcher and his muscular physique had made parents' evenings quite enjoyable that year. She smiled – Belle was her mother's daughter all right. 'Okay, sugar, well, you just make up a story in your head about you and Dave . . . Mr Butcher having a Romantic Liaison, and before you know it you'll be fast asleep and dreaming the most delicious dreams.' Rosalie glanced at her watch. She was already half an hour late for her own romantic liaison. Giuseppe would be going mad. She kissed Belle warmly, leaving a sticky film of lip gloss on her cheek. 'See you in the morning, sweetie.'

After she had gone Belle lay in the darkness breathing in the last traces of Chanel and wondering exactly what a 'Romantic Liaison' was. Concluding that it had to be some kind of rip-roaring adventure, she spent the next hour and a half inventing stories about herself and Mr Butcher on board a pirate ship searching the high seas for treasure, fighting cannibals and drinking the milk from coconuts.

It was during a game of Romantic Liaisons only a couple of weeks earlier that Belle had realised she needed to have an affair. Of course she had long since moved on from the swashbuckling adventures of a pirate's life – and the charms of Mr Butcher, come to that. She was about twelve when she discovered the true meaning of a Romantic Liaison, and from then on there had been no stopping her.

Over the years Romantic Liaisons had become as much a part of her nightly routine as cleaning her teeth. Almost every night before Belle drifted off to sleep she would escape into her own private world of fantasy. A world of romantic love stories in which she always played the starring role. In Romantic Liaisons Belle's current unrequited love would morph into a gushing, adoring admirer, and the one who got away would come running right back. Belle never got dumped during a Romantic Liaison, she was never cheated on, and she never, ever fanny-farted!

She'd even enjoyed several Romantic Liaisons with Johnny during the weeks between their first meeting at Global Telecoms and them finally getting it together. In the privacy of her bedroom she imagined liaisons on the photocopier, over her desk, even at a football match:

As Wolves scored the winning goal in the dying minutes of the game, Johnny swept Belle up into his muscular arms and kissed her passionately on the lips. 'I've been wanting to do that for ages,' he sighed into her ear. To the roars of the crowd their lips locked once again, finally unleashing the pent-up passion of the past few weeks. 'Let's go somewhere a little more private,' Johnny whispered breathlessly as he led her by the hand towards the exit . . .

Of course, those were the days before football had

ruined her life, taken away her husband and left her feeling so lonely and so damned frustrated. She had to be frustrated – why else would she have found herself only two weeks ago having a Romantic Liaison with her middle-aged, balding bank manager?

Look, I know I've gone over my limit, but I'm more than willing to pay it off in kind, Belle whispered seductively, walking around Mr Bradbury's desk to straddle his lap and loosen his tie. He quivered with anticipation as she slowly undid his shirt buttons one by one to reveal . . . To reveal a pale and flabby stomach.

'Ahhhhh!' Belle had screamed in horror, and sat bolt upright in the bed. What the hell was wrong with her?

'What the hell's wrong with you?' Johnny murmured in his sleep.

Belle sank back down feeling horny and horrified. Mr Bradbury was vile. His breath smelled of pickled onions and he was constantly sweating. She put her arm around Johnny and snuggled up against his back. Running her hands through the hair on his chest, she traced a faint path down his taut stomach, lower and lower until . . .

'Leave it out, love. It's the first game of the season tomorrow – I've got to conserve energy.'

Belle withdrew her hand as if it had been burnt. Rejected yet again for that fucking game. She lay in the dark, staring at the ceiling, fuming. She was so sick of feeling like this. She would never have imagined it possible to feel so much hatred towards a sport. As Princess Diana had once said, it was as if there were three of them in her marriage, and it was more than a little crowded.

At least Diana's rival had been human. How could you possibly feel threatened by a sport? The worst thing about it was that Belle felt as if *she* were the bit on the side, constantly taking second place to football. It was as if Johnny and football had been together for years, and Belle was just a fleeting distraction. 'Wives come and go,' she could just imagine him saying, 'but football's for life!' And so, like the naive, ever-hopeful mistress, Belle felt destined to a life of false expectation and disappointment.

Each year things had grown worse. When they first met, Johnny had just moved to London from Wolverhampton and had no team to play for. Their hectic social life also meant that he didn't have the time to travel all over the country to see his beloved Wolves play. On the odd occasion he did, Belle hadn't batted an eyelid. She wasn't an unreasonable person, and she didn't see anything wrong with him attending a handful of games each season. Besides, it meant she could spend all Saturday shopping with Ginny. But then she fell pregnant. Once Johnny had recovered from the shock of impending parenthood, he became determined to resurrect his playing career. It had always been a dream of his to play in the same team as his son. In a few years from now that dream could become a reality, and if it got him out of changing nappies . . .

Johnny first started playing for Rayners Park shortly after Harry was born. Belle had torn her hair out with the boredom and loneliness of being on her own all week, only to be deserted for half the weekend too, but nothing would stop Johnny playing. 'There's a lot worse things I could be doing. At least I don't knock you about. At least I'm not out gambling all our money away on the horses. At least I'm not letting myself go,' he would say, honestly believing that this would be of some reassurance to Belle. Great, Belle would think to herself, I hardly ever see my husband, we can never go away for a weekend together, he hardly spends any time with his son, but thank God I never married Gazza!

Then, halfway through the previous season, just when it seemed things couldn't get any worse – they did. Johnny announced that he was going to play Sunday pub football for the Pig and Whistle as well as Saturday football for Rayners Park, two weekly training sessions on Tuesday and Thursday nights and the odd midweek fixture on a Wednesday. Belle was incandescent with rage. How could he ruin the only day they had left to spend together as a family?

'But I'm in every Monday night – we can be together then,' Johnny had said, perplexed. 'Why don't you bring Harry down on a Sunday if you want a family day out?'

Deciding that anything was better than nothing, Belle had sulkily agreed, only to discover with horror the pointless charade that is Sunday pub football. For two hours she stood shivering in a cold, windy park, watching as a bunch of mainly unfit, beer-bellied slobs staggered about, pausing periodically to run over to the sideline and puke up the previous night's fifteen pints. Never again!

The six months that followed were littered with screaming-matches and moody silences.

'You don't love me,' Belle had screamed. 'If you did you'd want to spend time with me, not playing that stupid game!' But Johnny would simply raise his eyes in despair, dismiss his wife's near-hysteria as PMT, and set off for football as normal.

'But it's my thirtieth,' she had cried aghast when he told her he had to play in some crappy final on her birthday at the end of the previous season.

'This is a once-in-a-lifetime opportunity, Belle. They've even got Russell Grant to be the guest of honour,' Johnny had replied, astounded at his wife's lack of understanding. 'I bet Alan Shearer doesn't get this kind of grief from his missus,' he added, ducking just in time to avoid an airborne ashtray.

The thirtieth birthday incident was the straw that broke the camel's back. Rosalie, who had flown over from Milan especially, was outraged to find her beloved only daughter sobbing uncontrollably over a pile of unopened cards and presents.

'How can he be so mean and heartless?' she had

thundered. 'Playing a dumb game on your special day – why, he deserves to be horse-whipped! Now pull yourself together, Belle, honey, you'll make your eyes go all puffy and bloodshot.'

Belle snuggled up to her mother, comforted once more by the scent of Chanel and her warm Southern drawl as she drummed into her the importance of never letting a man ruin your life. Rosalie seemed to have so much insight into her feelings of abandonment and rejection it was uncanny.

'Honey, now y'all remember this, there's not a man alive worthy of your tears and heartache, and if that dumb-assed, no-good loser puts some stupid game before your feelings then you go out there, my girl, and you live life for yourself. Do you understand? *Carpe diem*, as Robin Williams so eloquently puts it in *Dead Poets Society*. Oh, Belle, did you ever see that movie? Why, I cried so hard I had to wear cucumber slices over my eyes for about a month after!'

That day at the end of the previous season had proved a turning point for Belle. Buoyed up by Rosalie's talk of seizing the day and seeking revenge, she vowed to herself that Johnny would never again hear her begging or crying for his attention. No, she, Marybelle Scarlett Ashley Elizabeth, deserved more than this, and if Johnny couldn't give her what she needed then she'd bloody well find someone who would!

9

Although it was only a twenty-minute walk from Belle's house, Anna felt as if she were entering another universe as she negotiated the glass-strewn entrance to her block of flats. There were no swags and tails draping these windows, just nicotine-stained nets and sheets of corrugated iron, and rather than clambering roses, graffiti plastered the walls like tattoos. PAKIS OUT! and FUCK OFF TOTTENHAM! they screamed as Anna slowly made her way up the stairs, a sleeping Grace in one arm and a folded buggy hooked over the other. Edging her way past a group of kids smoking and swearing on the balcony, she instinctively lowered her eyes.

'Give me da fuckin' spliff, man,' one of the boys squeaked, all bum-fluff and bravado. Although he couldn't have been a day over twelve, Anna still felt intimidated. She dreaded walking past these packs of stray kids even more than she did a building site full of workmen demanding she get her tits out.

'Don't diss me, man!' the boy shouted, sounding like Ali G on helium as he squared up to one of the others. Closing and double-locking the door behind her, Anna breathed a sigh of relief – Tom wasn't home yet.

It was seven o'clock before the Football Widows had finally disbanded. After Belle had furnished them all with a detailed and rather lewd explanation of her adulterous desires, she had issued her instructions for the next meeting. Each of them had to come up with a plan for achieving their Passion Pursuit, and they also had to think of ways in which they might help the other Football Widows achieve theirs, such as finding Belle a 'well-endowed lover'. Much to Anna's relief it was agreed that Maz would carry out an act of Widow's Revenge.

Anna switched on the hall light and promptly switched it off again. Having spent the past four hours in the rainbow spectrum of 22 Emerald Avenue, the sight of her own poky, cluttered hall came as a complete shock to the system. How had she let it get in such a state? What would Belle and the others think if they could see the way she lived? She shuddered at the thought.

Careful not to wake Grace, Anna crept down the hall past the row of boxes that had been languishing there since the move. Boxes containing her previous life, all packaged away neatly, out of sight, almost out of mind. She glanced at the labels on top of each box – A-LEVEL ARTWORK, ST MARTIN'S COURSE- WORK, STORYBOARDS. Had she really once been organised enough to catalogue the contents like that? It seemed impossible to believe now, and about as pointless as the thought of unpacking them.

Anna gently laid Grace down in her cot and clambered on to an old toolbox of Tom's to drape a towel over the empty curtain rail. She was stung by a sudden pang of guilt. Grace's room should be a riot of colour by now, a menagerie of stuffed toys, with Winnie the Pooh curtains fluttering in the breeze, not an old bath towel hanging precariously on a rail.

Anna's head had begun to thump slightly from the wine. For the first time in years she was going to have a hangover, but she didn't mind because for the first time in years she also had a social life and possibly even some new friends. Never had the onset of a headache felt so good. Anna headed for the living room emboldened with a new sense of purpose.

Summoning all her courage, she turned on the light, and the room was flooded with an unforgiving hundred-watt glare. She forced herself to look at the wallpaper; its faded grey and red stripes complete with yellow stains bore a rather unsettling resemblance to a pair of old man's pyjamas. The equally hideous brown swirly carpet was barely visible beneath the multitude of toys, Rizla packets and old copies of the *Racing Post* scattered about. How could she have let Grace play in such a mess? Anna felt as neglectful as the mother in *Trainspotting* who let her baby crawl among abandoned hypodermics. Well, not any more. When she'd told Belle she wanted to be a good mother it hadn't been a complete fabrication.

She did want to be a better mum to Grace, and at least it was vaguely attainable – unlike wanting to be an artist. Anna cringed at the mere thought.

Still, she was pretty confident she could redecorate the living room – anyone could give a room a lick of paint. Besides, she had the distinct advantage that it couldn't really look any worse. Maybe she ought to do a stencilled border like Belle's? Anna imagined Belle decorating her living room, somehow managing to make dungarees look sexy, her hair swept back in a bandana, playfully flicking terracotta paint at a man dressed from head to toe in Wolves leisure wear while Neil Diamond crooned away in the background.

Inspired by this image, Anna headed for the stereo, clearing up the trail of discarded CD cases along the way. She flicked the tuner until she found Capital Gold. As the Beach Boys harmonised about 'Good Vibrations', Anna armed herself with a knife, a bucket of soapy water and several industrial-sized bin-liners and set to work.

'Fuck me!'

'Club Tropicana, drinks are free,' Anna warbled at the top of her voice, experiencing a sudden twinge of old age. Since when did Wham! qualify for golden-oldie status? She paused in her wallpaper scraping to consider this rather worrying prospect.

'Fuck me!' Tom repeated from the doorway, re-moving his baseball cap and scratching his head in bewilderment. 'Anna? What's going on?'

Anna almost dropped her knife in shock. 'Tom. Sorry, I didn't hear you come in.'

'I'm not surprised with that crap on.' Tom slung his sports bag on to the newly visible living-room carpet and walked over to the stereo. 'How about a bit of Oasis?' he said, rifling through the neatly stacked CDs.

Anna nodded and allowed herself a small sigh of relief. Oasis was Tom's good-mood music.

'So what's going on? Don't tell me, they've had a *Changing Rooms* special on BBC Choice?' Tom chuckled to himself as he slumped down on the sofa and kicked off his trainers.

'No. I just thought it was about time I sorted this place out, that's all,' Anna replied, cautiously resuming her wallpaper peeling.

'Oh. Right. So what happened to you earlier? Why weren't you at the match? It wasn't the same without my girls there cheering me on.'

God, Anna thought, he really was in a good mood. 'I'm sorry. I got halfway there and Grace was sick all over the place. I thought it was probably best if I brought her back here.' Anna's heart pounded away to the bass line of Oasis as she busied herself with a particularly awkward piece of wallpaper. She daren't turn her crimson cheeks to face Tom.

'Is she all right?'

'Oh, yeah – I think it was just the heat.'

Tom breathed a sigh of relief and pulled a battered

packet of cigarettes from his jeans pocket. 'How about the Gooners, eh?' he asked, expertly peeling away the side of a cigarette and tipping the tobacco on to a king-sized Rizla.

Anna froze. For the first time ever she had forgotten to check the Arsenal score. 'Yeah,' she muttered, with a nervous smile.

'Four–nil. FOUR. FUCKING. NIL!' Tom grinned at her over the half-built joint. Anna loved watching him skin up. She found it hard to believe that such huge, calloused hands could perform so delicate a task with such ease.

'I tell you what, babe, we're gonna go all the way this season. We'll show that fucking Man United.' Shadows danced about Tom's swarthy face as he held the end of the joint in the flame of his lighter. He blew out the flame and sucked greedily on the spliff. 'Come over here,' he rasped, exhaling great clouds of smoke as he spoke. Just like a cartoon dragon, Anna observed. The plastic covering on the sofa squeaked as she perched down beside him.

'Right here,' he coaxed, pulling her closer. 'I'll sort you out with some paint next week. We've got shit-loads of magnolia knocking around at work.'

'Oh. Actually I was thinking more of orange or yellow or something. Brighten the place up a little?' Anna suggested.

'Yellow? Do me a favour. It'll look like a fucking canary massacre! Nah, you can't go wrong with magnolia – goes with anything.'

Anna bit her lip.

'So what have you done with all the crap in the hall?' Tom enquired.

'I managed to get most of it in our bedroom cupboard,' Anna murmured. Inhaling Tom's smoke was making her feel drowsy.

'I don't know why you don't just bin those pictures – it's not like you're ever going to need them again, is it?'

Anna began picking at an irritating piece of sponge protruding from the arm of the sofa. 'No, I suppose not, but I thought it might be nice to keep some of them for old time's sake – something to show Grace when she gets older.'

'Don't you go filling my daughter's head with all that arty-farty crap. There's no way she's going to some posh university and coming back here too stuck up to talk to her old dad. It was the best thing you ever did when you jacked it all in.'

Anna's heart sank. 'I know, but . . .'

'Anyway, let's not worry about all that now.' Tom ground the end of the joint into the ashtray. 'It's our song.'

Anna closed her eyes as the opening chords of 'Wonderwall' filled the room. Suddenly everything felt warm and slightly fuzzy around the edges. Today had been a really good day. She had got to know some new people without completely humiliating herself, she had finally made a start on the flat, and Tom was being more sociable than he'd been in ages. Anna allowed herself to snuggle up closer as Tom rasped along with Liam Gallagher, his fingers lightly tracing their way up and down her arm. Anna inhaled the mixture of smoke and aftershave woven into his T-shirt and lost herself in the music.

'Wonderwall' had been playing on the tinny, grease-splattered transistor radio at Crossways Café the first time she had met Tom. He had serenaded her over the counter, accompanied by sizzling bacon, hissing kettles and the roar of traffic rushing by outside. Meanwhile Anna had blushed as red as the Formica table-tops and longed to take refuge in the kitchen. It was the dawn shift before her first lecture of the day, a bleary-eyed haze of buttering toast and brewing tea for the King's Cross regulars. Since beginning her part-time job at Crossways, Anna had effortlessly blended into the background. It was what she did best; observing life from the wings rather than flinging herself centre stage shrieking and giggling like so many of her fellow art students. Being the focus of Tom's attention had both unnerved and excited her. As he stood there hollering along to the radio, Anna stole surreptitious glances at him through her fringe. Like jigsaw pieces coming together in her mind – the slightly skew-whiff, paint-splattered cap, the tousled chestnut hair, the tanned, weather-beaten face and hazel puppy-dog eyes, the faded T-shirt, torn jeans and steel-toecapped boots – all formed a picture of somebody very grown up and very *brown*. As 'Wonderwall' reached its climax Tom had grabbed a squeezy bottle of ketchup from the counter and held it aloft as a microphone, showering himself in watery red sauce in his enthusiasm. Tom's workmates at a nearby table fell around laughing. 'That showed her, mate!' they cheered as Tom stood there, smiling sheepishly at Anna and dripping ketchup all over the floor.

'What's so funny?' Tom asked sleepily.

'I was just remembering the ketchup incident,' Anna spluttered in between giggles.

'Oh, bloody hell – what a nightmare! Mind you, at least it did the trick.'

'What do you mean?' Anna asked, convinced that she must have misheard him.

'You know what I mean. I got the girl, didn't I? Here, Anna, be a sweetheart and tickle my arm.' Tom extended his arm across Anna's lap and closed his eyes.

Anna traced her fingernails slowly over his skin. Across his chafed knuckles, along his tanned forearm, circling the criss-crossed cannons insignia and the words 'Gunners Forever' before travelling on up the granite-like bicep. Her fingers didn't stop when they got to his shoulder, continuing up his neck to his jaw, briefly coming to rest on the scar by his eye. Anna felt the familiar twinge of concern as she pictured a ten-year-old Tom cowering in the corner of the kitchen as his drunken father rained down punch after punch. With its assorted tattoos and scars, Tom's skin was like a canvas depicting his own life story, Anna mused, her fingers retracing their path down his arm. Tom let out a deep sigh and eased himself on to her lap. As she cautiously stroked his paint-flecked hair, Anna hardly dared hope that things might turn out all right after all.

10

'*Prime cuts of pork, with just the faintest trace of lemon . . .*'

Belle was having a bad day.

'*The delicate suggestion of citrus, combined with the finest-quality pork . . .*'

The weather had taken a sudden turn for the worse, the cold winds and driving rain bringing a sharp reminder that winter was lurking just around the corner.

'*In a bold new move, designed to take the meat industry by storm, Morrison's Meats are proud to announce the launch of their brand-new lemon-flavoured sausage.*'

Belle felt sick. She'd got back from the nursery run battered and bedraggled by the elements and suffering from severe premenstrual tension. Her stomach seemed to have swollen to melon-like proportions overnight, her breasts ached, and a spot the size of Mount Etna had erupted right on the end of her nose. For the third time she highlighted the text on the screen of her PC and hit the DELETE button.

'*The new sausage from Morrison's Meats is set to become a sure-fire hit this winter. A unique combi-*'

nation of the finest-quality pork combined with an exquisite intimation of lemon, conjuring up images of Mediterranean citrus groves and . . . and Wigan slaughterhouses . . .'

'Ahhhhhhhhhh!' Belle let out an agonised yell. Who had ever heard of a lemon-flavoured sausage? How the hell was she supposed to make it sound appetising when all it made her want to do was puke?

Since leaving Global Telecoms, Belle had reinvented herself as a part-time freelance PR. Inspired by the admittedly somewhat shabby brochure from the Weybridge College of Public Relations – as advertised among the classifieds in the *Evening Standard* – Belle had been assured that with one of their diplomas under her belt the world of PR would be a veritable oyster of opportunity. Apparently, Mrs Angela Butterworth of High Wycombe hadn't looked back since completing her correspondence course. And neither had any of the other rather odd-looking individuals whose gushing quotes and grainy photographs popped up with gay abandon all over the college prospectus.

After six months of dispatching assignments to a mysterious faceless tutor named Donald MacDougall, Belle passed the course with distinction, receiving a dog-eared diploma and an even sadder attempt at a press pass, emblazoned with the Weybridge College logo and looking suspiciously as if it had been laminated in somebody's garage.

Module Seven of the course, entitled 'Building

Your Own Client Portfolio', had advised approaching local businesses with innovative ideas for improving their public relations.

'*Ask your local restaurant if they've ever considered running a raffle for charity,*' the booklet suggested. '*This story is bound to appeal to the local press, providing the company with the enhanced reputation of someone who cares and, more importantly, a free advertisement.*' Belle thought of Mr Shah in the Rayners Tandoori and, realising that he had never once seen her in a state even resembling sobriety, thought better of it. Besides, she had bigger fish to promote. My God, she had a Weybridge College Diploma in Public Relations, passed with distinction. She was destined for far greater things than a raffle in her local curry house.

So why the hell did she find herself wrestling with writer's block over a press release about a lemon-flavoured sausage? Once the euphoria of receiving her diploma had died down – Belle had thrown a small launch party in celebration – she had soon realised that even a distinction from the Weybridge College of PR cut little ice with the likes of Robbie Williams or Jude Law when they had a new CD or movie to promote. So she took the advice of Module Seven and wrote down a list of all her business contacts. They were as follows:

> Mr Shah at The Rayners Tandoori
> Mark Morrison at Morrison's Meats

As there was no way on this earth Mr Shah would ever take her seriously – he'd witnessed her passing out into a biriyani, for God's sake – she concluded that Morrison's Meats were obviously destined to be her launch pad into the glamorous world of public relations.

The second-largest meat producers in Great Britain, Morrison's Meats were a Wigan-based company that supplied to all the main supermarket chains. Belle had looked after their telecoms account in her previous life at Global Telecoms and had struck up a very good working relationship with their extremely sarcastic and somewhat eccentric managing director, Mark Morrison. On the way to her first appointment with him, Belle hadn't been able to get the song 'Return Of The Mac' out of her head. By the time she reached Wigan she was convinced she was about to meet a black rap star, clad in a shiny tracksuit and dripping in gold rope. It came as some surprise, therefore, to be greeted by a middle-aged, red-faced, blustering man who wore braces, said 'chuffin' 'ell' incessantly, and had a large bronze statuette of a sausage on his desk.

They hit it off straight away. After a lifetime in the meat trade, Mark Morrison had little time for slimy southern salesmen, with their cheesy smiles and never-ending pig swill. Belle was a refreshing change from the smarmy lad at BT; she obviously didn't know her arse from her elbow when it came to telecoms, she swore like a trooper, *and* she had a great pair of knockers.

Belle couldn't believe her luck when she actually got the Morrison deal. She'd brought the wrong slides for her presentation, she'd repeatedly said 'bollocks' when her laptop failed to work properly, and to cap it all she'd told Mark Morrison that apart from the occasional bacon sandwich she was a vegetarian and proud of it. She'd broken just about every rule in her advanced sales technique manual, but she had remembered to wear a low-cut top and high-heeled shoes.

Morrison's soon became the only account Belle actually looked forward to hearing from.

'The chuffin' phones are down again, lass,' Morrison would bellow down the line like a father scolding his wayward daughter, and rather than fob him off with a load of excuses and lies, Belle would agree whole-heartedly that Global were the 'biggest heap of pigshit south of chuffin' Watford'.

When she'd told Morrison she was pregnant, he snorted with laughter, 'Up the chuffin' duff! That'll teach yer for tekkin' yer pork unprotected!' (Morrison had a rather disturbing way of relating almost everything back to a pig or a pig by-product.) The day before Belle began her maternity leave, a slightly drunk and emotional Morrison had rung her to say that if she ever found herself in the rather unlikely situation of moving to Wigan she would always have a job at Morrison's Meats. As far as he was concerned she was a 'chuffin' prime cut!' He was therefore only too pleased to receive a begging phone call from Belle some two years later offering her services as a freelance PR for at least one-tenth of the going rate.

For the past year Belle had been writing regular press releases and the odd internal newsletter for Morrison's Meats and up until now it hadn't been too bad. It was something to do now Harry was at nursery five mornings a week, and she enjoyed writing – just not very much about lemon sausages.

'The new lemon-flavoured sausage from Morrison's is just the thing you need to give your taste buds a kick-start in the morning. The delicate zest of lemon combined with top-quality pork. Lean pork, long and lean pork, pink and firm, firm and hard and pink and . . .'

What the hell was wrong with her? She had to be sick fantasising about a sausage – and a lemon one at that. God, she was dying for a shag. Yet again Belle hit DELETE. She leaned back in her chair and looked out of the living-room window. Outside, a gale-force wind was raging, sheets of rain lashing down on her newly decked patio. Autumn isn't supposed to be like this, Belle mused. Autumn is a time for crisp blue skies and sunlight reflecting on golden leaves. A slightly colder version of summer, really. It is a time for walking in the park hand in hand with your husband, dressed in matching Aran sweaters to keep out the chill and laughing gayly as you playfully kick your way through the carpet of leaves underfoot.

What a load of bollocks! There was only one park

Johnny would be frequenting this autumn and it would not be to stroll hand in hand with her.

There was only one thing for it, Belle thought . . . No, on second thoughts, two things for it . . . Oh, sod it, three things for it. She marched over to the CD player and automatically selected track nine, pausing it while she located her secret stash of fags from under the sofa, poured herself a stiff vodka and tonic and flung open the window. She lit her cigarette and took a long drag. It tasted foul, but it felt like the right thing for a desperate woman such as herself to do. Taking a large gulp of her drink, which went down far better than the smoke, she pressed PLAY on the remote control. 'You Don't Bring Me Flowers' echoed around the room. Belle felt a juicy great sob welling in her throat as Neil Diamond lamented that nobody sang him love songs.

The sob unleashed itself. Belle clutched her forehead in pure, unadulterated sorrow, completely ignoring the fact that if Johnny did ever sing her a love song she would probably piss herself laughing.

Belle gulped and wailed and smoked and sobbed her way through the entire song. Her life was the pits, but at least Neil Diamond knew what she was going through. Nobody could sing that passionately and not have experienced the loneliness and isolation she currently felt. Perhaps his wife was an obsessive baseball fan or something.

Feeling refreshed and invigorated, Belle decided to phone someone. It was pointless trying to find inspiration from a sausage all morning, and she might as well make full use of what little spare time she did have. Maz was at Wealdstone market and Ginny was busy organising a vets convention or something. Anna. She would phone Anna. She had said she would anyway, and besides, she was desperate to get a bit more information on the mystery member of the Football Widows. Johnny hadn't stopped talking about her boyfriend Tom when he'd got back from football on Saturday night. Apparently he was the life and soul of the party, not really the type Belle would have imagined a timid little thing like Anna with at all. No, there was definitely more to Anna than met the eye, and who better than Belle to find out what.

11

Belle was coming to visit. Belle, the proud owner of
swags and tails, solid pine furniture and a sumptuous
seven-foot sofa, would soon be standing in Anna's
living room. In just a few minutes Belle's feet would
be walking hesitantly across the threadbare carpet,
her bottom would be shifting uncomfortably on the
vinyl-covered sofa, and her eyes would be widening
in horror at the desecrated walls. Anna thought back
to the tatty stained wallpaper with a pang of nos-
talgia – if only it were still covering the pock-marked
plasterwork rather than stuffed in shreds in the bin.
She looked around the living room in despair. It was
still reasonably tidy, and most of the carpet was now
visible in all of its beige swirling glory. Thankfully
Grace's toys remained pretty much confined to one
corner, with Grace herself sat in the middle of them,
gurgling away merrily. Gurgling and grunting.
Grunting and now straining, her face growing increasingly redder with the exertion. 'Oh no,' Anna
groaned, recalling the scented candles dotted around
Belle's living room, filling the air with the balmy
aroma of jasmine and vanilla. A welcoming fragrance – quite unlike the overpowering odour of

excrement that was now surging its way towards the hall.

Brrrrrrrrrrring! The doorbell screeched, like an alarm warning of the dire humiliation about to strike. What was she going to do? Leave Belle on the balcony at the mercy of the pouring rain and the prepubescent posse who were bound to be loitering about sniffing glue or setting fire to cats? The doorbell rang again, a little more insistently. Anna had no choice; she would have to admit Belle to the stinking hellhole.

'Oh, thank God!' Belle cried as she burst into the hall, bringing with her a welcome waft of Chanel. 'I thought for one awful moment you'd had to go out and I'd be left outside to drown.'

Anna watched enviously as Belle pulled down the hood of her puffa jacket and shook out her mane of curls, half expecting her to gasp, 'Because I'm worth it!' She cursed herself for not having made the effort to wash her hair that morning; for not having made the effort to wash her hair since Saturday morning. Anna gestured to Belle to go through to the living room and hovered in the doorway nervously.

'Ah, that's better,' Belle sighed as she removed her jacket and sat down on the sofa. Two seconds later she was back on her feet, coughing violently and rummaging about in her bag. Finally producing a crumpled tissue, she clamped it over her face and continued to splutter. Momentarily transfixed by some kind of warped fascination, Anna looked on, intrigued – could it be possible to actually die from nappy fumes? Belle certainly looked as if she were being asphyxiated. *Think of something! Do something!* a voice screamed inside Anna's head, jolting her back to reality.

'Would you like a cup of tea or coffee or anything?' she asked, feebly.

Belle nodded from behind her tissue. 'Coffee would be great,' she gasped. 'I'm absolutely dying for a caffeine fix!'

Scooping Grace up as subtly as possible, Anna scuttled out to the bathroom. Seemingly oblivious to the foul smell, or perhaps sensing the acute embarrassment she had caused, Grace shrieked and waved her arms about gleefully as every last trace of the foul-smelling poo was scraped and wiped from her person, rushed from the flat and sent hurtling down the rubbish chute outside.

Returning to the kitchen and lurching straight from one crisis to another, Anna realised she had absolutely no idea where the coffee was. Why oh why did Tom have to be a tea addict? She began ransacking the cupboards, her anxiety levels reaching momentous proportions. This was a total nightmare. Why had she bothered trying to make real friends? It was all far too stressful. She could have been relaxing in front of Richard and Judy right now. They didn't mind when Grace did a poo. They didn't expect her to make interesting conversation. All she had to do was laugh occasionally at Richard's naff jokes. They didn't demand cups of coffee either. God, where was the damned stuff?

'Oh no!' Anna whispered, aghast as she stared at the blue-and-white-striped label. Not only was it coffee powder, but it was Kwik Save Extra Value coffee powder. She gingerly placed a teaspoonful in the only unchipped mug she could find, which by some awful twist of fate also happened to be emblazoned with the crest of Uxbridge Town Football Club, and added some boiling water. She gave it a feeble stir and nearly burst into tears. How could she possibly give someone 'absolutely dying for a caffeine fix' the insipid-looking beverage in front of her?

'Do you need a hand?' Belle called from the living room.

'No, no, I'm just coming. Do you take milk or sugar?' *Please, please take milk and sugar – anything to give it some kind of flavour*, Anna silently pleaded, sniffing the odourless liquid.

'Oh no, just strong and black, please,' Belle replied.

Typical. Anna said a quick prayer and added three more heaped teaspoons of coffee powder. This had quite a dramatic effect on the consistency, causing it to assume an uncanny resemblance to gravy, but it made no difference whatsoever to the distinct lack of aroma. Realising that she couldn't remain in the kitchen for ever, however appealing it might seem, Anna reluctantly returned to the living room to find a rejuvenated Belle crawling about on the floor with

Grace. The room reeked of Chanel and all of the windows had been flung open.

'Oh, thank you – my saviour!' Belle gushed unsuspectingly as she took the mug.

Anna held her breath.

'Jesus!' Belle spluttered, sending a shower of brown spots down the front of her grey-marl polo neck and faded Levi's. 'What the hell is this?'

'Super Saver Extra Value coffee powder,' Anna said sheepishly, and then, for some awful, inexplicable reason, she began to giggle quite uncontrollably. She just couldn't help herself. Great spasms of nervous laughter coursed through her body, causing her to bend over double, clutching at the door frame for support.

Belle raised her eyebrows quizzically. 'Did you say Extra Value or Extra Vile?' she asked, a smirk thankfully beginning to appear at the corners of her mouth.

Anna fought desperately for self-control. 'I'm so sorry,' she gasped. 'You said you were dying for some caffeine and it looked so weak. I ended up putting in about four spoonfuls.'

'I tell you what, let's scrap the caffeine idea. How about alcohol. Have you got any paint stripper?'

They both looked at the barren walls and burst out laughing. Anna hastily removed the mug of brown paste to the kitchen and returned with two bottles of Budweiser, a cloth and a bottle opener.

'That's more like it,' said Belle, ignoring the cloth

to open her bottle and take a hasty gulp. 'Listen, thanks a lot for letting me come round at such short notice. You would not believe the day from hell I've been having.'

Anna was amazed, Belle just didn't seem the type of person to have bad days. 'Why? What's happened?' she asked, intrigued.

'Oh, I don't know. I just woke up this morning with a real sense of doom. Another Monday, another week of exactly the same crap, only now the weather's gone all shitty too. Sometimes I feel like my sole purpose in life is to provide some kind of back-up service for Johnny and Harry. A sort of "laundered pants and packed lunch service", so that they can get along unhindered with their own exciting lives, while all I've got to call my own is a pathetic little job writing about sausages! Long story,' she added, in response to Anna's bewildered expression. 'Maybe I've just got the SAD thing – you know, where you get all depressed on cloudy days. Or maybe I've just got an excruciatingly boring life.' Belle sighed and took another swig of her lager. 'So how was the rest of your weekend?'

'Oh, not bad. I've been doing a bit of DIY,' Anna replied, nodding at the walls.

'Yeah, I thought someone had been busy. So what colour scheme are you going for?'

'Probably magnolia – it goes with anything,' Anna added, trying really hard to sound enthusiastic.

'Oh.' Belle sounded a little disappointed. 'I thought

an artist like you would have been a bit more adventurous – a bit more Anna Ryder Richardson.'

Anna blushed and began picking at the label on her beer.

'But magnolia's very nice, and like you said, at least it goes with everything,' Belle added hastily.

Anna looked at Belle and smiled. 'It's just that Tom can get loads of magnolia paint from work at the moment.'

'Oh, of course. He's a builder, isn't he?'

Anna nodded.

'Johnny was talking about him on Saturday night – they seem to have hit it off.'

'Yeah, everyone likes Tom,' Anna replied flatly.

'Oh well, you can't go wrong with a paint that goes with everything *and* it's free,' Belle said diplomatically.

Anna nodded. 'Shame it's so . . .'

'Neutral?' Belle offered.

'Yes, neutral.' Anna laughed. 'And bland.'

'Mmm, yes, definitely bland. But that's the price you pay for going with everything. So . . .' Belle shifted slightly to face Anna. 'Do you have any of your artwork about the place?'

'Oh no, it's still all boxed up – from the move.'

'Oh, that's a shame, I really wanted to see some of it.' Belle looked at Anna imploringly.

It felt so unfamiliar for someone to actually want to see her work rather than throw it in the bin, Anna couldn't help feeling slightly suspicious.

'Don't you have anything you could show me? A sketch or something? I've never known an artist before. You're so lucky to have a talent like that. It's like being a poet or a musician or something – born with a gift.' Belle's eyes glazed over dreamily.

'Okay, I'll see if I can find something,' Anna said, reluctantly caving in to Belle's powers of persuasion.

She retrieved one of the recently rehoused boxes from her bedroom cupboard. Blowing the layer of dust off the top, she set it down on the floor in front of Belle. 'Don't expect anything great – it's all really old stuff,' she warned. Running a key through the tape on top of the box, Anna experienced a small stab of excitement. It had been years since she'd laid eyes on the pictures waiting inside, and now, as she slowly folded back the flaps, she was greeted with flashes of familiarity. The cover of a well-worn sketchpad, the arm or leg of a favourite character, like catching a glimpse of a long-lost friend across a crowded street. Pulling out a folder covered with intricate doodles and elaborate lettering, her body tingled with recognition.

'The Snotlaws,' Belle read over her shoulder. 'Who are the Snotlaws?'

'They're a comic strip I started when I was a child,' Anna explained. 'I drew them for years. They were meant to be a satire on *The Waltons* and people who lived in my home-town – Walton on Thames. They became a bit of a hobby, I suppose.'

The truth was, the Snotlaws had been far more

than a hobby to Anna – they had been an escape from the choking claustrophobia of life as the only child of middle-aged, middle-class, Middle England parents. Part of her had always refused to believe that Shirley and Brian Perkins could be her real mum and dad. How could they be? They called each other 'Mother' and 'Father' and said things like 'Coughs and sneezes spread diseases'. They had a bowl of plastic fruit on the sideboard, which Shirley polished religiously every Thursday. They had prunes every other day to keep them regular, slept in identical twin beds and went on day trips to Worthing. She couldn't possibly be their offspring. She couldn't imagine them having sex, for a start. Everything about their life was so regimented and cold, from the set breakfast menu – poached eggs every Monday, bacon on a Friday – to the studious dissecting of the television schedules – neat red ticks against *Terry and June* and *The Two Ronnies* and a big fat line through *Grange Hill*. As Anna grew older she became convinced that she was either adopted or had been the victim of some tragic maternity-ward mix-up. Night after night she would huddle over her desk, pencil flying as she imagined how different her life would have been with her real family.

And so the Snotlaws were born. The Snotlaw children – all five of them – didn't have to go to school unless they wanted to. They could call their fun-loving, pot-smoking parents by their first names – Pendragon and Savannah – and they had a large menagerie of pets who were free to roam all over their rambling house. A house beautifully decorated by the children, with not a trace of floral Dralon or a plastic Cox's Pippin in sight. Anna's alter ego, Panther Snotlaw, was actively encouraged by her parents to question authority, she was forbidden from joining the Girl Guides, and never once given a crappy plastic geometry set for Christmas. Through Panther and the Snotlaws, Anna created a parallel universe for herself, a world in which she could be confident and strong willed. It wasn't until Panther decided to move to London to study art that fact and fantasy finally began to merge. Brian and Shirley were horrified. What was wrong with doing accountancy at the University of Milton Keynes, like Rita and Cyril's son Derrick? But Anna was adamant. Her escape route wasn't merely beckoning – it was positively shouting and screaming.

'Open it, then,' Belle urged. 'Please.'

Anna opened the folder and pulled out the top sheet of paper. It was a slightly faded sketch of Panther Snotlaw wearing an annihilated school uniform, torn fishnet tights, an enormous pair of biker boots, and burning a copy of the *Girl Guide Handbook*.

'Wow!' Belle studied the picture in amazement. 'This is brilliant. Who is she?'

Anna reached into the folder and brought out

some more sheets, this time proper storyboards. Belle grabbed one entitled 'The Snotlaws Firebomb Worthing', and began to read.

As Belle pored over her work, Anna felt a tremendous sensation of relief. She had been so afraid they would seem naff or amateurish after so long, but judging by Belle's gasps of admiration and shrieks of laughter time seemed only to have enhanced them.

They were nearing the end of the folder when suddenly the door burst open and a rain-soaked Tom stomped into the room. Rivulets of water trickled from his hair down on to his face, and his sodden T-shirt clung to his body. His eyes slowly scanned the room, taking in the opened box, the pictures in piles on the floor and the two empty bottles of Bud, before coming to rest on Belle.

'Oh – hello,' he said, awkwardly.

Anna's heart leaped right up into her throat. What was he doing home so early? She began blindly stuffing the pictures back into the folder, trying desperately to think of some explanation for Belle's presence. Enthusiastic Jehovah's Witness? Over-friendly Betterware agent?

'Hi,' said Belle, getting to her feet and smiling sweetly. 'You must be Tom.' She stretched out her hand in greeting.

Tom shook her hand warily.

'I'm Belle, Johnny's wife – Johnny from football?'

Tom's face broke into a grin of recognition. 'Oh. All right? Sorry, I didn't realise you two knew each other.' He looked pointedly at Anna. 'So how is the miserable old git? Has he got over Wolves losing yet? I thought he was gonna break down in tears on Saturday night.'

Belle laughed. 'I think he's used to it by now. He's more likely to cry if they actually win something!'

Tom grinned and ran his hand through his wet hair. 'So how do you two know each other, then?' he asked, looking straight at Anna.

Once again Belle came to the rescue. 'Oh, we met a couple of weeks ago at the football ground and I promised Anna I'd pop round to see her – see how she was settling in and all that.'

'Oh. Right. Well, you and your old man will have to come round one night for a curry or something. Once we've got the place sorted. I can't believe you're Johnny's missus. What happened to your accent?'

'God, I'm not from up there, I'm from London.'

'Blimey – you deserve a medal. It must be like being married to Noddy Holder,' Tom said – with a wink, Anna noted.

'More like Barry from *Auf Wiedersehen, Pet*.' Belle giggled and glanced at her watch. 'Shit, I'm going to have to go, I've got to pick Harry up from nursery. I'll call you in the week, Anna, about the cake bake on Saturday.' Belle turned to Tom as she put on her jacket. 'Anna's very kindly agreed to help me make some cakes for the school bring-and-buy sale,' she explained.

Tom nodded. 'Well, it was nice meeting you, Mrs

Farraday. You tell Johnny to remember his shin pads this Saturday – I'm not bailing him out again.'

Anna followed Belle out into the hall, not quite believing her luck. Belle had lied so convincingly and with such ease.

When they got to the door Belle turned to her and whispered in her ear, 'I loved your drawings – make sure you bring them with you on Saturday to show the others.'

Belle loved her drawings. Anna closed the door behind her, basking in the afterglow of the compliment. She wanted to leap about the hall with excitement and relief. She had had a friend over for a cup of coffee. Okay, a cup of putrid, gravyish liquid that had ended up splattered all over her new friend's pristine clothes, but in spite of that, and in spite of the fact that she had then laughed like some crazed hyena rather than offering any assistance, and in spite of the flat looking and smelling like shit, she still hadn't blown it. Belle had liked her pictures – 'loved' her pictures, in fact. Anna felt as if she had finally turned a corner; at last things seemed to be changing for the better. Nothing could ruin the feeling of elation she was currently experiencing – nothing, that is, apart from the sound of ripping paper coming from the living room, bringing Anna's soaring confidence screeching to a halt.

12

'What are you doing?' It was a stupid question really, as it was blatantly obvious what Tom was doing. He was standing in the middle of the living room slowly and deliberately ripping each of her pictures in half before letting them flutter to the floor where a delighted Grace grabbed at them wildly.

'What are you doing?' Anna asked once again, too shocked to come up with anything more astute.

'You stupid cow,' Tom muttered, in an unfamiliar controlled voice, ripping the last of the pages in two and flinging it to the ground. 'You stupid, stupid cow.'

Anna dropped to her knees and began scooping up pieces of paper blindly.

'How could you have invited my mate's wife round here when it looks like this?' He gestured at the walls. 'The place is a shithole.'

Realising that this was not some sort of fun game after all, Grace toddled behind Anna and clung on to the bottom of her skirt.

'But she knew we were in the middle of decorating. It'll look fine once I've painted it,' Anna replied, desperately trying to diffuse a situation she could barely understand.

'Oh, and where exactly are you going to get this paint from?' Tom yelled, towering over her.

'I thought you were getting some from work, you said . . .'

'There is no bloody work the job's finished, I've been laid off.'

'Oh.'

'But it's all right for you, isn't it? Sitting around on your arse all day, drinking beer.' Tom picked up one of the empty Budweiser bottles and shoved it under her nose. 'Drinking *my* beer with your new mate, looking at this pile of shit.' He grabbed the pile of torn papers from Anna. 'The Snotlaws!' He practically spat the words out. 'What a load of bollocks. When are you going to realise that you can't draw? YOU CAN'T FUCKING DRAW!' Tom pushed past her to the front door.

'What are you doing? Where are you going?' Anna heard her own voice calling after him, squeaky and shrill. 'Where are you going?' The squeak turned to a scream as she leaped to her feet and stumbled after him.

Tom stopped and turned suddenly, his face barely an inch away from hers. 'I'm going to do what I should have done a long time ago,' he hissed. 'What you should have done a long time ago. I'm going to bin them. Then maybe you'll get this arty-farty crap out of your head once and for all.'

'No, please.' Anna began sobbing, grabbing Tom's arm in desperation. Shaking off her hand as if he were shooing away an annoying little insect, Tom marched out, slamming the door behind him. Anna felt her knees buckle under her. Somewhere in the distance she could hear Grace whimpering and the awful clanging of the rubbish chute sending the Snotlaws to their cockroach-infested doom.

'He's lovely,' Belle whispered into the phone, 'really tanned and rugged, but with that cheeky little-boy look as well. A sort of mixture of Robbie Williams and Beppe Di Marco.'

Ginny, who in the past had admitted to a crush on Dave Lee Travis and therefore couldn't be taken too seriously in such matters, snorted sarcastically. 'Mmmm, sounds delightful. Well, I must say I never imagined Anna with someone like that. I had her down as more of a Rupert Everett, Morrissey kind of girl.'

'I know!' Belle exclaimed, immediately kicking herself.

'Oooh, I know!' Johnny echoed from his end of the sofa, gaping, rather gormlessly, Belle thought, at the television while jabbing frantically at the remote control. 'Just like Sybil bloody Fawlty,' he muttered to himself.

Belle flung a cushion at him and made a deliberate point of turning her back. This left her twisted at a rather uncomfortable angle and half strangulated by telephone wire, but nevertheless it would show him. 'I tell you what, the tasty Tom wasn't the only surprise about our Anna,' she continued enigmatically into the phone.

'Tell me more,' Ginny implored. At least Belle was pretty sure she could detect a slight undercurrent of imploring beneath Ginny's usual air of indifference.

'Well, I got her to show me some of her artwork. I didn't think I'd be able to at first – she's hardly got any confidence, poor thing, but I suppose that's often the case with artists, isn't it, tortured souls unable to cope with their brilliance and all that.' Belle ignored the loud sighs coming at her in stereo from the end of the sofa and along the telephone line. 'God, Ginny, her pictures were incredible.'

'Don't tell me – all fluffy bunnies and picturesque landscapes,' Ginny sneered, ever the Philistine.

'No, not at all – quite the opposite in fact. She showed me this comic strip that she's been drawing since she was a kid, about this spoof family. They were incredible. Seriously, that girl has got a real talent. She's going to bring them with her on Saturday so you and Maz can have a look.'

'Shhhhhhhhh,' Johnny hissed, flinging the cushion back at Belle. He really, really pissed her off when he did this. It was as if he couldn't grasp how she could prefer exchanging some red-hot gossip with a friend to watching . . . what was it he was watching? Belle shifted slightly to glance at the TV. Ah, yes, *Jimmy Hill's Ten Greatest Sporting Moments*. Riveting!

'So our mystery member has some very hidden depths indeed,' Ginny said, sounding like a cut-glass Hercule Poirot.

'She seems really sweet,' Belle replied, flinging the cushion back at Johnny. 'I think she just needs bringing out of her shell a bit, that's all.'

'Well, she's certainly met the right person – if you can't do it no one can.'

Belle's smile was rudely wiped from her face by a projectile cushion catching her squarely on the jaw. 'Jesus, Johnny!' she screamed.

'Oh, bloody hell, is he doing his "give me some attention now!" routine?' Ginny sighed.

'Yes, you could say that.' Belle shot Johnny a withering look. 'Talking of arseholes, have you found it in your heart to forgive Mike yet?'

'Let's just say I'm over the blind fury stage and I'm currently halfway through a programme of cold shoulder.'

Belle chuckled. Ginny's cold-shoulder treatment had been known to turn many a grown man into a fawning, apologetic wreck. 'So has he been allowed back into the bedroom yet?'

'You're joking – he's not even made it off the sofa.'

'What, you've not even let him have the spare room?'

'Good God, no. The man isn't worthy of a mattress, let alone a bed. And before you start – I know what you said on Saturday about not letting them get to you and taking affirmative action and all that, but you have to admit, you can't beat making them grovel and beg for forgiveness.'

'Poor bloke,' Johnny bellowed. 'Why don't you give him a break?'

Belle glowered at him. Was it really necessary for him to make his contempt for Ginny quite so obvious? Of course, it would be a different story if there were an England match coming up. He wouldn't be shouting sarky remarks then, not if there was a chance of Ginny getting him a ticket. Mind you, even her job pissed Johnny off. 'What a waste, giving a bird like that an office inside Wembley Stadium – it's bloody criminal,' he had sighed on more than one occasion.

'You women don't know when you're well off,' he continued, ignoring Belle's glare.

'Oh, we do,' Belle sniped. 'I can just about remember a time in the darkest recesses of my memory when I was well off – it was before I met you, obviously.'

Ginny laughed. 'You tell him. I don't know, Belle, how did we end up with such a pathetic pair? I bet Anna knows she's well off with her hunky Robbie Williams look-alike.'

'Yeah, I bet he knows how to treat a lady,' Belle agreed, shooting yet another filthy look along the sofa at Johnny.

13

As Belle and Ginny bade their hasty farewells to resume their exercises in husband-blanking, Anna was three hours into a *Dynasty* omnibus on UK Gold, her mind completely and utterly blank. She was far too scared of what had happened to allow herself to think about it, and an endless stream of naff eighties melodrama was providing the perfect escape. In the entire nine hours since Tom had stormed out the only thing to have sparked a flicker of interest was when Adam Carrington redecorated Jeff Colby's office in toxic paint. Anna allowed herself a brief moment to imagine Tom choking and spluttering to death in the freshly decorated living room while attempting to watch *Match of the Day*, but it didn't take long for despondency to return her to her trance-like state. With her kind of luck they probably stocked toxic paint in every shade apart from magnolia.

When Tom finally returned home Anna didn't notice the look of concern upon his face, the Homebase carrier bags on his arm or the long flat package he placed cautiously against the wall. Her eyes remained drawn like magnets to the television screen.

'Anna.' Tom's voice was barely above a whisper. 'Anna.' He dropped the bags to the ground and knelt down in front of her. 'Are you okay? I'm sorry – I'm so sorry.'

Anna tried desperately to block him out, to remain enveloped in her haven of outrageous shoulder pads and even more outrageous storylines. She silently challenged herself to name all the men Alexis Colby had slept with. Just as she got to the unfeasibly named Dex Dexter she became aware of something quivering against her. Wrenching her eyes away from the screen, she realised it was Tom, his face buried in her lap and his arms wrapped around her back, his whole body shaking violently.

What was he doing? Anna wondered. Surely he wasn't laughing at her? But then again, why not? She had to be the biggest laughing-stock going, actually believing for one second that her pictures were any good and daring to show them to a virtual stranger. No wonder Belle had asked her to bring them along on Saturday – to give the others a good laugh, that was why. But the longer Anna listened to the muffled gasps coming from her lap, the more she realised that it wasn't laughter after all. She reached out a hand and gingerly touched the top of Tom's head.

'Tom?'

Tom slowly raised his eyes to meet hers. 'I'm so sorry,' he gasped, great streams of tears running down his face. She had never seen him cry before, not even when Grace was born, and yet now he didn't seem able to stop. On and on they poured, down his face and on to her lap. Something stirred deep within Anna, the same pang of love intermingled with concern she felt whenever she heard a baby cry. The shouting, swearing monster of earlier seemed to have disappeared without trace, leaving a frightened little boy in its place.

'You've got to help me, Anna, please,' he begged, gulping back a sob. 'I don't know what's wrong with me – I get so . . .'

Anna began stroking his hair cautiously, wary of doing anything to provoke another outburst. 'It's okay,' she whispered, more in hope than in certainty, 'it's okay.'

Tom gently eased her down to the floor next to him and cupped her face in his hands. 'You're the only one for me, Anna – I don't know what I'd do without you. I don't want to end up like him. You've got to help me.' He gently loosened her ponytail and ran his fingers through her hair. 'Please don't leave me.'

Anna felt a warm, fat tear spill on to her face. All this time she'd been terrified he was about to leave her and now here he was begging *her* not to go. The thought of leaving him hadn't even crossed her mind. Why would it? All of a sudden she felt a genuine glimmer of hope. He did love her, he did need her after all. How could she ever have doubted him? She felt slightly ashamed at her lack of trust.

They clung to each other on the living-room floor,

under the flickering light of the television, kissing each other's tears away. Then, when there were no tears left, they lay alongside each other, their lips touching just enough to send little charges of electricity rushing about Anna's body, reawakening places that seemed to have lain dormant for years. Slowly and gently, Tom helped her to her feet, and Anna was so overcome with an intoxicating mixture of fear and yearning that she didn't even hear Krystal Carrington shrieking, 'Alexis, you bitch!'

After hours of kissing and stroking and soothing away the pain and hurt and resentment of the past few months, Tom leaped from the bed like an excited child. 'I forgot!' he exclaimed. 'I got you a present. Wait there.'

A few seconds later he returned, brandishing the Homebase carrier bags which he placed in front of her on the bed. 'You were right,' he conceded. 'That room could do with some brightening up.' And, like a magician pulling rabbits from a hat, he produced two large tins of paint. Tangerine Dream and Burnt Sienna. 'And . . .' With a final flourish Tom produced a sponge and stencil. 'I know how much you like to experiment.'

'But . . . but I thought you wanted magnolia? What about the money?' Anna ventured. Surely Tom hadn't forgotten that he'd been laid off?

'Oh, don't worry about that. I bumped into Terry down at the bookie's and he's given me a few weeks' work on an extension he's doing over in Hatch End. By the time that's finished the Barratts contract should've come through.' Tom crawled over the bed to hug her. 'I got you something else as well, to say sorry, you know, for the pictures.'

For a split second Anna winced as she thought of the Snotlaws shredded and languishing at the bottom of the rubbish chute, submerged in soggy teabags and greasy leftovers by now. Tom handed her a rectangular package wrapped in brown paper.

'Open it,' he urged.

Anna carefully undid the paper. A gilt-edged frame surrounding the most hideous picture she had ever seen slid into view. She didn't know whether to laugh or cry as she studied the shiny silver unicorn/winged horse hybrid swooping majestically across a garish Technicolor sunset. It was vile – the kind of picture her parents would proudly display over their stone-clad fireplace.

'Do you like it? I thought we could put it in the living room when it's finished. Aren't the colours blinding?'

Well, she certainly agreed with him there. Anna looked at Tom, his face so full of expectation, and her heart crumpled. He so badly wanted her to like his ghastly gift. How could she possibly tell him the truth?

She sighed. 'I love it. Thank you so much.'

14

'Mum – why don't poos have hair?'

'What?'

'Why don't poos have hair?'

Belle popped her fourth Anadin Extra of the day and took a large gulp of coffee. 'I don't know, Harry – they just don't.'

'But why not?' Harry stood in front of the dishwasher, hands on hips, demanding answers.

Belle sighed. This really was the worst possible moment for one of Harry's inquisitions. It never ceased to amaze her how a three-year-old could come up with such cryptic questions. Perhaps she ought to contact Chris Tarrant to see whether there were any vacancies for question devisers on *Who Wants to Be a Millionaire?*

And now, John Hardy from Paignton in Devon, for one million pounds – why don't poos have hair?

'Why, Mum, why?' Harry began tugging at her sleeve.

Belle felt a sudden urge to scream. There were just under two hours before the Football Widows were due to arrive, she was suffering from the worst period pains ever, the house was a tip, Johnny was still playing that bloody football manager game on the computer, and her son seemed to have developed an unhealthy anxiety over the follically challenged state of excrement! Belle slung the final dishes into the dishwasher and gave the counter a quick wipe. Suddenly she had a flash of inspiration.

'Because we don't eat hair, of course,' she said, proudly.

'But why?'

'Why what?'

'Why don't we eat hair?'

Oh, for God's sake, Belle thought as she crammed the remaining half of a king-sized Snickers bar into her mouth – the half she had promised herself she wouldn't eat. Right, that was the kitchen done, now for the living room.

As soon as she walked into the living room she felt her blood pressure crank up several notches.

'*And that was an excellent free kick from – WOL-VERHAMPTON WANDERERS*,' crackled a disjointed, tinny voice from the computer in the corner. Johnny was sitting hunched over the monitor, pausing only for an occasional glance at the television, where *Grandstand* was blasting away.

The computer game Football Manager was an absolute anathema to Belle. The day Johnny had brought it home and headed for the PC in a state of borderline hysteria, Belle had initially felt relieved. If it keeps him at home, rather than out playing the damned game, she had reasoned, then it was fine by her. But as with everything football related, within minutes Football Manager had managed to irritate the hell out of her. 'It's only pretend,' she had consoled when Johnny's initial excitement turned to abject misery as he took Wolves to the bottom of the league within the first hour of playing. That first day he had spent a grand total of seven hours, forty-seven minutes at the computer (Belle had been keeping an increasingly pissed-off eye on the clock). On one of the rare occasions he left the room to go to the toilet she sneaked over to the screen, thoughts of sabotage uppermost in her mind. Clicking on the team tactics button she had wondered why Johnny had chosen to go for the dull-sounding 5–3–2 formation when he could have chosen the delightful-sounding 'Christmas tree' instead. No wonder it was still 0–0 at half-time. Belle rectified the situation and returned to her armchair. Well, talk about sense-of-humour failure. It had taken Johnny about ten seconds to realise all was not right, but by that time Wolves had conceded two goals to Liverpool and were out of the FA Cup. Johnny was promptly sacked by the board and went to bed in a sulk. Yes, Belle hated Football Manager even more than she hated *Grandstand*.

She marched over to the television and switched it off.

'What are you doing?' screamed Johnny in a high-pitched Barry-from-*Auf Wiedersehen* special.

'Why don't we eat hair?' Harry whined, tugging at

her elbow. Belle felt the veins throbbing in her temples, fit to burst.

'*And that was a terrible piece of defending from – WOLVERHAMPTON WANDERERS – goal to – MANCHESTER UNITED. MANCHESTER UNITED – lead four goals to one*,' squawked the computer.

'Now look what you've made me do,' Johnny whinged.

'Is it because hair tastes like dog poo?' Harry asked, before falling to the floor giggling inanely.

Ignoring both of them, Belle pressed PLAY on the CD player and yanked the volume up to the previously uncharted territory of level fifteen.

'You Don't Bring Me Flowers,' boomed throughout the room.

'Oh God, no!' yelled Johnny, covering his ears.

'Oh God, no!' echoed Harry, writhing around on the floor.

'What?' Belle shouted, staring defiantly at Johnny. 'I've had to listen to that bloody game all morning and now you've got football on the telly as well. Well, it's my house too and I want to listen to some music. I am sick to death of football, football, football, all the bloody time!'

'Well, I'm sick to death of Neil bloody Diamond all the time. We've got hundreds of CDs. Why does it always have to be Neil Diamond and why does it always have to be this song?' Johnny demanded, switching the computer off huffily.

'Oh, well, you're a fine one to talk. How many times have I had to listen to that horrendous "Three lions on our shirt, jewels remain still gleaming" rubbish?'

'What did you just say?' Johnny asked, staring at her incredulously.

'I said, I can't possibly have played Neil Diamond any more than you've played "Three Lions".'

'Three lions what?'

'What do you mean, Three Lions what?' God, Belle thought, he's getting as bad as Harry.

'Three lions on our shirt, then what did you say?'

'Jewels remain still gleaming.'

'Jewels remain still gleaming?' Johnny began laughing in irritatingly high-pitched snorts. 'Jewels remain still gleaming?'

'Yes – so what? For God's sake, Johnny, aren't you going to be late for football?'

'It's Jules Rimet still gleaming,' Johnny informed her in the most annoyingly patronising voice imaginable. 'Jules Rimet as in the Jules Rimet trophy – you know, the WORLD CUP! Jewels remain, ha!' And he let out another snort.

'Get out!' Belle shrieked, flinging what was surely becoming the most flung cushion in North London at him. 'And don't hurry back!'

'Don't worry, I won't,' Johnny replied, still snorting like a demented horse.

Neil Diamond continued to bemoan his lack of

flowers as Belle sank down into the sofa, fighting back angry tears.

'Mum?' Harry asked, gazing up at her imploringly.

Belle sighed. 'Yes, sweetie.'

'Why don't poos have teeth?'

15

Anna swung into Emerald Avenue, a bag of assorted baking trays and tins clattering noisily on the handle of Grace's buggy. She hadn't noticed them when she'd been walking through the estate – it was impossible to hear anything over the competing din of kids shouting, car stereos blaring and the distant tinkle of glass somewhere being smashed. But in the tranquil, tree-lined oasis of Emerald Avenue the clanging metal was about as discreet as an Iron Maiden gig in a library. Anna could just imagine the chairperson of the Emerald Avenue Neighbourhood Watch on the phone right now to the local police station. *'Yes, she's obviously from the council estate, Officer – making a frightful racket. You couldn't dispatch a patrol car posthaste to remove her, could you?'*

Anna quickened her pace. Just as the tins reached a deafening crescendo she heard an almighty bang. Surely not a gunshot? Not on Emerald Avenue. She turned to see a metallic-blue Datsun, wreathed in a cloud of exhaust fumes, slowly proceeding down the road towards her. As it drew level it shuddered to a halt. The window wound down slowly and a bright orange head leaned out.

'Oh, fuck me!' exclaimed the head as it examined a handle that had broken off the door. 'Every time I open this bleedin' window! How are you doing, Anna?'

'Maz?' Anna squinted at the face beneath the carrot-like tufts; the purple reflector sunglasses made it pretty hard to tell.

'Jump in, darlin'.'

Casting a furtive glance down the road for any signs of Neighbourhood Watch officers waiting to pounce, Anna opened the back door of the car and bundled Grace, the baking tins and the folded buggy inside.

' 'Scuse the mess,' Maz shouted over the unmistakable warblings of Dolly Parton crackling from the car stereo.

It wasn't until Anna had strapped herself and Grace in that she realised when Maz said 'excuse the mess' she certainly wasn't exaggerating. A pair of faded pink dice hung from the rear-view mirror, bobbing about over a blanket of parking tickets that covered the dashboard and overflowed into a sea of wrappers and crisp packets littering the floor. Most of the windows displayed fading stickers advertising the joys of country-and-western music, and the seats were covered in lurid nylon leopard print. In a bid to prevent Grace from lunging at the overflowing ashtray next to her, Anna shifted slightly in her seat and felt the crunch of metal under her foot. It was an empty Coke can. One of several empty Coke cans, in fact. Anna couldn't help admiring Maz's bravery in stopping to offer her a lift. If it had been her car she would probably have driven straight past, eyes fixed firmly on the road, pretending not to notice any friends who may have been walking by.

'So how's your week been, then? Your old man been driving you mad with football talk? My Darren won't bloody shut up about the Arsenal. You'd think nobody had ever won four–nil before.'

'Tell me about it,' Anna said, smiling shyly at Maz's reflection in the rear-view mirror. In actual fact Tom had hardly mentioned football all week. Every night, when he got home from work, he'd helped her decorate the living room for a couple of hours before popping out to the chip shop for their tea. They'd sat on the floor, surrounded by a sea of paper, paint-brushes and dustsheets, munching on fat, greasy chips and swigging from steaming mugs of tea. Afterwards Tom would roll his customary post-dinner spliff, and for the first time since she had fallen pregnant with Grace, Anna had joined him for a smoke. Of course, it had gone straight to her head, rendering her completely incapable of speech, so she had lost herself in Bob Marley instead, watching transfixed as thin fingers of smoke lazily curled their way up to the ceiling. Every night they had ended up slumped on the floor, lost in the music and the smoke, like an extremely chilled-out version of *Changing Rooms*, with not a mention of football or any of the tension of the previous months.

'Oh, there goes Madam,' Maz announced as a black Saab convertible went zooming past them and pulled into Belle's drive. Anna watched as Ginny eased herself out of her car. She looked effortlessly elegant in a charcoal-grey trouser suit over a pale lilac polo neck and shiny high-heeled boots. As they jolted to a halt alongside her, she turned to smile a sickly sweet smile, her hair swishing like a curtain about her shoulders.

Maz sniffed. 'Do you reckon she irons that hair of hers?'

Anna laughed uneasily and released herself from the back of the car.

'Oh, Anna, hi, I didn't see you back there. The window's a bit grimed up, isn't it. Like the hair, Maz – very Chris Evans!' Ginny couldn't wipe the grin from her face as she stared at Maz's hair. 'Here, let me give you a hand,' she said, grabbing the bag of cake tins from Anna. 'Good grief, what are these for?'

Anna felt her face flare. 'I told Tom I was coming over here for a cake bake,' she mumbled.

'A cake bake?' Ginny shrieked. 'Whatever for?' When Mike had politely enquired about her plans for the day she had shot him a withering look and flounced from the room. He may have wheedled his way back into the bedroom, but she was still not in the mood for small talk. And even if she was she would just have told him to mind his own bloody business. Never in a month of Sundays would she have told him she was going to a 'cake bake'. How sad! She followed behind smirking, as a glowering Maz and a glowing Anna made their way to Belle's front door.

As soon as Belle opened the door her face broke into a broad smile.

'Oh my God, Maz – what happened? I thought it was supposed to be Florida Honey Blonde?'

'More like Florida Juicy Orange,' Ginny muttered.

'What did you say?' Maz snarled, turning so abruptly that she knocked straight into Anna and sent her bag of cake tins clattering to the ground.

Belle burst out laughing. 'I see you've come well prepared for the cake bake,' she said, bending down to help Anna retrieve the tins. 'I like your style. So tell me, Maz – what went wrong?'

As Maz recounted her woeful tale of the dearth of pre-application lighteners in Boots and how with hindsight Florida Honey Blonde was probably not the best colour to mix with Blackberry Blush, they made their way into the living room. Anna was somewhat comforted by the fact that it didn't seem quite as immaculate as the previous week; in fact parts of the room looked as if it had been hit by a mini-tornado, with CD covers, screwed-up balls of paper and cushions strewn all over the floor.

'I apologise for the mess,' Belle said, gesturing at the floor. 'I've been experiencing a few problems with writer's block this week. Help yourselves to drinks.'

'Don't tell me you still haven't come up with a

press release for that strawberry-flavoured hamburger?' Ginny said, as she mixed herself a spritzer and helped herself to a solitary peanut.

'Lemon-flavoured sausage,' Belle corrected. 'No, for some strange reason it just isn't filling me with inspiration.'

'It sounds all right to me,' Maz mumbled through a mouthful of popcorn as she poured herself a tumbler of wine.

Anna dithered over the different drinks on offer. She really ought to have an orange juice – if Tom came home and smelled drink on her breath he might get suspicious about the authenticity of the cake bake. Then again, one glass of wine wouldn't hurt, as long as she remembered to clean her teeth as soon as she got home. Besides, she was dreading having to tell Belle she hadn't done anything for her Passion Pursuit – she could do with a bit of Dutch courage.

Belle waited until everyone was seated and Harry and Grace had become suitably engrossed in a video before beginning.

'Okay, so how are we all getting on with our Passion Pursuits?'

Anna listened numbly as Maz told them all about her new part-time job as a cleaner which should hopefully pay for a 'pukka' sewing machine from Argos by Christmas. Then Ginny rather begrudgingly confessed to enrolling on a yoga course as stage one of her journey towards inner tranquillity. Then Belle explained that it was a little difficult for her to get anywhere with her own Pursuit at the moment as she didn't currently come into contact with any decent men – at all. But she was working on a comprehensive profile of her ideal lover so that she would instantly be able to identify him when he did eventually come along. And then came the words Anna had been dreading:

'So, Anna, how about you? Have you done any drawing? Did you bring the Snotlaws?' Belle enquired hopefully.

Anna hung her head in shame. 'No,' she muttered, 'sorry.'

'Oh.' Belle was unable to conceal her disappointment.

'What a pity,' Ginny added. 'Belle's been raving about your pictures all week. I was looking forward to seeing them.'

Anna had been so convinced that they couldn't really be interested in her work, that Belle had simply been being polite or, even worse, wanting to give the others a laugh, that the palpable air of disappointment in the room was quite unbearable. Even Maz looked sad.

'I'm really sorry – I've been so busy with decorating the living room I just haven't had a chance to do any drawing. And I was going to bring the Snotlaws – I'd put them out so that I wouldn't forget and I, er, spilt coffee all over them. By accident, er, I tripped up, on one of Grace's toys.' *Stop bloody rambling*, a voice barked in her head, *just shut up!* 'Sorry.'

'It's all right, darlin'. Blimey, no wonder you don't feel like drawing if you've been decorating all week,' Maz said, giving her arm a comforting squeeze.

'Oh, you poor thing,' sighed Belle. 'Are they ruined?'

Anna looked at her blankly.

'The Snotlaws. Are they ruined?'

'Oh – oh, yes, totally. I had to throw them out.' Anna replied, feeling a little sick.

'Oh, God – that is so sad! All those years of work! Well, don't worry, I'll help you all I can this week with Grace so that you can get cracking on some new pictures.' Belle seemed so genuinely concerned that Anna felt a pang of guilt for ever having doubted her and, even worse, for her own dishonesty. She took a large gulp of wine and prayed that the conversation would move on to something else.

'Okay, Maz,' said Belle, answering Anna's prayers, 'it was your turn for this week's act of Widow's Revenge – what have you got for us?'

Maz grinned and reached into her handbag, producing a slightly faded red-and-white Arsenal scarf. 'This,' she announced, 'is my Darren's lucky scarf. He's been wearing it to every Arsenal match since he was a nipper.'

'Oh no – not another boil wash,' Ginny said, sighing at the unoriginality.

'Not at all – what I have in mind is far more subtle,' Maz replied.

Ginny sniffed. Somehow she very much doubted it.

'What is it? What are you going to do?' Belle asked, rubbing her hands together excitedly.

Maz got to her feet. 'Do you know what? That wine's gone right through me. I think I'll just go for a piss.'

The room fell silent for a second as they all looked at Maz, clutching the scarf.

'Oh no!' Belle let out a shriek of laughter. 'You're not going to do what I think you're going to? Are you?'

Maz nodded and winked. 'It's the old quilted double velvet treatment for me. Or should that be double woollen?'

Anna let out a giggle and Ginny turned slightly green.

'See you in a minute,' Maz cried, and she marched out of the room trailing Darren's beloved lucky scarf behind her.

'Brilliant,' Belle said.

'Where's she going to put it?' Ginny whispered. 'You know, when she's finished with it. Surely not back in her handbag. That's, like, so unhygienic!' Mind you, Ginny thought with a shudder, God only knew what else Maz had lurking in that hideous plastic handbag of hers – perhaps a urine-soaked scarf wouldn't be all that out of place.

Upon Maz's return they all eyed the scarf curiously. It didn't look any different really. She had folded it up neatly and reached into her bag for a carrier bag into which she placed the scarf. Ginny breathed a sigh of relief.

'God, I needed that,' Maz sighed. 'It was like opening the bleedin' floodgates! Oooh, before I forget.' She produced a garish gift box from her handbag and turned to Ginny. 'I got you a little something – you know, to help you achieve your Passion Pursuit.'

Ginny eyed the gift box suspiciously. 'Oh – how sweet of you, you shouldn't have,' she said, taking the box cautiously and making a mental note to wash her hands as soon as she got the chance.

'What is it?' Belle asked, perching herself on the arm of Ginny's chair.

Ginny slowly removed the lid of the box. It was filled with tissue paper. Pushing some aside she caught a glimpse of another box inside which she fished out. It was hard to tell who screamed the louder, Belle with laughter or Ginny with horror as she dropped the box to the floor. There on the carpet lay the most enormous black penis-shaped vibrator that Anna had ever seen. Seemingly no attention to detail had been overlooked, from the tiny veins protruding from the sides to the shiny, bulbous helmet on top. There it lay, big and black and proud, in the middle of Belle's living room, under the banner 'BLACK BEAUTY – WHO SAYS BIG CAN'T BE BEAUTIFUL?'

16

'Ginny's never come during sex, you know,' Belle whispered over Anna's shoulder as they glided slowly up the escalator. 'Harry! Hold my hand, please!'

Anna turned to look down at Belle. 'What do you . . . how do you know?' she asked, trying in vain to prevent herself from blushing.

'She told me,' Belle replied, feeling an instant stab of guilt at having betrayed Ginny's drunken confidence. It had taken half a bottle of Taboo, or for the average drinker the equivalent of an entire bottle of Jack Daniel's, before Ginny had finally admitted to faking an orgasm every time she made love. 'It just saves a lot of hassle and embarrassment,' she'd said defensively to a visibly shellshocked Belle. 'Besides, men don't really care if you have an orgasm or not, they're just waiting for the go-ahead to come themselves – it's just so much easier to fake it. We've all seen *When Harry Met Sally*. All you have to do is moan and roll your eyes around a bit.'

As Belle rooted through her pockets for her travel card she couldn't help feeling slightly ashamed. It had obviously taken a lot for Ginny to confide something of such an intimate nature, and yet here she was in the middle of Leicester Square Tube station merrily betraying that confidence. Belle knew it was wrong, but she just couldn't help herself. There was something so nerve-tinglingly thrilling about imparting a nugget of twenty-four-carat gossip; something so gratifying about causing the beholder's eyes and mouth to gape like those of a goldfish. Exactly like Anna's were doing now, as she stared down at her, desperate to be fed another titbit. When Belle came to think of it, Anna and Ginny *were* practically strangers – what she had done was no worse than sharing a piece of trivia about Posh Spice. And where was the harm in that?

Before Belle could convince herself that it was actually in Ginny's best interests to broadcast her sexual problems to all and sundry, she was wrenched back to reality by the sight of Harry making a frantic bid for freedom.

'Harry, get back here now!' she screamed as he lurched off the top of the escalator to be swallowed up by the crowd pouring forth into Leicester Square.

Anna ambled along behind Belle, thankful that Grace was still small enough to be physically restrained. Finding a vacant doorway where she could unfold Grace's buggy without being trampled underfoot, she inhaled deeply. Although it was no doubt laden with a cocktail of asthma-inducing pollutants, the air seemed pleasantly crisp and fresh compared with the suffocating atmosphere of the Underground. Anna turned to face the hustle and bustle of Leicester

Square and drank in the kaleidoscopic mixture of Mohicaned punks mingling with pin-striped businessmen, nonchalant students ambling past map-clutching tourists, and chanting Hare Krishna devotees bounding by stumbling drunks. This was the reason she'd come to London in the first place. This was the London she'd fallen in love with all those years ago through a steamy coach window on the way to a school theatre trip. In London nobody batted an eyelid if you looked different. In fact, the stranger you appeared the more you seemed to blend in. Yet in her home-town of Walton on Thames if you so much as parted your hair slightly off centre you were courting finger pointings and frosty stares. One Saturday, when Anna was about ten, a man wearing a Stetson and a pair of leather chaps had swaggered into Bejam's and purchased a bag of frozen sprouts. Other shoppers were sent into a frenzy of speculation and disgust, and it was the talk of many a coffee morning for weeks to come. Yet here in the West End, John Wayne himself could have cantered by and nobody would have given a second glance. (And if they did it would only be to point out that John Wayne had actually passed away some years previously.)

As she waited for Belle, Anna observed the passers-by, trying to imagine the response they would elicit in Walton: a Rasta carrying a large watermelon under his arm, a girl with poppy-red hair giggling into her mobile, an elderly couple frowning at each other and two men strolling arm in arm. Brief snatches of conversation filled the air like a radio being tuned . . . 'No of course I didn't, I didn't have any knickers on . . . I told you we should have made an offer for the mahogany one, it would have looked exquisite . . . God, why do you have to be so suspicious all the . . .? Now, Harry, you do as Mummy tells you or there'll be no ice cream ever again!'

'God, I'm going to swing for that boy,' Belle sighed as she drew level with Anna. 'Did I tell you he has a new imaginary friend?'

Anna shook her head as they began ambling their way up to Covent Garden.

'His name is Harry-Billy and he's a right little sod!'

Harry-Billy had first made an appearance on Monday evening. Johnny was at a football match (Harrow Borough versus Canvey Island), Harry was tucked up in bed, and Belle had snuggled down on the sofa with a cup of coffee, a Mountain Bar and both *Hello!* and *OK!* magazines. What was looking set to be a night of bliss was rudely shattered by a little voice calling down the stairs, 'Mummy, Mummy, Harry-Billy has just peed all over my bed!' Belle's heart had not just sunk, it had plummeted to the very depths of despair as the promise of a chocolate and celebrity-gossip fest was chased from her head by the nightmare prospect of bed-stripping, mattress-scrubbing and pyjama-swapping. She stormed upstairs to find Harry giggling nervously in the corner of his bedroom, pointing to a large dark circle in the centre of his sheet.

'Oh, Harry,' was all Belle had trusted herself to say, while a voice inside her head screamed a multitude of outrageous expletives. Ripping the urine-soaked sheet from the bed, she dreamed of marching to the football ground and rubbing it in Johnny's face. Why did all the most unpleasant tasks always fall upon her? Why was Johnny never anywhere to be seen whenever a bum needed wiping, a toilet needed cleaning, or a bed needed stripping? Because he was bloody well always somewhere else enjoying himself – that was why.

'It wasn't me, Mum,' Harry had whined. 'It was my friend Harry-Billy. He stood in my bed and peed all over me.'

Harry-Billy had paid them a visit every day since. On Tuesday he had eaten half the batch of chocolate-chip cookies Belle had baked in a frenzy of guilt over not being an enthusiastic enough housewife. On Wednesday Harry-Billy had drawn a picture of Tinky Winky in purple crayon on the kitchen floor. On Thursday he had shouted 'Go away, dog poo!' through the letterbox at the postman, and now, on Friday, he had apparently grabbed Harry by the hand in the middle of Leicester Square Tube and dragged him into the nearest sweet kiosk.

It had been Belle's idea to come to London. When she'd called round at Anna's earlier in the week to see how the decorating was coming along she'd been amazed by the transformation that had taken place. The living-room walls radiated warmth in expertly rag-rolled shades of burnt orange, while a stencilled border of dark green vine leaves curled its way around the centre, perfectly matching the new throw on the sofa. The only thing that detracted from the whole Mediterranean feel was the slightly bizarre picture of a silver unicorn swooping over a Technicolor sunset, but Belle had put that down to some quirky art student sense of humour. When Anna had told her of her plans to go to Wembley market to buy some candles and a rug, Belle had been quick with her response.

'Wembley, Shwembley!' she had retorted, glancing at the shiny unicorn. 'You don't want to go there, it's full of cheap tat. Why don't we go to Covent Garden instead? We can make a day of it – see the sights.'

As Anna removed her cardigan and tied it loosely about her waist, she congratulated herself on accepting Belle's invitation. The sun was beating down and there wasn't a cloud in the sky. Somewhere in the distance a busker was singing the most beautiful rendition of 'Leila' she had ever heard. It was perfect.

'Do you fancy an ice cream?' Belle asked, pointing to a nearby van.

'Good idea – I'll grab that bench over there.' Anna sat down and marvelled at how quickly things could change. Only a few weeks ago she had been trudging around the estate, lonely and depressed, and yet here she was now amidst the riot of noise and colour of Covent Garden with her brand-new friend.

'When we've finished these, can we take a look at the jewellery on that stall over there?' Belle asked, doling out the ice creams.

'Sure,' Anna replied. Tom had given her fifty pounds to buy bits and pieces for the living room. She was sure he wouldn't mind if she spent a fiver on a pair of earrings – it was ages since she had bought herself any new jewellery.

At that moment a man dressed in black from head to toe stopped next to the stall. He was tall and thin with slightly stoopy shoulders and dirty blond hair pulled back into a ponytail. Dropping his bag on the ground, he sat down next to it cross-legged and placed a black Balaclava on his head.

'Oh my God, do you think he's a bank robber?' Belle whispered hopefully.

'I don't know – I don't think so,' Anna replied. He didn't exactly look the bank-robber type, with his spindly limbs and straggly hair, but then you never could tell.

The man reached into his bag.

'Oh my God, he's getting his sawn-off shotgun,' Belle hissed, before dunking her flake in ice cream and taking a large bite.

However, instead of a rifle, the man retrieved two acrylic balls the size of tennis balls, one blue and one green, which he began to roll up and down the insides of his arms.

'Oh, he's a contact juggler,' Anna said excitedly.

'Oh,' Belle responded, yawning and closing her eyes.

Anna watched as the man effortlessly rolled the balls down the outside of his arms then, with a deft flick of the wrist, back over his fingers and up again. After about five minutes of this he got to his feet, removed a small cassette player from his bag and began to play 'Nothing Compares To You'.

'Oooh, I love this one,' Belle sighed, her eyes still closed as the haunting vocals filled the air. The man remained standing, moving his limbs so subtly that the balls appeared to take on a life of their own. Keeping perfect time with the music, they glided over his lithe body, backwards and forwards over the black silhouette of his gloved hands, up his arms, over his chest, even up on to his head. Anna's eyes followed, hypnotised by the glistening trail of green and blue. This was what life was all about, this was where she belonged. Not in some Surrey time warp surrounded by Alan Partridge clones or some grotty block of flats surrounded by prepubescent gangstas. She wanted to live in a world of buskers and street entertainers, a world of market stalls and pavement artists, a world of misfits and mavericks. She felt as if she had finally come home. Anna watched as the man held his hands in prayer position, swaying his arms this way and that, like a snake-charmer, with the balls obeying his every command.

And then, heralded by a strange yelping sound, the

spell was broken. The balls broke free, arcing sharply into the air, higher and higher, before plummeting back down until they landed smack bang in the middle of the jewellery stall, littering the pavement with pieces of silver. Anna turned back to the juggler, who was no longer on his feet, but lying in a crumpled heap on the ground, struggling to remove a little boy from on top of him. A little boy with a crazed expression upon his ice-cream-splattered face. Somebody was shouting about calling the Old Bill and criminal damages while a low, strangulated moan emanated from the heap of black limbs on the ground. And then, cutting through the commotion, came the sound of a child crying out in fear:

'It wasn't me, Mum – it was Harry-Billy!'

17

Ginny felt ridiculous. What on earth was a successful, thirty-one-year-old career woman like herself doing lying naked on a bed clutching an enormous black plastic penis? Could she really have been addressing a group of directors from ICI in the boardroom of Wembley National Stadium only six hours previously? What would they think if they could see her now? She shuddered at the thought.

The meeting had gone like clockwork – as usual. Overseeing corporate hospitality was the best part of her job – she loved the type of people it brought her into contact with. Successful, powerful people. People like herself. Although she wasn't a company director yet she knew it was just a matter of time. Two years, in fact, if she met her personal objectives target, and she always met her personal objectives targets. Since the announcement of Wembley Stadium's imminent demise she had been headhunted by no fewer than four different companies. Four different companies had sought out her talent and expertise, just as Wembley had five years ago, making her the youngest events manager in their history. History was what she had focused on in her presentation today, starting with the brief introductory spiel about the stadium's grand opening in 1924, accompanied by a couple of grainy slides of George V attending the opening ceremony and ending with the historical importance of this final year for the famous twin towers and how much it would add to the overall sense of occasion should ICI choose to do their corporate entertaining at Wembley. She liked the sense of symmetry this gave to her presentation, beginning and ending on a historical note. And the men from ICI obviously liked it too; they agreed to a block booking of an executive suite on the spot. Presentation and organisation was all it took. They were Ginny's two buzz words – she even used them as a screensaver, flickering across her monitor like some royal-blue mantra, keeping her focused at all times: 'PRESENTATION . . . ORGANISATION . . . PRESENTATION . . . ORGANISATION . . .'

She knew what the others in the office thought of her, the jealous, insecure bastards. She had nothing in common with them anyway – that had become blatantly obvious the afternoon they all came back from the pub and changed their screensavers to 'INTOXICATION . . . MASTURBATION . . .'

Ginny looked at the vibrator in her hand. What the hell was she doing? This was the kind of sordid implement those giggly secretaries Cheryl and Caroline, or Chezza and Cazza as they preferred to be known, would buy from one of the naff Ann Summers parties they were always going to. This wasn't her scene at all. How dare Maz have ridiculed her like that in front of Belle and Anna, the crude cow. Ginny's head began pounding. Why was life always so stressful? Why could she never meet any like-minded people? Even Belle, her closest friend, her only friend, sometimes seemed to come from another planet they had so little in common. She could never understand why Belle had abandoned a highly lucrative career in sales to sit around at home all day watching *Thomas the Tank Engine* and writing about meat products. Even worse, how could she have allowed herself to become financially dependant on Johnny. One of Ginny's greatest sources of comfort was the knowledge that her own salary was twice as much as Mike's. If he ever left her it wouldn't affect her in the slightest, whereas his standard of living would plummet dramatically. No, there were things about Belle she would never understand. Her friendship with Maz was another fine example. God, it made her mad, hearing all about the latest 'scream' they had had sitting around drinking and gossiping while she had been slogging her guts out at the office all day. For if truth be told that was what work seemed to be becoming – a long, hard slog. Ginny used to thrive under pressure, but recently things had changed – she couldn't quite put her finger on it, she just felt so angry all the time. Of course, living with Mike and his ridiculously sunny disposition didn't help. And he was a teacher, for Christ's sake – he was supposed to be the bitter, twisted one, not her. But nothing seemed to rattle him – no matter how snappy and irritable she became, he would just lollop about like some stupid great puppy desperate to be loved. The big wimp.

Ginny pummelled her cornflower-blue pillow. Her headache was becoming quite insufferable. So much for the relaxing benefits of yoga. It may have worked wonders for Madonna, but Ginny's first class had been an unmitigated disaster.

'*Relax*,' the New Age freak had urged. '*Let your mind and body come together through your breathing. Open your chakras and let the energy flow freely.*' Well, how the hell was she supposed to relax, lying spread-eagled on the floor in a room full of complete strangers? '*Clear your mind of all clutter and let it drain empty of all thoughts . . .*' Was he having a laugh? She was a busy woman. She had lists to compile, a proposal to compose, a CV to update. Besides, how was she supposed to clear her mind of all thoughts when he wouldn't bloody well shut up? Every time he said something it would spark off another flurry of activity in her brain. '*Picture yourself as a tree, swaying and bending in the breeze, but all the time firmly rooted in the soil . . .*' This instantly reminded Ginny that she had to buy a Garden Vac. Autumn was just around the corner and she simply couldn't bear all the mess it brought with it – all those awful soggy brown leaves littering the place. The very thought of her pristine lawn covered in leaf mulch made her tense every muscle in her body. '*You may find that your head is filling with stressful thoughts . . .*' Well, he'd got that bit right at least. '*Take those thoughts, wrap them up into parcels and visualise them floating away from you down a stream . . .*'

Ginny pictured a bundle of leaves, Maz, Mike's grinning face and most of her work colleagues smothered in brown parcel paper, bound tightly with string, hurtling down some rapids and crashing over the edge of an enormous waterfall. She could just imagine their frantic screams as they plummeted to their watery graves, but any accompanying sense of satisfaction was swiftly replaced by a sudden burning sensation in her bladder. All of this water imagery was making her quite desperate for a pee. Oh, why had she stopped at Starbucks for that extra-large moccachino? Once again every muscle in her body tightened in a bid to prevent her bladder from emptying itself all over her exercise mat.

This pointless charade continued for half an hour before they progressed to any form of exercise, and then all it consisted of was a series of the most torturously slow stretches imaginable with a lengthy rest in between each one! It took a full hour of stretching for Ginny to feel the slightest sensation of warmth, and then it was time for the 'cool down', which involved another half-hour spread-eagled on the floor. By this point all hope of relaxation was utterly futile as Ginny lay there calculating exactly how many calories she could have burnt had she spent two hours pounding the running machine rather than moving in ultra-slow motion and pretending to be a tree. She had returned home even more tense and frustrated than before.

Hence the appearance of the vibrator. Ginny studied the instructions on the back of the box. '*Not for internal use*' – God, how gross. How would it possibly fit anyway? '*Not for use on calf injuries*' – what the hell was that about? Did they mean calf as in the lower part of her leg or calf as in baby cow? It wouldn't really surprise her if they meant the latter. The kind of people who actually used these things were probably into all manner of unspeakable acts. '*Always clean with alcohol after use*' – what kind of alcohol? Surely not advocaat? Ginny shuddered at the prospect of the ensuing sticky mess. '*To operate, twist base for desired speed.*' Ginny nervously twisted the base of the vibrator approximately one millimetre. Nothing happened. She twisted it another millimetre. Again nothing. For Christ's sake! The bloody thing didn't even work, but what could she really expect from Maz, the cheap slut. Ginny gave it one final yank in frustration and suddenly the black plastic member burst into life, leaping out of her hands and on to the bed, where it lay vibrating loudly against the duvet.

'Oh my God!' Ginny gasped. It was noisier than a pneumatic drill. She fought desperately to regain control of the pulsating penis, twisting the base this way and that until it finally shuddered to a standstill.

She had to get it out of the house before Mike returned home from football training. Deciding to sneak outside under cover of darkness and bury the monstrosity in the back garden, Ginny began giggling quite hysterically. It gave an entirely different meaning to the concept of burying a bone. Perhaps she ought to try it first – just to see what all the fuss was about before banishing it from the house for good. She cautiously twisted the base until the vibrator gently hummed into life. Now what was she supposed to do? She gingerly placed the vibrator against her pubic bone and waited. Nothing happened. She felt completely ludicrous. If anything the intense vibrations were making her go numb. What a letdown. It was exactly like sex. All that hype leaving you feeling nothing but empty and dejected. She glanced down at the huge black implement between her legs with its bulging veins and enormous helmet, and suddenly, without warning, the image of her dead grandparents popped into her head. What if all that spiritual crap Belle liked going on about was actually true? What if the ghosts of her gran and grandad were watching over her now as she lay there stark naked with this thing throbbing away on her nether regions.

But before she had time to be flooded with feelings of revulsion something strange started to happen. A slight tingling at first, from somewhere deep inside her, reminding her of that funny sensation she used to get in PE sliding down the ropes. Then it grew stronger, changing from tingles to waves of pleasure rippling out across her body. Ginny closed her eyes and moaned as her whole being seemed to become engulfed in the most beautifully mind-blowing orgasm imaginable. She held the vibrator in place until every last blissful tremor had finally abated. Then, after turning it off and placing it back in its box, she curled herself up into a ball and for the first time in eighteen years she began to cry, great pillow-drenching sobs.

18

Belle looked at the fax for the fifty-seventh time before finally flinging it on to the dining-room table in despair. She had spent weeks coming up with ideas for Morrison's Lemon Zinger launch party only to have her proposal faxed back to her with 'NO CHUFFING WAY!' scrawled right across it. What was the point in being Morrison's PR consultant if he was simply going to overrule her every suggestion? And who was the one with the diploma in public relations from Weybridge College anyway? Her course hadn't actually covered launch parties as such, but Belle had read enough novels about sassy PR and media types to know exactly what they involved. Armies of industrious waiters laden with trays of champagne cocktails and exquisite canapés, weaving their way through hordes of achingly hip movers and shakers.

Belle had spent the past month acquiring sample invitations embossed in up-to-the-minute lilac and silver, accumulating recipes for an array of mouth-watering cocktails and putting together a complimentary gift pack to end all complimentary gift packs. Inspired by a description of the goody bags on offer at Elton John's Aids Ball, as featured in *OK!* magazine, Belle's proposed gift pack was to include a miniature bottle of scent, a box of Belgian chocolates and a Gap T-shirt. Any PR consultant worth her salt knew that the freebies on offer could often make or break a product launch, but Morrison was having none of it. He had not agreed with a single one of her suggestions. After faxing back her desecrated proposal, he had then issued a list of his own instructions. A list that Belle was now studying, slumped over the dining-room table in despair.

Whereas her guest list had included everyone from *Vanity Fair* to *Cosmopolitan*, Morrison's read more like a directory of the obscure publications featured on *Have I Got News for You*, with the editors from *Meat Manufacturers' Monthly*, *Pig Farming Weekly* and *Butcher's News* as guests of honour. Rather than embossed in lilac and silver, the invitations were to be printed on cardboard sausages. There were to be no waiters weaving, just a trestle table laden with miniature Lemon Zingers on sticks, and the only free drinks on offer would be Thwaites' bitter or water. 'If anyone wants a poncy cocktail or a lager-top they can chuffing well sod off back to London!' Morrison had scrawled next to this. A voucher for 50p off your next purchase of Morrison's Lemon Zingers was the closest that guests would get to a gift pack – Elton John and David Furnish would have been appalled.

Even the sound of the phone ringing could not raise Belle from her gloom.

'Well, are you going to answer it before it wakes Harry up?' she snapped at Johnny, who was lounging on the sofa in his work shirt and boxer shorts (orange peppered with miniature black wolves' heads), seemingly oblivious to the telephone pealing away right next to him.

'What's the point?' he replied, flicking through his copy of *Four Four Two*. 'It's bound to be one of your gossipy mates.'

For once Belle didn't feel like seeking solace in gossip, especially not with one of the Football Widows. For the past few weeks, while she had been fruitlessly preparing for her first launch party, the others had all been merrily beavering away at their Passion Pursuits. Maz had already saved fifty pounds towards a sewing machine, Ginny had been to a couple of yoga classes, and Anna was busy drawing something, although she was being very secretive about it. Whereas Belle, the founder member, the one who had got them all inspired in the first place, was absolutely nowhere nearer to achieving her goal. All she had to show for her Passion Pursuit was an increasingly detailed profile of her ideal lover. She made a mental note to add 'somebody who isn't a phone-phobe' at the earliest opportunity.

'Johnny, can you just answer the damn phone and tell whoever it is that I'm working and I'll call them back later.'

Johnny flung down his magazine and snatched up the phone. 'Belle Farraday's Gossip Hotline,' he barked into the mouthpiece, then his whole tone softened and his Black Country accent magically deepened. 'Oh, all roight, Dad. Yeah, two–nil . . . No, I helped make one of them, though . . . I know, gone to Chelsea, hasn't he, cockncy twat . . . Transfer list, yeah . . . Vauxhall Conference, I think . . . What about Scunthorpe, eh? Yeah, six–three . . . All roight, speak to you next week, Dad. Ta-ra.' Johnny replaced the receiver and returned to his magazine.

Belle sat staring at him in disbelief. She was in the perfect frame of mind to pick on Johnny, and what better opportunity? 'Unbelievable!' she said, shaking her head.

Johnny studiously ignored her and carried on reading.

'I said, you are unbelievable,' Belle repeated, undeterred.

Johnny sighed. 'Why's that, then?'

'Is that all you and your dad can talk about? Do you never feel the urge to discuss something other than football? Like his grandson or your mum perhaps? Every week it's the same. Is that the only way you two can communicate? Honestly, an eavesdropper could die of boredom listening in on you!'

As always, Johnny took the bait. 'Oh, and listening to you drone on to that drama queen of a mother of yours for hours on end is supposed to be riveting, is it? At least me and my dad just say what we have to say and then say goodbye. We don't spend all day analysing every bloody last detail of a person's relationship or their clothes or what they said to you and how.'

'What did you call my mum?' It wasn't as if Belle hadn't heard him call Rosalie a drama queen before, but tonight it was just the excuse she needed to vent her exasperation.

'A dra—' Johnny was about to swallow the bait, but then he remembered that he'd been dying for a shag all day. Insulting Rosalie was definitely not the best way of seducing Belle. He was beginning to wonder whether there *was* any way to seduce Belle these days. If she wasn't suffering from PMT, she was on the longest periods imaginable, with the window of opportunity between the two ever diminishing. 'Sorry, I shouldn't have said that,' he conceded, nobly.

Belle smirked and was about to fish out her ideal lover profile for its latest update when she felt something pressing into her back. *Oh no, he wants sex*, a voice inside her head groaned as she watched his arms wrap themselves around her chest. Then, predictable as ever, one of Johnny's hands wormed its way inside her dressing gown and groped at her left breast as if it were testing the ripeness of a peach. That's right, she thought, poke your penis in my back, maul me, that's bound to get me going. Don't think to ask me how my day's been or how I might be feeling at the moment. I mean, it's not as if I'm a proper person, is it? I'm just a Laundered Pants and Packed Lunch Provider, after all. With a sudden surge of anger, Belle pushed back on her chair, wheeling it over Johnny's foot in the process.

'Jesus, Belle, what's the matter with you?' he shouted.

For a brief second Belle panicked, wondering where that burst of anger had come from. Just as she was about to explain all about her frustration at not being taken seriously at work, or at home for that matter, Johnny continued his rant, administering the final nail in his 'chances of a shag' coffin.

'You could have broken my toe. And we've got a big away game this Saturday.'

Anna looked at the blank piece of paper in front of her and frowned. She chewed on the end of her pencil, stared at the burnt-orange wall, studiously avoiding the gaze of the garish unicorn/winged horse, and frowned some more. No matter how hard she tried she just couldn't force the band of nagging doubts from her head. *It's starting again, it's starting again*, they taunted. And every time she tried to block them out by putting pencil to paper they would come back even stronger than before. Like lawyers for the prosecution, summing up a catalogue of incriminating evidence. *Think of the late nights, the cold expression, the distracted manner. What about the betting slips and the silent phone calls? Or the way he flung his mobile over the balcony just because he couldn't get any reception.*

Anna put down her pencil and sighed. It was no

good, she wasn't going to be able to get anything done tonight. Carefully disassembling her home-made drawing board, she returned the tray to the kitchen and the pile of books it had been propped up against to the shelves. She then put the blank sheet of paper back in the envelope tucked inside a copy of *Marie Claire* and hid the pencil underneath the sofa.

Operation complete, Anna switched on the television. She cast her eyes down the TV guide that had once seemed so familiar but now contained a multitude of new delights. UK Gold were showing *Cagney and Lacey*, she noted. Suddenly things didn't seem quite so bad after all. Besides, they were going for a curry with Belle and Johnny tomorrow night. It would do them good to get out of the flat for an evening – help Tom unwind. Anna settled down for the opening credits, all nagging doubts driven from her mind. Or so she thought, until a straggler popped up from out of nowhere. *But what if it makes him worse?* it whispered ominously.

19

'Now, are you sure you don't mind doing this?' Belle hopped around the hall pulling on her boot as she ushered Ginny inside. 'Harry shouldn't be any trouble, he was out like a light.'

Ginny didn't mind in the slightest. In actual fact she felt rather guilty at never having baby-sat for Belle before – it was nothing personal, she simply had a bit of an aversion to kids.

'Of course not. It'll be great to get a bit of peace and quiet to update my CV – Mike's doing a stack of marking in front of the Manchester United game. We'd only have had a massive row if I'd been there. I can't understand how he can spend half his life slagging that team off and yet the moment they're on TV he has to watch them. Why?'

Belle shrugged and gave her a look specifically designed to convey the sentiment *Don't ask me, Johnny's just the same, but after all, aren't all men useless tossers?*

'You look great, by the way.'

'Do I?' Belle certainly didn't feel great. Her day had been a whirlwind of racing backwards and forwards to the nursery, studiously avoiding the other housebound mums hovering like vultures waiting to pounce on the slightest chance of adult conversation. In the two hours, ten minutes she was Harry-free Belle had managed to write out one hundred invitations on the back of cardboard sausages. In fact it had all been going swimmingly, when, without warning, the blanket of frost that had been stealthily coating the interior of her freezer like some arctic fungus decided to expand just enough to render closing the door completely impossible.

For two hours Belle had chiselled away, cursing the day she decided against a frost-free and kicking herself for allowing it to get in such a horrendous state yet again. By the time she had removed the mini-Antarctica from her kitchen and got Harry fed, bathed and into bed, she was left with exactly fifteen minutes to jump in the shower and sling on an outfit that wasn't covered in ketchup or antifreeze. The days when she would spend an entire afternoon exfoliating, waxing, plucking, conditioning, deodorising and moisturising in preparation for an evening out were well and truly behind her. The sad fact was that Belle had spent eight times longer grooming her freezer than she had herself. In her previous life she wouldn't have dreamt of going out with six days' worth of fuzz sprouting from her legs and armpits, not to mention the merry band of stragglers marching their way out from beneath her Marks and Spencer's cotton briefs. Once upon a time, an evening out with Johnny would have required the finest silk lingerie La Senza could provide and a bikini line waxed and plucked into submission. Mind you, those were also the days when love songs seemed loaded with meaning and the anticipation of sex evoked a shiver rather than a shudder.

'Take a seat,' Belle instructed Ginny as she touched up her lipstick in the hall mirror. 'I'll just go and check on Harry.'

Ginny ventured cautiously into the living room. The Man United game was blasting from the television and a clean-shaven Johnny, reeking of Insignia and resplendent in smart-casual Wolves leisure wear, was glued to the screen. Ginny sniffed. God, those cheap sprays were so repugnant; she didn't know how Belle put up with it. She hadn't allowed Mike to buy anything other than Giorgio Armani or Calvin Klein for years.

'Hi, Johnny,' Ginny said as sweetly as she could before perching on the sofa.

'All right,' Johnny grunted in response, not even bothering to look up.

Ignorant pig, Ginny fumed as she removed a folder from her leather attaché case. No wonder Belle wanted to have an affair.

Belle flew into the room, a breathless mix of Chanel and corkscrew curls. 'Come on, Johnny, the cab's here. Ginny, help yourself to food and drink. There's loads of defrosted chicken nuggets in the kitchen that need to be eaten. Now, I've got my mobile and the number for the Rayners Tandoori is next to the phone.'

Ginny couldn't help emitting a small sigh. What a waste of an evening going to that dive – it was only one step above the local Wimpy bar. 'I'll be fine – you just enjoy yourselves,' she said, her voice full of doubt as she followed them to the front door.

'Yeah, you too. I really hope Harry doesn't play up,' Johnny said with a smirk before slamming the door loud enough to wake the twins at number seventy-four, let alone a lightly sleeping three-year-old at number twenty-two.

'Are you sure everything's all right?' Anna looked across the table at Tom imploringly, trying desperately to think of a way to wipe the scowl from his face.

'I said leave it alone, didn't I?' Tom hissed back at her. 'Why do you always have to get on my case? I get enough shit all day at work.'

Anna watched in silence as Tom chewed on his fingernails, his eyes darting about the restaurant frantically.

'Can I have another beer, mate?' he called over to the solitary waiter on duty, a sweet-faced boy of no more than seventeen, who was slumped over the bar looking bored out of his mind.

'Yeah, sure,' the waiter replied, springing into life, grateful for something to do. 'And anything for the lady?' he asked somewhat hopefully.

'No, she's fine,' Tom responded before Anna had a chance to ask for another drink. She looked down at the film of orange juice lining the bottom of her glass and decided it was probably better to make it last rather than challenge Tom in his current mood. Resigning herself to dejected silence, Anna glumly surveyed the restaurant. Its dreary burgundy décor and overall lack of ambience only added to the cloud of doom hanging over the evening. When Belle originally suggested this night out it had seemed like a brilliant idea, but that had been over a week ago, before everything had started to go wrong again.

Anna wasn't exactly sure what had initiated Tom's bad mood, but she had a feeling it was something to do with the betting slip she'd found in his pocket when she was doing the washing. The one that read *£400 on Rebel Yell at 8–1*. Four hundred pounds. Anna had been momentarily stunned that Tom could have found that kind of money for a bet, but then she remembered the travel fund.

Tom had never lost the travel bug since spending six months in Asia when he was twenty-one, two years before they'd met. In the early days of their relationship they had spent many an hour lying on his faded Arsenal duvet cover, smoking joint after joint while he regaled her with stories of his travels. 'There's so much out there, Anna,' he had said, his voice buoyant with hope. 'I never want to end up a sad, bitter old fucker like my dad, spending most of my life inside the boozer or the bookie's – I want to get out there and see it all, man.' Anna had lain there, wide eyed at Tom's worldliness and terrified that one day she would turn up at his bed-sit to find him with his rucksack packed and a copy of the Lonely Planet guide to Thailand in his hand, ready to leave without her. But as the months passed Tom's plans began to include her too, and further hours were spent discussing the merits of Australia over the States and whether or not Thailand had become too touristy. Tom opened a savings account into which he deposited all his overtime payments. As soon as Anna left college to work in a local call centre she contributed as much as she could spare too. Even when she got pregnant Tom continued saving. 'Ours'll be the best-travelled kid in London,' he said proudly as he stroked her ever-expanding belly. For a long time Anna believed him, but as the months passed travelling became more and more of a pipe dream. There never seemed to be any extra cash, and looking after a toddler was hard enough in the relative comfort of a North London council flat, let alone a mosquito-infested hut in India.

'I'm going to the toilet,' Tom snapped, pushing his chair back into the wall so hard that the fringe of gold tassels hanging from the dado rail quivered violently. 'Fucking hell, I get better conversation from Grace than I do off you. You'd better sort yourself out before the others get here.'

Anna thought of Grace and her eyes pricked with tears. She should be with her now, not that awful baby-sitter Tom had brought home. She was one of his mate's girlfriends, all bold gold and brassy hair.

Anna prayed that Grace didn't wake up while they were out. She somehow doubted that the baby-sitter would have a clue what to do if confronted with a crying baby. She looked completely out of her head for a start, standing there in her Arsenal shirt staring blankly at Anna, but Tom had vouched for her and Anna hadn't dared question his judgment.

Sulking on her own in the back of the minicab, Belle suddenly felt the overwhelming desire to wail. As she listened to Johnny and the cab-driver chattering endlessly about football she felt as if she were intruding on *their* night out! When she had got into the back of the cab, she'd assumed Johnny would get in beside her. But oh no, he jumped right into the front, greeting the driver like some long-lost mate and asking whether he'd mind putting the football on the radio. Of course, the driver had been only too happy to oblige, leaving Belle like some stupid great gooseberry in the back. She might as well let Johnny take the driver out for a night of curry and football talk with Tom while she and Anna went back home for a laugh with Ginny.

Having a laugh was currently the last thing on Ginny's mind. Every time she attempted to update her CV her eyes were drawn to the kingdom of chaos reigning in Belle's living room. She'd initially cleared a work space on a corner of the dining-room table, but the piles of paperwork, countless chocolate wrappers and bizarre cardboard sausages scattered all about proved far too much of a distraction. Ginny couldn't see a pile of paperwork without thinking *file*, or a pile of wrappers without thinking *bin*, and as for the cardboard sausages – well, all she could think of was *why?*

So she relocated to the sofa, but that was hardly an improvement. Every time she tried to make a colour-coded note in the margin of her existing CV her eyes would find themselves drawn to the clutter of plants by the fireplace. There was just no order to them. Try as she might she could not ascertain any logical arrangement, in terms either of size, colour or species. It was as if Belle had placed them there all willy-nilly on purpose! And if that wasn't bad enough there was the state of anarchy that was the bookcase leering down at her, taunting her as it had done every single time she entered Belle's living room. Small books mixed with huge volumes, paperbacks alongside hardbacks, all just slung in with no regard at all to how displeasing it was on the eye. At least when Belle was present Ginny was able to restrain herself from a frenzy of rearranging, but now, left on her own, holding back was proving to be a torturous experience. Then of course there was the icing on the cake, or rather the ornaments on the mantelpiece, seemingly slung there at random. Well, they had to be – why else would there be just three ornaments on the left-hand side and an almighty eight on the right? The lack of symmetry was making her feel quite dizzy. Ginny put her CV back in its folder and placed it neatly on the arm of the sofa. There was nothing else for it . . .

Belle flounced into the Rayners Tandoori leaving Johnny to his fond farewells with the cab-driver only to find a rather dejected-looking Anna and an equally despondent-looking waiter.

'God, is this it?' she asked, gesturing at the empty restaurant. 'You look bored out of your mind, Rav.' Rav shrugged his shoulders and grinned as he set about preparing a large vodka and tonic. Belle turned to Anna. 'Where's Tom?'

'I'm right here, Mrs Farraday,' Tom replied, emerging from the back of the restaurant with a cheery grin on his face – much to Anna's surprise. 'What have you done with Johnny, then? Told him *Auf wiedersehen*?'

Belle shook her head and laughed. 'No, he's just outside paying the cab-driver.' God, Anna's lucky, Belle thought as she checked out the silhouette of Tom's granite-like physique beneath his shirt. She could just imagine him on the building site, top off, all rippling muscles and gleaming tanned skin – so much sexier than picturing Johnny sat behind a desk selling Internet solutions. Then Belle felt a stab of guilt – Romantic Liaisons with a friend's boyfriend were strictly off limits. She looked at Anna staring forlornly at the empty glass in front of her and wondered why she wasn't leaping around the restaurant for joy at having landed such a walking, talking Diet Coke moment. It was probably an artist thing – she was probably feeling a little melancholic or something.

'Are you okay, Anna?' Belle asked, sitting down in the seat next to her.

'Oh yes, fine, fine,' Anna replied hastily.

'She's a bit tired, aren't you, sweetheart? Too much sitting around watching Jerry Springer all day.' Tom chuckled loudly and winked knowingly at Belle. 'Oh, here he is.' He pulled out the seat next to him for Johnny. Tom and Johnny greeted each other warmly, and effortlessly fell into football talk.

'It was one–nil when I got out of the cab,' Johnny took delight in informing Tom. 'Shame they haven't got a telly in here, eh?'

Belle looked at Anna and raised her eyebrows, wondering why the hell she had suggested this night out. Oh, the blokes were going to have a great time all right, whereas she and Anna would have to talk about bloody kids and daytime television all night long. And she was itching to know what Anna had been drawing for the last few weeks, and of course tell her all about the latest additions to her ideal-lover profile. Belle looked at the menu in front of her and decided there and then to have a blow-out – the only possible avenue of pleasure available to her that night.

20

Ginny stood in the centre of Belle's living room and exhaled contentedly. Where there is discord, let me bring harmony, she thought, a warm smile of self-congratulation spreading over her face. Everywhere she looked order reigned. Papers had been filed, litter had been binned, cardboard sausages had been neatly stacked – she had been at a bit of a loss there. The plants now formed two neat rows either side of the fireplace, like sets of Russian dolls, the tallest rubber plants first, then the medium-sized ferns, dwindling down to the cacti.

The bookshelf had been by far the most laborious of her night's tasks. She had had to empty the entire thing and develop a rather convoluted classification process on the carpet, but seeing the books all finally rehoused in their rightful places gave such a terrific sense of satisfaction it made all the dust and dead insects seem worthwhile. (She had made a particularly gruesome find behind the *Encyclopedia Britannica* involving several decomposing woodlice.) Not only had Ginny ranked the books in order of size, but they had also been subcategorised by publisher. She cast a triumphal eye along the procession of penguins and smiled. When she had luxuriated in the bookcase for long enough she gazed at the mantelpiece proudly. Given that it housed eleven ornaments in total, it had made perfect sense to make one of them central with five on either side. Ginny had lined them all up on the coffee table for inspection. She had never seen such a bizarre mixture of knick-knacks. Why hadn't Belle gone for a theme, like she had with her collection of blue Persian glass? It made life so much simpler. Ginny finally decided that the ebony Buddha should form the focal point and had arranged the assorted candles, framed photos and trinket boxes on either side, again in order of size. Standing in the centre of the room, casting her eyes about the place proudly, she had to admit that, given her limited resources, she had done a damned good job. Now at last the karma was right for her to begin work on her CV.

Ginny wasn't really sure what came first, the blood-curdling scream almost shattering her eardrums or the deluge of ice-cold water blasting against the back of her head. Everything seemed to happen so fast, as the water gushed downward, soaking her back and then her legs, causing her whole body to spasm involuntarily. When the drenching finally stopped she turned slowly, nervously, completely unprepared for the sight that greeted her. There in the doorway, like a miniature Rambo in his Action Man pyjamas, brandishing a huge pump-action water pistol, stood Harry, grinning sheepishly.

'It wasn't me, it was Harry-Billy,' he uttered, before turning on his heels and beating a hasty retreat upstairs.

Belle looked at the dessert menu and sighed. This was the one drawback of going for an Indian – the puddings were crap. She looked at the rows of photos in the vain hope of discovering a slab of cheesecake smothered in cream or a squidgy brownie oozing warm chocolate sauce lurking between the uninspiring selection of ice creams in flowerpots. But no – the menu was exactly the same as it always was, completely devoid of anything delicious. That was another bizarre phenomenon peculiar to Indian restaurants – no matter where you went for a curry, be it Brick Lane or Bromsgrove, the dessert menu was identical. Why? Didn't they realise that for most women the pudding was the climax of the entire meal (if not evening)? Oh well, it looked as if it would have to be the frozen coconut yet again. The Coconut Supreme was the only dessert Belle vaguely liked as it bore a fleeting resemblance to a Bounty, unfortunately minus the thick layer of chocolate.

'The usual, madam?' Rav enquired, as he hovered next to Belle, notepad and pen at the ready.

'Oh, go on, then,' Belle sighed, sorely missing the tingle of pleasure that accompanied a request for Death by Chocolate.

'And any sweet for you, madam?' Rav asked

Anna. 'Or are you sweet enough already?' he added with a slightly embarrassed giggle.

'Oh, Rav, please!' Belle groaned.

Anna laughed. 'I think I'll try the kulfi,' she replied.

'Excellent choice, excellent choice, but then you look like a lady with taste,' Rav murmured, obviously thoroughly enjoying himself.

Anna couldn't help giggling, but then she saw Tom frowning at her and she realised how foolish she must seem, flirting with a boy barely out of school.

'And for you, gentlemen?' Rav said, turning to Johnny and Tom.

'Nothing for me, thanks,' Johnny replied.

Boring and unadventurous as ever, Belle couldn't help thinking.

'Oh, come on, mate – you've got to have something,' Tom urged. 'What about a liqueur? Or even better, what about an Irish coffee? Do you do Irish coffees, mate?'

Rav nodded hesitantly.

'Right, make it two Irish coffees, then,' said Tom, rubbing his hands eagerly.

Anna couldn't believe the transformation in Tom since the others had arrived. Throughout the meal he had regaled them with tales of his travels through India, all signs of his previous mood vanished without trace.

'So when are you two ladies going to start coming to watch us play?' Tom asked, lighting up a cigarette.

Johnny let out a snort of laughter.

A bit like a stupid fat pig, Belle couldn't help thinking.

'You've got some hope, mate. The day Belle comes to a match is the day I—'

'You have no idea how hard it is to keep a young kid amused for two hours on a sideline,' Belle snapped. Come to think of it, Johnny had no idea how to keep Harry amused full stop, such was his lack of involvement in his son's life. 'Tom, could I be really cheeky and pinch one of your fags?' Belle asked, ignoring the shocked stares from Anna and Johnny.

'Yeah, sure,' Tom replied, taking a cigarette from his packet and lighting it for Belle. 'Sorry, I didn't realise you smoked – I would have offered you one earlier.'

'She doesn't smoke,' Johnny said stonily.

'I do when I'm stressed out,' Belle replied, equally stonily.

Anna glanced at Tom, hoping to exchange one of those furtive 'Oh my God the other couple are about to have a massive row – let's sit back and wallow in our own sense of togetherness' kinds of glances, but to her disappointment Tom was staring at Belle, amusement twitching at the corners of his mouth.

'Well, how about the firework do, then?' Johnny enquired. 'You are going to come to that, aren't you? Harry would love it. Even you enjoyed it last year, didn't you, Belle?' Johnny looked at Belle hopefully.

Belle nodded. 'Yeah, the disco was pretty good,' she conceded.

'What firework do?' Anna asked.

'On the Saturday closest to Guy Fawkes' Night the football club has a big firework party with a disco afterwards,' Johnny explained, smiling warmly at Anna. 'You'll have to come along, Anna, bring Grace.'

Anna nodded and smiled back. Johnny was completely different to what she had expected. Belle's rather harsh descriptions had left her with the picture of a self-obsessed bore, dressed from head to toe in orange and black, but he actually seemed really pleasant – even his top was fairly discreet, with the smallest of wolves' heads woven on to the left breast pocket. 'I'd love to go,' she replied. 'I haven't been to a firework display for years.'

'Oh, I don't know – Grace might be a bit young for fireworks,' said Tom, the frown on his face immediately causing Anna's heart to sink.

'Oh – well, try and get a baby-sitter or something. Who's got her tonight?' Johnny asked.

Before Anna could reply Tom let out a cheer. 'Here he is!' They all turned to see Rav returning to the table with the two desserts. 'Hey, where's our coffees?' Tom asked, with mock indignation.

Rav looked momentarily panicked. 'They're on their way, sir. The chef's just adding the cream now.' In actual fact when Rav had left the kitchen the chef was fighting desperately to stop the cream from plummeting to the bottom of the glass for the fifth time.

Belle began chipping away at her rock-solid Coconut Supreme, immediately reminded of her afternoon of defrosting. She hoped Ginny was tucking into those chicken nuggets. It would be such a waste to have to throw them all out.

Ginny had stood in the middle of Belle's living room, dripping water and mouth agape, and for some reason all she could think of was that annoying children's hero from the 1980s, He Man. '*By the power of Grey Skull I have the power!*' echoed through her head as she remembered her two irritating little brothers tearing round and round the house screaming at the tops of their voices and brandishing those stupid plastic swords.

'Be quiet!' she remembered screaming as she desperately tried to cram for her O-levels, empty the washing machine and compile a shopping list while her mother lay in bed sobbing into her pillow over the latest man to abandon her.

On and on they'd screamed until Ginny could take it no more. She had marched into her mother's darkened room and pleaded with her to get out of bed, but as usual it was to no avail.

'Please, Ginny, you see to them,' her mother had sobbed. 'I don't think I can cope with all this, not now. I just need a bit of space to get my head together.'

And I don't, Ginny had raged, silently of course, as she abandoned her studying to fry up an enormous batch of Alphabites.

It was that same feeling of utter helplessness which she was experiencing now, standing there drenched in Belle's living room, Harry's shrieks still ringing in her ears and tears pouring down her face.

'I don't know what to do! I don't know what to do!' she cried, every grain of comfort and control gleaned from rearranging Belle's living room disappearing with each awful, shuddering sob. And then suddenly she knew exactly what to do.

'Harry! Do you fancy some chicken nuggets?' she called up the stairs before making a beeline for the deep-fat fryer in Belle's kitchen.

'You're having a laugh, aren't you?' Tom stared at the two glasses on Rav's tray incredulously. 'What the fuck *is* that?'

Rav looked at the murky brown liquid seeping over the tops of the glasses and smiled apologetically. 'I'm so sorry, sir, our chef is new. He has never actually made an Irish coffee before, but my uncle sends his apologies and says that of course they shall be on the house.' Rav removed the glasses from the tray and placed them by Johnny and Tom.

'I should bloody well hope so too – what the hell's he done to them?' Johnny stared at the glass in front of him, completely bemused.

'Sod being on the house,' Tom added. 'I reckon we should be paid danger money if he wants us to drink the bloody things!'

At this point Belle looked at Anna and Anna

looked at Rav and all three of them burst out laughing.

'Would you like to complain to the manager, sir?' Rav asked hopefully.

'Oh no, there'll be no need for that,' Johnny replied hastily.

'No, we'll just have the bill please, mate,' Tom said, raising his shoulders in despair.

Belle and Anna were still giggling when Rav returned with the bill.

'A beautiful English rose for a beautiful English rose,' Rav schmoozed as he handed a rather wilting-looking flower bearing a suspicious resemblance to a carnation to Anna. 'And one for you too,' he said, thrusting another flower at Belle.

'Huh! I see I don't get the special treatment any more, Rav,' Belle said, pretending to sulk. 'You're so fickle!'

Rav grinned at Belle. 'You shouldn't have such attractive friends,' he said, giving Anna's arm a playful squeeze. 'Only kidding, sir,' he added hastily.

Anna flinched. She didn't need to look up to know that Tom's face would be thunder.

'No worries, mate,' Tom replied jovially, with a trace of tension so slight only Anna was able to detect it. 'Bloody hell, Anna, how come the only one of us who doesn't earn a wage orders the most expensive thing on the menu? What am I gonna do with her, eh?' Tom said to Johnny, laughing, as he removed a bundle of notes from his wallet.

As Rav helped her on with her coat, Anna felt her heart sink ever lower. 'I can do it myself,' she pleaded, feebly, but knowing that the damage was already done.

Belle laughed. 'I suppose I'll have to put my own coat on now I'm out of favour,' she said sorrowfully.

'No, no, you're still my second favourite.' Rav grinned, helping Belle with her leather jacket.

'Cab's here,' said Tom, marching to the door.

21

Belle and Johnny walked into their living room and looked around in disbelief.

'What's happened?' Belle whispered, horrified. 'Everything's gone symmetrical!'

They took in the neatly stacked papers in the dining room, the new-look bookshelf, the plants all standing to attention and the perfectly balanced mantelpiece until their eyes finally came to rest on a bedraggled-looking Ginny, curled up on the sofa fast asleep next to an equally comatose Harry.

'Fucking hell!' Johnny exclaimed. 'We've been burgled by Anal Retentives Anonymous!'

'I said I'm sorry,' Anna pleaded, running to keep up with Tom as he strode across the forecourt to the flats. 'He was only joking anyway. I'm sure he's like that with all the female customers.'

'It's not him I'm worried about,' Tom snarled. 'He's just a kid. It's you – acting like a cheap tart, giggling all over him, encouraging him. You're a mother, for fuck's sake, and you were supposed to be with me.'

'I *was* with you.'

'Well, that's not what it looked like back there in front of Johnny and his missus. You really take the fucking piss – ordering everything on the menu when you know how tight things are at the moment. But why should you care? I'm the mug who has to pay for it all. Well, I tell you what, that's the last fucking time I take *you* out anywhere.' Tom stormed through the door to the flats, swinging it back in Anna's face.

'Ow! Tom, please don't be like this. I'm sorry. I really am. Can't we talk about this, please?' Anna's heart began pounding like a bass drum against her ribcage as she ran to keep up with him.

'I've got nothing to say to you,' Tom said, effortlessly taking the stairs three at a time.

'Tom, please, I've said I'm sorry,' Anna pleaded breathlessly as they reached the front door. 'Isn't there anything I can do or say to make it all right?'

Tom put his key in the lock and turned to face her. 'Just keep out of my way. If I were you I'd sleep with Grace tonight.'

Grace. Anna felt a surge of panic as she followed Tom into the living room. In all the confusion she had completely forgotten about the baby-sitter from hell.

The baby-sitter from hell was sat on the floor flicking through a copy of *That's Life!* magazine and chewing fervently on a piece of gum. From her vantage point above, Anna marvelled at the wide streak of black running like a landing strip along the centre of her head. If she left it much longer her roots would be longer than the rest of her hair.

The girl looked up and met Anna's gaze blankly before turning a dazzling smile on Tom. Well, it would have been dazzling if it hadn't been quite so full of amalgam. 'All right, Tommo,' she whined, pulling on a ridiculously high pair of platform trainers.

'Has Grace been okay?' Anna asked anxiously.

'Yeah, fine,' she replied, looking straight at Tom.

Tom smiled and reached out his hand to help her to her feet. 'Come on, then, Chelsea, I'll walk you home.'

22

'Blimey! What the hell's happened to your living room?' Maz asked, making a beeline for the armchair closest to the bowl of tortilla chips.

'What do you mean?' Belle asked, knowing exactly what Maz meant but hoping desperately that she was somehow mistaken.

'Well, why's it gone so bloody *symmetrical*? Have you got the mother-in-law coming to visit or something?'

'Er, no, not exactly.' Belle felt her face begin to tingle with embarrassment as she set about pouring the drinks. She daren't look in Ginny's direction.

'And what the hell's going on with the plants? They look like an identity parade standing in a line like that.' Maz made her voice go all squeaky. 'It was her, Officer, the busy Lizzie, she was the one what dunnit.' Maz turned, guffawing, to Ginny and Anna, only to be stunned into silence by the array of po faces greeting her. Maz turned her attention to the tortillas in a state of confusion – what the hell was wrong with everybody today?

'Well, it's a big improvement on the mess it was in before,' Belle said swiftly. 'Now, let's get down to business. First of all, how is everyone getting on with their Passion Pursuits?'

As usual the others all coughed, fidgeted and stared about the room anxiously, like patients in a dentist's waiting room, praying that theirs would not be the first name to be called.

'Okay, I'll start,' Belle offered enthusiastically, picking up a sheaf of papers from the coffee table. 'As you know, my Pursuit is to have a mad passionate affair, but as I never seem to come into contact with any men I've had to spend the past couple of months working on a profile of my ideal lover instead. Anyway, I've finally arrived at a prototype which I would like to share with you now because, my fellow Widows, in exactly one and a half weeks' time I will be working away from home at my first-ever launch party. And get this, I will be staying overnight in a swanky hotel.' Belle somehow doubted that the Wigan Travel Lodge had ever been referred to as a 'swanky hotel' before, but if it added to the romantic aura of her Passion Pursuit, then so be it.

Maz sighed. 'You lucky cow. I'd give anything for a night away from Darren and the boys in some posh hotel. Mind you, I'd be too busy trying out the room service to think about any 'ow's yer father. I suppose you'll be getting all of that on the house, will you – room service and that?'

'Oh yes,' Belle lied breezily. Although Morrison had begrudgingly agreed to pay for her motel room, he had made it quite clear that that was as far as her expenses went. 'I'm not paying for any chuffin' extras – you pay your own bar bill,' he had blustered down the phone.

'So do you think you'll actually get the chance to, you know, meet someone?' Anna blushed.

'Oh, I don't think – I know.' Belle's outward confidence belied the sense of desperation she was really feeling. The truth was she very much doubted that the Wigan Travel Lodge was going to be swarming with horny young men eager to embark upon an affair with a frustrated sausage publicist, but she was fed up listening to the other Football Widows reporting on their progress week after week while she had absolutely nothing to say.

'So go on, then – tell us all about this perfect man you're going to meet up in . . . where is it again . . . *Wigan*?' Ginny's sarcasm-laden voice managed to make Wigan sound about as romantic a prospect as colonic irrigation.

'Okay,' Belle replied, refusing to let even Ginny spoil her moment in the spotlight, 'I'll read it to you.' She cleared her throat and began to read from the paper in front of her. 'Profile of Belle Farraday's Ideal Lover. Hair: long and tousled. Eyes: must be of the hypnotic, come-to-bed variety. Body: lean and lithe like a well-bred whippet, must not be flabby or have excess body hair. Age: eighteen to thirty-five – although I will consider over thirty-five if in the Bill Clinton league,' she added as an afterthought. 'Accent: cockney, Geordie, Scouse, Irish, Yorkshire,

Scottish, Welsh, Cornish, American, West Indian, East European, Dutch.' Belle paused for a much-needed intake of breath. 'Anything apart from West Midlands, really. Clothes forward slash style: cross between manual labourer and starving poet – sort of Russell Crowe meets Joseph Fiennes.'

'Don't tell me,' Maz interrupted, 'definitely no Wolves leisure wear?'

'You've got it.' Belle smiled before continuing. 'So now for the most important bit of all – PERSON-ALITY!'

Ginny sighed. Wasn't that enough? What the hell did Belle want a personality for anyway? Surely it was just a penis she was after. But judging by the number of pages remaining in her ideal-lover profile it looked as if Ginny had thought wrong. She threw Anna a sideways glance and noticed that she too was sharing her sense of despair – in fact the way she was clutching her head in her hands she looked positively close to tears.

Belle beamed at them all before continuing. 'Well, first of all he must be completely unselfish without being clingy or wet. He must be kind without being a doormat, he must be a man's man but equally inter-ested in women, he must be a Pisces, but one who actually is romantic and sensitive . . .'

One by one, the three sets of eyebrows surround-ing Belle began to rise ceilingward as she proceeded with her list of unfeasible demands.

'. . . he must be interested in soap operas, but not

in a way that suggests he may be a latent homosexual. He must love talking on the telephone, but not so much that you never get a chance to call your mates. He must always place his underpants straight in the laundry, but not be tidy to the point of being anal . . .'

On and on Belle read with enthusiasm and passion while the others listened in muted disbelief.

'And finally,' she announced, after what seemed like an eternity, 'he must like Neil Diamond, but not in a way that implies he still lives at home with his mother and has a penchant for glittery shirts and nylon trousers. So! What do you think?' Belle placed the profile down on the coffee table and stared at the others expectantly.

Anna was the first to break the silence. 'He sounds lovely,' she lied, for some reason unable to erase from her mind the image of a skinny, homosexual Dutch man, washing his underpants in front of *EastEnders*.

'Yeah, good luck, mate,' was all Maz could manage.

'Yes, good luck indeed,' Ginny added. 'Let's hope that Wigan is also hosting its annual Piscean Fans of Neil Diamond Convention on the same night as your sausage launch, eh?'

Belle smarted – and to think she'd kept her plants in that ridiculous line-up just to save Ginny's feelings.

'Don't you think you're being a tad too fussy?' Ginny continued. 'After all – you're only supposed to be after a shag. Why the hell should it matter whether or not he picks his pants up?'

'Of course it matters,' Belle fumed. 'What's the point of cheating on Johnny with someone just as bad?'

'Well, it sounds to me like you're looking for a new husband – not just a bit on the side.'

It took a minute for Ginny's observation to sink in. Was she looking for a new husband? Did she really want to leave Johnny? Belle felt a twinge of something uncomfortably close to fear. Time to move on, she decided – this was suddenly getting far too heavy. 'So how about the rest of you?' she enquired.

'Well, the sewing machine fund's coming along nicely,' said Maz, 'and to be honest I'm quite enjoying my little job – the other girls are a scream.'

'What is it you're doing again?' Ginny enquired, in exactly the same tone she had used when referring to Wigan. '*Cleaning?*'

'Yeah, that's right,' Maz replied defiantly.

'Oh, how exciting!' Ginny enthused. 'That reminds me – I've got a little gift for you, Maz. I thought it might come in useful when you finally design your own outfit.' Ginny's mouth remained fixed in a smug little smile as she produced a package beautifully wrapped in gold paper and festooned in ribbons and bows.

'Wow!' Maz gasped, momentarily thrown off guard by the elegance of the gift wrap. 'Thank you.'

'Oh, don't mention it,' Ginny purred.

All eyes fell upon Maz as she ripped the paper off eagerly.

'Oh . . .'

Anna and Belle looked at the glossy hardback on Maz's lap. *Style for Beginners – a guide to elegance and taste*, the title read.

Ginny studied Maz's face, but when she spotted the desired flicker of hurt it failed to elicit quite the thrill she had expected. On the contrary, the look of disappointment on Maz's plump face coupled with the accusing stares from Belle and Anna made her feel quite uncomfortable.

Maz coughed loudly and took a swig from her glass. 'That reminds me, Ginny – how's the vibrator? Have you managed to have an orgasm yet?'

A horrified silence fell upon the room, not least upon Belle. Ginny would know that she had blabbed, that she had betrayed her drunken confidence. Belle hung her head and waited for the onslaught, but instead of a tirade of abuse, a loud sob echoed throughout the room. Not Ginny, surely? Belle looked up and to her surprise discovered that the sobs were in fact coming from Anna. Anna, who had sat there even quieter than usual all afternoon, was now holding her face in her hands and sobbing quite uncontrollably. Within seconds Harry and Grace were at her side, prodding her anxiously, closely followed by Belle, Ginny and Maz, offering tissues, wine and comforting hugs.

'Anna, what's the matter? What is it?' Belle enquired nervously. The way things were going this afternoon, she was almost afraid to ask.

'I'm sorry,' Anna gasped, accepting Belle's offer of a tissue gratefully, 'I'm just really tired, that's all.'

'Are you sure?' Maz asked, her over-pearlised eyes wide with concern.

Anna nodded and shakily took the glass of wine from Maz's hand. It wasn't so much a lie as an abbreviation of the truth. She was tired. Exhausted in fact. Three nights sleeping on the floor in Grace's room were beginning to take their toll physically; every bone in her body ached. But she was mentally drained as well. With Tom blatantly ignoring her during the fleeting moments their paths crossed she had been dying to get to the Football Widows meeting to seek solace in some friendly faces. All of this sniping and tension made it feel just as bad as home.

'Right,' said Belle, authoritatively, 'I think it's time we took a moment to remember exactly why we're here and who the real enemy are. If we can't stick together we haven't got a hope in our war against football, have we?'

Much to Belle's relief the others all shook their heads meekly, including Ginny. 'So with that in mind,' she continued, 'I would like to share with you an absolute brainwave I have had for our next act of Widow's Revenge.'

The others looked at her with a mixture of interest and relief.

'As you are probably aware, next Saturday is the

football club firework party, and it suddenly dawned on me that this would provide the ideal opportunity to do something slightly more daring than wiping our arse on a scarf or boiling a football top.'

'Or tying their bootlaces together,' Maz interrupted with a derisory snort.

Ginny clenched her fists in outrage; it had taken her ages to come up with the previous week's revenge act.

'Anyway,' Belle continued hastily, 'I think it's high time we stepped our campaign up a gear or two.'

'Like what? Do a Guy Fawkes and blow up the clubhouse?' Maz chortled, nudging Anna into a smile.

'Not quite, but you're on the right track.'

'Oh God,' Ginny groaned, 'I really don't feel comfortable with breaking the law, you know, Belle . . .'

'I'm not talking about breaking the law, I'm just talking about taking advantage of their bonfire.'

'What do you mean?'

'Well, what if we make our own guy – a sort of effigy to football – you know, England top, Gary Lineker mask, that kind of thing – and swap it with theirs at the last minute. Then of course we could always help them out with a bit of kindling – shove a few of their precious programmes underneath the firewood. Think about it. The do doesn't start until eight o'clock, by which time they'll all be half pissed and hardly at their most observant. Imagine what a laugh we'd have watching them all standing around a funeral pyre to football without a clue what was going on!'

Maz sighed. 'Fucking brilliant!'

Ginny naturally remained unconvinced. 'It all sounds very impressive, but are you sure we can pull it off?'

'Of course we can,' Belle replied confidently. 'They always build the fire a few days beforehand, so we can sneak down and plant the football memorabilia the night before when no one's about.'

'And don't worry about the guy,' Maz added. 'My boys have made it for the past couple of years, so I'll get Darren to ask them again. Then I'll helpfully volunteer to drop it down to the club on the night and make a few alterations on the way.'

'Excellent!' Belle exclaimed. 'What do you reckon, Anna, brilliant idea or what?'

Anna nodded meekly. She didn't have the guts to tell Belle that she wouldn't be there. Her unexpected crying fit of earlier had been embarrassing enough without admitting that Tom had forbidden her coming anywhere near the firework party.

'Right, so that settles it,' Belle announced. 'Let phase two of our campaign commence.'

23

As Belle made her way to the football club she felt about as jittery as the entire canine population of Harrow. With every rocket that exploded into the night sky her heart missed a beat. Would they pull it off? Had Maz managed to get the guy, or rather the Gary, into position without being seen? Would anyone have noticed the assortment of football memorabilia stashed at the bottom of the bonfire?

The previous night, Belle, Ginny and Maz had crept into the football ground under cover of darkness (and Balaclavas – Belle's idea) to ceremoniously conceal their sacrificial offerings under the pyre. Offerings that included various Arsenal and Wolverhampton Wanderers programmes, Johnny's hand-painted 1980 Wolves Subbuteo team, a *Non-League Club Directory* (containing a photo of the Rayners Park team), the instructions to the Football Manager CD-ROM, and token copies of all the football magazines available in W H Smith's.

The high Belle had experienced driving home from the covert operation had been unbelievable, but now, as she headed back to the ground, blind panic had taken hold. By the time she pulled into the carpark she half expected to find a fleet of police cars waiting, lights flashing and sirens wailing, and a manacled Maz being bundled into the back of a van. To her overwhelming relief it looked just like any other firework do. Kids waved luminous plastic wands and munched on hot dogs, while their impatient mothers stamped the cold from their feet. Groups of teenagers loitered about trying to look hard and trying even harder to look as if they were actually enjoying the cigarettes they puffed away on. The only sign of authority present was the handful of stewards clad in bright orange jackets drifting around aimlessly and no doubt wishing they were back in the warmth of the bar.

Belle got out of her car and, after the obligatory five-minute struggle to get Harry wrapped up against the cold, headed to the designated meeting point. Ginny and Maz were already there, huddled conspiratorially against the rickety wooden fence surrounding the bonfire. As Belle approached, she glanced at the top of the mound of firewood anxiously. To her relief a guy had been perched on top and, judging by the size of his ears, Maz's mission had indeed been successful.

'Aunty Ginny!' Harry shrieked, launching himself at Ginny's legs, memories of their late-night chicken nugget fest still fresh in his mind.

'Oh – hello, Harry,' Ginny replied, patting him on the head awkwardly. Since her baby-sitting experience she had become rather wary of Harry and the feelings of vulnerability he had unwittingly triggered in her.

'All right, Belle,' Maz mumbled through a mouthful of hot dog, her cheeks smudged red from a mixture of cold and ketchup. 'Anna still poorly, is she?'

'Yeah – I think it must be the flu, she sounded terrible on the phone,' Belle replied.

'Well, she wasn't herself last week, was she? Bursting into tears like that,' Maz reflected. 'I'm just the same – I always get really emotional when I'm coming down with something.'

'It's a shame she'll miss all the action,' Ginny said, tactfully trying to disentangle Harry from her legs without resorting to a good old clip around the ear.

'I promised I'd call round as soon as I get back from Wigan and give her a blow-by-blow account,' Belle said, fishing a baseball cap from her bag and clamping it over her curls.

'Is that a blow-by-blow account of tonight or Wigan?' Maz chortled as she lit a cigarette. 'Fuck me, it's cold!'

Ginny shuddered. 'Language, Maz! Harry's listening.'

'Are you still sad, Aunty Ginny?' Harry piped up upon hearing his name.

'What?' Ginny asked weakly. God, she hated kids.

'Are you still sad?' Harry repeated.

'Ginny's not sad, sweetie,' said Belle, rummaging in her bag for some chocolate to shut him up.

'He probably means miserable,' Maz retorted.

'She is sad! She is sad!' Harry shouted, stamping his feet. 'She was crying just like Grace does.'

Belle looked at Harry in despair. Where the hell did he get such a vivid imagination?

'Oh, look – they're coming,' Ginny practically shrieked with relief as a procession of pint-wielding men slowly made their way out of the clubhouse and began meandering towards them.

'I take it the guy went okay,' Belle whispered to Maz, pointing to the figure on top of the fire.

'Yeah, no problem. I had to put a jacket over the England top because I think even these pissheads would have noticed it, but we should get away with the Gary Lineker mask – it's not a very good likeness.'

'Excellent!' Belle's excitement suddenly waned. 'Oh, look, here come our lot.'

The women watched as Johnny, Mike, Darren and Tom made their way laughing and joking to the bonfire.

'Hey – it's Mrs Farraday!' Tom shouted, waving and grinning at Belle. To her embarrassment, Belle felt her face flush. In his woolly hat and lumberjack shirt Tom looked even sexier than ever.

'Cor! He's a bit of all right,' Maz whispered, reading Belle's mind.

'All right, love.' Johnny beamed as he walked over to Belle. Belle squirmed as he planted a huge kiss on the top of her head before scooping Harry up into his arms. 'Hello, mate, are you looking forward to the fireworks?'

Ginny looked at Belle, Johnny and Harry and for a split second she was hit by the strangest yearning. But yearning for what exactly? She hated Johnny, and Harry was beginning to terrify the life out of her, but seeing them all together was definitely bringing a lump to her throat. What the hell was wrong with her these days? If she wasn't careful she was going to end up an emotional wreck like Anna.

Belle shrugged Johnny's arm from her shoulder. 'Aren't you going to join your mates?' she asked, her voice as icy sharp as the night air.

'Oh – yeah, okay.' Johnny set Harry down, visibly shocked. 'I'll see you a bit later, then. Do you want a hot dog or anything?'

'I'm fine.'

Johnny trudged back round to join his growing band of team-mates on the other side of the fire. The air was becoming thick with cigarette smoke and football banter.

Mike was the next to venture over. 'Hi, girls!' he enthused. Everything Mike said came across as enthusing. It was the saucer-like eyes and Cheshire-cat grin that did it; even his hair seemed over-enthusiastic, springing from his head in energetic little spirals. 'It should be a great night! Are you okay, sweetheart? Not too cold?' Ginny shook her head. 'Excellent! Well, I suppose you want to be left alone to have a good old natter?' Ginny nodded. 'Great! I'll catch you later, then. Enjoy the fireworks!' And with a last dazzling grin he bounded back over to Johnny.

'Blimey – he seems really sweet,' said Maz, failing miserably to conceal her shock. 'All right, babe!' she yelled over to Darren. 'No pissing in the bonfire this time, please!'

Darren's chubby red face broke into a grin. 'I won't if you won't, mate!' he replied, raising his glass to Maz.

Oh my God, Ginny thought with a shudder, it's Wayne and Waynetta Weeble!

'Here we go,' Belle whispered, as George, the club secretary, shuffled his way to the front of the bonfire. He then proceeded to make the same speech he made at every club do, with the same tired jokes about what a shame certain players' football skills didn't match their drinking skills and what a hoot they'd had that time they played at Chalfont St Peter and Sharkey had been arrested for nutting the ref. Belle looked at Maz and Ginny and rolled her eyes. *Just light the damn thing, you boring old git!* Finally her wish was granted and, to a roar of grateful applause, George lit the fire.

The Football Widows watched with bated breath as, crackling and sparking, tongues of flame began to lick away at the wood.

'Look – there goes Mike's Cup Final programme,' Ginny whispered excitedly. Belle followed her gaze. Tucked under a large plank of wood just a few feet in front of them she saw the edges of a football programme, glowing red as they began to curl inward.

Belle, Maz and Ginny huddled together, giggling. 'BURN! BURN!' they hissed, like the three witches from *Macbeth*.

'Look at them,' Ginny sneered as Johnny, Mike and Darren stood laughing and joking, completely oblivious as their most prized football programmes (not to mention Subbuteo teams) began to meet their fiery fate. Belle stifled a pang of guilt as she pictured Johnny's beloved little figurines melting into a pool of plastic.

'Look out, slapper alert!' Maz sniggered. Belle and Ginny turned just in time to see Chelsea swanning past, her bare legs glowing in the dark like two fluorescent strip lights.

'Has she made a pass at your Mike yet?' Maz asked mischievously.

'No, she most certainly has not – she probably realises that he's way out of her league. Unlike some others I could mention,' Ginny retorted, looking pointedly at Darren resting his pint on top of his beer belly.

'How can she come out on a night like this with nothing on her legs?' Belle asked, in amazement. They all watched as Chelsea's luminous white legs made their way back to the clubhouse. 'No wonder she's going back inside.'

'And now, ladies and gents,' George shouted, returning to the front of the crowd, 'I would like to announce the commencement of the fireworks. I hope you all enjoy the show.'

On cue Harry tugged on Belle's coat. 'Mum, I need a wee.'

'What? But the fireworks are about to start.'

'I need a wee.'

'Can't you just hold on for five minutes – you don't want to miss the fireworks, do you?'

'I NEED A WEE!'

'Okay, okay. I'll be back in a minute,' Belle said to the others, before marching Harry off to the club-house.

'Jaysus Christ, Dale. It's Gary fucking Lineker!' a completely pissed Irishman slurred as he staggered into the space vacated by Belle.

A horrified Ginny hastily repositioned herself on the other side of Maz.

Dale, a six-foot skinhead with the tattoo of a cobweb covering most of his face, looked at him, bewildered. 'Blimey. 'Ow many 'ave you 'ad, Ferg? That ain't Gary Lineker, it's that geezer what tried to blow up Buckingham Palace, innit?'

24

The clubhouse was completely deserted. Tables were littered with abandoned drinks and 'Love Me Tender' echoed eerily in the background. Belle looked at a cigarette smouldering forlornly in an ashtray and shivered. It was all a bit too *Mary Celeste* for her liking.

'Now hurry up,' she ordered, bustling Harry through the bar in the direction of the toilets. Just as they reached the ladies' the door swung open and out walked Tom.

'Bloody hell!' Tom stopped in shock. 'What are you doing here?'

'Jesus!' Belle gasped. 'You nearly gave me a heart attack. Harry needs a wee. Anyway, what are *you* doing here? This *is* the ladies'.'

Harry pushed passed them into the toilet, clutching his crotch and moaning.

Tom sniffed loudly and began to laugh.

God, you look cute, Belle couldn't help thinking, admiring the dimple in Tom's cheek and the way his eyes crinkled at the edges when he smiled.

'God – it looks bad, doesn't it? Don't worry, I haven't got any bizarre fetishes for women's toilets or anything – it's just that someone's hueyed all over the gents' and I thought as there was no one about . . .'

Belle looked at Tom and giggled. 'Hmm, well, what's it worth to keep quiet?' she asked, a little too coquettishly.

Tom leaned against the door frame. 'Well, that depends on what you want,' he replied, staring at her intently. Then, with a laugh, he retrieved a packet of cigarettes from his shirt pocket. 'Another fag perhaps? I won't tell Johnny if you won't.'

Belle laughed. 'Yeah, okay, I'll just get Harry.'

'No!' Tom barked, 'You're all right, I'll get him – I need to get a tissue anyway. I'll meet you back in the bar.'

Belle wandered over to a window and looked outside. At the far end of the field the crowd stood entranced, necks craned as the fireworks erupted into the sky like glitter. Belle recalled the excitement she had felt every Bonfire Night as a kid. But now the colours all seemed strangely muted, the oohs and ahs of the crowd manufactured somehow. Just when had her life become so bland? When had her senses become so deadened?

'Penny for them.' Tom suddenly appeared at her side holding Harry's hand. 'Or perhaps you'd prefer a B & H?' He held out a cigarette.

Belle took it and smiled. 'Oh, I don't know – just wondering where my life has gone, really.'

'Tell me about it!'

'Mum, can we play hide-and-seek again?' Harry whined, tugging on her sleeve.

'Not now, Harry – maybe later.' Belle studied Tom's face as he moved in to light her cigarette. There was something about the smooth tanned skin wrapping his chiselled cheekbones that made her want to reach out and touch it. To stroke the scar running parallel to his eye. He looked up and caught her gaze.

'So what have you got to be so down about? Haven't you got your launch thing this week?'

Belle was momentarily stunned. Tom had actually remembered her launch party, unlike her husband, who seemed to drift through life in some kind of football-induced trance. Despite the fact that their house had been overrun with cardboard sausages for the past week, Johnny hadn't mentioned a word about her going away – not a single question about how her preparations were coming along or how she was feeling at the prospect of her first real work in four years. 'Yeah, that's right. Two whole days in sunny Wigan.'

'So how are you feeling about it? Are you nervous?' Tom asked as he held the door open for her.

God, this man had to be the closest thing to perfection a woman could want. A walking, talking Diet Coke moment, who actually took an interest in you too. But he's a walking, talking Diet Coke moment who also happens to be living with your mate, Belle reminded herself sharply. 'Yeah, to be honest I am a bit. It's the first time I've ever done anything like this,' she explained, shivering as the cold air hit her face.

'Don't worry, you'll knock 'em dead. I think it's brilliant what you're doing.' Tom sniffed loudly and rubbed his nose with the back of his hand.

'So have you got the same thing as Anna?' Belle asked as they slowly made their way across the field.

'Eh?'

'That flu thing?'

'Oh, that. Yeah, I think so.' Tom stuffed his hands in his pockets and glanced about the field edgily. 'Anyway, I'd better get back to the lads.'

'Yeah, sure. Thanks for the cigarette – and don't worry, your secret's safe with me.'

'What secret?' Tom asked, a look of alarm flickering across his face.

'Your ladies' toilet fetish, of course.'

'Oh, right, thanks. Listen, good luck with the launch.' Tom patted her on the shoulder gently before pacing off to join some rather unsavoury-looking teenagers loitering at the back of the crowd.

As Belle made her way back to Ginny and Maz, Harry looked up at her imploringly. 'Mum, please can I play hide-and-seek again?'

'What do you mean, again? We haven't played hide-and-seek for ages.'

'With that lady?'

'What lady?'

'The lady in the toilet.'

Belle stopped in her tracks – what the hell was he talking about? Tom had been the only person in the toilets and there was no way even Harry could have mistaken him for a lady!

'There wasn't a lady in the toilets, Harry.'

'Yes, there was – she was playing hide-and-seek with that man.'

Belle looked down at Harry and shook her head. 'Honestly, Harry, you're going to have to stop making up all these stories.' Tom couldn't have been in there with a woman. Could he? Belle instinctively glanced back towards the clubhouse. Light glared from the windows into the darkness, not a soul in sight. Just as she was about to turn back she noticed a silhouette slinking past each window through the bar until the door at the end opened, the accompanying blaze of light revealing a pair of milk-bottle-white legs.

25

Anna was having a really good night, and the irony of this fact had not escaped her. After all, this was the night she'd been banned from going out with her only friends by a boyfriend who couldn't even bear to sleep in the same room as her. *And* she was missing the highlight of the Football Widows campaign to date. Yet for some unknown reason it also turned out to be the night she finally rediscovered her ability to draw.

Theoretically she should have spent the evening littering the carpet with sodden tissues rather than endless sketches, with tears streaking her face, not ink, but the minute she stationed herself on the sofa – studiously avoiding the remote control – to construct her makeshift drawing board, something inside her clicked. All the self-doubt that had plagued her for the past few months, causing rigor mortis to invade her hand every time she picked up a pen, vanished without trace.

Perhaps her body simply couldn't take another night of crying its eyes out in front of *Dallas* (UK Gold was showing the entire first series as part of their Texan Soap Week), before lying cold, uncomfortable and sleep-free on the makeshift bed next to Grace's cot. Every night she would lie there, rigid as a corpse on her slab of cushions, waiting for the heart-stopping rattle of Tom's key in the door and hoping in vain for him to poke his head around the door, declaring Bobby Ewing-style that the past two weeks had just been a dream. But of course he hadn't, and her living nightmare continued.

Until tonight. Tonight she knew exactly where Tom was and, secure in the knowledge that he wouldn't be home for ages, she decided to have one more go at drawing. Without warning the new character she had been toying with for the past month finally forced his way from the confines of her mind, dancing through her pen and out on to the paper. One by one, all the thoughts and ideas that had been flickering through her head like old film reel finally began to take shape.

As her hand flew across the paper, Anna was vaguely aware of the splutter of fireworks echoing across the estate, but nothing could distract her. On and on she drew, until suddenly she had a completed storyboard. She gazed at her new crea-tion bounding through the comic strip in front of her and rubbed her eyes. 'Where the hell did you come from?' she said to herself, before slumping back on the sofa in an exhausted heap. A wave of contentment swept through her body as she curled herself up into a ball. *I can draw again, I can draw again*, hummed through her head like a mantra, wrapping her in a blanket of deep, peaceful sleep.

'Ahhhhhhhh!' Anna felt as if her scalp were being torn from her head. 'What the . . . ?' She blinked furiously, trying to find her focus in the semi-darkness. The outline of the sofa disappeared from under her as she was wrenched to her feet by her ponytail. Dazed, she half turned, half stumbled around, clutching the back of her head in agony. 'Tom?'

'Been busy, have we?' Their eyes met in the semi-darkness, hers dazed and confused, his wild and staring.

Anna felt almost delirious with shock and fear. The video clock read 2 a.m. Oh God, she had fallen asleep. How could she have been so stupid? Her stomach lurched.

'Answer me!' Shadows chiselled his face, giving him the appearance of a wooden etching.

Anna stepped back instinctively, drawing her dressing gown more tightly around her.

'Look at the state of you.' In the darkness a finger jabbed at her shoulder blade accusingly. 'Lazing around at home all day in front of the fucking telly or drawing your stupid little pictures.' A piece of paper was thrust under her nose. 'Look at it – it's kids' stuff.' She heard the rustle of paper being kicked across the floor. 'Why can't you be like Johnny's missus? She's got a kid and she manages to get off her arse and do a proper job *and* she still looks a million fucking dollars.'

Outside, a banger exploded like a shotgun blast. Anna felt her whole body shuddering uncontrollably. 'What's happening to you?' she sobbed. 'Why are you being like this?'

'What did you say?' Tom closed in on her menacingly.

Footsteps thudded along the balcony outside, followed by a bang so loud it reverberated through Anna's ribcage. A flash of light illuminated the room, like the blinding flash of a pouncing paparazzo, and for a split second it was as if they had become a photographic image, Tom motionless in front of her and Anna frozen in fright.

And then, BANG! She was up against the wall, Tom's hand gripping her neck. An explosion of tiny stars erupted before Anna's eyes as her head ricocheted forward. As the stars began to fade, Tom's face emerged pressed up close to hers, his piercing stare pinning her to the wall like ten-inch nails.

'Nothing's happened to me.' His voice seemed muffled, as if she'd been immersed in water. 'It's you. You're the fucking problem.' Then, with a final little shove of disgust, he turned and was gone.

26

'Belle Farraday, International PR Consultant, pleased to meet you.' Belle offered her hand in greeting to the elegant executive in the hall mirror and smiled her most dazzling smile. God, she looked good. So what if the suit had cost twice as much as she was going to be paid for the next two days, it was an investment, wasn't it? After all, when her client base had expanded to more than one and she had finally branched out from the meat industry she would need a decent suit. It would hardly be appropriate to entertain Hollywood types in the Ivy clad in a one-wash wonder from Mark One, now, would it? In preparation for the Lemon Zinger launch, Belle had applied the same principle to her hair. Although she had been using Kurl Up 'N' Dye for years and knew more about her stylist Sandra's sex life than Sandra's fiancé Wayne, it didn't really seem fitting for an up-and-coming PR consultant to have her hair highlighted amidst a sea of blue rinses. So Belle had made an appointment with the impressively titled Director of Colour Styling at Toni and Guy. It had been a terrifying experience. Enrique Benitez, the aforementioned director, had strutted around her haughtily, like some Latex-clad cockerel, before seizing a pair of scissors from his hip belt and snipping randomly at her hair. 'When did you last have this cut?' he practically sneered, gingerly fingering a tendril as if it were a bedraggled piece of seaweed. 'It really is in the most hideous condition.' A shamefaced Belle had shrunk back into her chair, pining for a natter with Sandra about Wayne's foreskin piercing. At Kurl Up 'N' Dye the only question Belle was ever asked was where she was going to on holiday. She never had to face an interrogation about which conditioner she used, or more to the point *didn't* use, or have her split ends waved in front of her eyes, or be patronised about the perils of home tinting.

However, admiring the final results in the mirror made all the humiliation worthwhile. Enrique had worked wonders taming Belle's cascade of curls into a recognisable style, and the subtle flecks of gold framing her face looked fantastic. The application process had been far less painful as well – why couldn't Sandra highlight hair in little strips of foil rather than yanking it through a rubber cap with a crochet needle?

Belle stepped into her not-too-high-heeled shoes and sighed. Her transformation from Laundered Pants and Packed Lunch Provider to high-flying go-getter was complete.

'Mum – what's happened to your legs?' A bewildered Harry appeared at the top of the stairs, rubbing sleep from his eyes.

Oh no, surely she hadn't laddered her tights already? Belle checked her legs anxiously in the mirror, but the ultra-sheer black Lycra appeared to be intact. 'What do you mean, sweetie?'

'Why have they gone all black?'

Belle didn't know whether to laugh or cry. Had it really been that long since she'd worn a pair of tights? Of course it had. There'd been that week about two years ago when, inspired by a feature on Yasmin Le Bon in *Hello!*, she'd decided to become a glamour mum and wear nothing but skirts and heels every day. Her new look had lasted precisely one hour – the time it took to nearly lose Harry under a juggernaut while she disentangled her kitten heel from a drain cover.

'I've got tights on, Harry, my legs haven't gone black,' Belle mumbled, applying a final coat of lip gloss.

'But why?'

'Because I'm going to work today.'

'But who will look after me?'

'Daddy's going to be here.'

'But who will look after me?' Harry cried, his voice quivering with alarm.

Belle felt her heart begin to sink. She'd been trying not to think too much about leaving Harry in Johnny's care for two days – it was enough of a worry when she left them both for the occasional two hours to go shopping. It wasn't that Johnny was deliberately neglectful, but once he started thinking about anything to do with football he tended to become completely oblivious to all else. All week horrifying scenarios had kept popping into her head. Johnny steering Wolves to the promotion play-offs on Football Manager while Harry merrily set about rewiring the toaster. Or Johnny rifling through his *Non-League Club Directory* to find out whether Halesowen Town's ground provided hot snacks while Harry attempted to abseil from his bedroom window on his Tweenies duvet cover. When she hadn't been transforming her image, Belle had been rushing about the house wedging plastic safety covers into every available electrical socket, locking all the upstairs windows and compiling a list of instructions so comprehensive that Johnny would probably need two days just to read it.

'Bloody hell – that's a bit over the top; you look like a dog's dinner,' Johnny said, appearing at the top of the stairs clad in a pair of Wolves shorts and yawning loudly.

'What is?' Once more Belle glanced anxiously at the mirror.

'The outfit. You're only going to the launch of a sausage.' Johnny sat down next to Harry, his sleep-lined face a combination of defiance and derision.

Well, this was just fucking typical. For the past four years she'd put her career on hold to bring up their son and wait on Johnny hand and foot and now, when she wanted to go to work for two days – *two poxy days* – he had to be petty and mean about it. Belle slung her lip gloss into her handbag and yanked her coat off the stand.

'I don't want you to go!' Harry began to wail.

'Don't worry, mate, we'll be fine on our own. We'll have a great time,' Johnny said a little unconvincingly, throwing his arm around Harry and pulling him close.

Belle looked up at them both – Harry gazing at her imploringly in his crumpled little Thomas pyjamas making her want to bound upstairs and smother him in kisses, and Johnny glowering at her in those ridiculous shorts making her want to run upstairs and smother him period. Snatching up her brand-new leather attaché case, crammed full of leftover cardboard sausages, Belle flung open the front door. 'I'm going to work,' she announced, but those four little words she'd been longing to utter all week no longer seemed to elicit quite such a thrill.

Ginny stared blankly at her computer screen. 'Hobbies and Interests' – why didn't she have any hobbies and interests? Oh, sure, she had loads on the CV in front of her – painting, feng shui, interior design, the obligatory French films and reading, but it was all bullshit. What did she really do in her spare time? Yoga. For some reason she was still going to those mind-numbingly boring classes each week; they were the only thing that helped her get to sleep at the moment, but putting yoga down as a hobby these days was a bit like putting breathing down. What did she do that was remotely interesting or fulfilling? Nothing, unless of course you counted membership of a secret society of football haters. Well, that would look great on the CV of someone who worked for Wembley plc, someone whose office actually looked out on to the 'hallowed turf'. Ginny swivelled round to the window and gazed down at the lush green blanket spread out beneath her. 'Hallowed' indeed. It was a bit of grass, that was all. She just couldn't understand the big deal; the big hoo-ha that had erupted when Wembley agreed to sell up earlier in the year. All Mike could think about was the fate of those two monstrous towers – he hadn't given a shit that her job was on the line, that she had to work for months unsure of who her next employer would be, or whether indeed she'd have one for much longer. As the new year approached it was becoming increasingly unbearable. The hype surrounding the FA Cup Final was bad enough anyway, but this season Ginny felt as if she might drown in the sea of nostalgic, sentimental bullshit currently engulfing the marketing department. All the nauseating droning of the promotional literature about the agony and ecstasy witnessed by the 'hallowed turf' over the years. Well, she was going through enough agony of her own, thank you very much, and there was no way she was going to stick around until Cup Final day. The question was, where was she going to go?

Ginny scrolled up a bit higher on her CV. Courses. *Self-Assertiveness, Time Management, Man Management, 'Sell Yourself', Neurolinguistic Programming, Know Your Market, Promotion for Profit*. There was a time when Ginny would have read this list with pride. Her CV had been the perfect promotional tool with which to market herself. 'Hobbies and Interests' had merely been a necessary irrelevance, a bit like the bumph on a menu informing you that the restaurant you were about to dine in prided itself on its ambience. Prospective employers didn't care if she hadn't really been on a six-week glass-painting course at her local tech. They all knew that 'Hobbies and Interests' was just a way of pretending you were a well-rounded person with a life outside your job. The trouble was, Ginny wasn't sure that she wanted to pretend any more.

A tinkle of laughter drifted across the office. Ginny peered over her desk partition to see Cheryl and Caroline poring over their Freemans catalogue. For the first time ever Ginny felt an overwhelming desire to march over to Caroline's desk and order herself a five-pack of pastel-coloured vest tops. *See*, she wanted to shout at them, *I am just like you really, I know how to have a good time too*.

'PRESENTATION . . . ORGANISATION . . .' suddenly flickered across Ginny's screen, and in that instant she was hit by a blinding realisation. It's all a load of complete and utter bollocks, she thought.

This is what life is all about, Belle mused as she laid her Pret-à-Manger sandwiches, bottle of Evian and gleaming copy of *Cosmo* out in front of her. She would have preferred to get *OK!*, they had an exclusive interview with Della Bovey, but *Cosmo* seemed far more in keeping with her new image. Besides, she was sure their twelve-page feature on female circumcision in West Africa would be riveting. As the train pulled out of Euston, Belle leaned back in her seat and closed her eyes. A sexual encounter on a train had always been one of her favourite 'Romantic Liaisons' – what if she were destined to meet her ideal lover on the 8.30 to Wigan?

Belle gazed at the tall handsome stranger sitting across from her. Unscrewing her bottle of Evian, she took a sip, allowing a drop of water to trickle from her mouth provocatively. His piercing blue eyes fixed upon her, caressing her, undressing her. Then suddenly he got to his feet, and with the merest tilt of his head he signalled for her to follow him through the swaying carriage. As Belle got to her feet a bolt of electricity charged through her La Senza knickers – no, sod it, this was a fantasy, after all – *her La Perla baby-doll. She knew what he wanted, all right, it was written all over his face. Sex. In the toilet. Now.*

''Scuse me – is this seat tekken?'

Belle jumped out of her daydream straight into her worst nightmare. There swaying in front of her, complete with fag behind ear and McEwan's in hand, was an extremely pissed Scotsman. Great tufts of ginger hair sprouted from his head like clumps of carrots, clashing horribly with his alcohol-pickled beetroot of a face.

'Er, no,' Belle practically moaned.

'Then you won't mind if I join yer!' he bellowed, launching himself into the seat opposite her. 'Cheers!'

Belle picked up her magazine and began pretending to read feverishly. Shit. Shit. Shit. Well, this was just great. Any tall, dark stranger who happened to meander through her carriage in search of a seat now would assume she was with this . . . this Russ Abbott-like freak!

'Ar need a piss.'

Oh God!

'Ar said, Ar need a piss.'

Belle peered over the top of her magazine. Russ Abbott-on-acid was leaning over the table towards her, his can balanced just precariously enough for every jolt of the train to shower her mango-and-brie ciabatta with lager.

'Er, the toilets are just back there.' *So why don't you just piss off.* Belle gestured feebly towards the rear of the carriage.

'Right. D'yer know if the bar's open yet?'

It's 8.59 in the morning, you fucking alky. 'I'm not sure, sorry,' Belle squeaked.

'Ken I get yer a drink?'

You must be joking. 'Er, no, thank you.'

With a resounding belch, just loud enough to attract the attention of the entire carriage, he hauled himself unsteadily to his feet. 'Yer fuckin' ginger dyke!' he hollered at Belle before lurching off down the aisle.

Belle was apoplectic with rage. *Ginger?* How dare he! She hadn't just spent the best part of a hundred quid for a Director of Colour Styling to tint her hair copper and gold so that some pissed-up arsehole could call her ginger! Seizing all her belongings, minus the McEwan's-marinated ciabatta, Belle fought her way up the lurching train, not stopping until she found a table occupied by a sweet-looking elderly couple. Taking the window seat opposite, she filled the remaining vacant seat with her bags and coat. With a deep sigh she closed her eyes and let the rattle of the train soothe away her stress. Now where was she?

27

As the private jet touched down at Los Angeles airport, Brad wrapped his perfectly toned arms around Belle. 'Thanks for all your work on my new movie, and hey,' he whispered breathlessly, 'thanks for joining the Mile High Club with me.'

'Don't mention it,' she sighed, her cheeks aglow with a post-coital flush . . .

'Ladies and gentlemen, we will shortly be arriving in Wigan,' announced a monotone drone from the Tannoy system. 'Please ensure you take all of your belongings with you upon leaving the train.'

In a mad scramble, Belle gathered up her possessions and headed for the door. Barring the unsavoury incident at the start, her journey had been extremely pleasant – the miles had flown by.

As her heels clicked their way up the platform, Belle shivered with excitement. So what if she wasn't sweeping through the arrivals lounge in Los Angeles on Brad Pitt's arm? She was still on her way to her first proper public relations assignment. For the first time in her life she would be doing a job she really enjoyed. Belle smiled sympathetically at a sour-faced cleaner wearily sweeping up the flotsam and jetsam of discarded McDonald's cartons and flattened fag butts. Poor thing. But her smile soon faded as she followed the taxi sign out of the station. A grey mist hung in the air, the kind of rain that was too fine to warrant an umbrella, but just damp enough to transform Belle's glossy hundred-pound hairdo into a frenzied frizz. She glanced anxiously at the deserted taxi rank – where the hell were all the cabs? Pulling up the collar on her coat, she thought wistfully of LA sunshine and luxury limousines. If only. People scuttled by clutching half-opened umbrellas, hurrying to escape the blustery spray. Finally a car pulled up, the hissing of its tyres on the wet road an ominous reminder of sausages frying.

'Where to, love?'

'Morrison's Meats, please.' *Oh, if only it could be MGM Studios.*

'Right you are.'

Within minutes they had wound their way out of the heart of Wigan and were speeding along smaller country roads. When Belle had last visited Morrison's in her role as a telecoms account manager it had been a scorching hot August day and the fields were ablaze with colour. But not today. This kind of dank drizzle made even the most picturesque landscapes appear bleak and un-welcoming.

'You up from London, then?' the cabbie asked, catching Belle's eye in the rear-view mirror.

'Yes,' Belle replied somewhat nervously. She knew

only too well that once you got north of Watford admitting to being a Londoner was akin to revealing a penchant for eating small children.

'Thought so. So what are you up here for?'

Belle took a deep breath and concentrated on her accent. The trick was getting the right balance – too posh and you were a stuck-up southerner, too common and you became a cockney twat.

'I'm here for a product launch. Morrison's have got a new sausage coming out.' For the first time Belle felt able to talk about the sausage launch with pride. Something told her that the driver's bulky frame, spilling over the edges of his seat, had to be the proud testimony to many a fry-up.

Sure enough, he seemed suitably impressed. 'Really? He does a tasty bit of sausage, does Morrison. Press, are you?'

'No, er, I'm a public relations consultant.' Belle's mouth curled into a smile as she uttered the magic words.

'What, like that Prince Edward's missus?' The cabdriver sounded even more impressed.

'Sophie?' Belle replied nonchalantly. 'Yes, same kind of thing. I run all Mark Morrison's publicity campaigns. I'm helping oversee the preparations today, and tomorrow I'll be dealing with press enquiries at the launch itself.' Belle leaned back in her seat and smiled. After all, cabbies didn't have a monopoly on bullshit.

* * *

'Chuffin' 'ell – you look like the pig's trotters!' Morrison's huge red face broke into a welcoming grin, like an overripe tomato splitting its skin.

Belle stood in the doorway, momentarily confused. His tone seemed complimentary enough, but being likened to pigs' feet was hardly an improvement on Johnny's dog's-dinner jibe of earlier.

'Come here, chuck, let's get a good look at you,' Morrison called from the far end of the empty function room, while mopping his brow with a spotty handkerchief.

As Belle made her way down the hall she surveyed the décor curiously. It looked like a slightly posher version of a workingmen's club – which was exactly what it was, really. As well as a factory, warehouse, office block and, of course, slaughterhouse, Morrison's Meats also had its very own social club, complete with function hall. Round pub-type tables lined either side of the wooden dance-floor, each one adorned with a large glass ashtray and four beer mats shaped like pork pies. A bar protected by an iron grille took up most of the wall to Belle's left; to her right dark red velvet curtains draped the windows, slivers of light filtering through the gap in the middle where they didn't quite meet. Picture frames covered any available wall space between the windows. Belle did a double-take, but it was as she'd first imagined – each frame proudly displayed the packaging from a meat product. Morrison's faggots,

Morrison's quarter-pounders, Morrison's streaky bacon – the selection was endless. There was also a wide variety of own-brand labels from most of the supermarkets.

Morrison himself was leaning against a small stage at the far end of the room. A dense cloud of cigar smoke hung above his head, and suspended above that was a huge cardboard sign showing a Lemon Zinger being struck by a lightning bolt.

'Very eye-catching,' Belle observed, gesturing to the sign.

'It was a chuffin' nightmare getting that bugger to stay up,' Morrison blustered, grabbing Belle's hand and shaking it enthusiastically. 'It's great to see you again, love. Here, sit yourself down, have yourself a beverage. MAVIS!'

Belle jumped out of her skin as Morrison's voice boomed around the empty hall. Within seconds a door next to the bar burst open and out scuttled Morrison's long-suffering personal assistant, Mavis Penthorpe.

'Get our Belle summat to drink. What would you like, love – still partial to the old vodka?'

Belle nodded. 'Yeah, vodka and tonic would be great.'

'Right, and I'll have another pint, please, Mavis.'

Mavis smiled weakly and retreated to fetch the drinks.

This was the life, Belle mused as she let the tonic fizz over her tongue; quaffing with a managing director in his own private bar, while all around the minions were toiling.

'So,' she said, her head buzzing with thoughts of press briefings and promotional soundbites. 'Where shall we start?'

'Well, love, I'm afraid I'm going to have to leave you on your own for a bit – one of the mincer's has gone on the blink again – but there's plenty for you to be getting on with. Here.'

Belle followed Morrison up on to the stage.

'Now, how good's your cutting out?'

'My cutting out? Okay, I guess.' Actually it was excellent – she had had enough bloody practice during endless cutting-and-pasting sessions with Harry.

'Great. Well, what I need you to do is cut out all these name badges for me.' Morrison pointed to a pile of cardboard sheets, printed with row upon row of name-badge-sized sausages. 'Then, when you've done that, I need you to fill each of these blank spaces with the names on this guest list and then stick a safety pin on the back of each one.'

Belle took a moment to regain her composure. 'Anything else?' she finally whimpered.

'Oh yes – arrange them alphabetically on that there trestle table by the door. It'll make it easier for you in the morning when you're giving them out.'

'When I'm giving them out?' Belle's voice was barely audible.

'Yes. I thought name badges would make it easier

for me and Tony – let us know exactly who we're talking to from the off.'

Belle grimaced. She remembered Tony Bradshaw, the Financial Director, from her telecoms days. The cowboy-boot-clad, chauvinist pig who had refused to have any dealings with her simply because she was a woman.

Completely oblivious to Belle's horrified expression, Morrison continued, 'Then once everyone's arrived I thought you could help Mavis and the girls out behind the bar.'

Belle necked her remaining vodka. 'But what about the press? Won't you need any help with them?' she practically pleaded.

'Not really. Actually, I tell a porky. *The Grocer* are doing some kind of behind-the-scenes feature on the launch. I've got that daft sow Ruth Henshaw interviewing me tomorrow, but the photographer's supposed to be turning up today – they want to get some before-and-after shots or summat. Can you look after him when he gets here – make him a cup of tea or summat?'

It was enough of an effort for Belle simply to nod at Morrison – the only public relations she was to be involved in was making a cup of tea for a photographer from *The Grocer*. THE GROCER!

'All right, then, love, I'll be off to factory. Help yourself to any grub from behind the bar. I'll be back to see how you're getting on at about five.'

Belle watched Morrison disappear from sight.

Johnny had been right. What was the point in wasting all that time and money on her appearance when all she would be doing was cutting out sausages and serving up pints? She should have stayed at home where she belonged with her son. Oh God, poor Harry, cruelly abandoned to his football maniac of a father. Belle fished her mobile out of her bag and frantically dialled home. No reply. Why was there no reply? They were at Casualty. Harry was lying on a trolley in a corridor somewhere, bleeding to death while she was cutting out cardboard sausages in Wigan.

Belle let herself behind the bar and poured herself a stiff drink – she had to find some way of making this nightmare slightly more bearable.

Two hours, five vodkas and two hundred sausages later, Belle collapsed into a heap on the stage. She was exhausted and her eyes stung from focusing so hard. Drinking on an empty stomach hadn't helped matters either. If she just had a little lie-down, closed her eyes for just a moment, she'd be raring to start on the name-writing. She curled up on the floor surrounded by a sea of little sausages. Just five minutes was all it would take . . .

Belle was dreaming that Mark Morrison had fallen into a giant mincing machine and she was turning the handle when suddenly a blinding flash pierced her closed eyelids.

'Wha . . . ?' Belle stumbled to her feet, squinting furiously.

'Sorry – I just couldn't resist. You wouldn't happen to be Belle Farraday, would you?'

As Belle's eyes adjusted to the half-light she could just make out the silhouette of a man standing right below her in front of the stage. Although his face was deadly straight, his cornflower-blue eyes sparkled with pent-up laughter. And what eyes. Belle flushed with an awful mixture of excitement and embarrassment as he slowly came into focus. Although he must have been nearing forty his face was that of a young boy's, with the kind of mouth that was just itching to break into a cheeky grin. His hair was dark grey, flecked with silver, slightly tufty from an outgrowing crop. He was wearing a loose-fitting blue checked shirt over a white T-shirt and faded jeans, and around his neck dangled a huge camera.

'Oh my God, the photographer!' Belle gasped, distraught.

'I'm Luke Ryan,' he said, stretching up a hand in greeting. 'I'm from *The Grocer*. Mr Morrison said you'd be expecting me.' He spoke with a Mancunian lilt – not unlike Liam Gallagher, Belle noted.

'I was. I am. I was just, er, feeling a little faint, that's all.'

'Are you okay?' Luke's eyes filled with concern, only slightly tinged with amusement.

'Oh yeah. It's just that I had to cut out two hundred sausages and my eyes had gone all funny and I thought that maybe if I rested them for a bit, it would, you know . . .' Belle rambled inanely as her mind went into overdrive. It was as if the profile of her ideal lover had got up and walked off the page. The question was, what the hell was he doing working for *The Grocer*?

28

'I'm a freelancer,' Luke explained as he laid a row of completed badges on the trestle table. 'Have you got any more Cs over there?'

Belle shook her head dreamily. He was a freelance photographer; an unfettered spirit roaming the world, with just his camera as companion. It was so *Bridges of Madison County*. 'So who else do you work for, then?' Belle pictured Luke darting about through the Amazonian rainforest on an assignment for *National Geographic*.

Luke ran a hand through his hair and visibly squirmed. 'At the moment mainly the women's weeklies, *That's Life*, *Take a Break* – that kind of thing.'

'Really?' Belle could barely contain her excitement. 'So do you take the photos for all those bizarre true-life stories?'

''Fraid so,' Luke admitted, grinning sheepishly. ' "I slept with my boyfriend's grandad" "I stabbed my boyfriend in the buttocks" – I've covered all the biggies.'

'I remember that one about the buttocks. What was she like? Weren't you nervous?' Belle asked, struggling to play it cool.

'Not until she went and got the knife – and showed me the stale bloodstains still on it.'

'Oh, gross!' Belle shuddered with glee as she handed Luke a badge. 'Sorry, I missed Jenny Clark from *Good Housekeeping*. You must meet some really strange people.'

'Oh yeah, all sorts. I even had a meeting with this PR consultant once and found her fast asleep in a sea of cardboard sausages.'

Belle blushed. She wished he wouldn't keep grinning like that – it was playing havoc with her hormones.

'To be honest, for half of those photo shoots the magazines use models.'

'You're kidding? Why?'

'Well, often the person wants to remain anonymous, or in some cases they just look too . . . how can I put it . . .?'

'Hideously unattractive?' Belle offered.

'Exactly. Do you remember that one about the woman who slept with half the men in her village?'

'Yeah – the *Horny Hussy of the Hamlet*.'

'That's the one. Well, it turned out that in real life she looked like a cross between Olive from *On the Buses* and Ozzy Osbourne. The editors didn't think anyone would believe that she'd lost her virginity, let alone shagged half a village. I ended up getting my mate's wife to pose for the picture wearing a wig.'

'What, you don't have to use proper models?'

'No, not at all. In fact the magazines prefer it.

Apparently the readers identify better with real people.'

'Wow!' Belle was amazed – she couldn't wait to share her new-found insider secrets with Maz.

'Here, let me get a couple of shots of you doing the badges,' said Luke, unscrewing the lens cap on his camera.

'Oh, do you have to?' Belle moaned. She was feeling far too mellow, not to mention half-cut, to think about posing for a photo shoot.

'Well, it's either that or I have to submit that shot of you asleep on the stage.' Luke grinned at her mischievously.

Belle frowned at him across the table. 'Don't you dare. All right, how do you want me?' The words resonated around the empty hall, laden with all the innuendo of a Carry On film. She half expected him to lurch at her shrieking, 'Oooer, missus,' but Luke just stared at her for a moment before looking away embarrassed.

'Just carry on what you're doing,' he said, getting to his feet. 'I want to make it as natural and relaxed as possible. Don't even look at the camera.'

Appearing relaxed when a distraction like Luke was prowling around proved virtually impossible. How was she supposed to concentrate on boring name badges while a lithe body like his sprang upon chairs and crouched on the floor searching for the perfect angle? There was something kinkily voyeuristic about the whole notion of him focusing on her through his lens while she pretended to work.

Belle writhed about on the four-poster, clad in the finest French lingerie, while Luke clicked away, murmuring his appreciation. 'You don't know what you're doing to me,' he moaned. Then, unable to contain himself any longer, he flung his camera aside and leaped on to the bed.

'CHUFFIN' STONE ME!'

Belle and Luke jumped as Morrison loomed in the doorway, a huge artificial sausage under his arm.

'This thing weighs a chuffin' ton. I hope you'll be all right in it tomorrow. Last thing we want is you keeling over on us.'

'What did you say?' Belle asked, staring at the sausage incredulously. Surely those weren't eyeholes cut out of the middle?

'I said I hope you'll be all right in this here outfit tomorrow. We don't want you wilting like a piece of honey-roast on a hot day, now, do we?'

Anna gazed blankly at her reflection in the bathroom mirror. It was funny, really, she thought as she examined her lank hair and sunken eyes. Once upon a time she had been the shy only daughter of a strait-laced couple from Walton on Thames escaping to the finest art college in the country; a whole world of opportunity finally at her feet. Or so she had thought, afloat on her cloud of youthful optimism. And yet here she was three years later, to all intents and purposes a battered wife. Funny how these things crept up on you without you even realising. She'd always thought of battered wives as lifelong victims; she'd never stopped to imagine their former lives. It was a bit like the way you forgot that old people were once young, had sex lives, got pissed. She had been so dismissive, writing them off like that, even condemning them for not getting up and leaving. But she knew better now. Now she knew all about how you could love someone so much you constantly made excuses for them, forgave them. Even when you knew for sure that it was bound to happen again. Even when you suspected they were having an affair and had to turn a blind eye to the mysterious silent phone calls and the nights spent away from home. Funny how the mental abuse, the contempt they rained down on you, only made you more dependent on them and more powerless to leave. So you ended up turning your back upon the people who really did love you – your parents, old friends. Funny.

Somewhere in the distance a telephone was ringing – on and on. Why didn't somebody answer it? The ringing seemed to grow more intense, until Anna finally realised it was her phone. Well, let it ring. They'd probably just hang up on her again anyway. Then she thought of Grace asleep in her bedroom. If she left it much longer the phone would wake her up, and an irritable toddler was the last thing she needed just now. She decided to take the call and then leave the phone off the hook for the rest of the night.

'Hello?'

'Anna, is that you? You sound really faint.'

It was Belle, effervescent as ever. Anna wanted to shout *WRONG NUMBER!* and hang up. She took a deep breath.

'Yes, it's me.'

'Great. Can you talk at the moment? Oh, please say you can. The most amazing thing has happened, is happening, is about to happen. Oh my God, you will not believe it.'

Anna listened numbly, holding the receiver slightly away from her ear. Belle's incessant chattering was making her head ache.

'That's great,' she said unenthusiastically when Belle finally paused for breath.

'And,' Belle continued, 'he's staying in the same hotel as me tonight. Talk about fate or what? I'm meeting him for a drink at eight o'clock. Oh my God, I'd better go and get ready. I don't believe it, Anna – I might finally be about to fulfil my Pursuit, I might finally get some passion in my sad life.'

Something inside Anna suddenly snapped. 'What exactly *is* so sad about your life, Belle?'

'Anna, what's the matter? I thought you'd be pleased for me.'

'Well, actually, at this moment in time I feel more sorry for Johnny and Harry than I feel pleased for you. Now, if you don't mind, I've got things to do.'

Anna slammed down the phone and burst into tears. What had she done? Belle was her only friend.

Why had she lectured her like that? But were they truly friends? The more Anna thought about it the more she realised that Belle would never normally befriend a loser like her – she'd just wanted to make the numbers up for the Football Widows. Why would someone with an exciting career and a big house, someone who looked 'a million dollars' as Tom had put it, want to be friends with a nothing like her?

Anna turned on the TV. 'I'll be there for you,' chirped the Rembrandts. Oh, great, Anna thought cynically. *Friends* had just started.

Belle stared blankly at the bedside phone. What was all that about? What the hell was wrong with Anna? She picked up the receiver and pressed REDIAL only to get the engaged signal. Feeling slightly shell-shocked, she called home.

'Hello,' Johnny barked.

'It's me.'

'Oh, right.'

'Is everything all right? How's Harry?'

'Harry's great. He's asleep now. He was upset you didn't call earlier.'

Belle could hear the familiar commentary of a football match in the background. 'I did try earlier – there was nobody there.'

'Oh, whatever. Anyway, did you want anything specific? I've got Tom and Mike over and we're trying to watch the Arsenal match.'

'Right. I'll go, then.'

'Right. 'Bye.'

Belle flung the phone down. Sod him. Sod Anna. Sod the lot of them. She was going to have fun tonight, and nothing and nobody was going to stop her.

29

'Truth . . .' Luke's eyes glinted across the table at her. 'Or Dare?'

Belle lowered her gaze coyly. Their table groaned with empty bottles and glasses and the congealed remnants of their long-forgotten meal.

'Truth.' As if she would pick dare. They had spent long enough exchanging pleasantries; now she wanted to know all about his darkest secrets and desires.

In the three hours they had been in the bar the conversation had flowed so effortlessly Belle had gleaned plenty of background information on Luke. She knew that he was one of five children, that his elder brother had emigrated to Canada, and his three sisters were all married with kids. His parents had finally given up pleading with him to settle down – 'I think they've decided I must be gay. God knows what me mam's been telling the local priest. No doubt I've been the subject of many a tortured confession,' Luke contemplated wryly – sending a shudder of panic down Belle's spine. It would be just her luck to spend the entire evening attempting to seduce a homosexual.

She knew that his favourite song of all time was 'You Can't Always Get What You Want' by the Stones, and after this revelation she hadn't dared ask him what he thought of Neil Diamond. Belle had learned that Luke ran his hand through his hair when he was embarrassed and that one of his front teeth was slightly chipped. Although he had never done any paparazzi work as such, his scariest photographic assignment had been when a tabloid newspaper hired him to take a few shots of the top-secret location for the *Teletubbies*. He had been chased by a pack of Rottweilers and had his camera smashed by a security guard who looked just like 'Laa-Laa on steroids'. Luke liked going to the cinema on his own in the middle of the day – 'when everyone else is out grafting'. He loved Martin Scorsese films and cheese on toast and hated Marmite with a passion.

'Okay.' Luke leaned so close that Belle could almost taste his tantalisingly musky aftershave. 'What do you feel is missing from your life?'

'How do you know there *is* something missing?'

'I don't know for sure,' Luke said, rearranging a row of empty beer bottles. 'I'm just working on a hunch.'

'Oh, I don't know. A proper career in public relations that doesn't involve dressing up as a sausage?'

Luke frowned. 'You know the penalties for lying in Truth or Dare are tougher than a ten-year stretch in the Bangkok Hilton?'

Belle sighed. Talk about cutting to the chase. Couldn't he at least have given her a naff warm-up question like who would she rather shag, Grant Bovey or H from Steps? Still, if that was the way he wanted to play it. 'Oh, all right, if you must know, passion and excitement are what's missing from my life right now,' she said, staring at him defiantly.

'That's better,' Luke replied, taking a swig from his beer.

'Right, your turn. Truth or Dare?'

'Truth.'

'What's missing from your life?'

'Oh no, you can't ask the same question – everyone knows that,' Luke retorted, smiling smugly.

Okay, smartarse, Belle thought, let's see you squirm. 'Have you ever taken any sexy photos of a girlfriend?'

'Yes.'

'Oh.' Belle couldn't believe she was the one blushing furiously, not him.

'Truth or Dare?' Luke asked, cool as a cucumber.

'Truth.'

'What do you do to try and fill this void in your life?'

'What do you mean?' Belle asked, playing for time.

'I mean, how do you try and create some passion or excitement for yourself?'

Belle abandoned all hope of her cheeks returning to their normal hue. If she hadn't consumed the best part of a bottle of vodka there was no way she would even contemplate answering this one, but she had, so she did. 'I play a game called Romantic Liaisons.' God, even Ginny didn't know about Romantic Liaisons.

'Romantic Liaisons? What's that?' Luke asked with yet another of his heart-stopping smiles.

'Uh-uh.' Belle shook her head sternly. 'Only one question at a time. Truth or Dare?'

'Truth.'

Belle simply had to find out before she went any farther. 'Do you like football?'

Luke burst out laughing. 'Well, that was a bit close to the mark. Of course I do, I'm from Manchester, but I support the local team – City.'

Belle's heart didn't just sink, it plummeted right to the very soles of her feet.

'But I like other things too,' he added, his expression suddenly intent.

'Like what?'

'Uh-uh. Only one question at a time, remember. So what exactly do these Romantic Liaisons involve?'

'Hold on. How do you know I didn't fancy a dare this time?'

'Well, do you?'

'No.'

'Well, then.'

Belle shifted uncomfortably in her seat. Part of her felt excruciated but another part of her, a hidden part that Luke seemed to have uncovered with remarkable ease, felt reckless and abandoned. She allowed this part of her to answer the question. 'They're basically sexual fantasies that I play out in my head ... they help me to relax,' the more restrained part of her added as an afterthought. Luke was looking at her even more intently now. 'So what else do you like apart from football?' she asked quickly, eager to shift the spotlight and praying he didn't say *Star Trek*.

'Sex.'

Oh God. Belle felt as if she were going to hyperventilate. Everything about him was turning her on. His soft, suggestive voice, that ruffled hair, the small silver hoop glinting in the top of his right ear, his long fingers casually peeling the label from his bottle of beer. God, what she would give to feel those fingers unpeeling her clothes. Right now.

'So would you have a Romantic Liaison involving me?'

'I already have.' The answer popped out before she had time to censor it with an embarrassed giggle and a mumbled denial.

His hands were still now, resting on the table, just inches from hers.

'Would you like to take a sexy photo of me?'

'I already have.'

Belle didn't know which of them got to their feet first; it felt as if some unbridled force of nature swept into the Wigan Travel Lodge, whisking them up into the air, carrying them through the bar and past the deserted lobby. (Of course, it could just have been a drunken haze.) Either way they suddenly found themselves in the corner by the lift. As Luke pressed up against her, she could feel his whole body shivering. Belle gasped as he traced the contour of her cheekbone with the tips of his fingers, bringing them to rest on her mouth. Then he moved his hand behind her head, burying his fingers in her hair as he moved her face closer to his. For a second they stood there, staring into each other's eyes, too consumed with lust to feel any kind of awkwardness or embarrassment. Luke bent his head down to hers and gently kissed the corner of her mouth. Unable to restrain herself any longer, Belle reached up to his face and pulled it towards her.

The kiss seemed to last for hours. At first it felt strange. He tasted different to Johnny; his tongue was thinner, gentler, a better fit. A perfect fit. Belle felt like Cinderella trying on the slipper. Everything felt so right, so preordained. Finally Luke pulled away, pressing the CALL button on the wall next to Belle.

'I've been wanting to do that all evening,' he whispered, holding her close.

With a shrill 'Ding!' the doors opened and they practically fell into the empty lift.

'Truth or Dare?' Luke whispered, as the doors closed behind them.

'Truth.'

'Would you ever cheat on your husband?' he asked, brushing a curl away from her face.

At this moment in time I feel more sorry for Johnny and Harry than I do for you.

For some awful, unexplained, completely inconvenient reason, Anna's words suddenly seemed to boom like a Tannoy around the lift. Belle froze, just long enough for a stab of sobriety to recapture control of part of her mind. What the hell was she doing in a lift in Wigan, snogging some virtual stranger? *No! No!* another voice shrieked. *This isn't just some naff knee-trembler, this is destiny, the fulfilment of your dream.* But it was too late. Belle thought of Harry curled up in bed with his bum in the air and Johnny, the miserable shit, sprawled across their own bed in those stupid Wolves shorts, muttering, 'Referee, offside,' in his sleep. Her body was crying out for Luke but her mind was exerting its power of attorney.

'Actually, I think I'll take a dare,' she muttered feebly, extricating herself from Luke's arms.

While Belle was doing her best to curb her passionate desires, two hundred miles south Ginny was preparing to unleash her own upon an unsuspecting Mike. Lighting the last bluebell-scented tea light – she had arranged four on each of their bedside cabinets and a neat row of eight lined the shelf at the head of the bed – Ginny relaxed back on the crisp blue bed linen. *Tonight I am going to have an orgasm during sex,* she told herself, while practising the breathing technique she had learned at yoga. *I am going to let go, my* body will be a leaf adrift on a flowing river, I will let nature take control. Ginny's eyes shot open. It was no good. This hippie bullshit was just not doing it for her. She carefully removed her vibrator from underneath the pile of neatly folded knickers in her underwear drawer and quickly and efficiently brought herself to the brink of climax. Just as she returned the vibrator to its hiding place she heard Mike arriving home from Johnny's. She listened as he carefully shut and locked the front door and tiptoed across the hall. Ginny arranged herself in what she deemed to be a suitably seductive pose across the bed and waited. And waited. Where the hell was he? Why hadn't he come straight up to bed? She looked at the alarm clock – 12:10 a.m., the display glowed. That explained it. Ginny had a rule that on the rare occasions when Mike came home later than midnight he had to sleep on the sofa so as not to wake her. Well, she'd just have to go and get him, then.

Ginny slunk downstairs. What was she going to say to him? This was all uncharted territory for her. She wasn't sure whether she had ever actually initiated sex before. What did you say in this kind of situation? What would Belle say? *Come and take me now, baby? Give it to me long and hard?* Ginny grimaced. Maybe she ought to just stand there coyly in her satin negligee and let him work it out for himself. She opened the door to the living room and turned on the light. Like a rabbit trapped in headlights, a startled Mike sat bolt upright on the sofa.

'Oh God, Ginny, I'm so sorry. I tried to be really quiet. I would have been home before twelve, it was just that Tom wouldn't stop drinking and I'd said I'd give him a lift home, and I know I should have rung, but then I thought that maybe you'd had an early night and wouldn't appreciate being woken up by the phone and . . . oh God, I'm really sorry . . .' Mike's head drooped like that of a disobedient child waiting to be disciplined.

Ginny remained frozen in the doorway. What the hell was wrong with him? He seemed so petrified he hadn't even noticed her blatant seduction attempt. She coughed loudly to attract his attention.

Mike clutched his head in his hands. 'I know, I know, I've let you down again, but Ginny, I promise you, I'm nothing like your dad. I just went round to Johnny's to watch the football. I should have come straight back after the game. I'm sorry.'

Ginny looked at the quivering wreck on the sofa and suddenly felt a curious mixture of guilt and affection. Was this all her doing? Had she reduced Mike to this – this wretched specimen before her? Did he really love her so much that he was willing to live like this, put up with this? She knelt down on the floor in front of the sofa and took Mike's face in her hands.

'Come upstairs, you silly old sod,' she said, her voice unfamiliarly gentle. 'I've been waiting for you.' *And stop gaping at me like some kind of demented goldfish*, she couldn't help thinking.

30

Belle pushed the glistening sausage around her plate. Bloody Morrison's, she thought, putting her knife and fork back down. Her stomach felt as if it were hosting a production of *Riverdance*. She didn't know what she was more apprehensive about, the Lemon Zinger launch or having to face Luke. There was no sign of him in the crowd of suited business people swarming around the restaurant, complimentary newspapers tucked under arms as they piled their plates high from the breakfast buffet.

Why oh why had she turned Luke down? All those months of waiting and longing for some passion and excitement, and what did she do when the opportunity finally arose? She opted to play knock-down-Ginger on the entire third floor of the Wigan Travel Lodge. Luke's dare hadn't been too bad, all things considered. She could hardly have blamed him if he had got his own back by making her walk through reception in the nude, or something equally humiliating. Getting her to wake up the entire third floor had been letting her off lightly, really. When Belle had finally gone to bed – alone – she had hoped that the cold light of day would make her see the wisdom of her decision and feel relieved that she'd remained loyal to Johnny. But all she felt was stupid and depressed. When she returned home nothing would have changed, she would still feel as lonely and unfulfilled as before, only now she would have the added torment of *if only* hanging over her. And then of course there were the other Football Widows. What kind of an example was she, encouraging them to pursue their passions when she was too gutless to do the same?

Belle returned her attention to the cooked breakfast before her. She supposed she really ought to eat something – it was going to be an extremely long day. As she speared the sausage with her fork and prepared to take a bite a voice whispered in her ear:

'Just think, in a couple of hours' time that'll be you.'

Just the sound of Luke's voice made Belle's heart skip a beat, and as he sat down opposite her, all freshly shaved and newly showered, she wondered whether it might actually be possible to explode with frustration. Images of Luke lathering shampoo through his hair as soapy water trickled down his naked torso flickered through her head like a poor-quality porno film. Stop it, stop it, stop it, she thought, slicing her sausage savagely.

'So how are you feeling this morning?' Luke asked chirpily, grabbing a piece of cold toast from the rack.

'Completely shit, if you must know,' Belle replied,

pouring herself coffee from the stainless-steel pot. 'Coffee?'

'Please. Hung over?'

'Hung over, nervous, dreading today – disappointed.'

'Disappointed?' Luke asked casually, reaching for the butter dish.

'Yeah.' Belle took a sip of her coffee and nearly retched; it was worse than Anna's.

'So what are you disappointed about?' Luke asked, trying in vain to spread a lump of rock-solid butter on his cold triangle of toast.

'Missed opportunities,' Belle replied gloomily. 'Letting my head rule my heart.' Without warning a tear rolled down her face and landed with a plop in the yolk of her fried egg. Covering her face with her hands, she wished she had never come to this godforsaken place. To think she had actually been looking forward to this unmitigated disaster.

'Come on,' Luke said, taking both her hands in his, 'come with me.'

Sunlight streamed through the half-opened curtains in Luke's room, falling like a spotlight upon the bed, illuminating the floral bedclothes strewn with rolls of film and camera cases. Luke cleared a space on the corner for Belle to sit down. The moment he put his arm around her she was off.

'I'm such a disaster,' she sobbed. 'My marriage is a farce, my husband has stronger feelings towards football than he does towards me, my career consists of dressing up as a sausage – and I'm a crap mother.'

'Now I'm sure that's not true,' Luke said gently, leaning over to get her a tissue from the bedside cabinet.

'Oh, it is. All my son will eat is chicken nuggets – he hates vegetables and will probably develop scurvy and it will all be my fault.'

'Well, how do you work that one out?'

'I never bothered to purée vegetables for him when he was a baby. I bought him jars of babyfood instead and now he has really bland food tastes.'

Luke nodded gravely. 'Oh, I see.' He removed his mobile phone from his shirt pocket and started dialling.

'What are you doing? Who are you calling?'

'The NSPCC, who do you think? Jesus, you can't expect me to keep that kind of information from them.'

Belle smiled weakly.

'Here.' Luke handed her a tissue and slung his phone on to the bed. 'Now, I'm the last person qualified to give advice on marriage, and to be totally honest I'm not really interested in your ungrateful husband – or your malnourished son.'

'I'm sorry, I shouldn't have expected you . . . I'll get out of your way.' Belle got to her feet. What had got into her, acting like a complete emotional wreck in front of Luke? Talk about a guaranteed turn-off. She may just as well have confessed to being a fully certified bunny-boiler.

'No, you don't understand.' Luke caught hold of her hand and pulled her back down next to him. 'I'm not interested in your domestic problems because I'm only interested in you. To me you're not a wife or a mam, you're Belle, Sausage Queen extraordinaire. If I had my way I'd keep you in this room and do things to you that you've never had done to you before – not even in your wildest Romantic Liaison!' Belle looked at him and laughed. 'But you obviously need time to get your head together and I don't want you doing anything with me that you might live to regret. Although I somehow doubt that would be possible,' he added with a grin. 'Now, are you going to go and get your stuff so we can get our arses over to Morrison's? I'm dying to get a few shots of you in that designer sausage.'

As they held each other tightly for a moment Belle closed her eyes, and slowly but surely a feeling of warmth and calm began to creep up through her body, finally filtering into her mind. Really, when she stopped to think about it there was something gloriously tragic about this whole scenario. Finally meeting the man of her dreams when she was already sworn to another. At least when she got back home she could entertain herself with possibilities rather than torture herself with guilt.

'Right, lads and lasses, if I could have your attention for a moment.' The whole function hall flinched as Morrison's microphone emitted a shriek of feedback.

'Whoops, sorry about that. Now, I'd like to thank you all for coming to the launch of our new Lemon Zinger. That reminds me, what time is it when there's a Morrison's Lemon zinger on top of Wigan clock tower? Summat to eight. Summat to ate, geddit?'

From inside her sausage behind the bar, Belle groaned. How much longer was this torturous event going to go on for? Even the man from the *Butcher's News* looked bored, slumped over a table in the corner, clutching his pint and chain-smoking furiously. As Morrison waffled on about pork quality and fat content, Belle gazed through her eyeholes at Luke flitting about the hall taking pictures.

'Fill her up, Belle,' a voice barked. Belle looked up to see Morrison's Financial Director, Tony Bradshaw, waving an empty pint glass at her, his wrist adorned with a gargantuan gold bracelet.

Belle grudgingly took the glass and began pulling a pint of bitter. It had to be his sixth of the morning, the drunken old sot. Suddenly the theme from *Goldfinger* began emanating from Bradshaw's jacket pocket.

Bradshaw pulled out his mobile phone and flipped it open with a flourish. 'Hello, Bradshaw speaking,' he muttered. 'YOU WHAT?' he suddenly roared, smashing his fist down on the bar.

Murmurs of vague interest rippled through the room as one by one the guests turned to face the bar. Even Morrison stopped talking. 'HOW? HOW

MANY?' Bradshaw continued, beckoning at Morrison furiously.

'Er, sorry about this, everybody,' Morrison stammered. 'If you'll just excuse me for a moment. Help yourselves to the free snacks, I'll be back in two shakes of a pig's scrotum.' Morrison hastily replaced his microphone on its stand and made his way over to the bar. 'What the chuffin' hell's the matter?' he puffed.

'That was Terry Jones – the pen's come loose in the slaughterhouse again and a dozen pigs are running amok in the carpark,' Bradshaw whispered just loud enough for Belle to hear. 'I'll get down there and help the lads round them up. Don't worry, I'll run the buggers over if I have to, but for God's sake don't let anyone out of here until I get back.'

Beads of sweat erupted on Morrison's face like dewdrops on a freshly picked red pepper. 'How am I supposed to chuffin' well keep 'em here? I've nearly finished speech.'

'I don't know, tell them some more flaming jokes or summat.'

Morrison hurriedly made his way back to the stage. 'All right, ladies and gents, now where was I? Oh yes, a man walks into a pub with a Morrison's pasty under his arm . . .'

At last, Belle thought, a chance to laugh at somebody else's misfortune. She only wished she could witness Bradshaw in his flashy suit and heavy gold jewellery chasing a dozen pigs around the carpark.

And then, in a bolt of inspiration, it hit her. As Martine McCutcheon once said, this was her moment, this was her perfect moment. Now where the hell was Luke?

31

'I'm home!' Belle stepped into the hall and kicked off her shoes. Her feet were killing her and her whole body was crying out for a long hot soak in the bath.

'Mum! Mum!' A flurry of footsteps heralded Harry's arrival at the top of the stairs clad in a miniature Wolves kit and a pair of red wellies. 'Mum, where have you been?'

Belle took the stairs two at a time to wrap him in a hug. 'Harry, you're freezing. Why aren't you wearing a jumper and trousers?'

'Dad got me dressed. We went to McDonald's and I had two ice creams.'

'Where is Dad?'

'Playing on the 'puter while Harry-Billy paints my bedroom.'

'What?'

'Come and see, come and see. I borrowed the little paints from your room, what you paint your toes with.'

Harry's room reeked of nail varnish. What he had actually painted wasn't quite so bad; at least he had concentrated his efforts on one square foot of wall, easily small enough to be hidden by a poster. It was the cluster of open bottles abandoned on their sides spilling little pools of colour on to the carpet which caused Belle to shriek like a banshee.

'Johnnyyyyyyyyyy!'

And then everything she had vowed she wouldn't let happen happened. On the train journey home, in between scribbling furiously and phoning Luke with various instructions, Belle had decided she would try her hardest to get on with Johnny upon her return. She was far too excited to waste any more time on animosity. She had prepared herself for Harry to be dressed in his Wolves kit – after all, it was the only time he would get to wear the bloody thing. She was even prepared for a bit of a mess, but this – this was taking the piss.

'I haven't got time for this now, Belle, I'm going to be late for training,' Johnny replied, actually having the nerve to sound like the aggrieved party as he flung a jock-strap and towel into his sports bag.

'*You* haven't got time – what about me? I've been working all day long and I've still got loads to do tonight.'

'Well, I've been cooped up in this house all day long looking after Harry. I need to get out.' Johnny marched into the bathroom to get his deodorant. 'Now, don't start the minute you get in the bloody door. Here, try this,' he said, handing her a bottle of nail-varnish remover.

Belle stood on the landing completely speechless as she watched Johnny leave. Of all the selfish, lazy, ignorant . . . and worse was to come. When she repaired to the kitchen to make herself a stiff drink, she found the sink and draining board completely covered in mud.

'What the hell? Harry, where did all this mud come from?'

'Dad was cleaning his football boots. Can I have some sweets?'

'No, you cannot, it's time for bed.'

Harry broke into a wail. 'But Dad let me have loads of sweets.'

'Oh, I bet he did. Well, Dad isn't here now.'

'I want my dad,' Harry wailed. 'Go back to work, Mum, I don't need you any more.'

Belle glared down at Harry. You fickle little bastard, she thought, before remembering that he was only three years old and was probably extremely aggrieved at having been deserted by his mother so unexpectedly.

By the time Belle had disinfected the sink, unpacked her bags, smeared nail varnish into Harry's carpet and bought her way back into his affection by reading him four bedtime stories and feeding him a packet of chocolate buttons, it was practically nine o'clock. She felt exhausted and more than a little deflated, but she knew she couldn't give up now. Putting 'Love On The Rocks' on the stereo (on repeat) and closing down Football Manager on the computer, she went into her word processor and began typing furiously. By ten o'clock she had completed her press release and was ready to check her e-mails. To her relief her inbox contained one new message from ryanpics@aol.com. Belle clicked on OPEN and began to read.

Belle,
They've turned out blinding, especially the one of the car. I've sent you the best four. Let me know how you get on.
Luke
PS: Truth or Dare?

One by one Belle clicked open the attached pictures. They were better than she could ever have imagined. As Neil Diamond embarked upon 'Love On The Rocks' for the twenty-second time, Belle clicked on REPLY and with a wistful little smile typed, 'Truth!'

32

'I don't fucking believe it!' Maz barged past Belle into the living room brandishing a copy of the *Sun*. 'You're famous – or at least your sausage is! Oh – all right.' Maz spotted Ginny sitting on the sofa and nodded warily.

'Afternoon,' Ginny replied curtly. Then she saw what Maz was wearing and couldn't prevent her mouth from twisting into a sly little grin. 'Tell me, Maz – do you have any knickers on under your, er, kilt?'

Maz stood there defiant in her lime-green tartan, complete with electric-blue sporran. 'God, no – never wear the things. I like to keep a well-ventilated vag!'

Ginny felt sick to the very odour-controlled core of her pantyliner. What the hell was wrong with Maz? Were there no depths to which she would not sink?

Sensing she had her adversary on the ropes, Maz deliberately plonked herself down in the armchair opposite with her legs ever so slightly apart. Not enough to reveal her carefully co-ordinated Black Watch high-waisters, but just enough to make the uptight cow squirm all afternoon.

'So come on!' Maz shrieked. 'Tell us about the

launch. How did you pull it off?' She glanced at her newspaper and guffawed.

'Er, could I have a look?' Ginny asked nervously, trying desperately not to look anywhere in the vicinity of Maz's legs.

Belle glowed with pride as Ginny pored over the paper. Never in her wildest dreams had she imagined that she would get the Lemon Zinger on to page five of the *Sun*, not to mention page eleven of the *Independent*, but her frantically prepared press release on Thursday night had paid off.

As soon as she'd woken up that morning, Belle had raced to the corner shop – not even bothering with her obligatory coat of mascara – to purchase a copy of every daily newspaper on sale. Then, heart pounding, she had returned home to study each one from cover to cover, searching for any mention of the words 'sausage', 'Morrison' or 'Lemon Zinger'. When she saw the piece in the *Sun* her screams had brought Johnny flying out of bed, expecting to find the house ransacked. When Belle had shown him the article she had been hurt and confused by his reaction. She may as well have asked him to read his horoscope, such was his lack of interest; he gave it only the most cursory of glances before turning straight to the sports section. She hadn't even bothered showing him the piece in the *Independent*, and for one awful moment it seemed as if Johnny's black mood would cast a cloud over Belle's PR coup. But then Morrison had rung.

'It's chuffin' marvellous publicity!' he boomed. 'I've

had North West News on phone asking me to be interviewed for their "And Finally" section. I don't know how you pulled it off, love, but you can expect a hefty bonus for this – just don't tell our Tony!'

Then Belle had received an e-mail from Luke saying, 'Not bad for a walking, talking sausage!' and suddenly her feelings of euphoria came flooding back. Johnny may not have been overly impressed but Belle was proud of her achievement – a write-up plus picture in two out of nine nationals was not bad going for her first-ever product launch, and at last she had some cuttings to file.

Although she must have read it several hundred times already, Belle couldn't help glancing over Ginny's shoulder. 'Lay Off My Sausage Rolls!' the headline blazed.

It was a case of 'Porky's Revenge' at the recent launch of the brand-new Lemon Zinger sausage. While guests enjoyed a free nosh-up courtesy of Morrison's Meats – makers of some of Britain's tastiest bangers – all hell was breaking loose outside. In a 'ham-fisted' escape bid a dozen pigs ended up running riot in the staff carpark. Financial Director Tony Bradshaw was 'pig sick' when one cheeky porker left his calling card right by his brand-new Roller!

Accompanying the piece was a photo of Tony Bradshaw beside his Rolls-Royce, glowering with rage as he tried to extricate his foot from a steaming mound of pig shit. As Belle read the tiny print alongside the photo, 'Picture: Luke Ryan', she felt a tingle of pride and excitement run up her spine.

'God – talk about different reporting styles,' Ginny remarked sniffily. 'I don't suppose you will have seen today's *Independent*,' she said, passing a copy to Maz. 'I take it you're familiar with *Animal Farm?*'

'Oh yeah, Darren brought a copy back from a stag weekend in Amsterdam once. I couldn't believe what they did to that poor gerbil.' Maz grappled with the broadsheet, privately wondering how the hell people managed to read the things; it was the size of a bloody tablecloth.

Sausage Launch Takes on an Orwellian Twist
There was an air of *Animal Farm* at a Wigan sausage launch this week. Morrison's Meats, one of the largest meat manufacturers in the UK, were proudly unveiling their latest product, the Lemon Zinger, when an unexpected rebellion from a dozen pigs, led no doubt by Napoleon, caused havoc in the carpark outside. Financial Director Tony Bradshaw, pictured right, declined to comment when asked if he agreed with the maxim 'four legs good, two legs better'!

Well, what the fuck was that all about? Maz thought, perplexed, before passing the paper back to Ginny. Then it dawned on her that something, or rather someone, was missing. 'Where's Anna got to – she's not still poorly, is she?'

Belle's face fell. 'I'm not exactly sure. I haven't been able to get hold of her since I got back. To be honest, I think she's avoiding me.'

'What? Why?' Ginny enquired, as she expertly turned the *Independent* back to the front page and neatly folded it in two.

Belle took a deep breath and launched into her tale about Luke and how she'd thought he'd be a dork, working for the *Grocer* and all, but in actual fact he'd turned out to be an uninhibited free spirit; a freelance photographer who also happened to work for some of the top women's glossies. She also told them of the animal-like attraction between them; the 'frisson' that had been present from the moment they met and how, when she'd phoned Anna to share her good news, she was greeted with a lecture on the sanctity of marriage. Or words to that effect.

'I always had her down as a bit strait-laced,' Ginny observed, edging up the sofa away from Maz. Why did she have to keep crossing and uncrossing her legs like some Highland version of Sharon Stone?

'No – there's something wrong. I know Anna's quiet, but she's not a prude and she's definitely not the type to be judgmental.' Even though there was nobody else in the house, Belle lowered her voice enigmatically. 'I think she may be having problems at home.'

'What, with her mega-hunk?' Ginny asked wryly.

'He's a bit of all right, isn't he? I tell you what, I

wouldn't have any problems at home if I had his face to sit on!' Maz shrieked, flailing her legs about wildly.

'Oh, for God's sake! Is it really necessary for you to refer to your . . . your vagina at every available opportunity?' Ginny exploded.

'All right, all right, don't get your knickers in a twist,' Maz chortled.

'Anyway,' Belle interrupted, annoyed that this ridiculous feud between Ginny and Maz was diluting the impact of her big news, 'after I spoke to her I kept trying to think of some reason for her acting like that and then I remembered Bonfire Night.'

'Bonfire Night? But Anna wasn't even there,' Ginny said, bemused.

'Yes, but Tom was, and something strange happened in the clubhouse. I didn't think much of it at the time, but with hindsight . . .'

'What? What was it?' Ginny and Maz asked in unison.

Belle breathed a sigh of relief at finally having united them in rapt curiosity. 'Well, I don't know if you remember seeing that old slapper there. You know, old Milk-bottle Legs?'

'Chelsea?' said Maz. 'Yeah, I remember, dressed like a dog's dinner as usual.'

Ginny made a strange spluttering sort of noise.

'Yeah, well, do you remember her going back into the bar just before the fireworks started?'

The others nodded.

'Shortly after that I had to take Harry to the toilet and just as I got to the ladies' I saw Tom coming out.'

'What, out of the ladies'?' Maz asked, breaking into a grin.

'Yeah – he said someone had been sick all over the gents', but he was acting a bit jumpy.'

'Yes, but wouldn't you if you'd just been caught coming out of the gents'?' Ginny reflected.

'Maybe, and like I said I didn't think anything of it at the time. It was only when I got back outside and Harry told me that a lady had been playing hide-and-seek in the toilets that I started getting a bit suspicious.'

'Didn't you go into the toilets with him?' Maz asked.

'No, that's what I mean, it was like Tom didn't want me to go in there – he kept me chatting outside and then he volunteered to go and get Harry, said he needed to get a tissue or something.'

'Oh dear,' Maz said, looking concerned. 'You don't think Tom's taking advantage of Chelsea's blowjob-for-the-boys bonus scheme, do you?'

'I don't know, but it would explain Anna's behaviour if she does suspect something's going on.'

The three Football Widows sat in silence for a moment.

'No – I just can't see it,' said Maz, shaking her head. 'Why would someone like Tom bother with a tart like her? Especially with a sweetheart like Anna waiting at home. It doesn't make sense.'

'Yeah, I know,' Belle said, nodding in agreement. 'And he seems like a really nice bloke. He was a right laugh the night we went out for a curry. I'm probably just jumping to the wrong conclusion.'

'You don't think it's just Anna, do you?' Ginny mused. 'I mean, doesn't she strike you as being a little, I don't know, unbalanced? What about that time she just burst into tears for no reason? And let's face it, Harry has got a rather overactive imagination at the moment, what with his imaginary friend and everything.'

Belle nodded. Ginny was probably right – maybe Anna was a little unbalanced; she was certainly very highly strung.

'So come on, then, spill the beans,' said Maz, breaking the silence. 'Did you shag this photographer geezer or not?'

'Well, I, er . . . no.'

'Oh.'

The disappointment in the room was palpable.

'Let's just say I'm currently enjoying the best damned foreplay I've ever had in my life!'

33

As soon as Anna saw the Christmas card lying on the doormat she knew it was from Belle. Although it had landed face down there was something about the thick creamy envelope, sealed with a shiny holly leaf and sparkling with glitter, which bore all the hall-marks of a Belle production. So she hadn't given up on her, after all. Anna felt a confusing mixture of fondness and regret.

She had successfully managed to avoid the Football Widows for nearly a month now. Whenever there had been a knock on the door she had sprung into action – calling upon her vast repertoire of Jehovah's Witness avoidance techniques, she would cower in the corner and put both the television and Grace on mute (Anna had taken to stocking a supply of lollipops in the living room especially). Although she daren't go anywhere near the vicinity of the window, she always knew when the caller had been Belle – the scent of Chanel would linger on the balcony for hours. Avoiding the phone calls had been a lot easier – she had simply pulled the plug from its socket in the wall. Then every few hours she would plug it back in to dial 1471. It was bizarre, really – despite the lengths she was going to to avoid

Belle, like a sulky teenager giving her boyfriend the cold shoulder, Anna always felt a small pang of relief when the recorded voice informed her that her number had called.

It had been over a week since Belle's last attempted phone call and Anna had become resigned to the fact that she may have finally given up. After all, even Jehovah's Witnesses go away if you ignore them for long enough. Although part of her was terrified by this prospect, another part of her was relieved. It was enough of an effort keeping things on an even keel with Tom right now, let alone trying to explain herself to Belle. Home life appeared to have returned to an uneasy calm, but fear and unease continued to crackle away in the background, like interference on a radio. Although Anna had been allowed back into their bed, it was hardly comforting lying there alone night after night wondering where Tom was and who he was with. He had taken to disappearing for days on end, returning unannounced for a shower and change of clothes. He offered no explanation for these absences, and Anna was far too scared to ask for one. However, the minute her head hit the pillow her imagination would go into overdrive. She pictured Tom in a bar somewhere, flashing that grin, as he regaled his travel stories to a bevy of other women. Women with proper jobs and fun-loving personalities, women who looked like 'a million fucking dollars', as Tom might say. One particularly bad night, just after the Wigan incident, it had even crossed Anna's mind that Tom might be with Belle. In the throes of hysterical exhaustion it had all made perfect sense. Tom was obviously attracted to her and Belle was dying for an affair – it all seemed so horribly inevitable. But in the cold light of the following day Anna felt nothing but guilt and shame for even entertaining such paranoid thoughts.

She turned the envelope over and examined the gold script swirling its way across the front. She missed Belle so much – the drama, the gossip, even the Neil Diamond. Hands trembling slightly, she pulled the card from the envelope and began to read:

Dearest Anna,

I hope you are okay. I keep trying to get in touch but you never seem to be home. We are all really missing you. As you probably know, the 'men' are all going to the Arsenal match on Boxing Day so we are planning a get-together around here. It would be great if you and Grace could come. (Harry has been pining for her.)

Anyway, if I don't speak to you before, have a wonderful Christmas and all the best for the new millennium!!

Lots of love,
Your friend
Belle xxx
PS: I didn't go through with it, you know.

Anna put the card down and sighed. She really didn't deserve a friend like Belle. She had contributed nothing to the Football Widows, lying and making excuses about her drawing, never taking part in an act of Widow's Revenge when even Ginny had managed to tie Mike's bootlaces together, and not helping with the 'funeral-to-football pyre'. Then, to cap it all, when Belle had phoned her from Wigan for a good-natured chat, she had given her a lecture on her morals. Anna cringed. What must they all think of her? How could she possibly face them again?

'Any post for me?' Johnny asked, cramming a whole slice of toast in his mouth and showering the front of his suit in crumbs.

'No, just one for me,' Belle replied as she walked back into the kitchen, studying the unfamiliar hand-writing on the envelope. It was obviously a Christmas card, but who from?

'So anyway, I'll be going to the Arsenal match on Boxing Day with the rest of the lads and, er, I've been meaning to tell you something, but it keeps slipping my mind.' Johnny paused to devour another slice of toast.

'Yes?' said Belle, ripping open the envelope only to hastily stuff it into the pocket of her dressing gown.

'Hoosh it fom?' Johnny enquired, showering more toast crumbs down his front.

'What?' Belle hastily dropped to her knees to rummage about in the saucepan cupboard, her face aflame.

'Who's it from? The card?'

'Oh – Morrison's,' Belle replied from the depths of the cupboard.

'He hasn't sent you another bonus, has he? I don't think I could stomach another sausage for at least a year!'

'Ha bloody ha!' Belle retorted. Her 'bonus' of fifty pounds' worth of Morrison vouchers was still a sore point. Suitably recovered from her furtive flush, she got to her feet. 'So what was it you've been meaning to tell me?'

'Oh yeah.' Johnny began edging sheepishly towards the door. 'Well, er, Rayners Park have fixed up a friendly against Chalfont St Giles on New Year's Day.'

'Oh, okay.'

'It's just that I won't be able to go O.T.T. on New Year's Eve now – we'll probably have to do something local.' Johnny twitched nervously by the door like a horse about to bolt.

'Yeah, whatever.'

'But I thought you had your heart set on going up to London to see Bob Geldof set the Thames on fire,' Johnny ventured, with a nervous giggle.

'Oh, I'm not all that bothered, to be honest,' Belle said breezily as she returned the margarine to the fridge.

'Seriously?' Johnny's face lit up like a Christmas tree.

'That's brilliant. Thanks, thanks a lot. I do love you, you know,' he murmured in her ear as he smothered her in a crumb-coated bear hug.

Belle freed herself and brushed her dressing gown clean. 'Don't mention it,' she said, smiling sweetly. 'Shit, look at the time. You're going to be late for work.'

'Oh yeah.' Johnny studied her face closely for the faintest trace of a strop. After all, Belle was world champion at the smile through gnashing teeth, but she certainly seemed happy enough as she danced about wiping toast crumbs from the counter. Ecstatic, in fact. ' 'Bye, then,' he offered, cautiously.

'Yeah, 'bye, have a nice day.'

As soon as she heard the front door shut behind him, Belle retrieved the envelope from her pocket and tore out the card. The picture on the front showed her fast asleep on the stage at Morrison's underneath the Lemon Zinger banner and surrounded by a sea of cardboard sausages. The festive-style greeting at the top of the card read: 'Don't Forget the Sausagemeat this Christmas!' Inside Luke had simply printed: 'Truth – have you woken up yet?'

Ginny looked at the glossy card in her hands and fought the urge to rip it into shreds. It was all so insincere and naff. A photo of those bloody twin towers with a picture of Santa in his sleigh superimposed over the top. If that wasn't bad enough, inside there was the printed 'personal' greeting from the board of directors at Wembley, wishing her health and prosperity for the new millennium. Health and prosperity? What did they care about her health and prosperity? They hadn't given a shit about it when they'd been deciding to sell up, had they? In previous years she'd always coveted her company Christmas cards, granting them pride of place in her meticulously arranged displays, but not any more. How could she have been so naive? Just because the directors of Wembley plc had sent her a standard-issue Christmas card it didn't mean they cared. She held the card up to the light. It was exactly as she thought – even the signatures had been printed. In their eyes she was no different to those brain-deads Chezza and Cazza. Ginny glanced over at them – Christmas baubles dangling from their ears, computers festooned with tinsel, singing that bloody Slade song over and over again. Well, she for one was not having fun. A new year was approaching and for the first time ever Ginny had absolutely no idea what she wanted to do with the rest of her life. She usually loved this time of year – it was a time for making lists, resolutions, plans, a time for reaffirming her goals, reasserting control over her destiny, but this year it all seemed as meaningless as her poxy company Christmas card.

Ginny stared out of the window on to the pitch below and tried to work out how she could make this Christmas more meaningful. Perhaps she ought to go home and dry out some oranges in the airing cupboard and spray some fir-cones silver before slinging them into a basket with a sprig of holly like that daft Scotswoman had done on GMTV that morning. Or maybe she ought to spend hours toiling over a Christmas cake that would take her and Mike until Easter to finish eating. But no, filling her house with Christmassy smells was still completely superficial. Christmas was about Christ, for Christ's sake, not naff basket arrangements. If she wanted a truly meaningful Christmas, then she would have to fill her holiday with Christian deeds. She would have to be caring, nice, forgive those who trespassed against her and all that. Ginny thought of Maz flailing about in her kilt and shuddered. But first she would have to get horribly drunk.

'Is anyone going to the pub at lunch-time?' she called out weakly, and for the first time since Gareth Southgate had missed his penalty a deathly silence fell over Wembley.

34

Anna stared at the television guide glumly. She knew it was Christmas Eve, but was it really necessary for quite so many 'Christmas specials'? And as for the films on offer, she couldn't think of anything she'd less like to watch than *It's a Wonderful Life*. To cap it all, *EastEnders*, the one programme guaranteed to remind her that there were others worse off than herself, wasn't on for another twenty-four hours. She flicked over to MTV, but even they were 'Sim-ply ha-ving a won-der-ful Christmas time'.

Anna turned the television off with a sigh. De-prived of her usual source of distraction, she found guilt beginning to edge its way into her mind. Grace deserved better than this. She wouldn't always be too young to know any better. Next year she would want to know why there weren't any decorations up, or why she didn't even have a Christmas tree. She might even want to know where her daddy kept disappear-ing off to for days on end. And then, of course, there was the awful nagging fear that Tom might one day turn on Grace. Anna shuddered. She knew she had to get them out of there, but where to? She felt like the princess in some postmodern ironic fairytale – *Ra-*

punzel, Rapunzel, let down your lank hair – but of course no Prince Charming was going to scale the graffiti-clad walls of her tower to whisk them off into the land of happy ever after. It was all down to her, and the responsibility was terrifying.

A loud clatter from the balcony shook Anna from her gloom. Moments later the front door swung open, ricocheting against the hall wall.

'Bollocks!' she heard Tom mutter. Anna's heart began to beat the familiar tattoo, signalling the start of a cacophony of panicked thoughts. *What's he doing home so early? Look at the state of this place. Why didn't I bother making him any tea? I should have stayed dressed, put some make-up on, washed my hair.*

'Here, Anna, give us a hand,' Tom called from the hall.

Anna peered out cautiously and did a double-take in shock. The entire hallway was filled with an enormous, slightly misshapen Christmas tree.

'Help me get it into the living room,' Tom's disembodied voice called out from among the branches.

Anna felt the overwhelming compulsion to giggle hysterically as she took hold of the tree trunk and began pulling it towards the living room. Of all the things she'd expected to happen that evening – and actually there hadn't been all that many – this certainly wasn't one of them. She'd been beginning to wonder whether she would even see Tom over Christmas; Tom plus tree had been far too much to hope for. As they wrestled the branches through the door, the carpet was showered with needles.

'Shit!' Tom uttered glumly. 'I think I overdid it a bit.'

Once in the living room the tree seemed to take on even more gargantuan proportions, stooping awkwardly as its top reached the ceiling, like a basketball player surveying an eighteenth-century cottage. Tom emerged from the other side smiling ruefully.

'I just wanted Gracie to have a tree.'

Anna had to stop herself from gasping out loud when she saw him. He looked so different, so haggard and worn. His hair seemed to have crossed that fine boundary between tousled and unkempt, and his face was smudged with stubble and shadows.

'Shall I get rid of it?' he asked, staring forlornly at the tree.

'No!' If there was one thing that Anna knew amidst all the confusion and mess, it was that this wasn't just a monstrous Christmas tree wedged in the centre of the living room, it was also an olive branch. 'It's lovely,' she added.

'I, er, got some lights and stuff from Woolies,' Tom said, edging his way back into the hall to retrieve a carrier bag full of decorations. 'I thought we could . . . you know.'

He didn't seem able to look at her; in fact, he seemed unable to focus on anything much, his eyes darting nervously this way and that. Anna fought to control the surge of concern welling up inside her.

She mustn't let her guard down, not even for a second. Remember what happened last time, she thought sternly, remember what he did to you.

'Shall we get started, then?' she asked cautiously.

'Yeah . . . yeah, great, let's do that . . . yeah.' Tom seemed even more nervous than she did.

They nudged the tree over to one side of the room, but it was so wide its branches still reached into the centre, completely obscuring the view from one side of the room to the other. As Tom set about unravelling the fairy lights, Anna busied herself attaching green plastic hooks to baubles.

'So – what's new?' Tom asked, finally breaking the silence.

'Oh, nothing much.' Anna didn't know whether to laugh or cry at the absurdity of it all. Too scared to do either, she simply bit her lip.

'Seen much of Johnny's missus?'

'No, not for a while now.'

'Oh.' Tom began winding the lights around the tree. As he walked past, Anna caught a waft of stale drink.

'Johnny was saying at training the other night she wants you to go over there Boxing Day, while we're at the Arsenal.'

'Oh yeah, she mentioned something about that in her Christmas card. Don't worry, I'm not going.'

'What do you mean, don't worry?' Tom asked as he wound the end of the lights round the top of the tree.

Shit, she'd said the wrong thing. Somehow the bauble in Anna's hand split in two. She'd assumed Tom wouldn't want her going out, seeing other people, talking to other people. She thought he'd be grateful she'd reverted to her life as a hermit.

'I think you should go,' he continued, turning the lights on. 'Enjoy yourself – we don't want people thinking I've done away with you or something.'

No, not when all you've done is smash my head against the wall, Anna thought bitterly. She gulped before reluctantly conceding, 'Okay, I'll call her tomorrow.'

'Great. Give us some of them and I'll get started on this side,' Tom took a handful of baubles and disappeared off behind the tree. As they worked on in silence, Anna's heart began to sink. This wasn't going to be some great reconciliation after all. There weren't going to be any tearful apologies this time, unless . . . Maybe *she* ought to instigate it?

Taking a deep breath, she crouched down by the bottom of her side of the tree, pretending to adjust a piece of tinsel. At least this way she didn't have to face him.

'I've, er, been doing a lot of thinking recently, about us and what's been happening, and I just want you to know that I still really love you, and so does Grace. We need you, Tom, and we miss you.' Anna felt a tear trickle down her face. If only he would come around and hold her for a minute. It wasn't too late to make a fresh start. 'It's not too late to make a fresh start. I'll do anything you want, anything to make it work. Just tell me what I'm doing wrong. Please.' Her voice echoed pitifully around the room, but Tom remained silent. Anna hugged her knees anxiously. She had overstepped the mark, she should have just acted as if nothing had happened. He was going to go mad again. She closed her eyes and waited for the onslaught, but still Tom said nothing. Summoning up all her courage, Anna peeped around the side of the tree. Tom lay slumped against the side of the sofa, fast asleep, fairy lights flickering upon his face.

35

Belle switched on the computer, took a sip of Bailey's and cast a loving glance down the living room at the magnificent Christmas tree twinkling in the bay window. Her mother would be proud of her efforts – it was a proper American-style tree, branches laden with hand-crafted decorations, stripy candy canes and spicy cinnamon cookies, with not a tatty piece of tinsel in sight. Then Belle shifted her gaze to the sofa and let out an exasperated sigh. Like a hairy great blot on her Christmas card landscape, Johnny lay reclined against the cushions, hand tucked down the front of his Wolves tangas, engrossed in his new *Non-League Club Directory*.

'Tell me, why exactly did you need another copy of that book?' Belle asked sarcastically.

'What do you mean?' Johnny asked, fumbling with his balls with one hand while turning the page with the other.

'I mean, how can you possibly need another *Non-League Club Directory* when you already possess the entire back catalogue to 1985? Couldn't you ask your dad for something a bit more useful, like a drill or something?'

'Well, why do you find it necessary to buy *OK!* magazine every week? At least this is only an annual purchase.'

Belle stared at Johnny in disbelief. 'But *OK!* is the Reuters of celebrity news. I have to get it every week to keep abreast of all the latest developments.'

'Well, that's exactly why I get the *Non-League Club Directory* every year – to keep abreast of all the latest developments,' Johnny retorted.

'Oh, and what might they be? Oh no, don't tell me – Amersham Town have finally started selling hot dogs? Or perhaps Clacton Rangers have opened a club shop?'

'Clacton Town.'

'What?'

'Clacton Town – there's no such team as Clacton Rangers!' Johnny responded with a derisory snort.

Belle stared at him languishing on the sofa, hand down pants, and for a split second she felt like taking that stupid great book and wedging it right up his arse. It didn't take long for her to reconsider. It was ironic, really. When she'd first met Johnny she couldn't wait to get into his pants, to get her hands on those firm buttocks of his, but now, five years down the line, that whole part of his anatomy made her stomach churn, from his rancid farts to his Dyno-Rod-requiring shits – not to mention those ridiculous pants he insisted upon wearing. How true, Belle thought with a sigh, that the thing that attracts you to a person always ends up repelling you in the end.

'Tell me,' she sneered, 'is there the remotest possibility that you could stop playing with yourself in public? How am I supposed to get Harry to leave his willy alone if he sees you doing that? Anyway, the others will be here soon. Hadn't you better go and get dressed?'

With a tortured sigh Johnny flung his directory to the floor and retreated upstairs. Belle allowed herself a smug little smile of victory before logging on to her e-mail. To her immense relief her inbox displayed a new mail from Luke. Sexy, free-spirited Luke. One thing was for sure – whatever he was doing right now it would not involve lying on a sofa with his hand down the front of a pair of orange-and-black striped pants. Belle clicked open the mail, shivering with anticipation. Her latest 'truth' to Luke had been to ask him to describe his ideal sexual fantasy. Hardly original, she knew, but it was a crucial part of the game of cat-and-mouse they were currently engaged in. As she waited what seemed like an eternity for the mail to open, she prayed it would involve her. She was not disappointed.

Belle,
I would whisk you off to an abandoned cabin in the heart of the Lake District. When we got there we would put everything on hold – our other lives, our other personalities, all the crap that gets in

the way of really experiencing life – and we would just follow our instincts. I would place a blindfold over your eyes in order to heighten all your other senses and then I would spend hours just playing with you, touching you, exploring you, until I discovered everything that makes you tick. Then, and only then, I would remove your blindfold and make love to you over and over again. Together we would reach a state of such total ecstasy that we would lose our grip on reality. Nothing else would matter any more, nothing else would count, just you and me. Us. TRUTH OR DARE?

Bloody hell!

'Belle, have you seen my blue shell-suit bottoms, the ones with the hole in the crotch?'

Johnny's plaintive cry fell upon deaf ears. This electronic foreplay was beginning to play havoc with Belle's powers of concentration, not to mention her pheromones. Luke was getting her so damned horny she felt fit to burst. If only she had the courage to do something about it. Perhaps all she needed was a little coercion. Before Johnny returned and she had time to think better of it, she clicked on reply and typed 'DARE!'

'Thanks for the lift,' Anna mumbled as they drew up outside Belle's house.

'That's all right – you make sure you behave yourself, now.'

Anna glanced at Tom to see whether he was joking, but his face remained fixed in a frown. 'Yes, of course. I probably won't stay all that long anyway.'

Tom had spent most of Christmas Day asleep, waking only for his dinner of turkey roll, oven-ready roast potatoes and processed peas. With her only recent source of income being Grace's child allowance, Anna had tried to turn her Christmas dinner budget of five pounds into a fun challenge – a sort of *Ready Steady Cook* Christmas Special. But Tom obviously wasn't in the mood for fun, not even on Christmas Day. When Anna had suggested they pop around to his parents' for the usual post-dinner tumbler of whisky in front of the Queen, she had been greeted with an un-expectedly vitriolic response. 'What, go and wish that fucker season's greetings?' Tom had snarled. 'You've got to be joking.' And with that he had returned to bed, leaving Anna to ponder the latest development over a game of Teletubbies with Grace.

Although she knew all about Stan's dubious meth-ods of discipline, Anna had never been aware of any lingering bitterness on Tom's part. If anything, he seemed slightly in awe of his dad, and was always quick to offer an excuse for his heavy-handed beha-viour, claiming to be grateful for being 'toughened up', and anyway, how else was his dad supposed to keep four sons under control? For a brief moment

Anna comforted herself with the possibility that Tom had been harbouring some deep-rooted resentment towards his father and she had just been bearing the brunt of it. All she had to do was make him open up to her and together they could work through it. God knows, she'd seen enough episodes of *Oprah* to know all the right things to say. But then she recalled Tom's blank expression throughout dinner, the way he looked at her with such obvious contempt when she read out the joke from her cracker – it hadn't even been that bad, as far as cracker jokes went – and she felt sure she was clutching at straws. There was a new coldness in Tom's attitude towards her, an emptiness between them, and it filled her with dread and fear.

This wasn't the only thing filling Anna with dread and fear as she trailed up the path behind Tom. She was about to see Belle for the first time in nearly two months, for the first time since that awful telephone conversation. As they waited for the door to be opened, Anna stared at the Christmas tree blazing like a beacon in the bay window to her right, and she couldn't help comparing it to their own pathetic eyesore cluttering up the living room, spewing needles all over the carpet every time anyone so much as coughed.

A key rattled in the lock and Anna's stomach performed a back flip. It was even worse than the first Football Widows meeting. What was Belle going to say when she saw Anna standing there? More to the point, what was she going to say to Belle? *Sorry about the lecture I gave you last time we spoke and sorry for blanking you ever since, but hey, merry Christmas!*

36

'Anna!' Belle cried, charging past Tom to enfold her in a hug. She smelt of a delicious mixture of Chanel, Christmas cake and Bailey's. Anna closed her eyes and for a second wished she could just fall asleep in that position for a long, long time. But then Belle stepped back, holding her at arm's length, the intensity of her stare making Anna squirm.

'You came! Oh, it's so good to see you. Come inside. All of you. Merry Christmas, Tom, merry Christmas, Grace.' Belle took Grace from Tom's arms and led them into the house. 'Harry, look who's here.'

As Anna followed Belle into the living room she felt like a child entering Santa's grotto, and she had to bite her lip to stop herself gasping out loud. Candles in holders of woven holly flickered on the mantelpiece, spicing the air with cinammon and frankincense. Dotted around the room were the most exquisite decorations Anna had ever seen. A musical carousel tinkled away on the coffee table while a red-faced Santa waved mechanically from the fireplace. Glass dishes crammed full of sweets filled every available surface, their multicoloured wrappers glistening like jewels and attracting Harry and Grace like magpies. And as for the tree, everything about it was perfect – the size, the shape, the array of intricately hand-finished stars, baubles and figures adorning each branch. For the first time that year Anna felt as if it was really Christmas.

'Oh, Belle – it looks amazing,' she sighed.

'Merry Christmas!' Johnny called from the doorway. 'Belle, I'm borrowing your Walkman so I can keep a check on the Wolves score.'

'You won't need that, mate, I can already tell you – you'll be winning two–nil and then in the last five minutes you'll let in four. That's the way it usually goes, eh, Belle?' said Tom, breaking into a throaty chuckle.

Belle nodded and laughed. 'Can I get you a drink, Anna?'

Anna stood in the centre of the living room temporarily rendered speechless by Tom's reincarnation.

Belle touched her gently on the arm. 'Anna?'

'Oh, sorry, just a lemonade, please,' Anna replied, balancing awkwardly on the arm of the sofa.

'A lemonade?' Belle practically shrieked. 'But it's Christmas.'

Anna could feel Tom's eyes boring into her. 'No, honestly, lemonade's fine.'

'Don't tell me – a bit too much of the old Christmas cheer yesterday, was it?' Johnny remarked with a grin.

'Yeah, something like that,' Anna responded feebly.

'You should have seen the state Belle got into. I don't know, you birds can certainly put it away. All right, then, Tommo, let's make a move. I said we'd pick Mike and Daz up from the station.'

'Right you are. Come here, Gracie, give your old man a kiss.' Tom hoisted Grace into the air and planted a huge kiss on her forehead. Gurgling with delight, she patted him on the head and squealed, 'Dadda! Dadda!'

Belle sighed. 'Ah. She's a real daddy's girl, isn't she?'

Grinning broadly, Tom turned to Anna. 'See you later, then, sweetheart.' *Sweetheart?* Anna froze as Tom kissed her lightly on the cheek. He hadn't touched her since Bonfire Night, let alone kiss her, and now all of a sudden he was playing happy families. Her cheek stung where his lips brushed against it. What the hell was he up to?

And then the men were gone and it was just her and Belle, sitting there awkwardly, both of them apparently engrossed in the assortment of new toys littering the carpet in front of the fire.

'So . . .' Belle was the first to break the silence. 'Did you have a nice Christmas Day?'

'Yeah – pretty quiet. How about you?'

'Yeah, same here. My mum was meant to be coming, but she ended up having to check her partner into rehab – she lives with a rather temperamental fashion designer in Milan.'

'Oh, that's nice.' Anna could have kicked herself;

she had been so determined not to make any slip-ups. 'I mean living in Milan must be nice – not the fact that your mum's partner's in rehab, or that she couldn't make it for Christmas. That must have been horrible . . .' Anna bit her lip nervously; it was hardly the best of starts.

'Yeah, but it was probably for the best – her and Johnny don't exactly see eye to eye and there's enough tension around here at the moment without my mum getting her two cents' worth.'

Anna looked around the room disbelievingly; she couldn't imagine a less likely setting for tension. With its soft candlelight and festive décor it felt more like the blurry backdrop for a Daniel O'Donnell video. Then she looked at Belle staring forlornly into the fire and instantly her nervousness fell away.

'Is everything all right, Belle? Look, I'm so sorry about that awful phone call. I had no business talking to you like that and I felt so ashamed afterwards I just couldn't face seeing you. Belle?'

Belle wiped a tear from her face. 'No, you were right. It is wrong to cheat on people and I didn't do anything with Luke in the end, but sometimes I feel so lonely and unloved and Johnny just doesn't seem to notice or care. He's too wrapped up in his damned football. Oh, Anna, I don't know what to do. Luke is the first man I've met in ages who actually seems interested in me as a person. He doesn't think of me as a mum, or a wife, or . . .'

'A Laundered Pants and Packed Lunch Provider?' Anna offered with a smile.

'Exactly. And I'm finding him harder and harder to resist – we e-mail each other all the time and I know that if I wanted to I could still make something happen between us. And to make matters worse he'll be moving to Canada in a few months and I'm just so scared that if I don't get it together with him I'll spend the rest of my life wondering what could have been.'

Belle was sobbing now, and Anna searched frantically in her bag for a tissue. Finally locating one that wasn't too badly soiled, she took it over to Belle and knelt down on the floor beside her. It was awful seeing Belle like this, Belle who was normally so full of vitality, so strong. If *she* caved in, what hope was there for the rest of them?

'So what happened to all your talk about pursuing our passions and following the men's example?' Anna retorted, as sternly as she could. 'We're the Football Widows, for goodness' sake. What happened to affirmative action and not taking any crap?'

Belle smiled weakly. 'Do you actually remember the rules, then?'

'Of course I do. We're supposed to be living by them, aren't we?' Please let this work, Anna prayed. It was becoming increasingly difficult to keep up the façade. Like an exhausted relay runner nearing the end of her lap, she desperately needed Belle to grab hold of the baton and run with it.

'So are you saying I ought to cheat on Johnny?' Belle asked hopefully between her tears.

Anna thought of Tom and a spark of anger ignited somewhere deep within her. She knew she was powerless to fight back or do anything for herself, but Belle wasn't. Belle had always been strong and successful, and yet here she was practically crumbling in front of her eyes. Anna couldn't let her end up in the same situation as herself; so weak and depressed that she lost all will to fight.

'I think you have to do whatever it takes to make you happy, and if Johnny isn't willing to listen to you, then you take whatever else you can. After all, you only live once.'

A loud hammering on the door rudely interrupted Anna's rousing rhetoric.

'That'll be Maz,' said Belle, leaping to her feet. 'God, Anna, it's so good to have you back. Right, for the rest of the day we are going to have FUN!'

Maz bounced into the room clad in a saucy Santa outfit, with tufts of crimson hair protruding from beneath an illuminated bobble hat. She was followed closely by Ginny. Both of them did a double-take when they saw Anna.

'Anna!' Maz hollered. 'Where have you been, darling? We've all been so worried about you. Here, have you been on a diet or something? You look even skinnier than ever!'

'She looks fine,' Ginny said sweetly. 'Welcome back.'

Anna nodded and blushed. 'Thank you.' There was something different about Ginny, something about her hair. The normally pristine bob appeared quite dishevelled, and Anna could have sworn she saw at least half an inch of regrowth snaking along her centre parting. Of course, it could have been the dim lighting.

After a brief exchange of turkey nightmares – Maz had flirted with food poisoning by stuffing the entire cavity without altering the cooking time, while Belle had inadvertently roasted the giblets complete with plastic bag – various gifts were produced. Although the others seemed mortally embarrassed, Anna wasn't bothered in the slightest that they hadn't got anything for her. She hadn't been able to afford to buy any of them gifts, and besides, it was hardly as if they knew she was coming. She did have her present for Harry, though, and in her eagerness not to be the only person not bearing gifts she thrust it into Belle's hands.

'This is for Harry,' she stammered. 'It's nothing much. I'm afraid money's a bit tight at the moment.' Anna held her breath as Belle unwrapped the present.

'*The Misadventures of Harry-Billy*,' Belle read out loud. 'Oh, Anna, did you make this yourself?'

Anna nodded and turned as scarlet as Maz's hair.

'Look, Harry, Anna's made you a comic about Harry-Billy.'

Harry leaped on to Belle's lap, and Maz and Ginny gathered around her chair. Anna winced as Belle began reading the story out loud. It was like torture *Listen with Mother* style: *Are you sitting excruciatingly uncomfortably? Then I'll begin.* Harry was the first to start giggling, followed closely by Ginny and Maz. Anna looked up in alarm, but they seemed to be laughing in amusement rather than derision.

'Look at his cheeky little face,' Maz guffawed.

'Oh my God, he's going to pinch that old lady's arse,' Ginny gasped, but for once her face seemed full of admiration rather than scorn.

'I told you she was brilliant, didn't I,' said Belle, sounding like a proud parent. 'Anna, this is incredible. It's like a proper children's comic. Is this what you were working on all that time?'

Anna nodded shyly. 'I'm sorry it's not on decent paper. As soon as I get the money I'll have it printed up properly.'

'God, don't worry about that, it's excellent as it is. He loves it,' Belle said, nodding at Harry. 'After all, it's not every day your alter ego gets his own personal comic, is it?'

'Well, I don't know,' Maz said with a chuckle. 'Us Football Widows are doing pretty well for ourselves, what with your PR coup and now a professional artist on our hands.'

'Not to mention a clothes designer in the making. How's the sewing-machine fund coming along?' Belle enquired as she attempted to unwrap a particularly sticky toffee.

'I've done it, mate, and I tell you what, it's not a

minute too soon. I don't think I could face another day in that cleaning job. Right bunch of dirty buggers those insurance brokers turned out to be – the things I found floating around in their bogs you wouldn't believe.'

'Ooh, that reminds me,' Ginny said, a rather strained smile etched upon her face. 'I've got a little something for you, Maz.'

Maz's face instantly fell. 'Oh?'

As Ginny handed her a Harrods carrier bag the whole room fell silent, waiting for the sting in the tail.

Maz peered into the bag unenthusiastically and removed a package wrapped in tissue. As she peeled away the wrapping she gasped in amazement. 'Fucking stone me!'

'What is it?' Belle asked nervously.

Anna held her breath.

Maz pulled out a swathe of sky-blue satin, her mouth gaping open in surprise.

'I thought you might want some fabric for your first outfit,' Ginny mumbled. 'If you don't like it I can always take it back – unfortunately they didn't do leopard print.'

'No, no, it's lovely,' Maz stuttered, practically paralytic with shock. 'Thanks a lot.'

'Well,' said Belle, 'I think we should all have a toast to the Football Widows.'

'The Football Widows!' everyone cheered in unison.

'Here's to the new millennium!' Belle cried.

'So are you looking forward to the New Year's Eve do at the football club, Belle? You'll never guess who's dee-jaying.' Maz chortled.

'What?' Belle's arm froze on its way to her mouth, leaving her drink suspended in midair.

'The New Year's Eve bash – don't tell me you don't know. Daz told me your old man's been organising it.'

'Why, that sneaky little shit,' Belle fumed. 'Of all the low-down, dirty tricks. He told me they had some friendly on New Year's Day and so we'd have to do something local. He never told me he meant the bloody football club.'

'Vince Dean's doing the sounds so at least you'll get to have a boogie to Neil Diamond,' Maz consoled.

'It might be quite a good laugh,' Ginny added cautiously.

Everyone turned to stare at her.

'Don't tell me you're going?' Belle asked incredulously.

To Anna's utter amazement, Ginny began to blush, quite furiously in fact. 'Well, yes, I said to Mike that I would – he seemed to have his heart set on it.'

'And since when has that ever bothered you before?' Belle thundered. 'Oh, I'm sorry, it's just the fact that Johnny didn't bother telling me that's making me mad. I feel so stupid.'

That makes two of us, Anna thought bitterly. She

hadn't dared broach the subject of New Year's Eve with Tom. She had taken it for granted that his plans wouldn't include her, but now that it seemed they would include all her friends while she stayed at home with Angus Deayton, a cloud of gloom began to descend.

'Right, well, this calls for revenge. Pass me that phone book, Ginny.'

They all watched bemused as Belle leafed through the phone book and began to dial.

'Oh, hello, is that Highbury? I wonder if you could put a message out for my husband over the PA system at half-time? Oh, that's great. Yes, his name's Johnny Farraday and he's sitting in the North Bank. Could you just say that his wife Belle sends her love and wants to congratulate him on finally passing his NVQ in Beauty Therapy. That's right – BEAUTY THERAPY!'

37

Dear sir or madam,

I am writing to you regarding any opportunities you may have for freelance artists. I am a graduate from St Martin's College with first-class honours in Art and Design and I specialise in cartoons and comic strips. Please see enclosed a copy of my latest work, The Misadventures of Harry-Billy . . .

Belle frowned. She was obviously still suffering from the after-effects of her Millennium Eve binge. Four days later. Her writing was about as dull and listless as her hair. The whole point of this letter was to secure Anna some work – a pile of rejection slips would hardly constitute the perfect belated Christmas present.

Belle had been touched by the effort Anna had gone to with the Harry-Billy comic – it must have taken her hours to come up with all the stories, and the pictures were superb. What made it all the more special was the fact that Anna was obviously not in the best of health. Belle had been shocked by how gaunt she'd become; that flu bug had obviously knocked her for six. Belle had decided that what she really needed was some kind of boost to start the new year on a positive note. The idea of approaching publishers first came to her when she discovered Harry poring over the comic, completely oblivious to his Thomas video blasting from the television and the countless new toys scattered about the floor. It was the first time she had seen him reading out of choice. Proof, surely, that Anna had what it took to be a children's illustrator. The trouble was, she was so damned insecure. Belle knew that Harry's enthusiasm alone wouldn't do the trick, but if an established publisher expressed an interest in her work . . .

But in order to achieve that her covering letter had to be powerful. Anna's story had to be more personal, more moving, more J.K. Rowling. Belle paused for a moment; she was sure Anna wouldn't mind a few white lies – the end justifying the means and all that. Any fool could see that she would have got a first-class degree if she hadn't dropped out of college – her illustrations were amazing. All it would take was a little further embellishment of her personal situation to grab the publisher's attention. Belle resumed typing:

Since graduating from St Martin's College with first-class honours in Art and Design I have put my career on hold in order to be a full-time mother to my two-year-old daughter, Grace. Although endlessly rewarding, life as a single parent can also be a wearying experience. I am determined to provide for my daughter materially as well as emotionally, and a career as a freelance illustrator would be the perfect way of achieving financial security through my passion for drawing. It would also enable me to continue caring for my daughter rather than leaving her at the mercy of some flibbertigibbet childminder while I go out of my mind with worry, stacking shelves in my local supermarket.

I have enclosed a sample of my most recent work, The Misadventures of Harry-Billy. *Please excuse the poor quality of the copy, but as you can appreciate, on such a limited budget my daughter's food and clothing must take precedence over art materials and paper.*

I look forward to hearing from you in due course, Yours sincerely, Anna . . .

It suddenly dawned upon Belle that she didn't even know Anna's surname, but when she looked up Tom's on the back of an old Rayners Park football programme it seemed ideal. Anna Grant, freelance artist. With all the romantic connotations of Cary . . . or Hugh, it gave her a real *je ne c'est quoi*. Besides, Anna and Tom had to be planning on marrying some day soon.

Belle printed off ten copies of the letter and decided on an early night with a trashy novel. Johnny still hadn't returned from the football. Wolves had beaten Hereford United 2–0 in the third round of the FA

Cup, so no doubt he had stopped off somewhere for an impromptu celebration. Just as she was about to shut down the computer, the electronic equivalent of a gentle thud on the doormat informed her of a freshly delivered e-mail. Her heart raced. There was only one person who would be sending her mail this late at night. Luke.

Belle,
Your dare, should you choose to accept it, is to be my model for a reader's true-life story in *That's Life* magazine. I think you'll enjoy the story, and don't worry, you will be provided with full disguise, including wig!!
L
PS: I got my ticket for Canada today. I leave February 14th.

Belle looked at the screen, looked away, then looked at the screen once more. But it still bore the same grave tidings. Luke was leaving, he was really going, and on bloody Valentine's Day as well. Talk about taking the piss! She had known all along that their flirtation couldn't last for ever, that one way or another it would have to come to an end, but did it have to be quite so soon? Since she'd met Luke she had been allowed a brief reminder of that heady rush of her pre-parent, pre-wife days. She had taken to lounging about on the sofa smoking surreptitious cigarettes while listening to a selection of her favourite eighties power ballads. Wailing along through plumes of smoke to Foreigner and Chicago, Neil Diamond hadn't had a look-in as Belle reverted to some kind of tortured teenage state. She had even taken to wearing her Walkman on the nursery run, staring pitifully at all the downtrodden mums with their saggy leggings and bleary eyes while Fat Larry's Band *Zoomed* its way through her headphones on a direct line to her heart. She couldn't go back to being one of those poor, unfulfilled women. She couldn't go back to the endless conversations about whether little Billy could wipe his bum yet and how many ounces they had managed to shift at this week's Weight Watchers.

Luke wanted her to be his model. Belle took a moment to contemplate her dare. A model in a proper women's magazine. Okay, so it was of the gloomy rather than glossy variety, but still. Okay, so she would have to wear a wig, but it would be a damned sight more subtle than wearing a sausage!

Just then the door crashed open and Johnny came careering into the room.

'Wem-ber-ley, Wem-ber-ley, we're the famous Wolver'ampton and we're going to Wem-ber-ley!' he slurred before slumping on to the sofa in an orange-and-black heap.

'Oh my God, look at the state of you.' Belle shuddered. 'Where have you been?'

'Don't start, not tonight. Not on this night of dreams.'

'What on earth are you talking about, Johnny?'

'This night of dreams, this day of dreams – the third round of the FA Cup. The round where David can beat Goliath or where Brighton and Hove Albion can stuff Newcastle three–one. The round where the little teams can become giant-killers. The round where anything is possible.'

'Yes – even Wolves can manage a win,' Belle remarked dryly. This was all she needed on top of her recent devastating news, a night in bed with a drunken Johnny – his thunderous snoring only interrupted by an hourly stagger to the bathroom in order to piss everywhere but the toilet bowl. Belle was about to volunteer to sleep on the sofa when she noticed Johnny staring at her, an indecipherable expression upon his face. She wasn't sure whether it was anger or disgust. Her heart skipped a beat and she hastily logged out of her e-mail. Surely he hadn't been able to read it from the other end of the room?

'Is everything all right?' she asked nervously.

Johnny uttered a low, blood-curdling moan, still staring almost trance-like in her direction. 'Oh. My. God,' he finally uttered.

'Johnny, what's the matter? You're scaring me.'

Appearing close to tears, an ashen-faced Johnny stumbled to his feet. 'Bloody hell, Belle, I just did a fart and I think I've followed through!'

As she watched Johnny race from the room clutching his buttocks, it was as if a light came on in Belle's mind. Why had she wasted so much time procrastinating over a man who obviously didn't care a jot about her, was completely obsessed with a game, and now, it would seem, couldn't even control his bowels? All at once she knew exactly what she had to do, and this time no stupid pangs of conscience were going to stop her. She was going to follow her heart, pursue her passion, and nothing, but nothing, was going to get in her way.

38

Belle took one look at her reflection and screamed. In less than an hour she was supposed to be making her modelling debut, but instead of looking like Caprice (whose beauty secrets she had been following to a tee all morning) she looked more like that stupid twat from *Fantasy Football* – the one with the goatee and moustache. The only difference being, *her* goatee and moustache were a rather startling shade of blue.

It had all been going so well. Having fallen hook, line and sinker for her story about a day's shopping with Ginny, Johnny had whisked Harry off on a flying visit to his parents in Wolverhampton. Belle had taken full advantage of having the house to herself for once. With 'Total Eclipse Of The Heart' on repeat, she had retired to the bathroom to drench her hair in conditioner, pack her face with mud and luxuriate in a foam bath before embarking upon an intensive programme of hair removal. It wasn't until she had tackled her armpits, legs, bikini line and eyebrows that her problems began. For some time now Belle had been aware of a faint shadow emerging along her upper lip. Admittedly the hair was relatively fair; in normal light and from a distance of more than a couple of feet it could hardly be seen at all. But under intense lighting and in close-up it was quite a different story, as Belle discovered while carrying out a pre-photo-shoot recce underneath the bathroom spotlight in the magnified side of Johnny's shaving mirror. Not only were there the distinct beginnings of a moustache, but also a thin line of hair blazing a trail down the centre of her chin, linking up with two little clusters on either side.

Belle scoured the photo of Caprice for the slightest hint of a whisker, but to no avail. Facial hair was obviously a complete taboo in the world of modelling. There was no question about it – the beard would have to go. But how? A razor was out of the question – the thought of her and Johnny jostling for space in front of the shaving mirror every morning was too awful for words. Legging it down to the local chemist, she decided to go for the mini wax strips, tempted by the promise of hair-free skin for *weeks* afterwards. As if all this hadn't been quite stressful enough, she then had to endure the utter humiliation of purchasing mini wax strips for the *face*. It made tampons and condoms seem a veritable breeze. Handing the packet to the stubble-free nymphet behind the counter, Belle held her breath and gazed at the floor. The way things were going she wouldn't have been at all surprised if the shop assistant had held the packet aloft and yelled, 'Mr Ahmed, how much shall I charge this bearded lady for her facial wax?' Mercifully she was spared this agony, but by the time she got home any relaxing benefits she had gained from the morning had been driven away by a mild bout of hysteria. She was going to be late for her first modelling assignment – she was going to be late for Luke. Completely disregarding the instructions, Belle wrenched the strips of paper apart and proceeded to apply them to her upper lip and chin. However, rather than removing any unwanted hair, they left her coated in sticky blue wax.

And worse was to come. When Belle attempted to remove the wax with a wet face flannel it just seemed to set even harder. Exfoliators, pumice stones and even a scouring pad from the kitchen were set loose upon her face, but they only served to create a red ring of inflamed skin around the waxen beard. Belle wanted to cry, and if she hadn't already applied her shockingly expensive but non-waterproof eye make-up she probably would have done. It was only while plumbing the depths of despair that it dawned on her to read the instructions. 'Please use the enclosed wipes to remove any residue of wax and leave the skin silky smooth', it stated quite clearly in black and white, right underneath. 'If wax appears sticky, place in the refrigerator for 30 minutes.'

By the time Belle arrived in Chiswick, she was nearly an hour late, had the pulse rate of one of those geriatric marathon runners about to keel over, and her mouth and chin were plastered in foundation, only partially camouflaging the angry rash that lay beneath. All the euphoria and anticipation that had made her lose half a stone in a week had vanished without trace. She felt hairy and ugly and very, very nervous. Suddenly Luke seemed like a complete stranger. Although they e-mailed each other almost every day, it had been nearly two months since she had actually seen him. Like a collection of old photographs, the images of him she had lovingly stored in her memory had become faded and worn around the edges.

Belle had always imagined Luke living in a converted warehouse somewhere, only accessible by one of those rickety old lifts where you had to haul the metal grille shut yourself. She envisaged emerging from the lift to find herself surrounded by polished wooden floorboards and black-and-white prints of naked women hanging from whitewashed walls. The only furniture on display would be a huge bed in one corner, and perhaps a rubber plant or two lurking by a glass wall overlooking the Thames.

In fact 8A Tregenna Gardens turned out to be an imposing town house displaying elegance of the faded, peeling and chipped variety – not to mention a vast array of doorbells. Finally locating the name card for L. Ryan, Belle pressed the adjacent button and almost immediately heard the sound of footsteps on stairs, thudding in time with her pounding heart. The door flew open to reveal Luke – a barefoot vision in black T-shirt and combats. He stood there beaming for a second before gingerly stepping on to the bristly doormat and wrapping his arms around her.

'I thought you'd chickened out,' he whispered in her ear, his breath sending shivers down her spine.

'Oh no,' Belle replied, self-consciously covering her mouth with her hand. 'Something came up at the last minute, that's all. I had to, er, unblock the sink.'

'Come inside, it's bloody freezing out here,' Luke said, ushering her into a dark hallway.

She followed him up a narrow flight of stairs, taking full advantage of the opportunity to admire his bum. Although Luke was thinner than Johnny, he was wiry rather than puny, padding up the stairs two at a time with the ease of a panther. A door stood ajar at the top of the stairs, strains of the Rolling Stones drifting out on to the landing.

'Go ahead,' he said, ushering her into the flat. The front door opened straight into a spacious, high-ceilinged living room. The wooden floor was covered with an ethnic-style rug, and in each corner a cluster of different-coloured spotlights curled their way around chrome stands, like electronic clambering roses. The effect was extraordinary as the red, green and orange emanating from each corner mingled in the centre, filling the room with a warm glow. A huge terracotta sofa squatted between two large sash windows, a framed print of Bob Marley hanging on the wall behind it. Although there were no taste-fully shot naked ladies, there were several black-and-white prints of various landscapes dotted around the walls which Belle assumed to be Luke's.

'Nice place,' she murmured appreciatively.

'Yeah, I've enjoyed it here – it's not bad for London,' he added with a grin.

Belle noticed a crate loaded with books and CDs in the corner and her heart sank. He really was leaving, then. Part of her had been hoping it was all just an elaborate ploy to get her to come over.

'Can I get you a drink?' Luke picked up an unopened bottle of Smirnoff from the assorted mess on what Belle assumed to be a coffee table and offered it to her awkwardly.

'Yeah, that would be great.' A large vodka was just what Belle needed to anaesthetise her nerves. 'So, tell me all about this Secret Confession, then. Who am I supposed to be?'

Luke chuckled as he sloshed some vodka into a mug. 'Well, maybe it would be better if you read it yourself.' He rummaged through the pile of newspapers, CD covers and cigarette packets on the coffee table until he finally located a sheet of typewritten text. 'This is the copy by the magazine's in-house writer. With these kinds of stories the main character is always anonymous and they always use a model for the photo. They tend to be slightly dodgy,' he explained.

Belle rubbed her hands with glee – the juicy ones were always far better than those naff stories about long-lost twin sisters reunited. Taking a swig from her mug, she began to read.

I was always the ugly duckling at school, the one left standing by the wall at discos, while all my mates smooched their way through 'Careless Whisper' with their latest fellas. Then just as I turned sixteen my boobs seemed to grow overnight from a size 32A to a 36D. Suddenly boys began to notice me, and one boy in particular, David West, captain of the school football team and all-round hunk.

'Can I have this dance?' he whispered in my ear at our school-leaving disco.

'Oh yes,' I swooned, and as I swayed in his arms I felt like the happiest girl alive. Suddenly all those years of being the school wallflower seemed worth it, if it meant that I ended up with hunky Dave West. After the disco we went to the local park, drinking cider and smoking fags. One thing led to another and before I knew it we were making love under the stars.

Belle fumbled in her handbag for a cigarette and swallowed back a lump in her throat – this story was so sweet.

But the very next day, when I went back to the park, Dave was with his football mates and acting all macho. I couldn't believe that the same lad who had been so lovey-dovey just hours before was now calling me a 'dirty dripper' and making fun of me in front of all his mates. I went home and sobbed my heart out all over my Take That pillowcase and duvet set. Two nights later Dave turned up at my house drunk. He was full of apologies but explained that although he really fancied me he had his image to think about – the captain of the school football team couldn't really be seen with someone like me. I was too 'rough' to be his proper girlfriend, but he wanted to know if I would agree to keep seeing him on the quiet.

I was so head over heels in love with him I immediately agreed. Even when he had other 're-spectable' girlfriends, he would still come and see me for a bit of nookie on the side. Altogether we saw each other on and off for nearly four years. Then one summer, shortly after Dave returned from a lads' holiday in Ibiza, I started to get an annoying itch on my private parts. I couldn't believe it when my doctor said, 'You've got herpes' – I thought it was just a bad case of thrush.

Belle choked on her drink – herpes? That was even worse than facial hair!

I was gutted, and for a long time I couldn't face going out or seeing anyone. I'd had enough of fellas to last me a lifetime. Then one day my mate Shirley asked me to come and watch a local football team with her. 'Go on, it'll cheer you up,' she coaxed. 'Some of the players are well fit.' So I tagged along, and while I was standing there, watching those pathetic men staggering around the pitch like they were David Beckham or something, I had a brain-wave. Suddenly I thought of the perfect way to get my own back on those arrogant pigs who think they're God's gift just because they can kick a ball around. I'd throw away my herpes treatment and with the help of my big boobs and a few tight football tops I'd give them a taste of their own medicine – and one they wouldn't forget in a hurry!

'Oh my God, that's so sick – but so inspired,' Belle gasped. Surely this had to be the ultimate act of Widow's Revenge? She couldn't wait to tell the other Football Widows. Then it dawned on her. 'I can't pretend to be her. What if my mother-in-law sees it?'

Luke laughed as he joined her on the sofa. 'Don't worry, I've got a great selection of wigs, and anyway, it will say by the side of the photo that it was posed by a model. Go on, I dare you.'

Belle looked at Luke staring at her expectantly with those bloody great eyes that didn't just say come to bed, but come to bed and don't stop shagging me until next Christmas. The way she was feeling at that precise moment she found herself physically incap-able of refusing him a thing, but posing as a demen-ted herpes-infected fiend was hardly very Caprice.

39

'I really don't think I can hold this position much longer,' Belle groaned. Every muscle in her face had seized up, her arms ached and her scalp had been rendered completely numb through insufficient blood supply. Lying on the floor beneath her, Luke paused to offer up an encouraging grin.

'Not long now,' he soothed. 'I'm nearly there.'

Belle sighed. She had no idea the glamorous world of modelling could be quite so exhausting – no wonder all the supermodels had to take anger management classes and cocaine. The whole experience had been quite an eye-opener. Literally. For the past two hours Luke had arranged her in a variety of poses with her brief being to look as 'deranged' as possible. If she stared psychotically for too much longer her eyes would probably plop out on to the carpet. She really hadn't seen the need to focus on her facial expression anyway; surely her ridiculous outfit made her look deranged enough, what with the skintight Man United top (age eight to nine years), obscenely short miniskirt and white stilettos, all thoughtfully provided by the fashion department at *That's Life*! Not to mention the canary-yellow wig. It had taken her the best part of an hour to cram her intensively conditioned, gleamingly serumed curls underneath the damned thing. But the real *pièce de résistance* had to be the packet of Zovirax – 'fast-acting and effective treatment for genital herpes' – that she had spent the last two hours dangling ominously over a wastepaper basket.

Belle had assumed Luke would just take a few snaps from a couple of different angles. She hadn't figured on the endless lighting tests, leading to minute adjustments of the shiny silk umbrellas and numerous spotlights stationed all about her. When he was finally satisfied with the quality of the lighting he then proceeded to use an entire roll of film on each individual shot. Belle would then have to change position for the whole procedure to begin all over again. So far she had been photographed standing menacingly by the door, gazing menacingly out of the window, perching menacingly on the edge of the bath, and finally sitting menacingly on the sofa with Luke lying on the floor at her white-stiletto-clad feet, snapping away at the most unflattering angle possible.

'Please, Luke, my arms are going to drop off if I have to hold this wastepaper basket for much longer,' she pleaded through gritted teeth, her deranged stare becoming more and more authentic by the minute. 'What the hell's the matter with you?'

Luke had put his camera down and was rolling

about on the floor roaring with laughter. 'If you could only see yourself,' he gasped, clutching his sides.

Well, this was just great! Belle bet Caprice never had to put up with this type of insolence. 'Oh, well, don't worry, no doubt I will soon, along with the half a million other *That's Life* readers,' Belle retorted, praying that the wig would prove a convincing enough disguise.

Luke, meanwhile, appeared to have lost all self-control as he writhed about on the floor in spasms of laughter. 'I'm sorry,' he spluttered, 'it's just your wig, it's gone all lopsided.'

Belle flung the packet of Zovirax at him and pouted. 'You're really loving this, aren't you?' she hissed. 'Well, just you wait until it's your turn for a truth or dare.'

'Why, what are you going to do?' he asked, making a sudden lunge for her wrist and pulling her down on top of him.

As Belle's body moulded itself into Luke's, all her pent-up irritation exploded into lust. Despite her skew-whiff canary-yellow wig, skin-tight football top and Liz MacDonald-style footwear, she felt instantly transformed from STD-infected loon to lascivious sex goddess.

'I'm afraid the wig's got to go,' Luke murmured, giving it a playful tug and allowing her hair to tumble its way back to freedom. 'And the stilettos,' he added, reaching down to gently slip the shoes from her feet.

'How about the football top?' Belle whispered shamelessly.

'Oh, that's definitely got to go.'

Belle obligingly raised her arms, enabling Luke to peel the red nylon from her body. For a split second he stared up at her, eyes glazed, and then their lips locked, taking up where they had left off back in Wigan. Belle trembled as his arms encircled her and effortlessly rolled her on to the floor beside him.

'Oh God, Belle,' he groaned as he pressed his lean, hard body up against her and fiddled with the catch on the back of her bra. Belle held her breath – this was definitely not the time for any embarrassed fumbling. But within seconds the tension in her bra loosened and she felt Luke's hands slipping underneath to cup her breasts. 'Oh God,' he moaned once more as his mouth began devouring her, his tongue winding its way around hers, gently at first, then probing harder and faster.

Belle wrapped a leg around his back, pulling him in closer. She wanted every part of their bodies to be touching, every part of them to merge. It was as if all her frustration of the past couple of years could finally be released – pure, unadulterated lust racing in like a tide to wash it away. Never had she felt so out of control of her own body. Nothing mattered apart from feeling Luke inside her.

And then, in one fabulously quivering orgasmic moment, it was over. Belle lay in Luke's arms, sated to the point of euphoria. She wanted to stay there for ever, she wanted to bury her face in his silver hair and cover the top of his head with kisses – she wanted to cry *I love you* at the top of her voice.

I love you? Belle opened her eyes and glanced at Luke lying next to her, his chest rising and falling rapidly as a satisfied smile beamed from his lips. And then, as quickly as it had swept into her body, the tidal wave of lust turned and drained away, leaving a dull, aching emptiness in its wake. The realisation was crushing. Belle didn't love this man; she hardly even knew him. All they had ever really talked about was sex. They hadn't ever sat up all night discussing politics or who was the greater legend, Neil Diamond or Noddy Holder. The body lying next to her suddenly felt scarily unfamiliar. This wasn't the man who had stood by her when she found herself pregnant and terrified at the tender age of twenty-five. He hadn't held her hand throughout a twelve-hour labour and only fallen asleep twice. He couldn't read her facial expressions like a book, telling by the slightest curve of her smile whether it was genuine or forced. He didn't know that her favourite part of a Snickers bar was the nougat or that she would do just about anything for a back rub (including watching *Match of the Day*). Belle didn't want to be having mind-altering sex with a virtual stranger, she wanted to be having it with her husband, the father of her child, somebody she could snuggle up to afterwards, telling him how much she loved him.

Luke cleared his throat and raised himself to a seated position. 'Would you like a cup of tea?' he asked awkwardly.

Belle nodded as she fumbled about the floor for her clothes.

'Do you take sugar?'

'Yes, one, please.' Belle watched sorrowfully as Luke padded over to the door, a flattened packet of herpes treatment stuck to his left buttock.

By the time Belle got home it was almost midnight. After checking on Harry, she slipped out of her clothes on the landing and crept into bed. Lying rigid as a corpse, she listened to Johnny's rhythmic breathing, the air rustling like leaves in the darkness. For a brief moment she relaxed – he was asleep, she had got away with it. But then the truth hit her like a sledgehammer. She had got away with what? *She had cheated on her husband*, something she had vowed she would never do, and now things would never be the same again. She would have to bear this burden of guilt for the rest of her life, and for once this was a drama Belle could do without. How would she ever be able to look Johnny in the eye again? Tentatively snuggling up behind him, she pressed her head against his back and listened to his heart pounding away like a muffled drum. One day that heart would stop pounding and so would hers. One day this would all be over, and how much time would she and Johnny have wasted on petty dramas and lashing out at the one person they truly loved? Belle closed her eyes and clung on to Johnny as silent tears spilt on to her face.

Johnny lay there motionless in the darkness as Belle's tears trickled a warm path down his back. Why was she crying? More importantly, why was she crying silently? Belle never cried silently. She liked to wail and scream and sob and moan. He knew she hadn't spent the day with Ginny either. When he'd phoned Mike on his way back from Wolverhampton about the dodgy offside decision in the Spurs–Chelsea game, he'd said Ginny was at some yoga workshop in Bath. So where the hell had Belle been?

She had been acting strangely ever since that bloody lemon sausage launch – practically driving him out of the house to play football on a Saturday and not batting an eyelid if he trained two evenings a week. She'd even brought a cup of coffee into the bathroom last Sunday and told him to take his time over the football results! No, something was definitely not right. For the first time in four years Johnny found himself in the bizarre situation of thinking about his wife rather than football as he teetered on the brink of sleep. And not even the tantalising prospect of Wolves making it to the quarter-finals of the FA Cup could drive the terrible sense of foreboding from his mind as he finally drifted into an uneasy slumber.

40

'Ginny – your Freemans order's arrived!' Caroline trilled across the office. Ginny jolted upright from her semi-slumbering state, slumped over several dozen unread marketing memos. Maybe this wasn't going to be such a tedious Monday morning after all, she thought, as she hauled herself to her feet. The previous day's yoga workshop had left her in such a blissful state of nirvana it was comparable only to the time she had taken one of Belle's prescription painkillers and inadvertently attempted to walk through a plate-glass window.

As Ginny glimpsed the package awaiting her among the menagerie of fluffy animals on Caroline's desk she felt like a kid in one of those soppy Christmas movies, and it took every ounce of self-control to prevent herself clapping her hands with glee. Of course, she knew exactly what lay beneath the cellophane wrapping – if only she'd found out sooner that Freemans featured a Betty Jackson collection – but it still didn't spoil the thrill of having something to unwrap.

Caroline gasped as Ginny tore open the parcel to reveal a pair of black organza-trimmed palazzo pants.

'Wow – they're gorgeous,' she sighed, running a cubic zirconia-encrusted nail over the fabric.

'Yes, they are,' Ginny murmured in agreement, and having them delivered straight to the office certainly beat traipsing around boutiques all day long.

'Oooh, by the way,' Caroline whispered conspiratorially, 'Cheryl's just been sent the new Ann Summers catalogue and it's got some of those fur-trimmed handcuffs you were on about.'

Ginny beamed. 'Excellent! When's she having her next party?'

'I don't know, we'll have to have a word. Coffee, sweetheart?'

Ginny nodded as Caroline rummaged about in her Barbie purse for some change.

'Do me a favour, love – keep an eye on me phone. It's been ringing off the bleeding hook all morning.'

'Sure.' Ginny sat down in Caroline's chair and gazed at her very first mail-order acquisition lovingly. All about her the office thronged – a discordant orchestra of mobile phones simultaneously piping out Mozart, *William Tell* and that bloody awful *Grande Valse* while people scurried by giving yet another guided tour to yet another journalist writing a piece on the 'tragic' demise of the National Stadium. This was the kind of atmosphere Ginny once would have thrived on, but not any more. She couldn't even be bothered to tweak her CV – in fact, all she could think about these days was sex.

Now she had finally discovered what all the fuss was about she just couldn't get enough. It was a bit like the Freemans catalogue, really. Ginny had always viewed sex in much the same way as she had a three-pack of vest tops – dull and pretty pointless – never realising that lurking there all the while was the mind-blowing equivalent of a spanking new designer collection. Just as she felt compelled to place her very next order immediately, she simply couldn't wait to get Mike back in the sack. After all, she did have an awful lot of lost time to catch up on. Ginny had begun picturing Mike manacled to the bed by a pair of fur-trimmed handcuffs when she was rudely interrupted by the pealing of Caroline's phone.

'Good morning, Wembley National Stadium. How can I help you?' she rattled into the receiver, completely uninterested.

'Oh, good morning,' came a rather nervous-sounding voice from the other end of the line. 'I'm calling from Full Time Hospitality. We have an executive suite booked for the FA Cup Final.'

'Oh, really.' Ginny gazed into space as she visualised Mike writhing about on the bed, stark bollock naked.

'Well, the thing is, due to completely unforeseen circumstances, our company has had to go into receivership,' the voice continued.

'Oh dear.' Ginny airbrushed a leather blindfold into her fantasy picture of Mike.

'So I'm afraid we'll have to cancel our booking with immediate effect.'

'Oh, okay.' Perhaps she could smear him in some of that chocolate body paint as well. Of course, she'd have to invest in some plastic sheets first.

'Anyway, I'm sure you won't have any problem filling it – they must be like gold dust at the moment, what with it being the last FA Cup Final on the hallowed turf and all.'

Ginny groaned inwardly. If she heard those words one more time . . . 'Right,' she said, scrawling on one of Caroline's Forever Friends Post-it notes. 'Full Time Hospitality. I'll process the cancellation immediately.'

As soon as Ginny had terminated the call she dialled Mike's school.

'Oh, hello, could I speak to Mr Woodward, please, it's his partner calling. Yes, I know he's in the middle of a lesson, but I can assure you this is a matter of the utmost urgency. Thank you.' As the harassed secretary went to extract Mike from the joys of Year Eleven history, Ginny stuffed the Post-it note into her pocket and smiled broadly. She fancied eating at home today, and she just couldn't wait to get her hands on Mike's lunch box.

Anna stared at the letter in disbelief. Who the hell were R.J. Ross Publishing, and why were they writing to her? She racked her brains trying desperately to recall which organisations she had most recently provided with her name and address. There was that toothy Mormon who had accosted her outside Boots last week, but why would he be writing to her under the guise of being a publisher, about her recent 'submission'? What recent submission? And why was the letter addressed to Anna Grant? She never used Tom's name. Intrigued, she opened the second of her bumper delivery of mail. Again it was from a publisher, and again it thanked her for her recent submission, but regretted to inform her that they currently had no opportunities for freelance work. Then, even more bizarrely, somebody had scrawled in Biro at the bottom of the letter, 'Sorry to hear of your current predicament stacking supermarket shelves, but don't forget, Van Gogh spent many years toiling down a mine before embarking upon a career in the art world. Your time will come!'

Anna scratched her head in bewilderment. What the hell was going on here? She opened her third letter – it was from Ken's Kitchens, thanking her for her recent enquiry and asking whether it would be convenient for a representative to call on Monday. It was Monday today. Anna groaned as she recalled the telephone call from a particularly over-zealous sales rep that had come right in the middle of Grace's bath. Haunted by the prospect of returning to the bathroom to discover Grace floating face downward in the water, Anna had had no choice but to agree with everything he said – it was the only way to get these people off the phone. Making a mental note not to answer the door all day, she tore open her final letter; again it was addressed to Anna Grant.

Dear Anna,

Thank you very much for your recent submission to D.C. Thomson & Co. I was very impressed with The Misadventures of Harry-Billy, *and in my role as commissioning editor I would be interested in seeing further examples of your work. Although we currently have no requirements for a 'Harry-Billy' character as such, we are putting together a new weekly comic for boys aged nine to thirteen years entitled* Wicked! *We are keen to develop a football-related character to feature in this publication – a Roy of the Rovers for the twenty-first century, if you like. When I saw Harry-Billy I felt you had captured exactly the kind of mischievous look I had in mind.*

If you are still interested in freelance opportunities at D.C. Thomson please could you submit a short strip of no more than ten illustrations showing such a character training for an important match, to reach me no later than 14 March. Feel free to use your imagination and make the character your own. If you have any queries please do not hesitate to contact me on the above number. I look forward to hearing from you in due course.

Yours sincerely,
Bob Cumming
Commissioning Editor

Like a yo-yo Anna's heart leaped, sank, leaped and then sank again. A publisher wanted to see some of her work, with a view to 'freelance opportunities'. It had to be a mistake. Why would they write to her out of the blue like that? She hadn't even made a submission. But then how did they know about Harry-Billy? Perhaps the letter was authentic. But then why had they got her name wrong? It had to be some kind of prank. A loud knock on the door barged its way into her befuddled mind. Oh no! Anna cringed – it had to be the kitchen people. Thrusting a lollipop into Grace's mouth, she cowered in the corner of the living room. They knocked again. And again. God, what was wrong with these people? Why couldn't they just leave her alone? Then, to Anna's utmost dismay, they began shouting through her letterbox.

'Anna, let me in, please!' the voice shrieked. Even the Jehovah's Witnesses weren't this persistent. Then, as the voice fell an octave or two, Anna detected a certain familiarity. It sounded just like Belle – a very tired and emotional Belle.

For the next hour Anna sat there dispensing tissues and tenderness in equal measure while listening attentively to Belle's torrid tale of sexually transmitted diseases, photo shoots and adultery.

'Oh, Anna,' Belle sobbed, her face bloated with tears, 'you were so right. I don't think I'll ever forgive myself for cheating on Johnny and Harry. I feel like . . . like . . .'

'Please don't say killing yourself,' Anna interrupted. 'That's definitely not the answer. Think of what it would do to everyone you'd leave behind. How would Johnny and Harry cope without you?'

'No, no,' Belle responded, shaking her head vigorously, 'I was going to say I felt like Cindy Beale from *EastEnders*. A shameless, good-for-nothing hussy. But even she had the excuse of being married to Ian – for all Johnny's faults there's no way he deserved to be betrayed like that. I only wish I'd taken more notice of what you said to me that night in Wigan.'

Anna cleared her throat nervously. 'Actually, Belle, I've been meaning to talk to you about that. You see, I wasn't really myself that night. I'd been having a few problems with Tom and I was just taking them out on you.' There – she'd said it, she'd finally confided in somebody about Tom. Anna glanced at the door anxiously, half expecting Tom to come bursting in from some hiding place in the hall.

'Oh no – oh, Anna. I had no idea. And here I've been moaning on about myself and all the time you've been . . . What kind of problems exactly?' Belle wiped her eyes and pulled herself upright in her chair.

'Oh, it's a long story. Tom's been under a lot of pressure lately. He's been laid off jobs unexpectedly and money's been really tight and the thing is—' Anna paused.

'What?' Belle coaxed, abandoning her tissue-draped armchair to join Anna on the sofa. 'What is it, Anna? You can tell me.'

'I don't think he loves me any more,' Anna whispered. 'I think he resents me for not working, for staying at home with Grace.'

Belle shook her head in disbelief. 'Oh, I'm sure that's not true. You've always seemed so happy whenever I've seen you together, and he obviously dotes on Grace. But if it is causing problems why don't you do what I do and work from home? Honestly, Anna, with your talent you could easily get some kind of freelance illustration work.'

The proverbial penny dropped. 'It was you, wasn't it?' Anna cried. 'You sent *The Misadventures of Harry-Billy* to all those publishers.'

Belle clapped her hands with glee. 'Oh my God – have you had any replies? Did you get any offers? Oh, please tell me you got an offer. It was meant to be a belated Christmas present – the last thing I wanted was for you to get ten rejection slips.'

'Ten? You sent my work to ten publishers without telling me?' Anna stared at Belle in disbelief.

Belle nodded sheepishly. 'I knew you'd never agree to it, but you've got to believe me, Anna, your pictures are brilliant. I couldn't just sit back and watch all that talent go to waste. So don't keep me in suspense – did you get any offers?'

Rendered completely speechless, Anna managed a nod.

'You did?' Belle leaped to her feet. 'Let me see it. Which one was it? What did they say? Did they fall for the supermarket story?'

Anna didn't dare ask; she simply passed Belle the letter from D.C. Thomson. Belle read it and whooped. 'Anna, don't you see, this is the answer to all your prayers. If you get this job, which you will, you can work from home and be with Grace – and you can ease the pressure off Tom a bit. Then you'll all be happy.' Belle sat back down again, beaming. She loved it when a plan came together, and if she could be responsible for bringing a bit of happiness into another family's life it went some way to compensating for her own monumental fuck-up. But why the hell was Anna crying? Tears of elation probably, or gratitude perhaps? But on closer examination Belle could see quite clearly that the tears streaming their way down Anna's face were tears of pure and unadulterated sorrow. 'Anna, what is it?' Belle leaned across to stroke her hair. 'I only told a couple of white lies in the letter – they'll never bother checking that you completed your degree, and they certainly won't be coming all the way down from Dundee to make sure you work in Kwik Save. Besides, does anyone really believe all that bullshit about J.K. Rowling writing *Harry Potter* in a café to save on heating bills? It's all about having a good story these days, that's all.'

'You don't understand,' Anna sobbed, not really understanding much of what Belle had just said herself. 'Tom really doesn't love me any more – he's having an affair.'

41

Belle blew the layer of dust from the top of the box of chocolates and stared at them in disbelief. They were even worse than the forecourt flowers of last year. Receiving a Valentine's gift from a petrol station had been bad enough, but Belle dreaded to think where this year's offering had originated. She studied the box for some kind of clue, but the print was completely illegible – all she knew was it certainly wasn't Belgian or Swiss. Sure enough, tucked away in the small print on the side of the box Belle could just make out 'Product of Iran', directly above what looked suspiciously like a sell-by date, 06/03/99. Iranian chocolates? Even worse, out-of-date Iranian chocolates. Well, that just about said it all, really. Surely this had to go down in the annals of history as the most unromantic Valentine's gift of all time. It wasn't as if Belle was some kind of rabid confectionery jingoist, loyally sticking to Cadbury's come hell or high water – but what was so wrong with Lindt or Suchard? It was so typical of Johnny to chance upon the sole suppliers of Iranian chocolates in London and, judging by the date and the dust, it was hardly as if he'd hit upon a new confectionery trend.

'Where the hell did you get these from?' she asked, her initial feeling of disappointment being rapidly displaced by one of intrigue.

'Mr Patel's – here's your card.' Johnny slung an envelope on to her lap and stomped over to the computer, discarding his jacket and tie along the way. As he waited for the Football Manager game to boot up, he loosened his shirt collar and let out a sigh.

Belle opened the card apprehensively, half expecting it to be written in Arabic. It might as well have been, it was so devoid of meaning and sentiment. 'For my Valentine', it read on the front above a hideous orange-and-mauve floral extravaganza. Inside, Johnny had simply scrawled his name – on his lap during an extremely bumpy Tube ride home by the look of it. There was no 'love', no kisses, none of the jokey little messages of previous years, thanking her for putting up with his farts or promising to make more of an effort with the dishes.

'*And WOLVERHAMPTON WANDERERS win the toss . . .*' the automated voice of Football Manager barked across the room, and Belle felt a sudden surge of outrage. She had spent the past week practically drowning in guilt over her liaison with Luke, especially since she had seen what Tom's suspected adultery had been doing to Anna, but for what? It wasn't as if Johnny knew what she had done – as far as he was concerned she was still the same devoted wife she'd always been – and yet how did he choose to demonstrate his feelings towards her on Valentine's Day? A box of out-of-date Iranian chocolates and a night in listening to that bloody computer game. Belle stomped over to the stereo and put 'You Don't Bring Me Flowers' on at full blast, reasoning that if it didn't drive him out it would at least drown him out.

'Oh, for fuck's sake!' Johnny bellowed. 'Not this fucking song again!' He leaped to his feet and marched over to the stereo to turn the CD off. Belle waited patiently for him to get back to the computer before grabbing the remote control and pressing PLAY. Once more Neil Diamond's throaty drawl filled the room.

'Right, that does it!' Johnny marched back over to the stereo, his face puce with rage. This time he not only stopped the CD but removed it from the stereo and flung it into the dining room.

'What the hell do you think you're doing?' Belle screamed. How dare he manhandle her Neil Diamond CD like that – it was the Greatest Hits collection as well.

'I'm confiscating it.'

'You're what?' Belle shrieked, practically out of her mind with indignation, not to mention the slightest hint of excitement – Johnny was normally so damned unconfrontational.

'I've had a shit day and all I want to do is come home and unwind. I do not want to spend an evening listening to that bollocks while you sit there feeling sorry for yourself like some spoilt little brat.'

'Me? Spoilt? Ha! Spoilt by whom exactly?' Belle leaped to her feet, brandishing her Valentine's gift. 'Oooh, Mr Ambassador, with these out-of-date Iranian chocolates you are really spoiling us! I don't think so somehow.'

'Oh, don't you . . .'

'*Goal to WEST BROMWICH ALBION. WEST BROMWICH ALBION lead one goal to nil.*'

To Belle's surprise, rather than returning to the computer to make a substitution or a tactical change, Johnny switched it off.

'You have got to be one of the most spoilt, ungrateful brats I have ever known.'

'What?' Johnny's harsh words whistled about her face like a slap, causing the air to rush from her lungs in shock. 'How dare you,' was all she could manage to gasp.

'You know what, Belle, I'm not some fucking Prince Charming who's going to waltz in here every Valentine's Day laden with flowers and gifts just because Clinton Cards say I should. I'm just a normal bloke, stuck in a job I hate, trying to do the best for my family. I'm sorry if that's not glamorous enough for you, but you ought to try living in the real world for a bit.'

'Living in the real world?' Belle retorted, sufficiently recovered from her verbal winding. 'Now what real world would that be? The one where

I'm stuck at home all day long while your career goes from strength to strength? The world where I constantly come second best to a game. A *game*, for Christ's sake. Have you any idea how demoralising it is to have to explain to your friends that your husband won't actually be with you on your thirtieth birthday because he's playing a poxy game?'

'It's not just a game . . .'

'Oh, don't give me that "it's more important than life and death" bollocks. What could possibly be more important than your own family?'

Johnny got to his feet, a towering inferno of rage in his work shirt and Wolves pants. 'You don't get it, do you? I don't have anything else. I hate my job. I hate it. I have to go into that office day after day and listen to those stupid twats droning on about the amount of commission they've earned or the number of birds they've shagged. And if that isn't bad enough, every month the bosses put our targets up, so every month I have to bullshit even more. It does my head in, Belle. Don't you remember what it's like, or have you conveniently wiped it from your memory?'

Belle stared at him blankly. Of course she remembered what it was like in the dog-eat-dog world of sales, but she'd assumed things had improved for Johnny since he'd been promoted to team leader. He'd certainly never voiced any discontent before – well, not this strongly anyway. Before she had a chance to respond, Johnny continued with his verbal barrage.

'Of course, it's okay for you, isn't it? I mean, while I've got the responsibility of paying the mortgage every month you can just swan around here playing at your dream job, getting paid in sausage vouchers. Let's face it, Belle, the most stressful decision you have to make each week is whether to get *OK!* or *Hello!* magazine. If I didn't have my football and a get-together with some ordinary lads every week I'd go insane.'

Belle glanced nervously at the coffee table, where both *Hello!* and *OK!* were proudly on display. Luckily Johnny seemed too blind with fury to notice them.

'I've been working bloody hard to try and get my career off the ground,' she offered cautiously. 'I know it's a job I enjoy, but it doesn't make it any easier. I've had to do it all myself, and look after Harry and you and this place. And I've got another client since the Lemon Zinger success so it shouldn't be long before I'm making a regular income.'

'Oh yeah, great – we're never going to want for sausages or bog rolls again,' Johnny replied sarcastically.

Belle smarted. When Mark Morrison's friend at Pattingham Paper Products had offered her a freelance contract she had assumed he was the director of a stationery firm, not a toilet roll factory. 'I don't think you're being very fair,' she said quietly. 'I could just laze about on the sofa all day eating Hobnobs and watching *Tricia*. At least I'm getting off my arse trying to do something with my life.'

Johnny sank down on to the end of the sofa like a deflated whoopee cushion. 'Exactly – don't you see how lucky you are to be able to do that? God, what I wouldn't give to be able to jack in that crappy job and try and make something of *my* life.'

'But you have,' Belle responded, baffled. 'How many other people of your age earn the sort of money you're on?'

'I'm not talking about money – I'm talking about dreams. I have to tell you, Belle, when I was a nipper I did not run around the park pretending to sell the other kids telecoms solutions. I was Bobby Charlton scoring the winning goal at Wembley, I was Pelé rising like a salmon to score the opening goal in the 1970 World Cup – I was Kenny Hibbitt scoring against Man City in the 1974 League Cup Final.' Johnny suddenly seemed dangerously close to tears as he held his head in his hands. 'I know it may seem pathetic to you, but playing for Rayners Park is the closest I'm going to get to living my dream.'

Belle let out a laugh.

'Oh, great – I try and explain how I'm feeling and all you can do is take the piss,' Johnny shouted as he got to his feet.

'No, no, sit down. I wasn't laughing at you. Well, I was, but I was laughing at me too,' Belle attempted to explain.

'What do you mean?'

'Well, look at the pair of us – there's you dreaming of being Pelé and ending up playing for Rayners Park and there's me dreaming of being PR to the stars and ending up writing press releases for lemon-flavoured sausages and bog rolls.'

Johnny chuckled. 'Hmmm, lemon-flavoured bog roll, now there's an idea.'

They both looked at each other and laughed, the type of nervous laughter normally associated with funerals and fatal diagnoses.

'I do love you, you know,' Johnny muttered. 'You and Harry – you're everything to me. I might not always show it, but —'

'I know.' Belle watched him gazing forlornly at his lap and she suddenly realised that the intensity of feeling that had been so glaringly absent with Luke was hovering between them, right there, and the best thing was – it was between her and her *husband*. Belle was still in love with her football-obsessed, rancid-arsed husband, and it felt great.

'Come here, you silly old sod,' she said, stretching out her arms. Johnny shuffled nervously along the sofa and took her hands in his.

'Belle, there's something I've got to ask you.'

'Yes?'

'Have you met someone else?'

Belle's heart skipped a beat. 'What do you mean?'

'Another bloke. Have you met another bloke?'

'What on earth gave you that idea?'

'Oh, I don't know – it's just that you've seemed different lately, more distant, colder. And we haven't shagged since last millennium.'

Belle grimaced at Johnny's crude exaggeration before realising that technically speaking he was of course correct.

'I thought you might have found yourself some poncy Neil Diamond look-alike or something.'

Belle laughed and pulled Johnny closer to her. God, his eyes were green – not that unlike Brad Pitt's, in fact. 'Come here,' she murmured, closing her eyes and waiting to feel his lips on hers.

'Belle.'

'Yes?'

'Can I ask you one more thing?'

'Yes. What?'

'Have you seen my 1980 league-winning Subbuteo team – I can't seem to find it anywhere.'

'For God's sake, Johnny, just shut up and kiss me!'

42

It was hard to believe it was only the first week in March. Even the estate seemed bearable – the clear blue sky and brilliant sunshine really bringing the grafitti to life and beautifully highlighting the burnt-out carcasses of abandoned vehicles. Picking her way through the shards of glass twinkling like fairy lights all over the children's playground, Anna smiled down at Grace.

'Hally! Hally!' Grace chirruped excitedly from her buggy.

'Yes, poppet, we'll see Harry in a minute. Mummy's just got to buy some stamps first.'

It wasn't just the weather that had improved in the past two weeks. Like the first crocus of spring, a glimmer of hope had cautiously probed its way into Anna's mind. The letter from D.C. Thomson had given her something to focus on – a flickering light at the end of her tunnel of gloom. If she concentrated hard enough she could just make out the words EMERGENCY EXIT.

As Anna swung the buggy around the corner, expertly avoiding the used condom by the foot of the slide, her heart sank. A gang of kids appeared to be holding some kind of huddled debate right outside the newsagent's. Anna took a deep breath while the familiar mantra filled her mind – *avoid all eye contact, avoid all eye contact*. With her heart performing its usual military-style tattoo, she shuffled past the boarded-up bookie's, the launderette and the chippy. Out of the corner of her eye she saw a cluster of designer trainers shift slightly to allow her past. To her immense relief they continued with their conversation, obviously far too preoccupied with their hushed talk of charlie and E to even notice her.

As Anna attempted to open the shop door with one hand and manoeuvre Grace's buggy inside with the other, a familiar voice cut through the muttering.

'Anna?'

'Tom?'

Like an extremely alternative Scout leader, Tom stood holding court in the middle of the group. Although it had only been a week since she'd last seen him, Anna was struck by how different he appeared. Perhaps it was the fact that he was surrounded by kids, or maybe it was the dark shadows lurking beneath his eyes and in the hollows of his cheeks which gave him the appearance of a caricature of himself as an old man.

'So,' Tom said with a half-hearted attempt at a swagger, 'how's my little princess?' He stooped down to kiss Grace on top of her head.

To Anna's dismay Grace gave a piercing scream

and kicked out at Tom. Tom stepped back, shocked and slightly embarrassed.

'She's a bit irritable today – teething,' Anna explained feebly. But somewhere deep within her a little voice couldn't help remarking, *Well, what the hell do you expect? You hardly show your face from week to week. No wonder your own daughter doesn't recognise you.*

Tom cleared his throat and nodded to the kids. 'I'll see you later, lads.'

Muttering 'Later, Tommo,' the gang shuffled off towards the play area to resume barbecuing the bin.

'So is everything all right?' Tom asked, slightly sheepishly, Anna noticed. 'Do you need anything? Cash?'

Instinctively Anna nodded and immediately felt a stab of self-loathing. She and Grace needed more than cash, they needed Tom at home with them, not hanging about with kids and God knows who else.

Tom took a wad of notes from his pocket and began peeling some away.

Anna gasped. For the past week she had been living on a packet of fish fingers and some stale hot cross buns while all the time Tom had been walking about like a mobile cashpoint. 'Are you sure?' she asked, her hunger far outweighing any residue of pride as she grabbed the notes.

'Yeah, no worries. Things are pretty flush at the moment. So, er, has my football kit been washed? Only I've got a match this afternoon.'

'Yeah, I know – I've laid it out on the bed ready for you.'

'Nice one. Well, I'll be off, then. I won't be back tonight, by the way – I'll probably see you tomorrow.' Tom ruffled Grace's hair. 'See you later, Princess. See you later.' He nodded awkwardly to Anna before turning on his heel and heading towards the flat.

All the way to the postbox Anna felt a rage welling inside her; initially directed at Tom, but as she reran their conversation through her head it turned upon herself. How many other women would put up with their partners disappearing off for days on end with no explanation, only to return waving a wad of notes and enquiring whether their football kit had been washed? How many other women would have been desperate enough to take the money, no questions asked, and have the football kit ready on the bed? How Tom must laugh about her with his new-found mates. 'I've got a right one here,' he'd probably sneered when he saw her coming. 'She's such a doormat I don't even have to bother giving her any bullshit excuses – I can just come and go as I please.'

Anna's hands trembled with a mixture of fury and fear as she withdrew an envelope from her bag. She'd show him, she'd show the lot of them. D.C. Thomson didn't think she was pathetic; they actually wanted to see some more of her work. Anna slapped a stamp onto the envelope and before she had time for any second thoughts crammed it into the postbox and let go.

Of course, as soon as it thudded to the bottom a swarm of fears buzzed into her mind, chasing away her feelings of indignation. What the hell had she done? The comic strip that seemed fine only a few hours previously suddenly became riddled with flaws. The central character was clichéd, the storyline was naff, the humour was corny. In short, it was crap. Her one big chance and she had blown it. She was still a week inside her deadline as well. Anna could have kicked herself for posting it so soon. Why hadn't she taken advantage of that week to make some much-needed improvements? Perhaps she should lurk about the postbox until the next collection and explain to the postman that she had made a dreadful mistake, but at 2.30 on a Saturday afternoon she could be in for quite a long wait. With a heavy heart, she continued on her way.

'Hally! Hally!' Grace shrieked as they turned the corner into Emerald Avenue. The route to Belle's house had been a well-trodden one over the past few weeks. At Belle's behest Anna had turned up on the dot of ten o'clock each morning to have Grace whisked out of her arms and be dispatched upstairs to the spare room to draw. On the first day she had stared blankly at the sheet of paper in front of her, racked with guilt at having lumbered Belle with Grace. After a couple of hours she had flung her pencil to the floor and marched downstairs to take

Grace back home. She had been completely unprepared for the scene that greeted her in the living room. It was a veritable Sindy and Barbie fest, the room awash with pink plastic and glittery fabric. Seated right in the middle of it all were a giggling Belle and Grace. Anna couldn't decide who looked the happier – Grace chewing on Ken's leg or Belle painting Barbie's nails with a red felt-tip. When Belle spotted Anna lurking in the doorway she whispered with a grin, 'This beats Thomas the bloody Tank Engine any day. Now get back upstairs and get cracking!'

And, having finally run out of obstacles and excuses, that was exactly what Anna had done. Even the fact that the character had to be football based hadn't fazed her. She pored over Johnny's old Roy of the Rovers annuals for inspiration and studied his soccer coaching manuals for useful tips until slowly but surely a new character began to sketch himself out in her mind. An older version of Harry-Billy, Hat-Tricky Ricky was a lovable rogue who was far more skilled at putting his opponents off with his outrageous antics than he was at actually playing football.

The past three weeks had flown by, and suddenly Anna had her first storyboard completed and the rough outlines for another two. Although it was football based, Belle had loved it. 'You've got to send it in now,' she had urged. 'Supposing they've got other artists on trial? It would look really impressive to get yours in first. It would show them that you can beat a deadline.'

Her words had seemed full of sense at the time and her enthusiasm had been infectious. As she drew level with Belle's house, Anna prayed that the impending Football Widows meeting would somehow help to replenish her rapidly fading enthusiasm.

43

'It's the first piece in my Springtide collection,' Maz announced, beaming proudly. The other Football Widows sat rooted to their seats on Belle's patio, freeze framed with mouths agape, like a naff advertisement for garden furniture.

Wrenching her arm back to life, Belle raised her glass to her lips and took a hasty gulp of wine. 'It's lovely, Maz – really original.'

It was original, all right, even by Maz's sartorial standards. Ginny's Christmas gift of sky-blue satin hadn't just been distressed, it had been positively distraught.

'The bleached bits are supposed to be clouds,' Maz offered helpfully.

'Oh, I see – and what about the shredded bits?' Belle enquired, pointing to the bottom of what could at best be described as a kimono and at worst a marquee. 'What do they symbolise?'

'Oh.' Maz blushed and looked slightly uncomfortable. 'I suppose all they really symbolise is that I still ain't got the hang of hemming.' And with that she threw back her head and roared, her bright yellow hair perfectly complimenting the ring of daffodils attached to her sash.

Stifling a giggle, Anna reached under the table and pretended to wipe Grace's nose.

'What the hell have you done to my satin?' Ginny's voice squawked across the patio like that of a strangulated starling. 'Have you any idea how much that cost?'

Belle and Anna glanced at one another and held their breath.

'Of course I haven't. I get my fabric from Wembley market, darling, not poncy bleeding Harrods.'

'Poncy? Bleeding? Harrods?' Ginny repeated, aghast.

'It's called imagination, Virginia, letting yourself go. You want to try it one day. Bleeding hell, ever since Belle started this Football Widows thing you've sat there all high and mighty in your Dolce and fucking Gabbana, bragging about your flashy job and flicking your ironed hair, but do you know what, I wouldn't want to swap places with you for nothing. Me and Darren might not have a lot and we might not drink in All Bar One Nine Two or whatever it's called, but at least we know how to have a laugh.' Maz plonked herself down on a sunlounger, causing several daffodils to burst forth from her sash.

Like spectators at a particularly gripping Wimbledon rally, Belle and Anna turned to face Ginny, but to their surprise, rather than rising up in preparation for her return volley, Ginny sat hunched in her chair like an old woman.

'I can't help it,' she stuttered. 'I don't know how

else to be. I look at all of you sometimes and I feel so jealous.'

Belle and Anna stared at her, mouths agape.

'Are you taking the piss?' Maz barked.

'No, of course not. I hate my life, I detest my job.'

'But what about your hair?' Maz offered, her tone softening a fraction.

'Oh, don't talk to me about my hair. It takes me hours to get it this straight. You know those pointless little charts you get in newspapers sometimes telling you how many years of your life you spend asleep or on the toilet or whatever? Well, I reckon by the time I die I will have spent at least two decades operating a set of straightening irons! And I will have spent the entire Third World debt on relaxing lotion and serum. Then, of course, I have the nightmare of my roots. I may as well take up residence at Toni and Guy. You don't know how lucky you are, Maz, being brave enough to put your faith in all those cheap home dyes. I really envy all of you for genuinely not caring about the state of your hair.' Completely oblivious to the three sets of raised eyebrows surrounding her, Ginny continued, 'You're all so chilled out. Take you, Belle. I wish I could live in this kind of chaos, I really do, but I just can't bear mess, it makes me feel physically ill.'

Belle glanced around the patio in shock. Okay, so there were a few toys strewn around and the honeysuckle did seem to be rampaging rather than clambering, but she had spent nearly fifteen minutes that morning sweeping away all the dead leaves and other winter residue.

'And you, Maz.' Maz stared at Ginny defensively. 'You might think that I look down on you, but I envy you too. No, really, I do. I think it's so cool the way you don't let your weight problem get you down. I only have to feel slightly bloated and I book myself in for a wheat allergy test. And Anna . . .'

Anna's face began to prickle with heat.

'I wish to God I could be as . . . well, as dependent as you obviously are on Tom. It must be great to have so much faith in a man. But no matter how hard I try I just can't imagine being subservient to Mike. Even though I loathe my job, the thought of having no financial independence absolutely terrifies the life out of me.'

'Who the hell do you think you are?' The voice sounded like Anna's and the words certainly seemed to emanate from Anna's direction, but nobody, herself included, could quite believe that she had uttered them.

'What did you just say?' Ginny asked, out of shock rather than anger.

The blood continued to flood Anna's face, rising up through her cheeks until a red veil covered her eyes. She was so sick and tired of being patronised. There was something about the smugness in Ginny's voice that reminded her of Tom: *Has my football kit been washed? – I won't be back tonight, by the way –*

I just can't imagine being subservient to Mike. Subservient!

'I said, who the hell do you think you are? How dare you insult us all like that? How dare you patronise me?'

'But I wasn't patronising you,' Ginny insisted.

'Yes, you were. You don't know anything about me or my relationship. You've got no right to jump to conclusions like that.' Anna sank back into her chair, fighting hard to restrain her trembling lip.

'But I wasn't insulting you all, I was complimenting you, I was telling you how much I envied you, for Christ's sake,' Ginny said, totally perplexed.

'Complimenting us? By saying that Belle is messy, Maz is fat and I'm some subservient little wimp?'

'Go, Anna,' Maz murmured in approval.

'I did not say you were a subservient little wimp, I said that I envied the way you could allow yourself to become so dependent on a man, and I meant it. You must really love and trust Tom to put yourself in that position. That's why I envy you, because no matter how hard I try I could never fully trust Mike.' Ginny's voice began to soar like the whistle of a slightly hysterical canary. 'And the worst thing is, he's done nothing wrong. I just can't ever seem to escape from my bloody childhood fears . . .' Ginny's voice finally petered out into a sob.

For a split second everyone sat in stunned silence before springing into life, a myriad of hands proffering tissues, wine, a soggy Monster Munch (Harry's contribution) and several slightly awkward pats on the back.

'I'm really sorry,' Ginny said, finally regaining her composure. 'I honestly never meant to be rude about any of you – I think I might be going slightly mad.'

'No, love,' Maz soothed, 'I think you're finally on the road to recovery.'

The two adversaries looked at each other and smiled.

'Friends?' Ginny asked hesitantly.

'Yeah, why not,' Maz said graciously.

Belle clapped her hands together and laughed. 'This is great, it's just like that episode of *EastEnders* where Bianca and Natalie finally made up after years of not talking.'

'Bianca and Natalie?' Ginny asked, aghast. 'I really don't see any resemblance . . .'

'Ginny!' the others groaned in unison.

'Sorry,' she muttered sheepishly.

'All you have to do is learn to let go a little bit at a time,' Belle said soothingly. 'There's nothing wrong with following your heart from time to time, you know. If you love Mike, prove it to him by putting a little trust in him. If you hate your job then get another one . . .'

'If you hate your hair have a crop,' Maz butted in helpfully.

Ginny smiled weakly. 'You're right – not you, Maz, although I might be tempted to go back to being brunette at least. Okay, well, what would you say if I came up with a way of leaving my job and providing the Football Widows with a coup d'état all in one go?'

'I'd say what the hell's wrong with fish and chips?' Everyone looked at Maz blankly. 'I bleeding hate that French food,' she explained, before cramming a large lump of Brie into her mouth.

44

It was early Monday morning and the Rayners Park Estate was awakening to the usual dawn chorus of breaking glass and blasphemy. Anna peered over the balcony to try to locate the source of the commotion. Down below, the milkman stood stamping his feet and brandishing his baseball bat, a pool of milk seeping across the carpark, like the scene of some dreadful dairy massacre.

'Come back here, you little toerags!' he raged, but his assailants had long gone. Anna sighed. Even the milkman looked like an extra from a Guy Ritchie film – she was quite surprised he didn't drive about in a specially customised armoured milk-float, clad in full combat gear. She let herself into the flat humming 'Ernie' and grinning from ear to ear. She hadn't expected to find Tom at home, and she certainly hadn't expected to find Tom kneeling over Grace's toy table with a rolled-up twenty-pound note shoved up his left nostril.

'Tom?'

Tom looked up. A thin line of snot, glistening like a slug's trail, trickled its way down from his nose to the corner of his mouth. 'All right, babes,' he gasped, wiping the snot away with the back of his hand. 'Where have you been? Where's Gracie? It's a bit early for you to be out and about, isn't it?'

'What are you doing?' Anna asked incredulously.

'Well, I thought that was pretty obvious. I'm giving my day a bit of a kick-start,' Tom replied with a defiant stare.

'But . . . but that's Grace's table.'

'So?'

'She eats off there. How could you?'

'How could I what?' Tom stood up suddenly, a little too suddenly, and leaned against the sideboard to steady himself.

Anna pictured Grace running a chubby little finger through the spilt 'sugar' on the table before licking it clean. 'How could you put that stuff on her table? What if she ate some of it?'

Tom pulled himself upright. 'I don't think you're in any position to get shitty with me, Anna. Or should I say *Ms Grant*.'

Ms Grant? 'Wh-what do you mean?' she asked, trying desperately to ignore the sickening realisation creeping over her.

Tom grabbed a scrunched-up piece of paper from the sideboard and flung it at her. 'Well, I don't really know. Why don't you tell me?'

Anna unfolded the paper. One look at the letter heading confirmed her worst fears. It was from a publisher. She'd assumed she'd received the last of them by now. In the past two months they'd arrived in a steady stream, but given Tom's nocturnal habits he was either out or out for the count whenever the postman called. It was bloody typical that one should arrive today. Anna skimmed through the letter: *Thank you for your submission . . . regret to inform you . . . currently no vacancies . . . all the best . . . etc., etc.*

'So, Ms Grant,' Tom sneered, 'looks like you've failed again, eh? How long have I been telling you you can't draw for shit? But you just wouldn't listen, would you? No, you had to sneak around behind my back sending your crappy little pictures to some poncy publishers. Who do you think you are, eh? Vincent fucking Van Gogh? And' – Tom leered at her – 'what the hell are you doing using my name?'

Anna felt the salty trickle of blood on her tongue as her teeth buried themselves into her bottom lip. *Bastard. Bastard. Bastard.*

'As if I'd ever marry a pathetic little drip like you. It's been bad enough having you hanging round my neck like some fucking noose ever since you got yourself pregnant. Talk about falling for the oldest trick in the book.'

'But you wanted a baby. You were the one who said that when I left college . . .'

'I wanted to go travelling,' Tom interrupted. 'I wanted to see the world. I did not want to be lumbered with a miserable cow and a snivelling brat.'

'A snivelling brat?' Anna repeated, unable to believe what she had just heard. What the hell was happening to Tom? He had never said a bad word about Grace before. She was supposed to be his little girl, his little 'princess' – any sniping had always been exclusively reserved for her.

Even Tom looked momentarily stunned. 'You know I didn't mean that. I love Gracie to bits, you know I do.' He slammed his fist down on the sideboard, causing the lava lamp to shudder. 'See what you do to me? You make me so mad you're even turning me against my own daughter. You're sick, you are. Sick. What am I gonna have to do to make you learn?'

A bolt of fear coursed through Anna's body before exiting her mouth in the form of an apology. 'I'm sorry, I . . .'

But what exactly was she sorry for? Leaving college when he asked her to? Obligingly getting herself pregnant when he requested they start a family? Or should she apologise for bringing his daughter up single-handedly while turning a blind eye to his frequent disappearing acts?

Anna looked at Tom – his once lustrous hair hanging lankly about his haggard face, his stained T-shirt, his hand inside his jeans pocket scratching his balls. Suddenly everything about him repulsed her.

'Go on, then,' she said, unable to calm the slight quaver in her voice.

'Go on what?'

'Do it. Do whatever you have to do.'

'You what?' Tom gaped at her in bewilderment.

Anna didn't care any more. She was so sick of this crap, of living in constant fear. It was as if the last two years of her life had been spent on some horrific tour of duty. Well, she was sick of dodging snipers' bullets and picking her way through minefields day after day. It was time to admit defeat. Let him do it. Let him do his worst – then finally this nightmare might come to an end. Anna closed her eyes and clenched her fists, her nails digging into her palms like blades. He was probably raising his fist right now, ready to take a swing. She felt a burning sensation in her bladder. Where would the punch land? Which side of her face would he choose? Maybe it would be both. Or maybe she'd have her whole head slammed against the wall like last time. Her heart beat like a grandfather clock counting down the seconds. *One, two, three*, she counted along in her head, desperately trying to remain focused, *four, five, six*. But still nothing happened. Anna squinted out of the corner of one eye. Tom was slumped over the sideboard clutching his face. She watched him with a detached curiosity. Could he be having some kind of reaction to the coke – an over-dose even? A glimmer of hope shivered its way up her spine.

'Tom?'

Tom spun around, his face slick with snot and tears.

'What's happening to me, Anna?' he snorted.

'You've got to help me. I need you, sweetheart, I need you.'

Anna watched him snivel. He was pathetic. Pathetic. 'You need *me*?' she asked incredulously.

'Yeah, babes, I do. I really do. You know I wouldn't hurt you. You and Gracie, you're everything to me.'

'So what have the last two years been about, then?'

'Eh?'

'Ever since I had Grace all you've done is go out of your way to hurt me. You've lied, bullied, cheated—'

'I haven't, I—'

'See, there you go again, lying to me. I'm not completely stupid, Tom. So where the hell do you go every night, then, if you've not been having an affair?'

Tom looked at the carpet, slowly tracing a beige swirl with his toe. Finally he spoke, his voice barely more than a whisper. 'It's over, Anna, she doesn't mean anything, she's just an old slapper. It was all a big mistake. You're the one for me, Anna – always have been, always will be.'

So it was true. Tom may as well have beaten her senseless; her entire body stung. All this time a tiny part of her had been harbouring the hope that it wasn't true; that he had been staying with friends or one of his brothers, that he just needed a bit of space and time to sort his head out. But all along he really had been sleeping with someone else. All of those images she'd tortured herself with night after night were true. Anna looked at him, sordid and snivelling in front of her, and all she felt was loathing and disgust, but for once it wasn't directed at herself. She wanted to lash out and hurt him for a change. She didn't need this pathetic snot-ridden mess – she never had done.

'Help me, Anna, please,' Tom begged. 'I know I've got problems, but it's not my fault, you know what I went through as a nipper.'

'You've got to be joking,' Anna retorted, grabbing a handful of Grace's toys from the playpen.

'What are you doing?'

'I'll tell you what I'm doing. I'm helping myself for once.'

'You what?'

'You heard. I'm helping myself and my daughter and I'm getting the hell out of here.'

'Oh yeah? And where are you going to go?'

'Didn't you know? Oh, but how could you? You've been with your tart all weekend. I moved out yesterday. I only came back to pick up a few more things.'

Tom snorted with laughter, his new-found humility rapidly evaporating. 'You've moved out? Where to? What the hell could you afford?'

'Oh, I know, stupid little me with my shitty little pictures and no job. How could I possibly afford to get my own place? Well, guess what? Not everybody seems to share your low opinion of me, Tom. In fact two publishers have just offered me freelance contracts. Not bad for a pathetic little drip, eh?'

Tom stood staring at her in disbelief, the cocky grin slipping from his face. A loud hammering on the door broke the silence, causing them both to jump.

'Anna, are you okay?' Belle called through the letterbox.

'Oh, I should've known that jumped-up little cow was behind all this,' Tom snarled. 'Well, I'll soon sort her out.' He marched to the door and flung it open. 'What the—?'

Belle, Ginny and Maz barged past him into the living room.

'Are you okay?' Belle asked anxiously, putting her arm around Anna's shoulders.

Anna nodded, gulping back a sob of relief and willing herself to hang on in there for a few more minutes.

'So who the fuck are you lot – Rent-a-Witch?' Tom asked with a smirk.

'You'd better fucking believe it, mate,' Maz snarled, her puce hair perfectly matching her cheeks.

'So you must be the wife-beater,' Ginny shrilled in a diamond-cut voice, as if she were socialising at some suburban soirée rather than lurking in the living room of a North London high-rise.

'You what?' Tom glanced at Ginny nervously.

'Oh, Anna's told us all about you, you low-down piece of shit,' Ginny continued breezily. 'How you like to bully women, you inadequate little scumbag.'

Anna wanted to scream at Ginny to stop – didn't she realise she was playing with fire talking to Tom like that? When she had finally confided in the others about her relationship with Tom, and they had plotted her great escape, she had begged them not to say anything too provocative. But instead of raising his fist, Tom's face broke into the sweetest of smiles.

'Look, I'm really sorry, love, but I'm afraid you obviously haven't been given the full story here. Anna's not the most stable of people, you see. She can't help it. It's an attention-seeking thing. I don't know what she's been telling you, but if you think I'd do anything to hurt her you couldn't be farther from the truth. Could they, sweetheart?' Tom stared at Anna intently.

'Oooh, listen to him trying to deflect responsibility. How tediously predictable,' Ginny mocked.

Belle laughed. 'It's classic *Oprah* material, isn't it? Still, what could we really expect?'

'Tell me, Tom, are you as dull and predictable as this in the sack?' Maz added, much to Anna's horror. She just wanted to get out of there as quickly as possible. Why were they going out of their way to wind Tom up when she'd warned them what he was like?

'Yeah, is that what's behind all this?' Ginny added. 'Isn't little Tommy up to scratch?'

Tom stood motionless as his face passed through various shades of purple. 'You'll be sorry for this,' he muttered to Anna, as he grabbed his jacket from the sofa.

'Oh, Tom, yet again so predictable,' Ginny sneered.

'And so fucking wrong,' Maz snarled, squaring up to him. 'If anything happens to Anna here, you'll be the one who's sorry. You see, the lads at the football club don't think too highly of wife-beaters. To be perfectly honest, my Darren's itching to get his hands on you. But I said no, let's give him one last chance. So here's the deal, Tom. You let Anna go and make a fresh start on her own and the lads will leave you alone. So how about it, Tom? What do you say?'

Tom looked at the Football Widows staring at him and edged towards the door. 'I'd say I'm better off fucking out of it,' he replied, with a half-hearted attempt at a scowl.

'Excellent,' Belle said, beaming. 'Oh, and Tom . . .' Tom paused in the doorway. 'I wouldn't bother showing up for the football club trip to Brighton if I were you. I don't think you'd be too welcome.'

And with one final slam of the door he was gone. Anna listened to his footsteps retreating along the balcony and suddenly it dawned on her – she would never have to hear that sound again. Nor would she have to jump at the sound of his key in the lock, or the clatter of tools as he slung his workbag down in the hall. She was free at last, and she didn't know whether to laugh or cry. So she did both.

'Oh, look, she's upset,' said Belle, rushing over to wrap her in a hug.

'It's for the best, love, it really is,' Maz soothed, clutching them both to her more than ample bosom.

'Yes, come on, Anna, where's your girl power?' Ginny added, scuffing her feet awkwardly on a particularly threadbare piece of carpet.

Belle, Maz and Anna looked at each other and laughed.

'Blimey, check out old Virginia Spice,' Maz chortled.

Anna smiled through her tears. 'I'm fine, honestly, I just need to get out of here, that's all.'

'Right, then – let's get the car loaded up. What do you want to take with you?' Belle asked, springing into action.

Anna cast her eyes about the dingy living room. She felt like a prisoner being asked upon release if they wanted a memento of their stay. The very notion suddenly seemed absurd. She glanced fondly at the television, her cell mate for the past year, before turning to Belle. 'Do you know what? I don't think I'll bother after all.'

45

'Belle, have you seen my vintage 1974 League Cup Final replica shirt?' Johnny bellowed down the stairs.

Belle glanced across the breakfast bar at Anna and grinned.

'No, dear. Isn't it hanging in the back of the wardrobe?'

A bare-chested Johnny came tearing into the room like Peter Stringfellow possessed. 'I have to find it. Don't you understand – 1974 was one of our sweetest victories of recent times. We'll never win today if I'm not wearing it.'

Belle stared at him quizzically, while continuing to butter a slice of toast. 'And you take the piss out of me for being superstitious? You'll be wanting to cut off one of Thumper's paws next.'

Anna glanced at Johnny anxiously. Although she'd been staying at Belle's for three weeks now, she still found it hard to accept the casual way in which the two of them traded insults and sarcasm. She had spent half the time on tenterhooks, waiting for Johnny to erupt. She put her uneaten Pop Tart back on her plate and prepared to dive for cover – surely when Johnny discovered the fate of his vintage 1974 whatever it would finally push him over the edge?

'Where the hell can it have got to?' Johnny wailed, for some strange reason looking in the dishwasher. 'I haven't worn it since Harry's christening.'

Belle casually topped up her glass of orange juice.

'I really don't know, Johnny, but to be perfectly honest I can't see what the big deal is – you've got hundreds of Wolves tops up there.'

'You can't see what the big deal is?' Johnny's eyes protruded from his head like a pair of gobstoppers on springs. 'Today Wolverhampton Wanderers are playing in the FA Cup Final – the last-ever Cup Final to be played at the world-famous Twin Towers – and you can't see the big deal? What on earth is the matter with you?'

Belle winked at Anna. 'Okay, I'm sorry, I suppose it is a major deal for someone accustomed to a lifetime of failure, but surely you must have another top that's synonymous with good fortune?'

Johnny scratched his head and thought for a moment. 'I suppose there's always the 1992 away strip that I wore when we stuffed the Albion four–two,' he mused before bounding back upstairs.

'God, that was close,' Anna sighed, before returning to her breakfast.

Belle laughed. 'That was nothing. Think what he's going to say later on.'

'Oh, don't – do you think we'll pull it off?'

'Of course we will – we're the Football Widows, aren't we?'

Anna nodded and grinned. 'Listen, Belle, thanks for everything you've done for me and Grace, letting us stay here while I sort my life out and all that.'

'Don't be daft. It's been great having you here; having somebody to talk to who doesn't live and breathe sport for a change. I'm going to really miss you when you go, and I don't know how Harry's going to cope without Grace.'

Anna looked at Harry and Grace creating an interesting mosaic effect in Frosties on the kitchen floor. 'Ealing's only a few stops down the Piccadilly Line, and just think of all the new shops we'll have to explore,' she said in what she hoped passed for the relaxed and confident tones of a freelance artist/single parent about to face the world on her own two feet.

'Yeah, well, you make sure you treat me to a whole new designer wardrobe when you get your first six-figure royalty cheque.' Belle laughed, buttering yet another slice of toast. 'God, what is wrong with me this morning? I can't stop eating – it must be all the nervous energy.'

Johnny re-entered the room clad in a sky-blue skin-tight nylon top complete with obligatory black wolf's-head motif.

'Oh my God!' Belle shrieked, trying to recall if she had ever subjected the 1992 away strip to a boil wash. She was pretty certain she hadn't, but it did seem obscenely tight.

Johnny gazed morosely at the undisputable beginnings of a paunch. 'I tell you what, Belle, I'm going on a major fitness campaign this summer. Ever since I turned thirty I can't look at a pie without putting on a stone.'

'Not to mention a pint,' Belle added cynically.

'That reminds me, where did I put those cans?'

'Down there,' Belle responded, pointing to a Thresher's bag in the corner. 'Are you really going to drink all those on the minibus?'

Johnny grimaced. 'Yeah.'

'But it's only nine o'clock in the morning.'

'Tell me about it, but it's traditional, isn't it? You can't go on a football club trip and drink pop – the other lads would have a field day.'

'That just says it all, really, doesn't it,' Belle said to Anna with a look of mock disgust. 'I bet every bloke on that minibus will be feeling as sick as a dog by the time they get to Brighton, but not one of them will have the guts to drink Coke.'

Johnny laughed and grabbed a slice of toast from Belle's plate. 'Right. I'm off, then. Just think, when you next see me Wolves will be champions once more. COME ON, WANDERERS! So what are you two up to today, then? No, don't tell me – you're going on a shopping spree followed by a night in gossiping and watching Jerry Springer, heh, heh!'

Belle smirked. If only he knew the truth. If only he knew that while he and the rest of Rayners Park Football Club watched the FA Cup Final pissed up in some bar in Brighton, she and her fellow Football Widows would be watching it live from an executive suite at Wembley. In the words of some tedious soccer bore or another – he'd be positively sick as a parrot!

46

'Excellent news!' Ginny gasped as she burst into the executive suite. 'Dozy Dave's the chief sound engineer.'

Belle, Maz and Anna looked up from their Irish coffees and smiled. Never had poor Ginny looked so flustered.

'Isn't he the one who put the Tannoy out for Wayne Kerr during Euro '96?' Belle enquired.

'Exactly,' Ginny replied. 'So, have you got the CD?'

'Of course I have, don't panic,' Belle soothed, offering her the miniature silver platter of after-dinner mints. 'Now, are you sure Darren Day's still got laryngitis?'

Ginny crammed a handful of mints into her mouth. 'Yeah, he's down in his dressing room practising his miming as we speak.'

'Ah, poor love,' Maz chortled. 'Here, Anna, gi's some more of that champagne.'

'Go easy, Maz – you're supposed to be a top corporate hospitality executive, not some down-and-out wino,' Ginny snapped.

'Sorry, boss. Wass the name of our company again?' Maz enquired between belches.

'Full Time Hospitality,' the others chorused.

'Okay, well, I guess I'd better go and do it, then,' Ginny muttered, slightly less than enthusiastically. 'Here, give us some of that champagne.' She grabbed the bottle from Maz and took at least two swigs.

Anna sighed. 'Oh, Ginny. You missed such a wonderful meal.'

'Sod the meal,' Belle retorted. 'What about the stars? I just saw Louise Adams *and* Beppe Di Marco in the Grandstand Bar!'

Ginny stared at Belle blankly. She'd obviously been in this god-forsaken job far too long – she couldn't remember the last time a celebrity sighting had aroused the slightest flicker of interest. 'Well, wish me luck – and if I'm not back in the next half-hour you'd better come and bail me out from Wembley cop shop.'

Belle got to her feet and pressed a CD into Ginny's hand. 'Break a leg,' she whispered before giving her an encouraging hug. 'Just keep reminding yourself how much you hate this place. Think how great it will be to get one over on them.'

'Yeah, good luck,' Anna added. 'We'll all be rooting for you.'

''*Asta la vista*, baby!' Maz bellowed before slumping into the remains of her chocolate torte and raspberry coulis.

As Ginny set off on her mission and Anna bustled Maz into the toilet to splash her face with copious amounts of cold water, Belle wandered over to the tinted-glass front of their suite. Although she was loath to admit it, she couldn't help being completely overwhelmed by the scene below her. The lush green pitch with its immaculate two-tone stripes was awash with colour as cheerleaders cheered, marching bands marched, and hundreds of balloons were released into the clear blue sky. According to Ginny the pitch would have been mown twice that very morning; like Gloria Hunniford's hairdo, not a blade was out of place. And as for the noise . . . When Belle had ventured out on to the terraces earlier it had been like plummeting down a log flume at one hundred miles an hour. The roars of the crowd had rushed up to hit her in the face, leaving her gasping for breath and pulsating with adrenalin.

Talking of which . . . Belle fumbled in her handbag for her binoculars. Could that tousled blond head down below her belong to Prince William?

'Oh my God! Girls, quick!' she shrieked.

Anna and Maz jostled around her, begging for a turn with the binoculars.

'It is – it's him,' Anna cried, completely forgetting her republican leanings.

Maz grabbed the binoculars and started scanning the suites on the other side of the stadium.

'What are you doing?' Belle demanded. 'He's not over there, he's right below us.'

'Sod Prince William,' Maz retorted. 'I'm looking for Jimmy Nail. The *Sun* said he was coming here with that Sting bloke.'

'Here, give me them back,' Belle said, grabbing the binoculars and scanning the pitch. 'Oh my God, Darren Day's on his way out. Quick, we've got to get changed.'

As Darren Day made his way across the hallowed turf, he felt quite overwhelmed by the enormity of the occasion. With any luck a gig like this should kill off those Cliff Richard comparisons once and for all – the FA Cup Final was hardly a rainy day at Wimbledon. Catching laryngitis was a bit of a bugger and he was dreading having to mime. What if he was slightly out of time or, even worse, got the words wrong and ended up looking like John Redwood attempting to sing the Welsh national anthem? *Abide with me; fast falls the eventide, The darkness deepens; Lord with me abide.* He just couldn't afford to fuck up; there was too much riding on it. Not only in terms of his career – he'd just spotted Dannii Minogue in the Grandstand Bar, definite fiancée material if ever he saw it. *When other helpers fail and comforts flee.* Oh God, only five minutes to go. He was really shitting himself now. *Help of the helpless, O abide with me.*

Back in executive suite number eleven, tension was running equally high.

'I've lost my veil,' Anna cried, adjusting her black pillbox hat in the mirror.

'Here,' Maz said, throwing her some black netting. 'I made a spare one just in case.'

'Where the hell is Ginny?' Belle snapped, pacing up and down the suite. 'She should have got back by now. He's about to start singing.'

At that moment the door burst open and Ginny rushed in. She took one look at the others and burst out laughing.

'God, you look fantastic – proper widows.'

'Quick, get your veil on,' Maz ordered.

'How did you get on? Did you manage to swap them over?' Belle asked anxiously.

'Yeah, no problem. I just told Dozy Dave that Posh Spice needed some technical advice for the studio she's having built in her new house. He was off like a shot.'

'Brilliant.' Belle glanced at the television suspended from the ceiling. 'Look, he's about to start. Quick, Maz, get your banner.'

Meanwhile, as a hush fell over the Outback Bar in Brighton, Johnny was having a major attack of the goose bumps. 'Abide With Me' had to rank alongside 'Cum On Feel The Noize' as one of the most moving songs ever written – it was a shame they couldn't have got Noddy Holder to sing it, really. The hairs on the back of Johnny's neck stood to attention as Darren Day stepped up to the microphone. Johnny's chest began to swell with pride as Darren opened his mouth and began to sing.

'You Don't Bring Me Flowers' began to resonate throughout the bar.

What the fuck?

No – it couldn't be happening. But it was. Darren Day was singing that fucking song. That fucking awful song at the FA Cup Final. What the hell was he doing? But on closer examination he didn't really appear to be doing anything much, apart from opening and closing his mouth like a particularly startled goldfish. As the Wembley crowd fell silent in disbelief, Johnny could quite clearly identify the voice ricocheting about the Twin Towers – he'd heard it often enough. It was Neil bloody Diamond. Somehow Neil bloody Diamond had managed to sabotage the FA Cup Final. Johnny's entire body coursed with rage – that man seemed destined to be the bane of his life.

'Well, this is most peculiar,' Richard Keyes muttered to no one in particular before informing the viewers that the FA certainly hadn't notified Sky Sports about any change in the programme. No, Andy Gray agreed, 'Abide With Me' was down there in black and white. While they continued to ponder this bizarre twist in events, the camera panned around the stadium, from an ashen-faced Darren Day to the sea of painted faces with mouths agape, while Neil Diamond continued to bellow out about how nobody ever talked to him any more when he returned home at the end of the day.

The camera came to a brief rest on a giggling Prince William before panning upwards along the Executive Gallery. Then suddenly the camera froze before zooming in on a suite. There, behind the tinted glass, four figures dressed in full mourning attire were leaping about, swigging from bottles of champagne and high-fiving around a banner that read:

'FOOTBALL WIDOWS OF THE WORLD UNITE!'

Epilogue
End-of-Season Signing for Chelsea

For the second time that week Ginny experienced the hitherto unfamiliar sensation of fear. Not that she was necessarily complaining as she squatted over the toilet, heart pounding. Events at the FA Cup Final had proved quite a revelation. The adrenalin rush she experienced when she deposited her resignation letter on the marketing director's desk before hotfooting it down a deserted Wembley Way clad in full funeral regalia and clutching a bottle of Moët & Chandon had beaten any self-assertiveness seminar hands down. And then, going back to Belle's and for once allowing herself to get well and truly hammered while watching an ashen-faced Darren Day being comforted by Dannii Minogue every hour on Sky News – well, all in all it had been the best day of her life. She had relinquished her vice-like grip on her destiny and, rather than being left feeling vulnerable and confused, she felt unexpectedly liberated. In one final act of letting go, Ginny relaxed her bladder muscles and began to pee.

'Have you had a slash yet?' Maz's dulcet tones sliced through the bathroom door. 'Bloody hell, girl – you'll be ready to drop by the time you get out of there!'

Ginny gritted her teeth and carefully replaced the cap on the indicator. She then placed the pregnancy test on top of the cistern and proceeded to wash her hands. Perching on the edge of the bath, she watched with interest as a thin blue line emerged in the first window. Turning her attention to the adjacent empty window, Ginny couldn't help frowning – the indicator looked so horribly out of synch with only one line. To her immense relief a second blue line obligingly began to appear.

'So? Are you saucepanned up or not?' Maz yelled, jolting Ginny from her state of symmetrical nirvana.

God, that was a point, Ginny thought as she fumbled about for the instructions. What exactly did two lines mean, apart from a pleasing sense of equilibrium? Holding the pamphlet in trembling hands, she studied the indicator.

'Yes – I suppose I am,' she said, her voice quivering from a mixture of fear, shock and panic, but most of all excitement.

Maz burst into the bathroom and thumped her on the back.

'Brilliant! I always fancied designing me own maternity range.'

Anna hauled her brand-new drawing board into her brand-new living room and sighed. It may only have been a one-bedroomed flat above a music shop in the shabbier part of Ealing, but it was her name on the tenancy agreement and hers alone. She could decide what colour to repaint the nicotine-stained walls, she could decide what music to play while she did it, and – best of all – she could decide where to position her drawing board.

Next to the large sash window seemed the obvious choice, with the golden shafts of sunlight forming a natural spotlight. And there was also the view. The music shop was situated on a street corner, sand-wiched between a variety of restaurants and take-aways – much to Maz's delight. The living room was at the rear of the building overlooking a maze of wrought-iron fire escapes and roof terraces. Although Anna didn't have a roof garden of her own, there was a large sycamore tree right outside the window with blossom hanging from its branches like great clusters of candyfloss. Everything seemed to shimmer with the depth of colour and newness of early summer, before the harsh August sun came along and bleached everything to a frazzle.

Anna leaned out of the window and inhaled deeply. Never had the cocktail of fried food and traffic fumes smelled so good. Snatches of the piano player's favourite, 'Chopsticks', floated up from the music shop like petals on the breeze. Anna wished that this moment could last for ever. And then, wouldn't you know it, a bloody magpie had to descend into the scene, strutting cockily along the branch right in front of her. He may as well have been wearing a sandwich board emblazoned with ONE FOR SORROW! Although Anna wasn't usually one for superstition, this moment was too important. She simply couldn't allow her new life to be doomed before it had even begun. There was no alternative – she would have to use Belle's ridiculous solitary magpie neutralising technique.

Anna pulled herself upright and gave an elaborate salute. 'Good afternoon, General!' she barked at the magpie. 'And how are all your children!'

'Good afternoon!' a voice shouted back. Anna stared at the magpie in disbelief – surely not? 'I'm afraid I have no children.'

It was uncanny – a talking magpie, and one with a Mediterranean accent at that. What kind of a place had she moved to? Then Anna saw something move out of the corner of her eye and the awful truth began to dawn. Turning slowly, she saw the owner of the Greek taverna across the way standing on his roof terrace grinning broadly. She watched motionless and mouth agape as he brought a tanned arm up into a salute. Oh my God, she was still saluting! Anna's arm shot back down to her side. She felt like collapsing to the floor in an embarrassed heap, but a voice in her head was saying, No, *those days are over. This is the new you – you are a freelance artist, a single mother, one of the Football Widows. For once in your life – PLAY IT COOL!*

'Oh, sorry,' she trilled, 'I didn't see you there. I was talking to the magpie.'

'It's one of those themed hotels,' Johnny explained as he and Belle wove their way through the hordes of people milling about Brighton pier.

'Really? Oh, cool!' Belle linked her arm through Johnny's. An unexpected shiver of teenage lust coursed its way down her spine. Although she was still plagued with the occasional pang of guilt over her affair with Luke, it somehow all seemed worthwhile if it led to her rediscovering her love for her husband. And here they were, about to embark on a dirty weekend in Brighton. Belle would never have imagined it possible a few months ago – especially the fact that Johnny had arranged it all as a birthday surprise. Then a sudden sense of trepidation descended upon her. 'When you say all the rooms have a different theme, well, there aren't any sports-related ones, are there?' Belle shuddered at the thought of attempting a weekend of X-rated sexual acts upon a king-sized bed in the shape of a wolf's head surrounded by orange-and-black décor.

'Don't be daft,' Johnny replied as he ushered her into an imposing Georgian terrace. Belle would never know how close he had come to booking the Muhammad Ali room, especially after the stunt she had pulled at the FA Cup Final. If it hadn't been for the fact that Wolves had somehow managed to massacre

Arsenal 1–0, Belle would have been spending the weekend in a recreated boxing ring.

Belle followed Johnny up the winding staircase to room number seven, her mind racing. What could the theme be? Why had the man behind the reception desk chuckled when he had given Johnny their key, and why had Johnny looked so embarrassed?

'Here – you go first,' Johnny said, standing aside to let her in.

Belle took a deep breath and flung the door open. A huge grin spread across her face as she took in the electric-blue sequinned duvet cover, the pop art mural of the *Jazz Singer* album cover and the life-sized cardboard cut-out of a middle-aged, heavy-set man clad in a spangled suit holding one arm aloft, like a glittery Statue of Liberty.

'A Neil Diamond room,' she gasped. 'Oh, Johnny!'

Chelsea signed the back of her prescription and handed it to the chemist, along with a packet of Sultry Sable hair colorant. Today was the first day of the rest of her life. All she had to do was rid herself of the clap and dye her hair a decent colour and she would be ready to go. Having successfully wreaked her revenge upon that arsehole Tom, she was finally ready to embark upon her true calling in life as a tabloid journalist. As soon as she had read her story in the current issue of *That's Life* magazine, Chelsea knew it was meant to be. The thrill of reading her own words in print had been unbelievable, and having had a taste she craved more. It was a shame the model they had used had been so ropy. Although she couldn't quite recall where, Chelsea knew she'd seen her face before. She was probably one of those brain-dead page-three 'stunnas' constantly pictured in the gossip columns staggering out of the Met Bar draped over some football player's arm. Chelsea snorted derisively to herself before sashaying out of the chemist's and into the blazing sunshine.